KT-510-968

If you liked *Forbidden to Touch* and *She Devil*
why not try

Hot Mistake by Cara Lockwood
Wicked Pleasure by Taryn Leigh Taylor

Lifelong romance addict **JC Harroway** lives in New Zealand. Writing feeds her very real obsession with happy endings and the endorphin rush they create. You can follow her at jcharroway.com, Facebook.com/jcharroway, Instagram.com/jcharroway and Twitter.com/jcharroway.

Formerly a video and radio producer, **Christy McKellen** now spends her time writing provocative, passionate, seductive romance. When she's not writing she can be found enjoying life with her husband and three children, walking for pleasure, and researching other people's deepest secrets and desires. Christy loves to hear from readers. You can get hold of her at christymckellen.com.

FORBIDDEN TO
TOUCH

JC HARROWAY

SHE DEVIL

CHRISTY McKELLEN

MILLS & BOON

First Published in Great Britain 2019
by Mills & Boon, an imprint of HarperCollins*Publishers*
1 London Bridge Street, London, SE1 9GF

Forbidden to Touch © 2019 JC Harroway

She Devil © 2019 Christy McKellen

ISBN: 978-0-263-27385-4

MIX
Paper from
responsible sources
FSC™ C007454

This book is produced from independently certified FSC™ paper
to ensure responsible forest management.
For more information visit www.harpercollins.co.uk/green.

Printed and bound in Spain
by CPI, Barcelona

FORBIDDEN TO
TOUCH

JC HARROWAY

MILLS & BOON

To Mel, for helping me to wrangle the Faulkner brothers into shape, and to Pete, IT genius—a knight on a shiny hard drive.

CHAPTER ONE

Reid

THE WORRY ON my brothers' faces tightens the shackles of my role as eldest and head of the Faulkner Group, but it's a role I was practically born to, so I hide the concern from my own expression and layer my voice with reassurance.

'The doctor said the best thing for Dad is to maintain his current routine. Let's keep him on the golf course or at his club until we know more about his prognosis.'

Drake and Kit nod. A Mexican wave of shudders seems to pass through all three of us, an unspoken acknowledgment that our newly retired parent may no longer be in command of all his faculties and what this means for the chain of luxury hotels that forms our family business. Our old man is only sixty—the experts calling his recent periods of forgetfulness early-onset dementia.

'And I'd like a second opinion, which I am happy to organise,' I say. 'Try not to worry. We'll take care of this.'

I'll take care of it.

Dad's always been there for us and for me in particular. This office, the biggest with the best views of London, used to be *his* office. I glance at the city, at the slice of the Thames, which is shrouded in a sheer curtain of haze at the record-high spring temperatures. How I'd love to play hooky, to shake off my business suit and head down to Chelsea marina…take a boat out, all four of us—me, Dad and my brothers—as we used to when we were teens…

The memories of happier times cement how signing out is not an option. I'll do whatever it takes to help Dad, just like he's always done for me.

A knock at the door heralds my assistant, Sue, with fresh coffee. She places her offerings on the table and begins to collect the old, half-drunk ones.

'You can't take on everything,' says Kit, his eyes a little tired. 'It's peak tourist season—we're all busy.'

I wave away his concern. I'm divorced—I have room in my life for extras, and the buck stops with me now. Dad taught me the ropes from the day I first accompanied him to work as a boy. And of the three of us, I owe him the most. I inwardly cringe, recalling the crappy end to my marriage and how he'd bailed me out of the subsequent close call for the Faulkner Group, one that could have been avoided if only I'd gone for a pre-nup...

'Sue, can you locate Harley Street's best neurologist and make Graham the earliest appointment available, please?' I look to my brothers, already raising my hand mentally to accompany him. 'I'm happy to go with him, or all of us could attend.'

'Absolutely,' says Drake, and Kit nods.

Sue hovers at my elbow.

I raise my eyebrow in question.

'Um...is Mr Faulkner popping in today?' Her eyes, which are laced with sympathy, dart between me and my brothers. We're a tight-knit company, our staff longstanding and loyal. Dad's episodes of confusion prior to his retirement won't have gone unnoticed.

'No—he's at his club today, I believe,' answers Kit.

Sue frowns. 'There's um...someone in Reception who claims to have an appointment with Mr Faulkner. Will you be taking it, Reid?'

'Appointment?' Unease stiffens my neck— my father has no more official Faulkner engagements. Drake's and Kit's blank faces tell me they're equally clueless, but it's not a feeling that sits well with me.

'*Does* she have an appointment?' I ask Sue, a growing sense of frustration clipping my tone. Dad entrusted this company to me, Drake and Kit. I won't tolerate cock-ups on my watch.

Sue returns to her desk in the outer office, and all three of us follow.

'Yes.' Sue shoots me an apologetic look. 'There's an entry on Mr Faulkner's schedule for a meeting with an interior-design company at twelve.'

'Why would Dad have engaged an interior designer?' says Drake.

I hide my wince at this unforeseen twist. It's *my* job to know everything that goes on at the Faulkner Group. My job and my personal preference to keep a tight rein on the company entrusted to me—a company Dad spent his life building from nothing.

'Do either of you know what this might be about?' I ask my brothers, compassion for my father flaring anew. He worked long hours for forty years to leave a legacy for his sons, steering the Faulkner Group to success and prosperity. This slip-up, albeit insignificant, provides further evidence of how he might have lost control towards the end.

'We did discuss renovations a board meeting

or two back in your absence,' says Drake, 'but I thought we'd shelved the idea for now.'

Kit nods. 'Yes. We never actioned anything.'

Sue's voice takes on a rarely heard flustered cadence. 'I'm sorry, Reid—the appointment must have slipped past unnoticed, what with Mr Faulkner's retirement. Should I…reschedule?'

'No need,' I say, shaking my head. 'Ring down to Reception and have this woman shown up to our waiting area.' I could cancel, but that level of unprofessionalism isn't typical for my tightly run ship. The sooner I see this woman, the sooner I can send her on her way.

I head past Sue's desk, ushering my brothers out. 'You two have enough on—so, usual drinks Friday?'

My brothers nod, reassured. I watch them walk away, pride that they've both recently found happiness—Drake in the first stages of love and Kit weeks away from becoming a father—affirmation that all will be well. Aside from walking in Dad's very large footsteps, steering the family business for my brothers and the generations of Faulkners to come is a privilege. We're going to be okay. Dad's going to be okay. I'll make sure of it.

The minute they're out of sight, my mind works on the newest problem to be solved. I turn to Sue. 'What can you tell me about this company?' I check my watch. I won't have time to do extensive research, as I prefer. But going in blind… Never a good idea. But could Graham have sanctioned major changes at one of the hotels without my knowledge? Has his confusion reached levels where he'd behave so…erratically and out of character?

My efficient assistant is already nodding, typing away. 'I've just sent you through a link to their website. I'm sorry, Mr Faulkner. It must have slipped past Graham's old PA.'

'No worries, I'm sure the mix-up can be easily rectified, but can you please ensure Graham has no other meetings on the horizon?' I rub a spot above my eyebrow at my mounting sense of irritation. What else has gone unnoticed? What else have I missed before recognising the extent of Dad's confusion went beyond pre-retirement pulling back of his workload? If I've been remiss, overlooked my usually competent father's decisions these past months, the 't's need crossing and 'i's dotting.

I shrug into my suit jacket, an expectant brow raised at Sue.

'The company is a small boutique business,' she says, scrolling down her computer screen. 'There's a news story—C&L Interiors, as it was then, winning some prestigious industry award in the small-spaces category.'

I nod, mind whirring. 'That's all? No big-name commissions?' Why would Graham choose a company with no track record for hotel renovations?

Sue shakes her head, looking apologetic.

My shoulders relax—whatever accolades C&L Interiors holds, they're small fry and in no position to undertake renovations on a Faulkner hotel. 'Send a companywide memo to Kit and Drake and the other heads—all new business requires my sign-off.' I ignore Sue's hastily concealed look of horror. I've allowed Dad's diagnosis to distract me and now I have this unscheduled meeting cluttering up my lunch hour.

'This mix-up will be dispensed with in ten minutes, tops. Why don't you take your lunch break now?'

I head for the waiting area through the open-plan offices acquired around the same time the Faulkner Group bought its third hotel. Until then, my father operated out of a converted suite at the Faulkner, our first hotel and the place Drake, Kit and I grew up.

I walk a little taller, remembering the day I joined the family business. As a naive twenty-year-old, I assumed I'd be sitting behind a desk, a carbon copy of my father's, with my business degree framed on the wall. Instead Graham took me downstairs and introduced me to the housekeepers.

I spent my first month changing sheets and cleaning bathrooms, my second trailing the concierge staff and another month working on Reception. He was right to teach me from the bottom up—he's taught me everything I know, which is our hotels inside out, especially the Faulkner.

I exit the admin offices, my resolve primed to undo whatever Dad has discussed with C&L Interiors. I smooth my tie—calling on my slightly rusty charm, anticipating victory.

I come to a halt on the threshold of the waiting area.

Blair Cameron sits on one of the leather sofas, her familiar face severe with concentration as she focuses on a tablet in her lap. I conceal my shock as my pulse hammers with the surge of attraction I've spent years ignoring.

Blair's family and mine go way back. The daughter of my father's friend, business rival, albeit a friendly one, and fellow golf crony, she grew up in similar circles, although she's closest in age to Kit, and it's been years since we've personally had any contact.

I straighten my tie and approach, scoping the length of her body, down spectacular legs, which I can tell, even from this distance, are bare. She's wearing a fitted red dress, her hair caught up in a high ponytail and sunglasses perched on top of her head, as if she's casually pushed them there on entering the building and perhaps forgotten their presence.

Heat stirs in my veins. Despite our ten-year age gap, her beauty has always caused a flicker of appreciation. I might have had my fingers burned by my money-grabbing ex-wife, but a woman like Blair is hard to ignore. A cool blonde—smart, classy, almost untouchable.

Still, appreciation is all it ever can be.

I arrange my features into something approximating a warm welcome and announce my arrival. 'Blair—it's been a while.'

She stands, her surprise that I'm not my father turning into a smile of greeting as she accepts my handshake with a flush. Her smile, slightly lopsided and pinching one cheek into an adorable dimple I recall she hated as a teenager, and the mildly taken-aback delight I spy lurking there, turns this morning's debacle into a minor hiccup.

'Reid. It's been years.' She laughs, a throaty sound that slides over me as surely as the glide of her palm as she disengages from our handshake. A fresh surge of heat pounds through me at her subtle coconut scent. Why didn't I greet her more fondly? Touch my cheek to hers, a woman who, because of our age gap, has been off my radar? For some inexplicable reason, I glance at her left hand—the last thing I heard from Dad, she was engaged—but there's no ring, only long, elegant fingers capped with red nail polish.

Interesting, but what am I doing?

I tuck my hand into my pocket and drag my head back into the game, noting the art satchel at Blair's feet. I vaguely recall her sidestep from working for her father, who owns a hotel in direct competition with the Faulkner, my suspicious nature kicking into overdrive and dampening the flare of attraction to Blair. Is that why she's here? To use Graham's forgetfulness and vulnerability as an opportunity to scope out the competition?

Fuck, I'm jumpy. Just because Sadie, my ex-wife, cured me from trusting members of the opposite sex, I shouldn't condemn her for industrial espionage just yet. I clear my throat, my suspicions beneath me.

'Well, this is unexpected.' I stretch out one arm, indicating she follow me back to my office.

'Yes—I was expecting Graham.' Her sideways glance, a sweep of those pretty eyes down the length of my body, forces my shoulders back a notch and fills my stride with swagger.

I nod as we walk side by side, the air tense with my new awareness of this woman. Has she ever looked at me with interest? I scour my memory for the last time I saw her, calculating I was still married and she was in a relationship with a guy she'd met at university.

At my office door, I pause so she can enter first, my smile concealing the cogs working in my mind on a revised game plan. How much of Graham's diagnosis should I reveal? She's no stranger. But my natural inclination is to play my cards close to my chest, especially when it comes to my father's uncertain health and the business it's my job to safeguard for my family. Yes, she's a family friend, but Graham may not want his medical condition bandied around, gossip fodder for London's hospitality sector.

'After you,' I say, lapping up the way colour heightens her high cheekbones as she passes me in the doorway. Her feminine scent wafts my way, reminding me of exotic beach holidays and tropical cocktails. But before I enjoy the mild flirtation I'm sensing, or offer a confidence by explaining the situation, I want answers.

Inside, she spins, taking in the empty room and then looking to me, but not before another quick tour of my torso. 'Will Graham be joining us?' Her long ponytail swings over one shoulder as she tilts her head and waits for my answer.

Hmm, I've still got it—but Blair would be the last woman I'd have thought would look at me that way. I'm way too old for her, and I definitely don't need a distraction as sexy as her with everything else that's going on.

I remove my jacket and hang it on the hook just inside the door. 'No. Didn't you hear? Graham has recently retired.' The first-name basis reminds me why she's here and how I'm very likely going to have to disappoint her, family friend or not.

Dad, what have you done…?

I wince, the reminder of what I owe him a lash across my back. Not only has he raised me and my brothers and built up our growing business, but also it wasn't so long ago that Graham Faulkner was there to financially bail me out of a disastrous marriage. But the sappy idiot I was soon learned that so-called love leads to misplaced trust, which leads to having your insides ripped out, picked over by vultures and vital parts of you taken as trophies. My stupidity, my naivety almost took down the Faulkner Group, almost took down my family. I needed him then and he needs me now.

A flicker of hesitation dulls Blair's pretty eyes. 'Yes, I was aware he'd retired. I just assumed.' She offers me another wide smile, not perturbed by the change of Faulkner.

I indicate she take a seat on one of the sofas near the window, my interest in the way she elegantly slides into a chair way too acute. What's wrong with me? Of all the days to have my head pleasantly distracted.

'Can I get you a drink?' I can't deny she's the whole package. Striking. One of those women people double-take in the street. I wonder again if she's single, cursing my lack of curiosity about her in recent years, not that I plan on changing my own relationship status any time soon. But perhaps something could be salvaged from this deal after all. At the very least I should take her out to lunch…

'Some water, please,' she says, tucking those long, slender legs together. I deposit her water and take a seat opposite. Now I know who I'm dealing with, tension eases from my muscles. Whatever she wants for C&L Interiors I can dismiss while I figure out if our flicker of chemistry is shared. That could certainly be indulged, as long as she understands its temporary nature.

'So why interiors? Didn't you already have a job for life in hospitality?' The Camerons are a large family and Blair is the youngest. Something in her eyes shifts. Instinct tells me I've touched a soft spot—excellent. Having a business opponent, even a beautiful one, on the back foot, is always advantageous. She's broken away from working with her family—is there a rift? Or is she still on the payroll? That control-freak part of me, the part screwed over by Sadie, again wonders if she's here to mess with the competition.

'I wanted to forge my own path, and I've always loved the creative aspects of my job. I'd be stifled in an office. And I offer the family a discount as compensation.' She lifts her brows, a mocking glint in her eye.

We chuckle together, but there's a thread of steel through her words. She hasn't taken the easy route, preferring to strike out alone rather than sit back on her laurels. And while she's young for a sole business owner, I can tell she's not a push-over. She's clearly a savvy businesswoman or she wouldn't have made it into *my* office.

I slide my eyes over the entire Blair package, caution warring with intrigue. The way she carries herself, the way she's dressed for a boardroom and her handshake are all clues that this woman values her business. The sky-high heels and the whimsical way she's simply pushed her sunglasses up onto her head tell me she's particular, but not rigid, at least when it comes to her own appearance.

I breathe my first sigh of relief—I have no time for high-maintenance women. Perhaps this is a chance to dust off that rusty charm, use it to my advantage, dispense with this misunderstanding and suggest that lunch.

'So, shall we start?' she asks, jerking me from pleasure and back to business.

'By all means.' I quash the flicker of sexual interest, my divorce having cured me of anything… romantic. Sex has become something I slot into my diary along with the gym, dental check-ups and haircuts, although perhaps a little more regularly.

When I don't initiate any conversation, Blair reaches for the art case and pulls an A3-sized board from it, laying it on the coffee table.

'I've sent through digital files of the technical work I discussed with Graham, but I also brought a mood board to give you an idea of the finished look.' She looks up, her fingers gliding over the fabric samples and paint swatches stuck to the board. 'Interiors are three-dimensional. Tactile.' Her eyes spark with enthusiasm, doubling her attractiveness and sharpening my powers of observation where she's concerned.

She continues. 'I prefer to feel something under my hand, to test its durability, to luxuriate in its texture, to imagine what it would feel like to lie upon, or walk upon barefoot…'

Her passion, her zeal, does something to my already heightened awareness—a fresh stirring below the belt. Would she trail those elegant hands over my bare chest the way she's caressing the fabric swatches?

I snap my attention back to what she's saying. Until this mistake is cleared up, my libido will have to take a back seat.

'Interiors are sensory, something you experience with your entire body. You can't appreciate these facets on an iPad.'

Her mouth is sensual. Mesmerising. My cock twitches in payment for my arse-over-tit priorities. I nod, her enthusiasm shifting something inside a dusty, neglected corner of my chest. She loves her work. I'll be sorry to disappoint her.

'I can appreciate that.' I shift in my seat, directing my frown to the swatch of fabric under my fingertips.

A blink, a sniff and my focus returns. Not to her passion or her rocking body, but the reason she's here. I abandon her mood board. Time to nip this in the bud. 'Excuse my confusion—I'm playing catch-up a little here. What exactly did you and Graham discuss?'

Her face falls a fraction, a hint of uncertainty entering her eyes, which seem to change colour in the light—are they blue or green? I can't decide. And why have I never noticed before?

'Well…he wanted me to start as soon as possible. I've managed to reschedule a few other projects, so—'

'Start what?' I brace myself for confirmation

of what I've already guessed, my fingertips gripping the armrests.

Her brows cinch, a tiny crease forming above the bridge of her nose. 'Renovations. On the Faulkner.'

Damn. I knew it. No way.

'You *are* joking?'

Confusion wrinkles her brow. 'No. Why would I joke?'

My enamel creaks from the tension in my jaw. 'I don't need to tell you it's peak season—the hotel is booked solid for the next three months.' I keep my face neutral while my mind whirrs at how much it might cost us financially to extricate ourselves from whatever Dad has set in motion, and how much it will cost me personally, in my time to… *deal* with Blair Cameron, which, outside of this cock-up, isn't a wholly unpleasant reality.

'Yes, I did question the timing.' She shrugs one shoulder. 'But Graham was adamant.'

I stroke my chin, contemplating my next move. No matter how gorgeous she is, no matter how, under different circumstances, I'd welcome *dealing* with this beautiful, passionate woman, there's no way she's laying a single elegant finger on my fucking hotel. The feeling that I'm a caged lion builds, an urge to quash this quickly and at all costs.

'I'm sorry, but Graham…' I clear my throat, my natural inclination to hedge. 'Let's just say he's currently indisposed.' No need to go into details of his health with a woman whose family, at least professionally, I could consider rivals. If she's unaware of Graham's health issues, the family friendship can't be that strong. My stomach pitches at the reminder of those health issues—I'd love to blank them out, pretend they're just a bad dream.

Her stare widens with sympathy. 'I'm sorry to hear that—I didn't know. I hope it's nothing serious.'

I incline my head, neither confirming nor denying, while my stomach knots with frustration that there's little I can do on that score currently. I focus on the easier to solve—and easy on the eye—predicament sitting opposite.

'So I'm afraid whatever arrangement you might have had…' I wave my hand over her colour-coordinated and detailed mood board '…is no longer required.' I slide the offering back along the table.

Her face registers quickly concealed shock. Her stare bounces up from the 'teal' and 'taupe' swatches and hardens, an expression I've never seen her wear before.

'Arrangement?' Her luscious mouth lingers over the word as she takes a slow sip of her drink, her lips caressing the rim of the glass, a distraction my libido in no way needs. She stares directly at me, as if I'm suggesting something illicit.

I'm tempted, and I have plenty of other illicit distractions if she's up for a brief fling.

But the look in her eyes tells me I face an admirable adversary. And I put business first. Always.

'We had no arrangement,' she says.

For a second a weight on my shoulders lifts at this easily rectified situation. 'Great—that's all sorted.' I smile—now seems like the perfect time to switch on the charm, to salvage something from this serendipitous meeting, to get to know the stunning Blair Cameron better. 'Perhaps you'd allow me to take you out for lunch, so we can catch up properly.'

My offer, layered with my usual confidence, seems to do the trick. Her pupils dilate, blocking out most of the blue-green hologram of her irises, her pulse picks up, thrumming rapidly in her neck, and her legs shift, presumably as she presses her thighs together. She's turned on by my suggestion, her mind perhaps imagining the same satisfying outcome, although her scenario is probably a little less graphic than the one rendering me stuck in the chair by the beginnings of a hard-on.

I lounge back against the leather. Who knew that what, only ten minutes ago, felt like a thorn in my side would end so…gratifyingly? That she doesn't seem perturbed by our age difference? And if it's just a fling, why should it matter?

My mind shuffles through my engagements for the rest of the afternoon, my dick stuck on the fact she didn't turn down my offer of lunch flat. There's nothing that can't be…reprioritised.

Then she sits a little straighter and tilts her head. 'Another time perhaps.' The eyes are back to flinty, although her pulse still trills nineteen to the dozen. 'Why don't we keep this about business, for now?'

For now…? Promising.

'You see, what Graham and I had was beyond an *arrangement*.'

The hairs at my collar stand to attention as the worst is confirmed.

'We had a contract.'

CHAPTER TWO

Blair

REID FAULKNER'S DECADENT lips thin, but he manages to keep his expression free of the irritation I'm certain he feels. He's not a man to be sideswiped, his reputation for dominating every aspect of the Faulkner Group well known. But I too have learned a few ruthless skills this past year, although none that can help me with my most pressing question—why does he have to still be so thigh-clenchingly hot?

Within thirty seconds of meeting him again, while I'd drooled at the way he fills his immaculate suit, I'd recalled his permanent air of supreme confidence, every stupid, misplaced and sometimes downright filthy fantasy I'd ever had about him roaring back to pulse-pounding life. Of course, back when I first noticed the eldest Faulkner brother was a bona fide fully grown sex god, he seemed permanently out of reach, and I finally abandoned my long-held crush when he married. But now…? With the way he's sliding that sexy stare over me, I have the urge to resurrect those fantasies. Funny how eighteen and twenty-eight seemed an insurmountable and naive dream, but twenty-five and thirty-five has…delicious possibilities.

I sit a little straighter, ignoring the way that, despite trying to wriggle free of our deal, he makes me feel a little more invincible. After all, this is business. My first priority. I wait for him to process my bombshell, while my own eyes burn with the pressure of maintaining his searing eye contact.

'A contract?' His expression hardens even as his stare lingers on my mouth so I almost feel the brush of his lashes. The cut of his voice—commanding, confident, seductive almost—makes my breath catch and leaves me wondering if I can't have the best of both worlds. Flex my professional muscles on this deal with an adversary as worthy as Reid Faulkner *and* explore what I'm pretty certain is a mutual attraction.

And why shouldn't I?

I'm no longer a besotted eighteen-year-old. Our chemistry, if kept separate from business, needn't be an obstacle. In fact, the opposite. Now I'm close to nursing Cameron Interiors back to full health, perhaps Reid Faulkner is the perfect reward I deserve...

I swallow and brace my entire body to combat the swirls of excitement twitching my muscles in response to our showdown. My pulse ricochets between my nipples and my pelvis, reminding me of my long year of celibacy, until I mentally slap myself and focus on pumping blood to my brain— the only part of me required for this particular encounter.

I open my tablet and, after a few swipes, offer him the screen for proof, but he bats me away with one large hand, which is big enough to leave me wondering how much of my waist it would circle and if it would swallow my entire breast...

Ignoring my soaring temperature, I clench my jaw with determination. I won't be dismissed, for all his years of business experience, and he wouldn't be the first person to underestimate me. As the youngest sibling in a large family, I'm used to fighting to be seen and taken seriously. Even my university professor cautioned me against trying to run before I could walk, to pay my dues at a big, well-established design firm, but I've always known I'd rather put in the hours and work hard for my own company, not someone else's. And if Reid Faulkner thinks I'm walking away from my first major deal since Josh and I parted ways, he can think again.

'Is there a problem?' I try not to allow the lurch of my stomach to register on my face—it's like a roller coaster in there. I secured this contract alone, fair and square, despite the competition. I won't be side-swiped for a second time.

'Nothing that can't be rectified.' His stare narrows as if dissecting me. 'But you should know we decided to shelve the Faulkner renovations until some time in the future.'

Panic flutters in my throat but I swallow it down. 'I wasn't party to that information.' I breathe, choose my words carefully, willing to fight but happy to remind him of his professional obligations, despite our family's connections. 'And I've already committed considerable hours to the Faulkner project. I've delayed other work to give it my full attention, as it deserves.'

I don't add that I've funnelled all my energy into secretly rebuilding my decimated business this past year—I won't be sidetracked by another man, not even a sexy suit who happens to make me feel eighteen again.

'The way I see it, Reid, we need each other.' I hold my breath. Even simply saying his name aloud leaves me achy and distracted, and the reminder we're more than business acquaintances flashes sparks in his eyes. But the bite of his tone puts him firmly back in charge.

'In what way?'

I hide my frustration behind my neutral facial expression—he's being deliberately obtuse. 'You have a hotel in need of renovation, and I have an interior-design business and a contract for those renovations. Plus, my commission is highly competitive—great news for the Faulkner Group. Surely there's only one outcome here that satisfies both of us.'

I feel the weight of his assessment to the tips of my toes. I can't work out if his mind lingers on business, where mine should firmly reside, or pleasure, a place I'm lured to every time he looks at me? The shiver of goose pimples along my bare arms tells me I'm struggling to ascertain which I want more, that I'd welcome the change of tack, once we've cleared up this misunderstanding.

Chemistry can be indulged or ignored. And the chemistry between us seems to have matured over the years like a fine vintage wine.

At his continued silence, my defensiveness kicks in. 'Is it an…experience concern? I assure you I'm more than capable of this contract. I'd be happy to provide you with references.' I should have known he'd underestimate me, see me as someone to be easily ignored and dismissed, just like many others have in my past. But I'm done being naive. No way will I ever put my business in the hands of anyone else. Especially not a man who, physically at least, does it for my poor, neglected body.

Reid narrows his steely eyes. 'It's not a question of experience.'

I ignore the way I feel naked under his scrutiny and how much I like it. 'Good, because interiors are personal—it's crucial you and I have a close working relationship.'

'Oh, we will,' he says on a husky promise that leaves me floundering to guess if we're still talking about interior design.

He brushes a speck of lint from his trousers, completely at ease. 'Nothing happens at a Faulkner hotel without my seal of approval. But, as you've brought up the size of your company, don't you think C&L Interiors is reaching a little far with a hotel of the Faulkner's calibre?'

'Cameron Interiors. I dropped the L.'

I ignore the jibe I've heard before. Yes, I'm young, my company small, but I work hard, even harder this past year. Ambition isn't a crime. I sit up taller—faking it. I can't confess, but his reticence is justified—Cameron Interiors isn't making waves, and, thanks to my hateful ex, who stole all our big clients despite promising we could still work together even though we were no longer a

couple, hasn't grown in proportion to the amount
of work I've personally invested. All the more reason I intend to walk out of Reid's sumptuous office with a start date agreed.

'What happened to the "L"?' His eyes spark.

Of course, he would ask the one question designed to throw icy doubt on my assertions I'm
capable of running the business I've taken a year
to rebuild single-handed.

I cross my legs, force my facial muscles to relax,
showing him I'm here to stay. 'Mr Lyle left the
company. Now it's just me—better and stronger
alone, and, as I've already pointed out, competi-
tively priced. So why don't you let me worry about
the details? I assure you that you'll be happy with
the final outcome.' I ensure my posture matches
my words in oozing confidence, when the reminder of my commitments if Reid insists on delaying the contracted work would crush me into
a snivelling ball.

His stare turns flinty as he pushes his hand
through his hair, which is dark with salt and pepper
at the temples. My eyes follow the passage of his
fingers, marvelling at how, even frustrated, he's in
control, still sexy and still throwing up roadblocks
to my most lucrative and prestigious contract since
Josh pulled the rug from under my feet.

'Mmm…' he murmurs, a sexy sound which reverberates through my entire body. 'What are we going to do with each other?'

My heart leaps, every thrum a thrill of excitement. Does that mean what I hope it means? Does Reid Faulkner finally see me? Can I have everything I want here? My contract honoured and my ego massaged through a little…fantasy fulfilment with Reid, of all men? Of course, the two will need to be completely separate—I learned my lesson from mixing business and pleasure with Josh.

The buzz of warning shudders through me—head to toe. I fully intend to win the battle for my contract, but can I walk away from the promise behind Reid's dark, searching eyes? A promise I once longed to see?

The promise of sex.

Good sex.

Great sex, even.

My libido's been dormant since Josh and I split, but Reid's interest swoops along every nerve ending, jerking me back to life. While I've toiled over my business, rebranded and reinvented while scraping my dignity back together, I've been oblivious to members of the opposite sex. How can *this* man change all that? Make me recall every second of my teenage infatuation? Make me want to indulge a sorely neglected area of my life?

Then my brain floods with images of my ex getting hot and heavy with his friend on my beautiful Italian leather sofa, and I close my eyes, breathing through the acidic burn in my chest. Seeing my fiancé's deceitful mouth on another man's had been shock enough, my sofa desecrated for ever, but it was the later betrayal, the professional one, which stole my tattered peace of mind, along with my pride and my clients, that lingers to this day, still shaping my decisions, still tainting my life.

Well, no more. Starting today as a bare minimum, I'm setting Cameron Interiors back on track to the big league. I open my eyes and look up at Reid, sucking in a breath, the contrast between the chill of my memories and the heat of his stare leaving me weirdly exposed.

'Look, I'm sure you're as busy as I am. So let's put this to bed, shall we?' I slide my palms down my skirt, fighting the heat at my chosen turn of phrase. 'All I need is your sign-off on my designs and the name of someone you nominate to oversee the project...' I smile up at him now things are finally going my way '...and I'll be out of your hair.'

Your sexy dark hair that's calling to my fingers...

His strong thighs spread, owning his space in the way of self-assured men, his elbow propped on one arm of the sofa while he strokes his chin as his eyes rake over me, slowly and with thorough sensuality, a move that lends him a roguish air completely at home on his angular face. 'If we're going to be working together, Blair…'

The way he says my name in a low, husky tone I've heard a thousand times in my late-night fantasies makes me wonder how he'd sound first thing the morning after—sleepy and sexy, his vibrating voice dragging my every nerve to delicious awareness… I flush warm all over, cursing my hormones.

'…we should get to know each other a little better.' He stretches out one arm along the back of the sofa, a move that tugs his shirt open a fraction at the neck where he's loosened his tie, affording me a glimpse of dark chest hair. 'Why are you no longer engaged?'

The roar of blood in my face scalds. 'That's a personal question.'

'Yes, it is.'

I consider ignoring it, reluctant to confirm how my relationship ended. I know Josh's change of heart, his confusion over his sexuality, is no reflection on me personally, but trusting him with our business even after I discovered him cheating, allowing him to steal most of our major clients— for that I've no one to blame but myself.

I hide my shudder behind a massive swallow of iced water while I consider that Reid already knows my sorry tale and has brought it up to throw me off my game, distract me from my contract and expose my naive lapse in business judgement, one I'm sure he'd never have made with all his years of experience at the helm of the Faulkner Group.

'Why are you no longer married?' I counter. Two can play at his game.

He laughs, tilting his head with a nod of respect, but stays resolutely silent—that subject is clearly out of bounds. Like mine, his one foray into matrimony seems to have cured his hunt for hearth and family.

I sigh, keen to draw a line under the personal veer of the conversation. 'It didn't work out—personally or professionally. Hence dropping the "L" from C&L.'

'I'm sorry to hear that.' Amusement leaches from his eyes, which now carry genuine dismay, telling me I might have judged him a little harshly. 'His loss.'

I accept his compliment with a tilt of my head. 'Yes, well, I dare say we're both better off.' I lean forward and deposit my glass on the sleek coffee table between us, new determination taking hold. I lift my chin, feigning confidence in my solo skills, and remind Reid of my credentials. 'And, luckily for the Faulkner Group, you get my undivided, award-winning attention. The reason, I think, why Graham selected Cameron Interiors.' I need to remind us both why I'm here. As far as I'm concerned, Graham's unfortunate illness, while upsetting, shouldn't affect the renovations. 'Why don't I show you some concepts I discussed with Graham—I'd love to hear your thoughts?'

With the personal stuff successfully navigated, he waves his hand for me to continue.

I stand and walk round the coffee table, settling beside him on the sofa and swiping at the screen of the iPad to bring up the images I want. Sharing the device necessitates closeness. That's what I tell myself as I'm buffeted by more Reid Faulkner than I can handle, at least half of my energy absorbed with maintaining a slow, even breathing rate this close to him, when all I want to do is lean in for an indulgent sniff.

'So this is a concept for the hotel entrance and foyer.' I hold the device in his direction, fighting the urge to scuttle away from or move closer to his body heat and tantalising masculine scent as he leans in to look, the slight rise of his eyebrows the only indication he's in any way interested or impressed. Now I'm free for a few seconds of eye-roaming, taking in the dark stubble on his chin, the harsh line of his jaw and the strong tendons in his tanned neck.

I collect myself, remembering I'm a grown woman with a business to run, and swipe to the second image. 'This is a selection of modern light fittings to replace the chandelier in the foyer—Graham was adamant he wanted a fresh, contemporary look throughout.'

When I look up he's staring at me, not the iPad. I smile, shift a little, my pulse pounding in my head at the way his eyes dip to my mouth every few seconds. For several beats he gives no indication what he thinks of the concepts I've painstakingly worked on for the last month. Then he blinks and the shutters fall, breaking the sexual tension, which had lifted every hair on my arm closest to him.

I cling to my control of the situation. 'If there are any changes you'd like to make—'

'Let's not get ahead of ourselves. You of all people know peak season isn't the best time for major works.'

I stare, fighting the urge to allow my jaw to hang open with shock. He can't rescind my contract. 'Well, yes, but Graham was adamant.'

Reid continues as if he's deaf to my every argument. 'Of course, loss of business for us is good for competing hotels.' He swivels to face me, leaning into the small space that separates us, a space now tense with professional mistrust and the fizzled-out sparks of that physical connection I'm now wondering if I imagined, leaving me hot and cold in the space of the same heartbeat.

'What are you suggesting?' How could I get carried away with my reawakened attraction to him, when all along he planned to veto the project? Assuming we were both on the right track for the renovations while indulging in our frisson of chemistry? Well, if he could ignore it to play dirty, I could ignore it to win.

Reid's eyes narrow a fraction. 'It's a double win for you—Cameron Interiors and your family's hotel benefit while the Faulkner is out of action. And, despite what Graham might have agreed to, now really isn't a good time.'

I force myself to remain calm. 'I only care about Cameron Interiors, and Graham didn't agree, he *insisted*—not that either is relevant in light of my contract.'

The tightening of his mouth should appease me—he's over a barrel, although icy trickles of doubt snake down my spine. If he chooses to contest, I can't afford much in the way of legal representation to fight him, just as I couldn't afford to hound Josh for the stolen business, neither financially nor in the humiliation stakes.

Reid's eyes have gone from blue to silvery grey. Hard. Unyielding. 'You can't deny there's considerable gain here for Cameron Interiors.' He has the decency to look away, but only temporarily.

'As there is for the Faulkner. I don't see why our

mutual benefit is of any consequence. There's a transactional element to any contract, otherwise why else would we bother?'

'Perhaps Graham jumped the gun.' His mouth twists, as if he's tasted something unpleasant, and I wonder what's really going on here. Why is he so keen to dispense with the renovations and me? 'I'd be happy to offer compensation for the inconvenience and for your time.'

Part of me is tempted by his buy-off. What better way to put a lid on this whole sorry episode and move on to fresh, more welcoming clients and to get away from his…addictive potency? Away from the lure of living out my teenage crush and embracing the inconvenient sexual attraction to Reid Faulkner?

But then I'd be no better than Josh. Deceitful. Taking something I hadn't wholly earned. No. I can handle this man, our chemistry irrelevant. I drag in a shuddering breath, bolstering my resolve, which had clearly been knocked off balance by the rage of my hormones. Whatever his motives, I'm here to stay.

'And your father's plans for the future of the Faulkner… You don't want to respect those?' I know what Graham wanted—to leave the Faulkner, their oldest hotel, in pristine condition—his last act as head of the company, future-proofing the jewel in the Faulkner Group crown for his sons.

His eyes narrow, his mouth thinning, as if by reminding him of his father's wishes I've asked for double his original offer.

'I know what's best for my family and my company.'

I nod. 'Yes. And I know what I discussed with Graham, and what *he* wanted.'

His eyes narrow but there's respect and heat layered in his irises. 'Quite spectacularly ruthless, aren't you?'

The way he enunciates every word makes me acutely aware of my body, my every heartbeat and breath—who knew sparring with him would be so...invigorating? Now he's thrown down the gauntlet, I can't resist. I scoot closer.

'You're right—I'm not too shoddy at negotiations, and I know what I want.' We're so close, his glittering eyes haze out of focus. His warm breath gusts over my tingling lips, lips I'm aware are parted to emit the rapid pants of my fired-up breathing.

Time passes. A thrilling face-off neither of us seems to want to lose.

I want to kiss him. The thought slams into me from nowhere.

At that second the office door swings open, snapping our attention from our intense staring contest. Our heads swivel in unison to the new arrival, the swing of my ponytail glancing off the side of Reid's face—that's how close we were.

Graham Faulkner stands in the doorway, his face wreathed in a smile of welcome and recognition. 'You two...' He waggles his finger, an indulgent grin on his face. 'Looking cosy.'

'Dad.' Reid jumps to his feet. 'What are you doing here?'

I follow, grateful to emerge from the sexual fog.

'I just popped in to collect a file.' Graham raises his eyebrows suggestively. 'Don't let me interrupt you two lovebirds.'

My face flames. Is that how we appeared? Was our chemistry obvious to anyone with eyes, despite the face-off that was taking place? Adversaries, more like... But now Graham is here, we can clear up this mess.

Graham grips my shoulders and presses a kiss to my cheek, catching me off guard. Last time we met it was handshakes and professional praise, albeit layered with the warmth of our longstanding personal relationship.

Reid slides me a look and then winces. 'No, Dad. This is—'

'Sadie, good to see you again,' says Graham, his smile warm. 'I'm so looking forward to your engagement party.'

Sadie...? Reid's ex-wife. Engagement party...?

I glance to Reid, my face draining of blood. 'It...it's good to see you again, Mr Faulkner,' I say. What the hell is going on?

Reid looks ashen, his smile brittle for his father. 'Dad...this is—'

'Now, now, Sadie,' Graham interrupts, 'I've told you before—we'll have none of that Mr Faulkner stuff. You're going to be my daughter-in-law. Call me Graham.' He hugs Reid and bustles back out of the room, muttering something about preparing for a meeting, which takes Reid's complexion from pallid to waxy.

At the threshold Graham pauses and spins, pointing at Reid. 'Bring Sadie for lunch on Sunday.'

'But—'

'I insist.' Graham holds up a hand, silencing Reid's protests. 'I want to get to know your future wife better.'

Beside me, Reid stiffens.

I step up alongside him, close but not touching, offering solidarity for this bewildering conversation, which renders me both speechless and sets my stomach in knots.

Graham's stare slides my way. 'What do you say, my dear? Reid's brothers will be there—it's a family tradition.'

I smile, caught between rational and sympathetic responses. Graham Faulkner clearly has no idea who I am or how he knows me. No idea that he taught me to play chess as a girl or gave me business advice when I left university. My stomach turns—something is clearly very wrong. This isn't the man I've known half of my life, a man my father considers a long-time friend, a man who has often treated me like the daughter he never had.

Reid's tension is a force field of repressed energy. I shift on my feet, a tangle of responses blocking my throat. What do I say? Should I remind him who I am and run the risk of upsetting or embarrassing a man I have great respect for, or simply play along with his confusion?

At my baffled silence, Graham's face drops, his bewildered eyes becoming glazed as they dip to the carpet.

'Please, just go along with it,' whispers Reid.

I swallow past my dry throat and nod. 'Absolutely. I'd love to. Thank you, Mr Faulk—Graham.'

His beam knocks ten years off his age, and, no matter how worrying this turn of events and how weird Reid's request, I've done the right thing.

'Fantastic—it's all arranged. See you Sunday.' He leaves, his whistle echoing through the distant offices.

In his wake, a vacuum sucks all the air from the room.

I stand frozen to the spot beside Reid, my mind

whirring over what just happened. Why did Reid
ask me to go along with Graham's misunderstanding? And what does all this—Graham's obvious
confusion—mean, not only for his health, but also
for my contract to renovate the Faulkner? I flush
at the selfishness of my thoughts, my gaze falling
to the carpet. I've just spent so long picking up the
scant pieces after Josh left, I've been counting on
this contract to finally put a line under my past.
To move forward, alone. Stronger. Independent.

Reid shifts beside me, looks down, wariness
clouding his stare. 'Thank you.' His breath gusts
from him in a long exhale, and I have the crazy
urge to reach out and comfort him by touching
his arm. But touching Reid Faulkner has always
been forbidden.

'What for?' All I did was gape and smile and
pretend I'm his ex-wife.

'For playing along.' He scrubs a hand over his
face, his eyes suddenly tired, fires off a text and
slips his phone into his pocket.

'I… No problem.' My mouth opens and closes,
the words springing to mind inappropriate in the
muddle of my mind. 'Is Graham…is he okay?'
Reid and I have never shared confidences, given
I'm closest in age to Kit, but Graham was always
kind to me growing up, even encouraging my ca-

reer dreams when my own family considered them an act of childish rebellion and mere frippery.

Reid turns to face me, shoulders back and hands slung in his pockets, wariness at the edges of his stare hinting at his vulnerability. 'He will be,' he says, shutting down the line of conversation.

Goose pimples prickle along my bare arms. What now? Do I walk away from my deal? Settle, again, for less than I deserve? Forget the contract I worked hard to secure when Graham Faulkner seemed to be a different man?

As I look at the lines in the corners of Reid's eyes, my heart thumps and my stance softens. Whatever is happening to Graham, it's taking a toll on Reid.

'I thought Sadie was your ex,' I whisper, my chest tight. I'm torn. Part of me wants answers, even though I know they'll signal the end of this lucrative, hard-won deal. And the other part—the part desperate to prove herself after the Josh debacle—wants to wallow in ignorance and simply start the job for which I've been hired. I swallow past the lump in my throat, telling myself Reid's personal family problems are not my concern.

But I can't ignore his look of uncertainty any more than I can ignore what this might mean for Graham.

'She is.' He clenches his jaw, his mouth a grim line.

Is that it? Don't I deserve a little more explanation after lying for him, albeit to save Graham from embarrassment?

'Is he…? He seemed confused. Is it temporary?'

Medication-related? A result of a blow to the head? The Graham I know was so supportive of my company and so enthusiastic for the renovations to the Faulkner.

Reid's lips press tighter together. I'm clearly not to be trusted with personal information. And that's fine. It reminds me that, chemistry or not, we're barely family friends, whatever Graham might have thought when he walked in.

I search for Reid's earlier vulnerability, but it's nowhere to be seen. I'm about to speak, to offer some appropriate platitude—clearly something major has happened since I last saw Graham—to tear up my contract and bill him only for the hours I've already put in, when he speaks first.

'I have another meeting now.' He scrubs at his stubbled jaw with one large hand. 'I suggest we reschedule for nine tomorrow in the boardroom. Let's see if we can't negotiate a middle ground—' he pins me once more with that hard-to-read stare, '—one that, as you said, satisfies us both.'

The way he utters the word 'satisfies' brings to

mind all kinds of lewd scenarios featuring Reid—
not the younger version, irresistible enough, but
this older man who no longer intimidates me. I
nod, my head still woolly and doubts over our
working relationship lingering. But if a temporary illness has befallen Graham, do I really need
to walk away from this deal? Won't he expect the
work to continue, regardless?

My mind races through various practicalities—
I've already employed contractors and secured supplies. I collect my bag and move towards the door,
my steps in no way as certain as when I arrived.

'Blair.'

I turn, but his face is unreadable with the exception of a flare of heat in his eyes, which my
erogenous zones latch onto.

He swallows. 'Thanks.'

He turns away and I leave, every certainty I
brought here in crumbs underneath the soles of
my heavy feet.

CHAPTER THREE

Reid

I STAND AS Sue ushers Blair into the smaller of the two boardrooms at the Faulkner offices, the slug of heat her appearance brings surging through my muscles and making me feel taller, as if anything were possible. It's an amplified version of what seeing her yesterday sparked, which tells me Blair Cameron and I may have unfinished business beyond hotel renovations.

Damn, I hoped I'd be over it today; instead, I note how her green dress accentuates the glow of her skin and brings out the same shade in her eyes. Her hair is down, the tousled swath casually draped over one shoulder, exposing one side of her neck and one earlobe, which is decorated with a dangling pearl.

Why do I have the highly inconvenient urge to suck on that earlobe and tongue the pearl, perhaps undoing the professional and put-together Blair, who I am certain has brought her promised negotiation skills to the table?

Sue leaves us, silently closing the door. I step closer, extend my hand towards my worthy adversary, almost looking forward to our spar.

Blair's fingers clasp mine, the heat in my palm increasing as if we're a chemistry experiment, our skin-on-skin combination creating our own energy source. With reluctance I drop her hand and pull out one of the seats around the conference table, more excited than I should be for today's negotiations.

She could have reacted very differently to last night's farce in my office, but she managed the whole affair with discretion. Drake and Kit and the lawyers agree—we're bound by her contract, and her designs, while modest to date, are good. Graham was clearly in sound mind when he contracted Cameron Interiors. I need to find a way to honour both the contract and his wishes, while, of course, getting what I want, too.

And where this woman is concerned, what I want has become somewhat…murky, at least physically. Damn, I almost kissed her yesterday just before we were interrupted by Graham. Her exquisite, previously forbidden closeness, her fiery, take-no-prisoners attitude, her eyes both excited and determined—I couldn't resist.

Blair Cameron is a potent and tempting package inspiring intrigue, fascination and respect. I tell myself it's my desire to draw a satisfactory line under this mix-up. I wait for her to settle before removing my suit jacket and sliding into my own seat, at right angles to her, swallowing the surge of lust. The family business comes first, and she's chosen the wrong challenger if she thinks this is all going her way. The table is long, rectangular, with places for twelve, but at this proximity I can see the flush of her skin, hear the soft intake of her breath and catalogue every nuance of her body language, which speaks for her. She has nowhere to hide—a perfect position of negotiating strength. Nothing to do with how fantastic she smells or how I'm drawn to those sparks of fire in her eyes. No, it makes sense to keep my enemies—or, in her case, someone whose professional motives could be considered ruthless—close. The last time my personal life encroached on the family business, I almost lost everything. And, although it will in no way be a chore, I intend to keep a very close eye on Ms Cameron.

And what of her personal motives? Could she possibly reciprocate my interest…?

She glances around and then pours herself a glass

of water from the carafe on the table between us. 'I thought you were joking about the boardroom.'

'Why would I joke? I take business very seriously.' She really doesn't know me, but that could be rectified.

She nods, shuffling her papers and giving away her nerves. 'As do I. So let's discuss that first.'

A surge of blood pounds in my dick at her words. First implies a second... And if not business, then perhaps pleasure.

Blair continues, 'I have discussed it at length with Graham, and of course I've been there many times over the years with my father, but why don't *you* tell me about the Faulkner?'

I oblige, certain my patience for the second agenda item will be rewarded. 'As you know, the Faulkner is our oldest and smallest hotel.' I recite some basic media-style facts by rote while my mind contemplates how enjoyable it will be to keep a close eye on this intriguing woman. 'It's something of an iconic landmark in Chelsea these days, and more than a business, more than a hotel, as I'm sure you understand—I grew up there.'

'Of course.' Her smile thuds my heart harder. 'Graham and I have discussed the hotel's sentimental value to your family in great detail. He even showed me some old photographs of the place when he first purchased it.' She pauses, taking a delicate sip of water. 'My designs are sympathetic to the heritage of the Faulkner. And I only have one major structural renovation to suggest.'

I bristle, feeling my overprotectiveness for my childhood home and concern over the changes my father may or may not have sanctioned rising up. I have no idea what state of mind Graham was in when he contracted Blair, but I know one thing: 'major' suggests delay, which means greater costs. The more these renovations are dragged out, the longer the hotel is out of business and the bigger her bill.

The reminder of a time when the roles were reversed, when it was *my* mistake with Sadie costing the Faulkner Group money, and my father had intervened to financially and emotionally bail me out of my marriage, stiffens my resolve to keep control of every inch of this project. I won't be hoodwinked again.

'Which is?' I swallow bile, wishing I'd been present at the initial discussions. The idea my father might have been vulnerable, made decisions he might not have contemplated a year ago, leaves me jittery with guilt, shrinking my dick quicker than a lapful of ice. Not that Blair necessarily took advantage of Graham, but she must have rejoiced when the call came. Renovating a Faulkner hotel is a major coup for anyone, least of all a small company.

'I plan to knock down the south wall behind the current reception desk in the foyer.'

I hold in my splutter of outrage and offer a cool stare, so she continues with her justification.

'There's just dead space behind—a cloakroom and storage room. And without that wall you'll achieve so much more natural light into an area that's a little gloomy, currently.'

'Hmm, I'm not sure I like the sound of that.'

Over my dead body springs to mind, but I'm the first to admit my knee-jerk reaction is all about preserving the hotel's heritage and looking out for my father.

She raises her eyebrows, a confident smile tugging at her pink-glossed lips. 'Trust me—I know what I'm talking about; you'll love the results, and opening up that space will improve the options for the foyer. You can have a separate concierge desk and a seating area.' She's showing her passion again, her excitement, or perhaps it's the ruthless streak that she might have the upper hand causing the sparkle in her eyes.

I rub my chin, drawn to every move she makes, my mind returning to the reel of fantasies I've had about Blair Cameron in the past eighteen hours. The idea of her in control is not an unwelcome image. That hair wild as she rides me, and those shapely legs gripping my waist, while I explore the sensitivity of those nipples I see peeking through the fabric of her dress. I spread my thighs a fraction under the table to accommodate the burgeoning tightness in my trousers.

Blair pulls out her tablet once more and slides it over the table. 'Take a look at the concept plans—try to visualise the end result.'

I glance at the images on the screen, still unconvinced.

My reticence wobbles her confident spiel, but she rallies. 'If it's the guest bookings that are concerning you, we can minimise delays by staging the renovations—close off one floor at a time to redecorate the guest rooms and then finish with the ground floor and the communal areas. Surely you can accommodate the minimal disruption by housing guests at your other hotels?'

She's determined to make this work. 'Searching for wiggle room to satisfy us both?' I say, my respect for her persistence and flexibility growing.

She flushes as though I've hit a nerve, leaving me curious about what exactly is running through her mind and if it in any way correlates to the pleasurable distractions in mine.

'It makes good business sense that we're both happy—repeat work from satisfied clients forms a large part of my business, so I would, of course, aim to give you everything you want.'

Her words, and the double meaning my brain interprets, make my blood pound harder.

'Ruthless and accommodating—admirable.' My smile seems to bring a delightful flush to her skin, but the bitter tang in my mouth reminds me that I've fallen prey to such ruthlessness before—never again, no matter how appealing the package. And ensuring Dad hasn't fallen prey to Blair's charms, her radical changes, will be my top priority going forward, no matter how good her designs.

'Yes…' she says, 'well…running my own business has taught me it's the only way to stop unscrupulous people taking advantage.' Her stare dips to the table. Perhaps because she's just intimated I'm unscrupulous and not to be trusted. If only she knew the lack of trust is totally reciprocated.

'Well, ruthlessness in a business setting is a worthy skill. One we share.' Best she understands from the start I'm not simply going to roll over because she waves her contract or cites our family connections. My suspicious mind hasn't abandoned all its wild theories—she could have cornered Graham at the golf club, played on his confusion, and now she's here to pick over the bones, for all I know. Perhaps she plans to sabotage her father's main competition by painting my beloved hotel lime green…

My lips twitch at that last absurd thought. That's *never* going to happen.

'Oh, I fully intend to extend the ruthlessness you admire to all areas of my life, believe me.' Her lips part, dragging my attention south.

Fuck. Is she flirting? And how can I have the best of both worlds here—the Faulkner safe and sound and under my strict control, and this woman temporarily in my bed? My attraction to her could become a distraction I don't need. Better to dispense with the inconvenience and focus on Dad and the renovations he's set in motion.

'But that falls outside the realms of this discussion,' she says.

I check the grudging respect for her building inside, quashing it back down. Blair Cameron may look like a strong wind could topple her from those heels, but there's steel running through her skeleton. Steel and ambition and fucking sexy spunk.

'Why don't you amend the contract to say the renovations will be staged so we can close the Faulkner to guests for the bare minimum of time?' she says.

I slide a file her way. 'I've already thought of that—the newly amended contract.' I lean back, a slug of satisfaction stretching my lips into a small smile, while I wait for the counter-proposal I know is coming. She's too smart, too driven to allow me off the hook so easily—after all, she has the upper hand legally, although she showed she can compromise too when she handled Graham's mistaken identity so thoughtfully.

'Great.' She eyes the paperwork and then looks up.

I relax into the leather, getting comfortable, and allow my stare to wander. That she isn't a pushover sharpens my focus, so I notice a freckle in the hollow at the base of her throat and find new colours hiding in her irises. I'm not expecting her question or the sharp change in direction.

'Is Graham still under the impression I'm his soon-to-be daughter-in-law?' She too relaxes back in the chair, as if all business deals conclude in this personal way.

The hair at the nape of my neck stands to attention. 'I don't see how what happened yesterday is relevant.' I'm not exposing my father to curiosity or gossip, or even to her well-meaning pity.

'You asked me to lie, to play along—that's how it's relevant.' Her index fingernail taps the table and she glances down, stilling the movement. 'I know you and I aren't close...' her eyes bounce back to mine '...but neither am I a complete stranger.'

I suck in a breath through my teeth, mentally conceding her point even as I try to wriggle free.

I *did* ask her to play along with Dad's misunderstanding. My father's presence in my office when he should have been at his club gave me enough of a shock, without the added double whammy of him mistaking Blair for Sadie, back when we'd first been engaged. I was reeling.

'No, perhaps our age difference is the reason we don't know each other well. You're young, in fact, to be running your own business, one of the reasons I was slightly bemused by your appointment.'

Her lush lips thin as if I've touched a nerve. 'I assure you I'm capable—Graham, for one, believes in me, and I respect him too,' she says, holding my eye contact. 'He's always been kind to me, made time for me, and I'd like to know how to respond when I see him again. I don't think that's unreasonable. In fact, I insist,' she says, putting me in my place once more.

Could she be any more fascinating?

I conceal my own uncertainty behind a shrug. I wish I had the answers she requires. But she's right—I have to give her something. 'He's…intermittently slightly confused and currently undergoing investigations.' I tap the table, my eyes narrowing. 'I'm afraid I can't give you any reassurances beyond that. So I understand if you prefer to walk away now.' Will she take the money and run? Will that be an end to this? 'My offer of financial recompense for the time you've already invested, of course, stands.'

She shakes her head before I've even registered the hollow pang that tells me a part of me wants to work with her on this project. Her insistence should ease my suspicions that she's in this for monetary gain. All my preconceived ideas about her, admittedly tainted by my past experiences with Sadie, were all rattled last night when she turned down my offer of financial compensation, and when she played along for the sake of my confused father. And now this morning, despite sticking to her guns, she's amenable and conciliatory, demanding further respect from me where she could have just clung to her bottom line.

My hands tense on the arms of the chair. But all I have to do is keep a close eye on her professionally—I don't have to trust her to enjoy her body.

'I'm happy to sign this revised contract.' She slides the folder closer, lining it up parallel to the edge of the table before relaxing her hands on either side on the polished oak.

I breathe a sigh of relief. 'Great. Then our business is concluded.' This couldn't go better from my point of view. Not only do I have a revised contract, but I've also cited myself as overseer to the work. She won't be able to change a light bulb without my prior approval.

'Perhaps.' Her eyes settle on mine, the rise and fall of her chest telling me I'm in no way imagining her sexual interest. I'm certain we want the same thing. And by the way this satisfactory negotiation has panned out, we could have what we want.

I incline my head, gracious in victory.

'Will I be required to act as if I'm…Sa…your ex again?'

Damn. How the hell am I supposed to answer that? I have no idea how my father will react from one day to the next. The doctors tell me a routine and a calm environment is the best medicine, but until I have that second opinion the last thing I want to do is upset Graham further, which is why I went along with the case of mistaken identity.

'Would that be so terrible?' I say. 'You handled it perfectly last night—something I'm very grateful for, by the way.'

I sense her hesitation, although she's doing a valiant job of trying to conceal it.

I add a layer of inducement. 'Now we've agreed on the specifics of the contract, if there's anything else I can do for you in return, just let me know.' Everyone wants something. What does Blair Cameron want if it isn't to sabotage my hotel?

She nods, looks away and then turns back to

face me with new resolve and a flash of excitement shining in her eyes. 'Actually, I do.'

Well, this should be interesting. I smile, heat building in my chest with excitement for the demands she's about to make.

'Now I'm intrigued. Go on.' My stare zeroes in on her full mouth, a mouth I'd like to feel on mine. The fire is there between us, a smoulder of embers waiting to be fanned to a blaze.

'I'm willing to…play along should the need arise. I wouldn't want to embarrass Graham or make things worse for him.' Her eyes harden. 'I prefer not to deceive him, believe me, but you've already put me in a difficult position.'

'So what *do* you want?'

She pushes her hair back from her face. 'If my work on the Faulkner meets your approval, you'll write me a client testimonial I can use however I see fit.'

'That's easy enough.' I'm failing to see where the rub is for me—she's agreed to all my terms, above and beyond. 'A glowing recommendation is something I'd do for any worthy contractor.' I'm sensing there's more. The second item, perhaps. 'What else do you want?' Everyone has a price, but can I afford hers? I hold myself still, certain her next demand will cost me one way or the other.

She hesitates, her lip caught under her top teeth,

'I—it's a little…unprofessional. Perhaps we should discuss it after hours.'

'Now works just fine for me.' I wait, curiosity a persistent drum sounding in my head. 'Tell me, Blair.'

My hushed command does the trick in loosening her tongue.

'Do you…find me attractive?' she asks with a tilt of her chin.

I conceal my astonished reaction. 'Attractive?' My blood roars. Sexy as fuck, more like. Fascinating, whip-smart and ballsy. What is there to doubt?

She nods. 'I could be wrong…about our… chemistry.' Her eyes dip to the tabletop for a fraction but then they're back, bolder than before.

I lean forward, place my arms on the table, my hands clasped together to stop myself reaching out and touching the strand of hair that has fallen over her cheek.

'You're not wrong. I've always thought you're a beautiful woman.' The heat in my chest slides below the belt. This is so inconvenient, but now she's verbalised what I hoped to hear, I'm done for.

The breath she's holding shudders out of her, the flutter of the pulse in her neck, the increased heat from her body, the subtle shift of her crossed legs all indicating she's as turned on as me.

'Ask your favour.' My patience snaps. The

sparks in her eyes deliver fresh blood to my groin. I'm either going to love what comes next out of those delicious lips, or my instincts are decidedly off...

'Well... I used to have something of a teenage crush on you.' She laughs then, despite the heightened colour in her cheeks. It's a delightful sound—a little throaty, almost dirty and so unexpected I laugh too. I didn't know about the crush. Yes, I recall for a while in my late twenties she blushed every time we crossed paths—which wasn't that often—but I figured it was an awkward phase. A teenager thing.

Then I quirk one eyebrow, waiting while this new piece of information floods my body with testosterone. 'Tell me what you want from me.' If it's what I'm thinking the answer is *hell, yes*. The fact that she knows what she wants and is negotiating it into our terms is the biggest turn-on so far. She's accruing quite a list of attributes.

But surely it can't be the same thing I want. The thing I've wanted since she looked up at me in the Faulkner Group waiting area with a flash of recognition and something else. Something bold and demanding, as ruthless as any business stipulation. Now I want to hear those other demands, hear confirmation from her sensual mouth.

She picks at a speck on her dress, something

so minute it's invisible. 'I'm correct in thinking you're single, right?'

I nod, watching her with renewed fanaticism. 'I've done the marriage thing—now I only do casual.' I incline my head, waiting while my heart hammers—I've never been propositioned like this before and to say I like it would be an understatement.

I lean a fraction closer and toss her a lifeline. 'We might be on the same page here.'

She nods, as if she's worked that out long before me. 'I'd like to propose a second contract. Just a verbal one will do.' Her eyes shine as she taps the paperwork on the table. 'Separate to the business one so no lines are blurred.'

'Why?' My interest peaks with the strengthening urge to taste her delicious-looking mouth.

'I beg your pardon?'

'Why do we need a second contract?' I know enough about her by now to know she won't fluster and dither at my direct question, but I need to know we're negotiating the same thing.

Her response blows me away.

'Because I have fantasies about you I'd like to play out.' Her voice is breathy now, and I not only know how driven and ambitious she is, but also how she sounds when she's turned on.

Before I can speak she continues the aural torture.

'If we're working closely together, something is going to happen sooner or later, and I prefer to keep sex separate from our working relationship. I don't want anything to interfere with the Faulkner renovations. Call it a no-strings arrangement if you like.'

I shift in my seat, arousal for once in what feels like a lifetime surpassing my need to control every aspect of my life and my business. Then I recall why we're here and what happened the last time I allowed my personal life—*Sadie*—to interfere with my family business. 'I don't often mix business with pleasure, and I'm usually the person in the driving seat when I do.'

I don't want her having any unrealistic expectations. Anything between us will be finite.

She holds my stare, lips parted and breaths shallow. 'That's why we need the second contract. And you *can* be in the driving seat.'

I swallow hard—she's incredible. Bold. Confronting. Captivating.

'Oh, I know I can.' I don't need her permission. 'If you want this, we do it my way.'

My mind helpfully provides a series of erotic images. The idea of making this woman's fantasies come true turns me to granite, so I have to spread my thighs under the table. My mind trips over itself. How will this even work? She's correct—it's

borderline unprofessional, not to mention the age
gap. *Fuck, who cares?* If she doesn't, I don't. And
we're consenting adults. It's just sex. I can keep
emotions off the cards, just as I have since Sadie,
so there's no chance of me being sucked in again.

She licks her lips, perhaps an unconscious
gesture…one that has a predictable effect on my
body. I grit my teeth and then relax my jaw so I
can speak. The sooner we're done negotiating, the
sooner we can put our verbal contract into prac-
tice. 'Tell me what you want this second contract
to include.'

She speaks without pause, telling me she's
played this conversation over in her head prior
to this meeting. 'One,' she counts on her fingers.
'No-strings sex. Two—it doesn't interfere with my
work on the Faulkner.'

My pulse thunders in my head. I shrug, keeping my body relaxed. 'No feelings, no strings, just
sex—easy.'

But she hasn't finished.

'Three—we work through my fantasies, but I'm
open to any you might have.'

Fuck me! She could actually bring me to my
knees… I arch my brow, fighting hard to maintain a neutral facial expression when all I want to
do is sweep the conference table clear and spread
her out. 'Anything else?'

She shrugs. 'I think that covers it.' She sucks in a big breath, trying to conceal the move. Her eyes dart, telling me she hasn't thought this through that far or she's hoping I'll simply take the lead. And I will.

Oh, we're going to have some fun.

'Up to the task?' she asks, eyes heavy with want.

Hell, yes. Is there a better way to keep a close eye on what Blair Cameron does to my hotel and exploit this unexpectedly fierce chemistry?

'I have no problem with the arrangement as laid out in this verbal contract.' I sound as if I'm dictating a memo, not discussing how to satisfy Blair Cameron's fantasies. 'You tell me about these fantasies and leave the rest to me.'

Her lips purse as if she's about to argue, even as her chest flushes with arousal.

I add another layer of incentive. 'I promise you'll benefit.'

'I will?' she asks, her tongue darting out to moisten her lip.

I nod, dropping my voice. 'Expect to come a lot.' I look up from her mouth to catch the flare of her pupils. 'Expect my very enthusiastic and frequent attention. Expect to have all your fantasies fulfilled.'

She smiles as though we're discussing paint colours or upholstery fabric, not how I'm going to give her so many orgasms she won't be able to walk on the heels she seems to love.

'Deal.' She holds out her hand, the fine tremor in her fingers almost invisible. 'Shall we shake on it?'

I take her hand and try not to smile when I hear the tiny catch in her throat as our palms connect. Before she can disengage from the most rewarding and electrifying handshake I've had in many years, I add another suggestion. I can't help myself. Blair Cameron is just too much—too tempting, too sexy and too much woman.

'I have a better idea.' I grip her hand a fraction tighter, allowing my fingertips to dance on her delicate inner wrist, because, now I've touched her with something beyond the professional, I want more. I want all of her. 'Tell me about one of these fantasies.'

My hard-on tents the front of my trousers underneath the table.

Her eyes widen as her hand slips from mine, and she sucks in a small, excited gasp that shoots straight to my balls. 'Now? Here?' She glances at the closed door, stands and smooths her palms down her thighs as if she's contemplating fleeing. But not Blair, although she must have guessed I'd be burning with curiosity to hear about these fantasies.

I nod, slowly, so she gets the message while my mind leafs through all the delicious possibilities. I swivel my chair, keeping my thighs spread so she can see the effect her particular negotiating skills have on me from her standing position. I give her a beat or two to take in the bulge I can't conceal, then I stand too, moving close so she has to look up if she wants to maintain her bold, almost challenging eye contact.

I'm close enough to kiss her, but I draw out the anticipation, even though I can't seem to stop looking at her mouth.

'I'd like to hear them all, but start with the first one you can remember.' My blood simmers. This verbal foreplay is not something I would usually indulge in at the office, but she's irresistible. She's thrown me completely with her bold request, and I'm not one to be outdone.

Her colour darkens, and I inch closer until her nipples brush my chest as she sucks in another shaky breath.

I tuck the strand of hair I've been longing to touch over her shoulder, loving the shudder that seems to rattle her entire frame as she inhales. 'Come on, Blair. Let's hear it.'

The minute lift of her chin, her go-to move of bravery, heralds her final act of surrender.

'I... I used to touch myself and think about

you.' Her confession is accompanied by a breathy sigh, which takes my body from keen to barely restrained. My fingers twitch to get hold of her sensational body, to touch every inch, taste her all over and hear her moans of pleasure.

'How old were you?' I'm almost scared to ask.

She shrugs. 'Seventeen…eighteen.'

Fuck. I couldn't even think of that then, but I can sure as shit do more than think about it today.

I nod, arch my brow, enjoy the gust of her warm breath on my lips. 'Show me.'

Her eyes go wide.

My pulse pounds through my head, driving me. 'Go on.' Excitement crackles between us like static electricity. 'See what happens.'

She flushes, her gaze once more drifting to the door. 'Now? I don't think I can, not here.'

Oh, no, this isn't the woman who's just negotiated a sexual dalliance between us as successfully as she's manoeuvred her company into a lucrative deal. This contradictory coyness won't do in light of what she's just told me. I want everything. Now.

I lean close, dip my head so my breath snakes over her exposed earlobe and her shudder wafts the scent of her hair over me.

'Liar,' I whisper, fighting the need to taste the skin of her neck.

She sways closer and I ease back, a tease, keeping my distance, torturing us both. For now. But the struggle is real, the deep and relentless need catching me off guard.

I continue in the same husky voice, 'It's your call, of course.'

She's panting now, her breath brushing my lips, and it takes every scrap of control I possess not to kiss her. But not yet. She's set a challenge, one my libido is raring to meet.

And I want to hear every detail of these fantasies. I want to know how her inventive and open mind works, especially the part that not only conjured up fantasies about me, but also had the mettle to proposition me in the Faulkner boardroom.

'Tell me.' I allow my hushed words to bathe the space between our mouths. 'Would you be in the bath or in your bed? Would I walk in and catch you with your hand down the front of your underwear? Would you stop touching yourself, or continue knowing I couldn't look away?'

Excitement sparks in her eyes. The space between her body and mine floods with pheromones, the air temperature rising and generating enough electrical activity to start a thunderstorm.

'Go on,' I taunt. 'Let me watch you now.'

She reaches for my forearms with both hands, as if she needs me to balance. But the look she raises to mine is pure challenge. She may have hesitated out of a sense of professionalism, but I can tell there's no way she'll allow me to wrestle control of her fantasy from her, and I'm happy to concede for the reward of watching this fascinating and beautiful woman claim her pleasure.

'Okay.' Her voice is husky with need or nerves, but she drops one hand to her side and slips it under the hem of her dress.

Triumph flares in my chest even as my knees weaken—she's astounding. Brave and determined and capable of anything. And fuck me if the fact she knows what she wants and isn't afraid to chase it isn't the biggest turn-on so far.

She drags in a shaky breath, her whole body trembling with its force. I look down to see her dress hitched up and her hand buried between her legs, but sheltered from my view by the bunched-up fabric.

I swallow hard. She's a dream. A siren. A goddess sent to test me.

I call on every scrap of strength I possess not to touch her, and force my voice to continue in the same low tone. 'What would you have done if I'd caught you touching yourself? What would you have said?'

She looks up with the need which is mirrored in me burning in her beautiful eyes. 'Kiss me.'

It's what I want to hear, the exact invitation I need.

I cup her face, holding her stare and tilting her head to the desired angle, but taking my sweet time even though I want to taste the lush lips only millimetres from mine with a ferocity I'm struggling to control.

'Just so you know, I've wanted to kiss you since I walked into the waiting area and saw you yesterday.' I give her no time to absorb my words, her tiny gasp signal enough that she's registered them. I slide my mouth over her parted lips and drag her body to mine so every soft inch of her is pressed up against the hardness she inspires.

One swipe, two, three… Who's counting?

She parts her lips further, accepting the push of my tongue inside. My fingers tangle in that swath of blonde silk and she whimpers under me, her whole body slack and her eyes, which have remained open throughout, glazing over.

I pull back, foolishly thinking I'm done with the kiss, only to tilt my head sideways and enjoy it from the opposite angle—an experience that's as good as the first time, because now she's practically writhing all over me and clutching at my hair with her free hand as she kisses me back.

Just one more taste. Just one more minute, then I'll put a stop to this and walk away.

Energy pours through me, electrifying every cell in my body. The reality of Blair Cameron has blown my mind. This room has never hosted such agreeable negotiations. I feel a new shiny brass plaque is in order to commemorate the great contract agreement of the Faulkner Group and Cameron Interiors.

But I want more now I've had one taste. I can't help myself. Knowing she's still touching herself under that dress, thinking of *me*, wanting *me*, recalling fantasies of *me*…

We part, panting and gasping.

'As good as you fantasised?' My voice is gruff. I'm at the office. It's before ten in the morning and all I can think about is laying her back on the oak conference table for a look under this dress.

Her mouth is swollen and I touch her lips, wiping the moisture from them with the pads of my fingers. They're smooth, red, a sexy haven I want to see slack with ecstasy, gasping my name and wrapped around my dick.

She nods, her head shaky, but then, in a bold move I should have expected, she sucks the pad of my index finger into her mouth and swivels her hips so her belly crushes my erection between us. 'Then I would have asked *you* to touch me.'

The groan in my head abolishes any reservation and spurs me on.

Her lips return to mine, her kiss sexy and bold, slaying me.

In one move I hoist her up and deposit her on the table, stepping into the space she creates for me by spreading her thighs. She doesn't care that she's creased her dress by bunching it up her bare, toned legs. She doesn't care that we could be disturbed at any minute. My own workplace principles are shot to hell by the heat coming from between her legs as I wedge myself closer. I can't get close enough.

I kiss her again, this time hissing at the ferocity with which she twists my hair. But revenge tastes as sweet as her mouth when I slide my hand up one thigh, my fingers joining hers tangling in the shoved-aside crotch of her damp underwear and her soft, slick centre.

This is madness. What the hell is she doing to me? Any minute now I'll come to my senses and stop.

She bucks against my hand, her fingers and mine sliding together to rub all the right places, and I wedge my hips closer to stop her slipping from the edge of the table. Then she snatches her own hand away so she can brace her arms behind her on the table.

'Yes,' she hisses around our kiss. 'Oh… Reid!'

My fingers glide over her swollen clit. A triumphant growl resonates past my tight throat. I pull away from her mouth to watch her pleasure streak across her beautiful face as I work the bundle of nerves. 'This is what you used to think about?'

She nods as I glance down to where all that deliciousness is exposed for my eyes only. I enjoy the view of my fingers working her, loving her gasp when I push one finger inside her and continue to circle her clit with my thumb.

'Yes…and I thought about you last night while I made myself come with my vibrator.' Her hips undulate in time with the rhythm of my plunging finger.

Fuck. I'm toast. This woman is almost too hot for me to handle. 'Oh, I'm going to want to see that some time.' I reward her with a second finger and revel in the cry snatched from her throat.

Her head falls back and I scrape my lips along the column of her neck, sucking in the essence of her soft skin. 'So you came to my office this morning with this very intention. Hoping to get what you wanted, to get me hard and get yourself off.'

'Yes. Oh…yes.' Her honesty slays me, her willingness to boldly and ruthlessly claim what she wants weakening my knees so I need to spread my feet wider to support her on the table's edge.

'Tell me you want to get off here, now, in my boardroom, where anyone could find us.' I tongue her earlobe, flicking at the dangling pearl.

Her hips gyrate faster and she grips fistfuls of my shirt so tightly, I wonder if I'll need to explain the missing buttons.

'I want to get off.' Her huge eyes are dark with arousal, clinging to mine. Begging. 'It's been so long.' She gasps. 'Reid, make me come.'

Fuck, she's magnificent. I can't stop now. I want to worship her, to witness her orgasm and how it undoes her put-together appearance. I want her as frantic and desperate as she's made me. And more than that, I want to fulfil her fantasy.

'Every time I have a meeting in here, I'm going to think of you, sexy as fuck on my conference table, taking what you want, your sexy mouth demanding an orgasm. No deal, no meeting will ever be the same. Understand?'

She whimpers, dragging my mouth back to hers with desperate tugs around my neck and shoulders. I kiss her and talk around our kisses, although her mouth is so wild, it's a struggle to get coherent words out. But my mouth runs away with itself, perhaps encouraged by the new deal we've struck. I can't seem to shut up.

'Next time you wear a dress, I want you to forget the underwear. I want to know that, if you're horny, there's nothing to get in my way. Nothing to stop me going down on you and tasting all this delicious sweetness between your legs.' I twist my wrist, scissoring my fingers and pressing down on her clit with my thumb.

She's there. With a sexy moan she throws her head back and comes, her tight muscles gripping my fingers while she rides my hand through the body-racking tremors. I kiss her through her climax, swallowing up her cries, each one a bolt of victory through my chest.

Spent, she collapses forward, her head heavy on my shoulder as her breathing settles. And then she looks up, vulnerable and breath-stealing and more beautiful than I've ever seen her.

I take my hand from between her legs, not ready to let her go just yet. I scoop my other arm around her waist, tugging her closer so we're nose-to-nose and I'm still sandwiched between her glorious thighs, what she does to me evident in my strung-taut body and my steel-hard dick. Stringing out the fantasy with my own erotic twist, I raise one wet finger to her mouth and trace her full bottom lip with her own desire. Her warm breath gusts over my fingertip and renewed excitement flashes in her eyes.

'Taste yourself.' My command, whisper-soft, murmured against her swollen lips makes her eyes widen.

She obeys, her tongue tracing where my finger has been. This time I trace her top lip and then I kiss her, every sense full of her——her scent, the vision of her flushed from her orgasm and the taste of her. All of her.

'Mmm…delicious…' I say around our kiss. 'I can't wait for more.' Then I step away and adjust myself, my own breathing ragged as I get myself back under control. If I don't stop there, we're at serious risk of being caught full-out fucking in the Faulkner Group's boardroom.

She frowns as I shrug into my suit jacket.

'What about you?' Her voice croaks as she slips from the table and pushes down her dress before loosely finger-combing her hair to conceal what has just taken place.

'I have a ten o'clock meeting.' Regret makes my voice a little gruff. I scoop up the signed paperwork and straighten my tie for something to do with my hands besides touch. She's way too tempting. And now I've had a brief taste…the roar in my head tells me how close I am to taking more. Taking everything. Blair Cameron could become an overwhelming addiction without careful management.

'Okay.' She turns away from me, head down, and busies herself with her bag.

Oh, no. She wants to live out her fantasies. Well, my first tactic is anticipation. Sure, I could clear my diary, take her home right now. That's what my body screams at me to do. But by the next time

I touch her we'll both be so primed…the reward will multiply exponentially.

I press up behind her once more, reminding her with the prod of my erection in the small of her back that, sadly, it's business as usual. The scent of sex and coconut shampoo lingers as I nuzzle her hair, seeking her soft, silky earlobe and the delicate pearl, which I tug between my lips. 'Are you free for dinner tonight?'

She gasps, melts back into me and then corrects herself, standing tall as she nods.

I allow my lips to linger, just below her ear—a sensitive spot if the trembles jolting her shoulders are any indication. 'I'll call you later. Have a good day, Blair.'

Her head snaps around, her eyes teetering on the edge of a glare. I wink and she smiles. How could she not? I'm pretty certain I just rocked her world. Her legs are obviously still a little unstable, because she's swaying on those heels she favours.

I leave the room, leave her to compose herself, while I ignore the wants of my own body and get back to my day. Who knew this deal would become so…rewarding?

I temper my wide grin. No one likes a smug bastard.

CHAPTER FOUR

Blair

Wear a dress, no underwear.

I READ THE text again for at least the hundredth time while tiny ripples dance down my abdominal muscles and everything below my waist tightens. I cover my face with my hands, threatening my carefully applied make-up, and groan.

What am I doing? What *did* I do?

My breath shudders into my lungs on a surge of shame. I confessed my long-held crush to Reid Faulkner. I negotiated sex into my Faulkner contract. I propositioned him and then I rode his hand on his boardroom conference table. And, of course, I agreed to play by his rules, the reason I'm in my current underwear predicament.

A hysterical giggle escapes past my fingers as I reread the text. I never believed Reid would go for my sexy proposition. I clutch my stomach, reliving the cascade of emotional turmoil I felt over our negotiations. Navigating the currents and rips of keeping my Faulkner contract solid while broaching the elephant in the room of our chemistry. The lingering niggle of fear I was wrong about our mutual attraction. The possibility he'd think our age difference insurmountable, or still see me as an easily ignored and mopey teen.

I slip my phone inside my bag to stop myself from reading the text again.

I'm over thinking. Reid was clearly on board with the sex-only arrangement. As long as he sticks to his side of the bargain and stays out of my plans for the Faulkner, I need only sit back and enjoy our fling.

Why, then, am I still wearing my underwear?

I sigh, applying another slick of gloss to my bottom lip for good measure. I've spent the year following Josh's betrayal working long hours, clawing back a client list, rebranding C&L Interiors and putting my personal life on hold. Now it's time to have a little of what *I* want and truly put the past behind me.

But with Reid, of all men?

He doesn't trust easily, that much is clear from some of the comments he's made. And I understand. I trusted Josh even after the cheating, accepting his seemingly heartfelt apologies, even counselling him through his confusion over his sexuality. I snort at my own stupidity. I spent hours ignoring my own needs while listening to his assurances that we could stay friends, still work together even though we were ending things as a couple.

My stomach pinches as I recall the shock of arriving at the office the Monday following our break-up to find no sign of him, current client files wiped from the computer and the business account stripped of funds.

I hover near the laundry basket, debating the pros and cons of following Reid's sexy request. I don't need his trust to enjoy this. I can make the most of our mutual attraction, reclaim my personal life as fiercely as I've fought to rebuild my business. Surely I've done the hardest part—admitting I fantasised about him and demanding he play the starring role as I live out those fantasies.

I close my eyes, recalling his kiss this morning in his boardroom…my pulse speeds and my internal muscles clench just thinking about the way his lips commanded mine just as I'd always imagined; the way he touched me, his big frame holding me; the way my body felt vibrantly alive for the first time in a year, reality outstripping every Reid fantasy I've ever had.

My stomach flips, excitement winning.

Before I can change my mind, I hike up my dress and slide off my lacy thong, tossing it in the laundry basket with a liberating finality. I smooth my palms over my hips, the sensual chill of the fabric lining my dress of choice joining the cool air between my legs—a sensual promise that makes my breath catch as if Reid is already in the room. Just like the promise of his text, the promise of his words.

'Expect to come a lot. Expect my very enthusiastic and frequent attention. Expect to have all your fantasies fulfilled.'

His car is waiting outside my ground-floor flat in Parson's Green when I emerge, determined to embrace the arrangement I set in motion. He steps from the back and greets me with a chaste kiss to the cheek. But his mouth twists in the rare but astounding smile I've always adored, his scruff-covered jaw scrapes against my skin, sparking my nervous system alive as if he has the unique key to my erogenous zones, and his warm breath tickles my neck as he whispers a gruff, 'You look beautiful.'

'Thanks.' I stifle my body's uncontrolled judder of pleasure that he, Reid Faulkner, wants me. My eighteen-year-old self would flip cartwheels down the street.

I stroke the lapel of his jacket, this one navy where this morning's had been charcoal. 'You don't look so bad yourself.' He's wearing a fresh shirt, the subtle scent of his cologne and undertones of something soapy telling me he's taken time out of his day to prepare for our 'dinner date'.

I slide into the car and press my thighs together, the cool leather on the backs of my legs going some way towards counteracting Reid's appearance, which floods my pelvis with gooey heat and hijacks my pulse with anticipation.

He settles beside me and signals to his driver but leaves the privacy screen down, and I try to hide my disappointment that he's not going to ravish me before we even make it to the restaurant.

'How long have you lived in Parson's Green?' he asks, setting the tone to polite conversation.

I answer, my hands clenched in my lap. I don't want to talk about the house I once shared with Josh. The house *he* encouraged me to remortgage to bolster our growing business and the debts he could so easily ignore when he walked away with our most lucrative clients.

'Where do *you* live?' I'm helpless against the way his mouth moves as he answers, remembering the decadent way he kissed me this morning—full pelt, like he'd been dying to do it since I stepped into the Faulkner Group offices the day before.

I half listen to him talk about Chelsea and how he and his brothers all live within a mile of each other, and close to Graham. I remember how close-knit they were growing up, although Kit and Drake seemed to squabble a lot, dragging Reid into the occasional argument on the rare occasions he was home when I visited.

'You've drifted—everything okay?' Reid's voice draws me back to our date. 'Nervous?' he asks, and I want him to touch me, to shove my body into that heady euphoria of this morning.

I latch onto the lifeline of his dark blue eyes and nod. 'A little. This is my first *date*—' I make air quotes to let him know I'm not shifting the goal-posts '—since Josh and I broke up.'

His hand lifts to push some hair back from my face but his fingers make no contact with my skin, to my endless frustration. 'That didn't end well for you, I'm sensing. Tell me about this dickhead of a fiancé who let you go.'

I grip my clutch bag and stare out of the window while I organise my emotions on the subject. Funny that admitting I was duped romantically is easier to confess than how naive I was business-wise, perhaps because, with the exception of Reid's father, no one in my life ever really believed I was capable of running my own business. Even Josh, when I first suggested we start our own company, baulked at the idea, only coming around when I offered the small nest egg I'd inherited from my grandmother as the necessary start-up capital.

'I caught him cheating, so no, it didn't end well. Does it ever?'

Shock registers on his face and I take comfort from it for a few flattering seconds.

'What an idiot.' He takes my hand, the simple gesture incendiary to my body temperature and soothing the sting of admitting past humiliation I should have dealt with by now, but clearly have simply shelved while working to rebuild my business every waking hour.

I clear my throat, seeking the same bravery I found in his boardroom this morning. 'I know it's going to sound naive, but after the initial shock of my discovering his betrayal we parted on good terms. Tried to stay friends for the sake of the business we'd started together after university, which was where we met.'

Reid's beautiful mouth twists. 'That's incredibly mature of you. I'm not sure I could have taken that attitude in your position.'

His compliment warms me, the years between us shrinking away for the first time. I change the subject, too close to admitting more and disabusing him of his regard.

'What happened with you and Sadie?'

Shutters seem to cover his eyes, reminding me this apparent closeness is an illusion—we're still virtual strangers. I know his father better than I know him.

'Also didn't work out, although not for the same reasons.' He shrugs. 'I dodged a bullet and it sounds like you might have as well. At least you hadn't married the guy.' His hand tightens around mine, his thumb swiping the back of my hand. 'It must have been hard though, losing your fiancé and your business partner in one fell swoop and having to go it alone.'

I half nod, half shrug. If only he knew...

'I channelled all my energies into the business— put in long hours, rebranded, raised the profile of the company. It's made me stronger and cured me from ever wanting a business partner again.'

His smile is layered with respect, causing heat to unfurl inside me. 'I can imagine, although being self-employed isn't easy—that's quite a burden of responsibility. At least I have Kit and Drake, and Graham taught me everything he knows. You've completely sidestepped from your family, branched out alone.'

I don't need the reminder of how irrelevant what I'm doing is to my large, self-absorbed family, who, as I'm the youngest, have always completely underestimated me. 'Well, it's all about scale, isn't it? You employ hundreds of staff. I have an office manager and a list of subcontractors. And Graham helped *me* out, too.'

'He did?' His surprise turns to what looks like awe. And I smile for their father-son bond. Of course, Reid and Graham must be close, working together all these years.

'Yes. I've always valued and respected his opinions—he's given me some valuable advice over the years.'

'Such as?'

I stall, dozens of memories crowding my mind, most of them linked in some way to the man sitting beside me. 'He always seemed to have time for me, even when he talked business with my dad—he once spent an hour explaining the way the stock market works to a fifteen-year-old me. When I earned a place at university he sat me down and told me to chase my passions, whatever they were, even if it was the path less travelled. He even came to my graduation ceremony—did you know that?'

Reid's eyes widen. He seems shell-shocked, as if I've told him something about his father's warm and giving personality that he didn't previously know.

I continue. 'When I qualified, I started work for a big company in the city—I hated it; I was creatively stifled and felt trapped. I'd chosen this career, against my own family's advice, and for a moment there, I thought I'd have to admit they were correct and go back to Dad for a job with my tail between my legs. Then I talked to Graham about the idea of starting C&L Interiors. Of course, he knew little of the creative aspects, but he offered plenty of sage business-related advice, put me in touch with a great business-mentoring organisation and was so enthusiastic and encouraging I felt I couldn't fail. But then, I've always found him generous like that.' I swallow hard at the sickening reminder that, of course, I could fail and almost had.

'Yes. Yes, he is.' Reid looks at me as if with fresh eyes. 'I was unaware you two were that close. I guess I've been a little out of the loop, socially.'

I can't hold back any longer—I have to ask, for my own peace of mind. 'Is Graham's confusion likely to be temporary?' The backs of my eyes burn and I have to swallow repeatedly to keep myself in check.

Reid glances out of the window at the passing traffic, perhaps looking for a distraction. 'The doctors say it's dementia.' He turns back to face me, his sculpted jaw tense. 'We're awaiting a second opinion.'

I cover my mouth in shock, my mind racing with the implications. 'I'm so sorry, Reid. That must be very hard for you, Drake and Kit, and, of course, Graham.' My eyes burn anew as I recall all Graham's kindnesses and considerations over the years. 'He's a lovely man.'

I want to pry some more, to ask about Graham's prognosis and what it means for him and the family. But the car pulls to a halt, ending our conversation and giving me a few seconds to pull myself together.

Reid exits and I follow, my hand still nestled in his. With my head reeling after what he's just confessed, I've barely found my balance on the pavement, when he steps closer, backing me up until my backside hits the car door and our chests collide. My breath hitches as all thought except of the man towering in front of me ebbs away. His warm, hard body pressing against mine from chest to thigh reminds me how decadent touching him feels. How forbidden even the idea of him has been for so long. How, after fighting and striving to make it alone, this past year has drained every sexual impulse from me, and the idea of handing over control to this man—albeit just in the bedroom—leaves me giddy with relief and anticipation.

I look up, achingly aware of his height, his broad chest, every spectacular masculine inch of him.

His arms encircle me, our entwined hands settling in the small of my back as he crushes me to his chest.

'Thank you.'

'What for?' His shirt smells fantastic, and I want to rub the scent all over myself so I can wake up tomorrow and relive tonight.

He pulls back and I'm left deprived of his heat under my cheek. 'For telling me how my father helped you.' The flash of uncertainty which momentarily crosses his features is so out of place, I almost convince myself I didn't see it.

'You're welcome.' I'm dying to ask questions. To press him for his confidence, but instinct tells me he'd disappear behind that controlled veneer quicker than the snap of a mousetrap. And the selfish, horny part of me is grateful I kept my mouth shut when I catch the intense look on his face a split second before his mouth descends and he kisses the air from my chest.

I cling to the sleeve of his jacket with my free hand as I kiss him back, any thought beyond how good it feels to be able to do this with him abolished.

He breaks away first, his chest heaving. 'Fuck, I've wanted to do that since you stepped out of your front door.' His lips brush mine again and he grins, almost apologetically. 'I'd planned to draw out the anticipation, but you're too irresistible.'

I laugh, all my nerves forgotten, and wipe the smear of my lip gloss from his mouth.

'Thanks.' He peels his body from mine and I almost hear our combined sigh of regret as we head inside. He guides me ahead of him, his hand in the small of my back. His fingers slide to the top of my arse, caressing, sending snakes of delight down to the backs of my knees.

I exhale through pursed lips as I settle myself in our discreet, booth-style table. Reid sits close enough that our thighs brush, his touch doing something wonderful to fan every flutter of excitement inside me so I'm desperate with anticipation. Not content with this, he spreads his legs in that way men sit, so now we're touching hip to knee and I'm left deliciously curious as to how much space he needs to create between his thighs. My mouth dries and he presses his leg against mine in a very deliberate move.

'Hungry?' he asks, his thumb idly swiping back and forth on my bare shoulder where he's casually slung his arm around my back.

I shrug, the keg of lust inside me filling to capacity. 'A little.' How can he do this to me, inspire so much lust with just a look and minimal body contact? Clearly a year without sex is too long. Clearly my fantasies were spot-on and the long wait to have them fulfilled was worth every second of yearning.

His stare hits me—seductive, bold, a challenge. 'Did you get my text?'

I nod, my brain fried by his heated eye contact, the scrape of his commanding voice and the reminder he wanted me bare and I willingly, almost giddily, complied. He's taking my fantasies and adding layer after layer of extras until I'm certain I'll combust from desire.

His eyes dip from my face, travelling at a snail's pace over my breasts and down into my lap, where my hands are clutched. 'Good, because I'm ravenous.' His eyes meet mine, and the flames in my belly reignite.

I forget how to breathe, revelling in the beam of his attention, just like this morning, when any other Faulkner employee could have disturbed us. My blood roars so hard, I completely miss the waiter asking for our drinks choice.

Reid keeps his eyes on me. 'What do you say?' He brushes a strand of hair from my cheek, fingertips grazing, in no hurry. 'Champagne?'

I nod, my mouth too dry for speech. Now he's touched me, kissed me, it's as if he can't keep his hands to himself. I resist the urge to fan my face or douse my body with the chilled water on the table. I know I wanted this, but at this rate I'll be a pile of ash before we've even ordered.

When we're alone, I gather some of my wits and

clear my throat. 'Just so we're clear, I'll be paying for dinner.' He can control the sex—something tells me I'll reap all the rewards tenfold—but I'm still a strong, independent woman. Of course, we may have to limit ourselves to the one bottle…

Reid snorts. 'I don't think so.' He inches closer, the heat in his stare constant, as if my suggestion carried negligible consequences.

'Dutch, then? This was *my* idea.'

Reid's stare narrows, searching, and then he dips his head so his lips graze my cheek. 'You said I could be in the driver's seat, so why don't you relax about the bill?'

The feminist in me baulks, deciding next time, if there is a repeat date, I'll put up more of a fight. Then I remember *I* suggested sex. We're here because I made him a proposition beyond business. And I conceded control so I could live out the very Reid fantasies making me hot and achy and embarrassingly damp between my legs…

Perhaps sensing victory, he grins, has the audacity to wink. 'Get used to it. Besides, we have more pressing matters to discuss.' His stare dances over my face, settling on my mouth, and he leans in so his lips brush my ear. 'Let's pick up where we left off this morning. You touching yourself, me walking in, watching, taking over…' His voice recites the events as if I needed the recap, but it's imprinted on my memory.

'So, tell me, how else did I touch you in these early fantasies? Because I need to touch you again.' His breath slides down my neck as he dips his chin and hums a sexy growl low in his throat while in-haling deeply.

He's sniffing me.

I shudder as my whole body tingles. My mouth opens but no sound emerges—I'm so turned on I literally couldn't speak even to warn him that the building around us was on fire. I check his expres-sion, seeing the need I glimpsed this morning as I came back down to earth after my orgasm.

'Here?' It's a croak. First his boardroom, now this restaurant… Perhaps he's some sort of exhi-bitionist. Do I care? As long as the boundaries of our game are so beautifully delineated. As long as I get what I want from this, from him.

He wets his lips and nods, his stare bouncing down to my mouth. 'I can't help myself.'

I look down to where his hand rests on the table, his fingers impatiently drumming. I nod too, so overcome with lust, I've forgotten all of the words in my vocabulary.

The other hand, which rests behind me on the seat, skates up my back and settles at the nape of my neck and then he's tugging me forward until our mouths touch in a slow, sensual glide of lips and mingling of warm breath.

I gasp as he releases me, nowhere near done with his particular brand of kisses, but he doesn't pull away. His eyes are intense as he looks to the place his mouth has just been as if he's just tasted the most delicious delicacy on earth and he wants more. His tongue peeks out and touches his top lip as he raises his hand and wipes a smear of lip gloss from my chin.

Pressure builds in my chest. I suck in a breath, preparing to touch my mouth back to his.

The waiter returns and Reid relaxes back into the leather beside me while I try my best to breathe normally and to not leave scorch marks on the leather.

Fucking hell. Have I ever been kissed the way he kisses me—with such delicious dichotomy? Devouring and demanding this morning, lazily thorough while pressed against his car, and slow and sensual in this quiet corner, as if I'm on the menu and he's determined to savour every bite. If I'd known it would be this good, perhaps I should have risked everything and thrown myself at him years ago.

The waiter pours the wine at Reid's request and then departs. I take a glug to settle my pounding blood before I lose consciousness and miss all the fun. I instinctively knew he'd be good…but this is a whole new level.

'So what would you like to eat? The seafood here is excellent.' Reid flips open his menu, eyes downcast, while his other hand settles on my knee under the table as if we've casually touched each other intimately a thousand times.

Warm. Confident. Thrilling.

Despite the way he touched me this morning, the intimacy is still alien enough that I freeze, the tingles from his palm print travelling up my thigh straight to my bare clit. He's inches away from touching my nakedness. In a public place. No closed door between us, and the other patrons only metres away.

I should push him away, but, as if controlled by a lascivious third party, my thighs spread a fraction.

'What are you doing?' I whisper, while bubbles of adrenaline pop in my veins.

His thumb strokes back and forth over my feverish skin with the familiarity and comfort of a lover, as if it's one of the million touches we share as a couple. But we're not a couple. We know only the superficial facts about each other. And this somehow adds to the potent hormonal mix.

He looks up from the menu as if I've requested nothing more banal than the time. 'I can't keep my hands off you, and you must have had more than one fantasy—I want details.'

It's so matter-of-fact, I'm sure my mouth hangs open, while all I can do is nod.

'I can't stop thinking about this morning,' he says. 'About what other fantasies you have. And just knowing you might be bare under here...' His stare darkens and he presses a silencing finger to my lips. 'Don't tell me—I want to find out for myself.' Then his attention flicks back to the menu while his fingers grip, pressing into my thigh like brands.

I check how low the white linen tablecloth drops, ensuring whatever he has planned won't be witnessed by the rest of the diners. I slide a cursory stare over the menu, the bone-melting lust stealing my decision-making capabilities. Not that food could make it past my tight throat. 'The chicken looks good.'

'Mmm...' he murmurs, his hand inching higher while he peruses the à la carte menu. 'I think I'll have the lamb.' He closes his menu and returns the intensity of his focus to me.

I can't help the shudder. I bite my lip and reach for my wine to cover my reaction.

'Feeling okay?' He too takes a swallow, the bob of his Adam's apple mesmerising.

'Fine.' About to combust, but fine.

'You feel better than fine to me.' His fingers stroke. His stare burns. His voice scrapes. Then slowly and deliberately he says, 'Open.'

One low, seductive word and I jump to his bidding as if I'm a conditioned lab rat desperate for my reward, spreading my thighs a fraction more so he can continue the caress of his palm.

'So smooth and silky and warm.' He leans in, lowering his voice to an intimate whisper. 'And now I know what awaits me at the top of this thigh... I'm struggling to work up much of an appetite for food, unless it's for dessert.'

The look on his face—pure, unrestrained lust combined with his stark declaration—drags a squeak from me and I lower my shaking wine glass to the table. My heart thuds as I struggle for breath around the intrusive visions of having Reid's cock in my mouth, having him desperate and out of control and as needy as I feel right now.

'Penny for your dirty thoughts,' he growls.

How does he know? How can he turn me on so effortlessly? How can I want him so fiercely?

I rest my elbow on the table and lean closer. 'I want your cock in my mouth.'

His fingers still, eyes blazing with lust.

I continue, spinning out the fantasy I can tell turns him on, too. 'I used to dream about coming to the Faulkner, finding you alone in your office and wordlessly dropping to my knees behind your desk.'

His groan, eyes heavy-lidded, is music to my ears.

I lean closer, drop my voice to a more intimate whisper. 'You'd splutter, ask me what I was doing, but you wouldn't stop me as I unzipped your trousers and took you into my mouth.'

'Fuck it, Blair. Touch me. Now.' He lifts one eyebrow, his command so gravelly, the sound buzzes over my nipples.

I glance around the dining room, but no one pays us any heed. No doubt we look like any other loved-up couple, out for a romantic dinner. We're so close on the seat, we could be holding hands under the table.

I place my hand on the steel of his muscular thigh, my stare holding his in challenge.

'Higher,' he bites out.

I obey, sliding my hand all the way up to the big, stiff length of him braced against the fly of his trousers.

His lips part as I stroke him with my fingertips, pressing my thumb to the spot below the head that drags a low growl from him. 'You're going to get your wish one day soon—trust me. First thing tomorrow morning I'll be getting a lock installed on my office door.'

'Don't bother,' I whisper, sliding my thumb over the head of his cock, certain his trousers feel damp, as if he's leaking already. 'Someone coming in was part of the fantasy. I'd keep going, concealed under your desk, and you'd try to continue a conversation while I took you to the back of my throat.'

He leans close, his mouth moving through the curtain of my hair. 'You wonderful woman. I've been sitting behind that desk hard for you all day— fucking uncomfortable feeling, let me tell you.' His confession makes me smile, the idea this urbane CEO spent the day discreetly adjusting himself around the office because of me adding another layer of turned-on to my weakened body.

'Why didn't you do something about it?' The thought of him stroking what I have in my hand while he thinks of me sends pulses of heat through my core. That I could inspire such…desperation after being invisible for so long. My throat dries and I swallow. Would he jack himself off hard and fast or pump slowly, his wrist twisting…? My thighs twitch, desperate to come together, but reluctant to dislodge the torturous, crawling passage of his hand.

'Because it's for you.' The brows once again rise as he pins me with a look packed with promise. 'I'm saving every drop for all the fantasies you have.'

I've been so turned on by his words, by touching him and learning what he likes, I've missed the fact his hand hasn't idly lingered in one place on my leg. When his finger brushes a whisper of touch over my exposed lips, I gasp as the sensation practically knocks me back in the seat.

'Here is my dessert,' his filthy voice husks, intimate, for my ears only. 'I'm ravenous for this. Was that also part of the fantasy?' His fingers circle while he speaks, and I fight to conceal the judders that rack my body as he strums my clit. I bite my lip, grasping hold of the pleasure, trying to keep it locked inside. Private.

'Tell me—did you ever fantasise about me putting my mouth on you?'

I offer a shaky nod, and triumph blazes over his face.

The waiter returns with some starters I have no recollection of ordering. I snatch my hand from Reid's crotch and he does the same from mine, but slowly, surely and with a confidence that leaves me wondering how many times he's done this public pleasuring routine before...

Lucky women.

Reid props his elbow on the table as the waiter deposits our plates. He looks directly at me, presses his thumb—the one that's just rubbed me close to melting—to his lips and swipes his tongue over the wet pad.

'Mmm…delicious.' It's subtle. Reid's polite smile for the waiter, his quick glance down at the food, covers his real meaning. But I flush all over, my body temperature now dangerously high.

And so it continues.

Over every course we tease each other beneath the table. I barely touch my food and, although Reid fares a little better, I'm certain he too struggles.

By the time he asks for the bill, he's dragged me close to the edge of climaxing at least twice, so I'm so desperate to come I've forgotten my own name.

My legs, as he guides me from the restaurant, are so wobbly I'm tempted to remove the heels I know make my legs appear longer in case I collapse before we reach the car.

When I'm panting on the back seat, my thighs pressed tightly closed to ease the burn, I glare at him, torn between begging and demanding he'll do something to finish me off.

'Fancy a nightcap at my place,' he says, 'or shall I drop you home?'

I appreciate the out clause, but home…? In this state…? The curl of his lip floods my body with relief.

'Nightcap sounds lovely, thanks.' My voice is an embarrassing croak and I want to swallow him whole in punishment.

He gives free rein to a full-out sinful smile. 'Egerton Crescent please, Terry,' Reid says to the driver before sliding closed the tinted privacy screen.

I practically sob with relief. Then I launch myself into his lap.

His hands grip my hips as I cover his mouth with mine, so desperate I drag my teeth over his bottom lip and pull back, panting, at his grunt of warning. 'That's for teasing me.' I rub his still hard length through his trousers and grapple with his belt buckle.

He's driven me so successfully to the brink of delirium all night, if he doesn't touch me soon I'm going to do it myself, right here in front of him, private or not.

He shoves me off his lap, tipping me onto the leather seat beside him and then following me so he can kiss me back. 'You want it here? In the back of a car? Another fantasy?'

'As opposed to a restaurant full of people?' I smile even though I'm a turned-on mess.

'Fair point.' His chuckle emboldens me to unleash some more honesty, as it seems to fire him up.

'I've fantasised about you in every conceivable

location.' Before I have a chance to tug his smug mouth back to mine, his hand slips along my thigh, heading north in the way he's tortured me through-out dinner.

'Oh, no. No way. There'll be no more teasing.' I spread my thighs, wriggling my dress up around my waist, until they're wide enough that he slots into place, his erection pressed up snug where I need him the most.

I reach for his fly, tugging while I kiss him, and giggle because his face is wreathed in amusement. It's not funny, but his smile is boyish, reminding me of a younger Reid—and seriously infectious. I grind my hips against his steely length. 'I need you now.' I look around for my clutch bag, where I'd stowed a condom before leaving the house.

Reid rears back, his hands grasping both my wrists and pressing them beside me on the seat. 'I fucking love your eagerness...' He rubs his lips over mine, his tongue a tease. 'But I'm still hun-gry.' The grin he shoots me steals my breath.

He keeps me pinned by the hands while he slides to his knees between my spread thighs. I'm light-headed, on fire, every inch of me alive with sparks. If he touches me with his mouth, I'm sure death will be imminent. But if he doesn't...either way I'm not long for this world.

'I thought I was giving you head...' I manage to say.

'Maybe later. But first I want to see exactly what's under here, up close and personal.' He releases my hands and spreads my thighs another few inches so he can wedge his broad shoulders between my knees. My thighs quake. I suck in ragged gasps, trying to contain the frenzy inside— one of *his* creation and one only he can quench.

Then the anticipation falters with a fizzle and a final pop.

Josh never went down on me. He always seemed eager for the main event, and I stupidly believed he was so crazy for me he couldn't wait. Stupid, naive Blair. The kick of shame slams into my ribs, stealing my breath, and I tense my thighs, preparing to push Reid away.

At his resistance, I look down, convinced this is too good to be happening and furious I still have unresolved Josh-related issues threatening to sour my delicious deal with Reid.

Reid grins up at me, his face alive with need as he shrugs out of his jacket and pushes up his shirtsleeves as if he's taking this very seriously.

Fuck, that's hot.

'Tell me to taste you.' His wicked eyes gleam as he kisses one knee.

I'm struck speechless by lust and lingering ripples of doubt. I don't think I can speak.

His mouth grazes my other thigh, lazily waiting as if he has all the time in the world, while his eyes dance with excitement.

He wants the words, wants my wildest imaginings.

'Taste me,' I croak, collapsing under the weight of his evident arousal. 'Make me come with your mouth—no one else ever has.'

He grins. 'Ah, I love a challenge.'

I bite back how I'm certain he can pull it off—this man could probably make me go off just by looking at me.

'Don't make too much noise,' he stage-whispers. 'We don't want Terry to know what's going on.' Reid looks like he doesn't give a shit if Terry has a front-row seat and eats popcorn, and that extra trill of excitement sets me aflame until I melt into the seat.

'Stop talking.' I want so much more from the sensual mouth he's slowly dragging up one of my thighs.

'Whatever you say.' He smiles, wraps an arm around my hips and drags me to the edge of the seat. At the same time, I cup my hand around the back of his neck and guide him forward with a whimper of desperation I can no longer hold inside.

Then his mouth is on me, and my vision tunnels as a gasp is sucked up from my lungs. I'm so busy absorbing the shock of pleasure when he spears his tongue inside then alternates with swirls and flicks over my swollen clit that I forget to breathe, and the roof of the car hazes out of focus as my lungs scream.

It's the best moment of my life.

Reid's sexy grunts of pleasure break the tension. I suck in a huge breath and look down to where he's eating me out with voracious appetite, stark hunger in his stare. He smiles up at me, wicked delight etched in every plane of his handsome face.

'Oh…my…' My throat closes.

My chest heaves, every fear confirmed. I *have* been short-changed. Served watery, lumpy mashed potato versus loaded French fries, unlike anything I've experienced before.

I open my eyes to make sure he's real.

He looks up, grinning again as he slides his fingers inside, stealing the last of my doubts. This is going to happen. This is *my* fantasy come true. I'm going to come on his mouth with him watching me. I've never been more certain of anything in my life.

I let go completely, lift my thigh over his shoulder and grind my hips, riding his face with abandon. Another cry rips from me and I come, my

back arched so my head presses into the seat behind and my hands brace—one flat on the widow
and one in Reid's hair.

O... M... G...

He hums a long, low sound that tells me he's as
pleased with himself as I am. I drag the last shudders from my body by jerking my hips against his
mouth and then push him away, the pleasure finally unbearable.

He tugs my dress down my thighs and sits beside where I'm still partially sprawled. But seriously, after that...am I really expected to move?

'Well, that was worth the wait. How did it live
up to the fantasy?' His smile floods me with renewed heat, and a niggle of concern that I might
be in over my head where this intense intimacy
with Reid is concerned. After all, my feelings, although immature, once carried that all-consuming
quality only a youthful infatuation can. I'll need
to stay on my guard and keep everything but the
pleasure off the table. One look at him and the
strong desire to gorge myself on Reid Faulkner
until neither of us can stand helps to set my mind
back on the correct track.

'It was okay for an old guy,' I lie, reaching for
him to kiss the self-satisfied smirk from his lips as
he laughs at my outrageous jibe. Can't have him
getting too cocky. And then I keep going, drag-

ging my mouth along his jaw and down his neck while I grapple once more with his trousers. 'Time to return the favour.'

Reid cups my face, bringing my eyes back to his.

'Much as that is a fucking awesome idea—' he wipes my lips with the pad of his thumb '—we're here.'

I look up to see we are indeed slowing, pulling off the road and driving into an underground garage.

'To be continued?'

CHAPTER FIVE

Reid

I'VE NO TIME to ask her what her slight hesitation in the car was about because the minute the door closes she spins to face me, yanks my neck down and pushes her tongue against mine. I'd never admit it aloud, but keeping up with her vast collection of fantasies could prove too much for me, as ancient as I am, not that I won't die trying, of course. And I can't stop touching her, my hands and mouth desperate to explore every inch until we know Blair Cameron thoroughly and completely.

And I'm a perfectionist, not content to simply cruise—I want to get inside her head, I want to push her to her limit and I want her so sexually sated that I'm the only man on her mind, no room for hesitations, old or not.

I sling one arm under her arse as she grips my waist with her thighs and head for the bedroom.

She tugs my hair, tilting my head back, and my mind scrambles for the nearest flat surface—we're not going to make it to the bedroom, which is upstairs but may as well be on the moon.

Strung taut by my own pledge, I carry her across the hall and kick open the door to the nearest room, almost dropping her, she's writhing so much. It's my home office, not the most practical, but the floor is carpeted and there's a chesterfield sofa in one corner, which is where I head.

'I'm sorry—you're too fucking sexy. This will have to do.' The minute I release her she slides to her feet.

I slide my hand down her bare arm, allowing it to linger palm-to-palm for a few beats. I'm rewarded with the flex of her fingers against mine. The barest of handholds.

'Why don't you strip for me, gorgeous? I want to see all of you.' I go first, shrugging off my jacket and unbuckling my belt.

'You first—keep going. I want to see what I've only felt up to now. See if it's as good as I've imagined.'

I grin—she's irresistible. 'I thought I was in the driving seat?' I unbutton my shirt. Us naked is a win-win for us, whoever goes first.

'You are.' She kicks off her shoes. 'Sorry. Habit, I guess, and eagerness to have that bad boy in my

mouth.' Her stare drops to my crotch as she thrusts
her clutch bag my way. 'There's a condom inside.'
She scoops her dress up and off and, before I've
even had the chance to take in her dark nipples and
the strip of hair between her thighs I'd felt earlier,
she's up close, attacking my fly once more.

I take her hand, stilling her hurried tugging, and
press her palm over my erection so she feels the
pulsing of my dick that's all for her. 'I love your enthusiasm, but I've got this.' I toss down the clutch
bag and retrieve my own condom stash from the
pocket of my trousers, pulling off my shirt.

'Sorry.' She chuckles. 'I've just waited so long.
I just want to make sure you don't run away before I've had my wicked way with you. All of you.'

I grin, the picture she paints fuelling my libido,
not that it needs any help.

My greedy eyes scour her nakedness and I can't
help reaching out to cup one perfect breast, my
thumb tracing the nipple dragging another shudder from her. 'You're so fucking sexy.' *What is she
doing here?* Thank fuck I didn't say that out loud.

She drags her bottom lip under her teeth, her
eyes wide and glazed with affirming lust. I suck
in some air and force my overexcited body back
from the brink, determined to show her a good
time, as promised, even if it means taking this at

a pace abhorrent to my restless body. But first I need to get into her head.

'I promise your patience will be rewarded,' I say.

Her eyes flare, a mix of turned-on and vulnerable. 'I know—I just…this is the first time I've been intimate with a man since…'

I nod. 'I understand.' That she's comfortable telling me about her ex's betrayal adds another layer of respect for her to what I'm already feeling. That she's comfortable enough to tease me about our age gap leaves me feeling as alive as if I'm touching her, kissing her. Alive like I haven't felt in years…

She shudders out a sigh. 'A year is a long time.'

I step close. 'A lifetime. And, as you've pointed out, I'm older than you, don't forget. I'm struggling to keep up with that insatiably filthy mind of yours.'

Her teeth take another tug on that full bottom lip, a small smile playing there as her stare drops to my straining fly. 'I'm sure you'll do just fine, although if it were up to me you'd already be inside me.' She blurts out a laugh, covering her mouth with one hand. And I grin with her—the fact that we can lighten such an intense moment for her into a shared joke sending me soaring.

'You're so forthright and demanding.' How can

I resist her when just her smile punches a hole through my chest?

'You're so hot, and hung. Stop talking.'

I obey, my libido grateful for the change of pace, and open my fly. I watch her face as I release myself with a sigh, my hand lingering for a lazy pump or two. Of course, my eager dick is done waiting and needs appeasing.

Her pupils flare with excitement.

'You like that?' I ask, certain of the answer.

'Yes.' She watches me stroke myself, short pants lifting her breasts, and then she drops to her knees, not even bothering to free me fully from my boxers before she wraps that luscious mouth around the head of my cock and moans, as if her need to taste me matches my need to have another taste of her sweetness.

I bite back the intense surge of pleasure at her heated mouth engulfing me. I guess we're still battling for control of the steering wheel. But if it feels this good, I'm happy to concede some of the time. The sight of her mouth on me burns into my retinas, smashing every tepid fantasy from my mind like blows from a baseball bat. I wasn't lying this morning—I've fantasised about her too, never imagining she'd ever reciprocate my attraction. Never imagining I'd get a shot with someone as astounding, jaded as I am.

I tangle my hands in her hair and hold the air trapped in my lungs while I rock my hips in time with the bobbing of her head. She looks up at me while she's sucking, a smile on her face and her eyes wicked. It's taking every shred of control I possess not to blow at the sight. It's a good thing we're just fucking—a woman like her could seriously threaten my single status if I was in the market for more. Wonderful woman could be made for me...

I cup her cheek, forcing my stare to stay on hers when the view of my cock disappearing past those lips is so tempting. I focus on sensation, grunting again when I touch the back of her throat and she hums, the vibration of the sound jerking new thrills alive along my length.

'That feels so good.' I widen my feet; clench my arse. 'You look beautiful with your mouth on me.' My voice breaks as her pupils dilate and her eyelids droop.

When she cups my balls, her fingers sliding behind to press down on my perineum, I grip her shoulders, pushing her back before I reach the point of no return and empty myself down her throat.

Fuck, where did she learn that trick?

'Not yet.' I drag her to a standing position and ease her back onto the sofa. 'You need to come one more time, first.'

She squeaks out a protest as I hand her the condom and shed the last of my clothing.

'I'm not sure I can. This is way better than my fantasies.' She wipes her swollen lips.

I grin—it's becoming a permanent look on me. 'I'm sure you can. I'd put money on it, because I'm going to make you, and then I'm going to come too, inside you.' I fist my attention-greedy cock, tugging faster when she stares with her lips parted around pants of excitement. I want to roll my eyes closed but the look on her face, her stare bouncing between my face and my cock, still shiny with her saliva, in my hand… I can't miss one second.

She whimpers, her own hand dropping between her legs, fingers pressing between her clenched thighs. 'Reid…'

I snatch my hand away before it's too late. She's too hot, too tempting and I want to come inside that tight haven that awaits me between her legs. I step close and she tears into the condom. When I'm covered I splay her back into the leather and kneel between her thighs, my mouth diving for one taut, straining nipple.

She cries my name as I suck the peak with everything I have. She's greedy, wrapping her legs around my waist, her hips lifting to grind her clit against my erection. I press her nipple to the back of my teeth and slide the head of my cock through her wet folds until she's moaning and whimpering, her eyes desperately clinging as well as her hands.

Releasing her nipple with drawn-out suction, I grip the base of my erection and line myself up with her drenched entrance. 'I'm sorry it's not a bed, but I need to be inside you now.'

She nods, eyes almost frantic with want. 'Yes... I don't care. This is perfect.'

My throat closes. *She's* perfect.

I angle the head of my cock inside her.

She tenses and I freeze, braced just outside the gates of paradise.

I grit my teeth. 'Everything okay?'

'Yes. It's just...you're...massive.'

I kiss her, tempering my grin and finding her clit with my thumb to remind her this is about our pleasure. 'Why, thanks.'

She smiles, shifting something in my chest. 'I kind of wish I'd known all this time—perhaps I'd have worked up the courage to jump you sooner.'

My ego inflates, even as I chuckle at the picture she paints, and I rub her clit and tongue that nipple once more, rewarding her honesty with as much pleasure as I can. She gifts the end of my cock with another gush of heat. I gather every scrap of willpower I possess to hold still. 'I'll go slow. At first.' I rub my thumb in a slow circle, loving the way she gasps and her pupils dilate as she looks up at me. 'And I have the feeling you and I are going to slot together perfectly.'

She nods, her trust pinching my ribs. Her hands find the cheeks of my arse and together we guide me home into her tight heat, our stares locked. We groan together, the wait worth it for the look of ecstasy on her face alone.

'You okay?' I pause, buried to the hilt, ensuring she's with me, even as my need roars so loudly in my chest I'm surprised I'm not sporting a mane and a mouth full of canines. But my patience is a brittle thread.

'Yes. This is better than I imagined.' Her eyes are wide, her voice breathy, and my chest fills with pride and longing to make this a night she'll never forget.

'Tell me. I need to hear that pretty mouth say the words. It's your fantasy after all.' I trace her bottom lip and she darts out her tongue, laving the pad of my fingertip.

'Fuck me, Reid. Don't hold back.'

'I can't—I want you too badly.' Her internal muscles squeeze me so I have to bite my tongue and recite in my head the one Shakespeare speech I learned at school to stave off the rush of pleasure. I dive once more for her nipple, alternating sucks and licks with plundering kisses, while I rock into her slowly at first, again and again. I brace myself on one arm, guiding her hand between our bodies. 'Touch yourself.'

Her fingers move on her clit and my free hand returns to her nipple, strumming in time with the frequency of her frantic breaths and choppy moans.

Only when I feel her tighten on my cock do I let go, powering into her until she climaxes with a cry, her nails digging into my hip.

'That's what I wanted,' I grit out, cupping her flushed face so her eyes stay on mine. 'Stay with me.'

She nods, bracing her arms on the sofa over her head so with every thrust she meets me head-on.

'Blair...' The fire builds. The sight of this beautiful, confident woman splayed under me, her skin flushed with her pleasure as she waits to witness mine, snapping the last thread of my control. I choke out the words. 'I'm coming. For *you*.' And then I follow her over, my face buried in her neck and flames racing down my spine.

Fucking hell... We'll be doing that again.

When we surface, the sweat cooling, I take my weight off her underneath me and sit back on my heels. I pull her into a sitting position and reach for a throw from the back of the sofa to drape around her, while I take care of the condom with some tissues from a box on the desk. It gives me time to find my breath, to compose myself after that fantastic lay… Otherwise we might have to start again, from the top.

When I return she's still checking me out like the three orgasms I've given her today have done nothing but whet her appetite. I hold out my hand, feeling ten feet tall, and she stands.

'Can you stay?' I fuss with her hair, sliding my fingers through the tangles I've created, although just fucked suits her perfectly. 'That was so good, I want a repeat, just to check I'm not dreaming.'

She laughs. 'I'm not complaining.'

I grip her chin, holding her still so I can enjoy her kiss. 'I should hope not. But we should make sure something that good is reproducible.'

She lifts one delicate shoulder, the one that's become exposed by the blanket slipping. 'A scientific experiment—I like it. Okay, but only if you're up to it, old man. I don't want to be responsible for depriving the Faulkner Group of its CEO.'

I grin, secretly delighted by her teasing. 'Old man, she says.' Then I swing her up into my arms and carry her, giggling, to my room as if I've dropped ten years.

It's four a.m. by the time we've exhausted my condom stash. I slide my fingers through the silkiness of her hair and contemplate dragging my weary bones downstairs to retrieve her clutch bag, which, she tells me, has two more inside.

It's bad enough she's as addictive as sex heroin, that fulfilling her fantasies has become my new favourite pastime. Where did she come from and how long can I juggle business and pleasure so I can keep her in my bed until I've quenched this fire roaring through my arid life?

Her eyes are still closed where her head rests on my sweaty chest, but she smiles, as if she knows I'm watching her.

'Those were some moves—I'll be walking like a cowboy for the rest of the week,' she says.

I laugh. I've done that more in the last few hours than in the last month, too. 'Glad I could oblige. Give an old man a second to catch his breath and I'll run you a bath.'

She scrapes her fingernails up and down the ladder of my abs, which clench every time she shifts, and rubs her soft labia over my thigh. My dick stirs. 'Fuck, I think you're actually going to kill me.'

She laughs and kisses me. 'You are pretty insatiable for a thirty-something.'

I grin and kiss the top of her head. Verbal sparring with her is almost as good as the horizontal sparring we've spent the last four hours indulging in. I roll onto my side so we're face-to-face, filling my hand with her gorgeous arse and tugging her hips close.

She's rumpled, so damned sexy and even more beautiful, if that's possible. 'There's plenty more where that came from if you have more lewd fantasies.'

She smiles, gives a half-laugh, but then she grows serious.

'You must think I'm nuts.' Her teeth trap her lip and I tease it free with the pad of my thumb.

'Not at all—that you know what you want and chase it is almost as sexy as hearing all those filthy requests.' I trace her bottom lip, pressing a playful kiss there to show her I'm in no way judging. Then I sober, my own betrayal a sour taste hijacking the sympathy I feel for what she went through with her ex.

'Was it someone you knew? The woman he cheated on you with?' Sadie, as far as I know, didn't cheat. But there are other ways to betray. Other ways to hurt and emasculate. Attacking the very heart of who I am—my family, my business, the father I hero-worship—is a well-aimed weapon.

Blair's eyes widen as she slowly shakes her head on the pillow. I press my forehead to hers so her face blurs out of focus and whisper over her lips, 'It's okay—you don't have to tell me. But if you ever want to talk—'

I hear her deep inhale and then the rush of words. 'It was a man—his best friend.'

I freeze, shock pinning me to the mattress, and then feel a stronger compulsion to drag her into my arms and hold her.

A sheen covers her eyes, holding me in place and locking the air in my lungs—I couldn't move if the roof started to crumble.

'I came home from work one day and found them on my expensive sofa sucking the face off each other. It wasn't a first kiss, if you know what I mean, and I'm guessing they'd have gone all the way right there on the Italian leather if I hadn't come home early. Needless to say, my local charity shop was delighted to receive such a stylish and generous donation the next day.' Her brave attempt at levity can't conceal her anguish, which beats at me like physical shock waves spreading out from the centre of an explosion and fuels my own anger until it's a hot ball in my stomach.

I cup her face, my thumbs brushing the hair back from her flushed cheeks. 'I'm so sorry you had to go through that. Betrayal hurts like fuck, especially from those who are supposed to love us.' No wonder she's so determined to make her business—a business she once shared with a man who let her down in the worst way—a success alone. No wonder she hasn't dated for a year and wants no-strings sex.

'It's okay.' She swallows and I want to drag her closer, but I keep still, listening, if that's what she needs. 'I should have known. All the signs were there.'

I stiffen. 'Your fiancé's confused sexuality was in no way your fault, you know that, right?' We're steering away from casual here, but I can't seem to stop myself, despite how her confession reminds me of my own misplaced trust years ago. I respect this woman. I like her—she's funny and independent, an unstoppable force. One who could seriously bulldoze through my life if I were in the market for a relationship and she could take someone older than her seriously for more than just sex.

My hands flex on her waist, impatient for more contact to dampen the swirl of mixed emotions turning my stomach.

'I know that, but we'd grown more like friends by the end. I told myself it was nice, comfortable, a sign of maturity, given we were only months away from our wedding. I even reasoned the sex would return when we weren't so swamped with work, not that he ever did what you did to me in the back of the car.'

She looks away, as if she's somehow embarrassed by her ex's shortcomings. I want to break something.

'We spent all day together, so when he wanted to socialise without me I thought nothing of it. But he was obviously struggling with how to tell me while looking for something else. I should have seen that him preferring to spend time with Mark meant they were more than just friends. But most of all I should have expected more than mediocre, demanded more. I'm ashamed that I settled for less.'

My jaw aches where I'm grinding my teeth. I unclamp it and breathe through the red haze of my anger. Of course, he couldn't help his feelings, but he should have come clean sooner. 'How long had it gone on before you caught him?'

'Initially he said a few weeks. But then he broke down and admitted it had been closer to months. He said part of him had always been attracted to men, but he thought he was bisexual and that he loved me. I tried to be mature about it, to support him—I could see it wasn't an easy thing for him to admit, least of all to me.'

I swallow hard, more questions springing to mind, but I don't want to make her relive painful memories, and the roll of my stomach, the way my own demons are clawing to be freed, tells me I'm skating too close to the boundary of casual sex. Even though this conversation borders on too personal for people sharing amazing sex but nothing more, I just can't seem to help myself from wanting to see inside her to figure out how she works.

I stare into her eyes, seeing more than a beautiful, smart, driven woman, a woman I've never truly looked at closely, and I have the uncharacteristic need to keep digging, keep learning all I can about Blair Cameron until I've discovered every fascinating facet of her personality. This realisation raises the hairs on my arms in warning, making me steer things back to safer ground.

'He didn't deserve you.' A simple but true statement. Any man who couldn't appreciate her amazing qualities, qualities glaringly obvious to me, despite the short time I've spent with her so far, was not worthy.

She laughs and my heart lurches into my throat because I've put that astounding smile back on her face.

'Well, that's true. So, what happened to you and Sadie?' Curiosity and caution war in her eyes. I consider dismissing her question. After all, I wasn't just betrayed on a personal level. Sadie went after my business, my *family* business, and almost succeeded—far more humiliating to admit.

'Just the usual,' I pacify, hypocrisy crawling over my skin like ants. I've been inside her, done intimate, personal things with her, and she's shared her darkest pain. Why is it harder to admit I was taken for a ride by a woman I thought I loved and trusted?

'Okay—you don't want to talk about it. I understand.' She withdraws slightly, and I tug her body back to mine. She's right. Of course she understands on one level, and I'm being a coward where she's fearless. Fuck, I'm too set in my ways, but if anyone could challenge me it's Blair, from the glimpses I've seen of her determination to date.

'No, I don't. But only because it's not very interesting,' I concede with a sigh. 'We split three years ago after a short and rocky marriage. She accused me of being a workaholic and putting the business before her, before everything.' My account is clipped, as devoid of emotion as I can make it, but I can see in her eyes she wants more.

'Did you?' She seems to hold her breath.

'Yes. Fuck, that sounds bad.' I rub at my eyebrow. 'You understand—running your own business isn't like other jobs. We have responsibilities, salaries to pay, people dependent on us. And the family business—it's who I am. Who I've been raised to be. Who I was when she met me.'

She nods, her intelligent eyes perceptive and blessedly free of judgement.

'Sadie liked the perks, but wasn't interested in the business.' Perhaps that was why she went after everything she could get—bitterness, a sense she'd been short-changed throughout our short marriage. Or perhaps she simply never loved me, only our lifestyle.

I'm dragged from my unpleasant reverie by the hushed voice of the woman in my arms. 'It must have been hard for you, the other day, hearing Graham mistake me for her. He was remembering a time when you two were happy together, wasn't he?'

'Perhaps.' The reminder of my father, of how his mind is stuck in the past and seems to have no recollection of the way Sadie behaved at the end of our relationship, snaps the door open on everything I want to forget but can't. I want to enjoy this moment—the aftermath of great sex, the pleasure of taking the time to hold Blair, to string tonight out as long as possible, to get to know her better— but instead I'm dragged back to the wide, gaping chasm of uncertainty in my life.

She runs her hand through my hair as if she's drawn to touch me, almost as if comforting me, but we don't know each other well enough for that. I stare deeper into her eyes, seeking the blissful escape of the pleasure we found in each other, and my cock stirs as if it's nineteen again. But I'm thirty-five. I have responsibilities. There's no margin for anything else.

I press a final kiss to her mouth, rolling away before my dick gets any more ideas.

'Where are you going?' The lingering un-derstanding in her eyes gives me pause, where it should scare me off. Because we've both been hurt, but getting close enough to care, to feel the protective stirrings building inside me, is a big red flag waving in my face.

'I'm going to run that bath. And then I'm going to let you sleep for a couple of hours before I drive you home.' I silence her objections with another brief kiss. 'All part of the fantasy service,' I add where she would have interrupted with some assur-ance of her independence. I wink for good measure, the uncertain quality of my pounding heart remind-ing me of my tattered and forgotten casual rule and how close I'm skating to the fine line of caring too much. Perhaps it's the age difference that inspires such urges towards her—completely ridiculous, because I've never met a woman more capable, or more determined to go it alone, than Blair.

'Thanks, Reid.' She accepts my change of subject with grace and a small, sexy smile that leaves me aching to climb back into bed and wring a bit more numbing pleasure from us both. 'I had a good time.'

I smile too, the finality of her statement and the absence of my answering relief scooping out my insides and leaving me hollow.

CHAPTER SIX

Blair

A FEW DAYS later I'm working on some last-minute
preparations at the Faulkner, and, despite the fact
that it's Sunday and not only is Reid unlikely to be
working, but is even less likely to walk into the hotel
where I'm occupying the deserted seating area with
my laptop, my eyes stray to the front doors every
five minutes.

I close down my emails, stretching out the kinks
in my back and recalling the astounding night I
spent in Reid's bed—the very reason said kinks
are there in the first place. Wow, did I get more
than I'd asked for? Talk about overachieving... As
I'd known he would be, Reid was as phenomenal
between the sheets as he is at the Faulkner helm.
It took two days before I stopped feeling the after-
effects between my legs, not that the erotic dreams

prolonging the experience even while I sleep show any sign of abating.

I stare at the insipid watercolour prints on the walls, my gaze blurring out of focus as I contemplate what other fantasies I can request. I might have to come up with one or two fresh ones, perhaps even a bit of kink, just to keep him on his toes… Don't want him becoming complacent, have him thinking he's *too* good, especially as he seems to have embraced my teasing him about our age difference.

The only downer was when he gently probed about Josh. I opened up to him where I've barely told anyone—friends or family—the full details of the split. A surge of acid burns my chest, reminding me I'm not quite as over his betrayal as I'd assumed. But I've worked so hard to put all that behind me, to focus on rebuilding what Josh stole and move on, there's no way I'm allowing what I have with Reid to be tainted.

Thinking of Reid's well-endowed prowess drags my mind off into fantasy land again. Which is presumably how I miss his approach.

'Off in your imagination again, I see.' His scent envelops me, warm and spicy, and his breath ruffles my hair. I stand, concealing the instant incendiary effect he has on my body with boring old fright as I clutch one hand to my chest. I hide my delight at seeing him, although it makes my breath catch.

'Sorry,' he says. 'I didn't mean to make you jump. I thought you'd seen me come in.' His smile kicks up one corner of his mouth and I wish he'd kiss me, remind me of the exhilarating thrill I feel every time we touch, but he stays at a distance designed to leave me achy and craving.

'No… I was…working.' Then an alarming thought occurs—perhaps he's done. Perhaps one night was enough for him. Perhaps we racked up enough orgasms between us that he's reached his casual threshold. I probe my own feelings, nowhere near done with him. I have years of yearning and crushing to sate. I'll just have to convince him to play out a few more fantasies…

He glances down at the blank screen of my laptop, one eyebrow arched. 'Ah…work…that's what we're calling it these days. More like daydreaming…off in fantasy land again?' He grins as if he has a front-row seat to every graphic play-by-play in my head—as he pretty much does, because I've told him—his eyes dark with his particular brand of intensity, seemingly equipped with laser beams, for all the protection my clothing offers.

I breathe a sigh of relief—he's not done yet either.

The teasing tone of our banter reminds me how

much we laughed together on the ride back to my place after the incredible night of mind-blowing sex. Reid has a tinder-dry sense of humour, with glimpses of self-deprecation that make me want to snuggle up to the massive man, as ridiculous as that sounds. It's then that I register he's wearing a grey T-shirt and relaxed black jeans. It's been years since I've seen him in anything other than a suit. He looks edible, and I can't help the shudder that originates in my core and passes through my entire body. Because I know what he looks like under those clothes—his big frame covered in toned muscle and a manly smattering of dark hair. I know what he's packing beneath his fly— the biggest, most beautiful cock I've ever seen. And no matter how naively I believed this would just be sex, neatly compartmentalised sex, things can never go back to the way they were between us. Because I've experienced forbidden, and it has the potential, if unchecked, to ruin me.

'Why are you working on a Sunday?' he asks, his hands slung casually in his pockets, dragging my willing eyes south.

'I'm just catching up on last-minute checks, and ensuring everything is ready for tomorrow. You're here too,' I counter his gentle reprimand.

He steps closer and I glance around. We're still occupying a professional or friendly space, but the air is tense as if any second one of us could close the distance, reach out and touch, making it clear to anyone who noticed that we've crossed a line and can no longer be considered acquaintances or even friends.

'I'm meeting my family for lunch. They're moments behind me.' He looks down at my hand hanging by my side, and I wonder if he intended to reach for it but stopped himself. My fingers twitch, the entire limb taking on an awkward, alien quality as if I'm a shop mannequin that's been posed in an anatomically impossible position, because I wish he'd taken my hand.

Of course. It's Sunday. Faulkner family tradition.

I look past him, my stomach trying to outrun my heartbeat. His family—Graham, his brothers—they'll be here any minute. See us together. Will they be able to tell what we've done? To see that we've crossed the line, left it far behind in the rear-view mirror? Will they think less of me? Still see me as the once mopey teen who'd traipsed after her father and mooned at the eldest Faulkner brother from afar? Will Kit and Drake doubt my capabilities, having known me as a youngster?

'How is Graham today?' His eyes are clear of the vulnerability he wore when he told me about Graham's diagnosis and his split from Sadie, so

I mentally cross my fingers that Graham is having a good day.

'He's fine, I believe.'

But there's no time for further discussion because the Faulkner clan arrive en masse—Graham, Reid's brothers and two women I assume are their partners, the hotel foyer at once full of easy chatter.

I busy myself, closing my laptop and stowing it in my bag, while the family, all casually dressed but still elegant, assemble around Reid. But I can't hide for long.

'Blair—how are you?' Kit recognises me immediately and swoops to kiss my cheek, his arm possessive around a striking, heavily pregnant brunette. 'Mia, this is an old friend of the family, Blair Cameron—you've met her father, James.'

'Lovely to meet you.' Mia pushes the hair from her flushed face, glowing in the way only a pregnant woman can.

We're joined by Graham, and I search his still handsome face for signs of confusion or recognition with a heaviness in my chest. Will he know who I am today? Reid and Kit seem to stiffen in unison.

'Good, so we're all here—let's head into the restaurant.' Graham smiles at me and clasps my shoulder with a warmth that leaves me floundering.

I glance at Reid and clutch my laptop bag before me, my feet itching to shuffle towards the exit.

Drake, Kit and the others head towards the hotel's restaurant and Graham places his hand in the centre of my back and encourages me to follow.

My mouth opens and closes without my saying anything. What should I say?

Reid leans close and whispers, 'Are you free? Care to accompany us for lunch?'

'I…' I stare, my eyes hopefully conveying my indecision. Am I being included as Sadie, or Blair, and won't the rest of the family think my presence odd?

'Of course she's coming. She's going to be joining the family soon,' says Graham.

So Sadie it is.

It's a beautiful day, but goose pimples form on my exposed arms as we enter the sun-filled dining room. Reid must sense my hesitation because he winks at me and smiles.

'Don't be nervous—if he remembers who you are, he'll still be delighted you're here. Come on— it's lunchtime. We can't have you working too hard.' He grins, drawing out my answering smile.

Graham heads to the table and pulls out a seat for Mia. I grip Reid's hand, stalling. 'What will Drake and Kit think about me being here?'

He frowns. 'They won't care either way. You're

a family friend who's also working for us.' He smiles then—not the polite, open smile of acquaintance or friend, but the secret, intimate smile of a lover—and I follow him to the table, reluctantly accepting my fate.

Reid pulls out the seat next to Mia, who smiles my way.

'When is the baby due?' I ask.

Mia collapses back in her chair as if she finds the mere effort of thinking about the baby's arrival in this heat exhausting. But she smiles, accepting the attentions of Kit, who kisses her and fills her water glass. 'Two weeks. I'm totally over it. So, tell me about your plans for the hotel? I love the old-world charm of the Faulkner, but I can't wait to see the place modernised.'

On my other side, Reid leans in, joining the conversation. 'I've already vetoed the lime-green paint.' His hand settles on the back of my chair, the intimate gesture making me freeze—one, in anticipation of his touch, and two, in case anyone else at the table notices. Reid offers me a playful wink, but from the corner of my eye I catch Kit's startled expression and the wide-eyed look he shares with Mia.

Heat creeps up my neck, my stomach griping with embarrassment so my appetite completely vanishes. Has Reid discussed our sex-only relationship with his brothers? Do they disapprove? I'm younger than Kit. I'm probably younger than Mia. I know we joke, but is it really a problem for him? And does Reid share his brother's reservations now he knows how foolishly trusting I was in my relationship? What would he do if he found out I was just as naive with my business too?

My body floods with the shame of a thousand stares.

I fake-bristle at Reid's comment to keep the conversation light and away from questions on the nature of our non-relationship relationship. 'Lime green, or chartreuse, as it's properly known, makes an excellent statement colour and can look stunning in a bedroom when teamed with fuchsia and orange.' I cast Reid a pointed look. 'But you're right, it is a more...*youthful* choice.'

Mia smiles, in no way trying to hide her amusement at Reid's expense, not that he seems in the least perturbed that we're mocking him—in fact, he's grinning. 'I love chartreuse,' she says. 'I'll have to invite you over when you're free—we haven't had time to decorate the nursery yet, not that I'm worried because babies can only see a foot in front of their face for the first few weeks. Perhaps while you're there, you could look over the entire house—I'd love to knock down a wall or two in the living space to let in more natural light, and Kit has a serious love affair with beige.' She offers Kit a sickly sweet smile, which he simply grins away, an indulgent look on his face.

I give Mia a nod of encouragement, wondering how much Reid has told his brothers about my designs for the Faulkner. Do his comments on paint colour hide a veiled truth? Does he really hate my designs, and why do I care when I didn't a few days ago? Unease and doubt build, crushing me until I feel small, an outsider in this room full of people who love and accept each other and have their lives all worked out.

Why am I here? Why did Reid invite me? And why has sex changed everything?

I struggle through the rest of the meal, exhausting my supply of small talk, although the Faulkners make easy companions.

We're just finishing a dessert when the thing I've most been dreading happens.

'So, Reid,' asks Graham, 'are you taking the beautiful Sadie here to the LHA gala next weekend?'

A collective hush falls over the table as everyone realises Graham's mistake. My stomach twists and I'm frozen, my dessertspoon hovering in the air. My skin crawls and my heart clenches for him, because the damage is done. Graham looks around the table at the expressions of his family, his own face turning dusky and a stricken frown of bewilderment dipping his brows.

Drake recovers first, prompting the conversations around the table to resume. 'Reid hates the London Hoteliers Association functions, Dad, as well you know.'

Reid shifts beside me, but I pipe up. 'That meal was delicious, Graham. Thanks so much for inviting me. I…um, I noticed a chessboard in the foyer—would you like to play?'

Graham nods, his face brightening. 'Of course, I'd love to.' Graham winks at me, and I feel Reid relax. 'I'll set up the board, my dear.' He leaves the table, still fit and agile and the apparent epitome of health.

I stand too, my heart heavy for the Faulkners.

Reid catches my wrist. 'Thank you.' The sombre look on his face, mirrored in both Kit's and Drake's expressions, is difficult to witness. I nod, too unsettled to speak, and wander out in search of a bathroom.

While I wash my hands my head replays the past hour, my concern for Graham's condition and Reid's obvious worry, which was evident in the number of times he slid his eyes his father's way during the meal. The uncertainty over Graham's prognosis and his bouts of confusion are taking a toll, perhaps the reason Reid seems both distracted and overprotective of the Faulkner. But at least I can help with the latter, manage the renovations as smoothly as possible and to the agreed time frame, releasing Reid from at least one burden. It's the least I can do and, although we've never been friends, perhaps we can be when this is over.

From the little I know of dementia, it's a progressive condition, so Graham is unlikely to improve. He's so young. Will he forget his sons as he's forgotten his ex-daughter-in-law and me? What will happen if he worsens and can no longer live alone?

I emerge from the bathroom minus any answers and head in the direction of the foyer to find Graham. Halfway there, I'm drawn to a halt by familiar voices coming from a quiet seating nook just outside the dining room. Nothing good ever comes of eavesdropping, and I'm about to walk on when I hear mention of my name.

'Blair Cameron—what's going on?' says Kit.

There's a pause filled only by the sound of my blood whooshing through my head and the metallic taste of apprehension.

'Dad saw her in the foyer and invited her to lunch.' Reid's voice—measured. Careful. 'They're quite close, by all accounts.'

I blink, my eyes hot. We are. Were, when Graham could remember me.

'I'm not talking about that. Are you seeing each other?' asks Kit.

Drake chuckles. 'Sleeping with the competition—didn't know you had the balls, big brother.'

I cover my mouth to stifle my gasp. Is that how Reid sees me? An adversary? Someone not to be trusted? Someone out to ruin his beloved hotel with lime-green paint? I'd assumed that was a joke. I know he's been hurt by Sadie, but the confirmation he expects so little of me *and* Cameron Interiors feels like a slap in the face after the vow I just made to ease his worry over the renovations.

Reid's growl of irritation echoes through the wall. 'Since when have you cared who I sleep with? It's none of your damned business—either of you.'

'Hey,' splutters Kit. 'Don't get defensive—we're just surprised that it's her, of all people.'

'Why? Because she's so much younger than me?' says Reid, with only the tiniest pause before he continues. 'Aside from what she does professionally to our hotel, my relationship with Blair Cameron has nothing to do with either of you.'

He, like me, must have seen the look of judgement on Kit's face earlier at lunch. Perhaps he's embarrassed to be caught out by his brothers. Perhaps he thinks someone younger can't be professionally as successful. And personally? Does he see my naivety with Josh as a barrier to taking me seriously as potential relationship material? Not that we're going there, but neither do I want or need a pity fuck.

Drake's voice turns sober. 'We're not prying into your private life, but since when have you brought someone to lunch? It's…heartening.'

'Don't read too much into it.' Reid's bored tone grates on my eardrums, and I want to interrupt and tell his brothers not to worry, that the eldest Faulkner is a great lay and I'll be sure to put him carefully back on the shelf once I'm done with him.

'So what about the renovations?' Drake's voice. 'Is everything on track? Are you finally happy she can deliver on time or will you be watching her like a hawk, controlling every move she makes?'

Despite their reassurances, I've heard enough. The younger two Faulkner brothers may not approve of my sexual relationship with Reid, but maligning my business is another matter. One I won't tolerate, from anyone.

I miss not only what Reid says in answer to Drake's question, but also my opportunity to interrupt and set the Faulkners straight, because at that moment Graham rounds the corner, presumably in search of his chess partner.

I struggle through a brief game of chess, accepting my defeat at Graham's hands while I formulate another battle plan. The sex was my idea. Reid and I are not in a relationship. He owes me nothing, least of all loyalty. But we agreed to keep the work separate. If we're off course before the work on the Faulkner has even begun, this is over.

I ignore the pinch in my stomach, which feels a lot like a mini version of Josh's betrayal, take my leave of the Faulkners and head outside into the late-afternoon sunshine. Have I made another mistake? Am I being naive where Reid is concerned? Have I wrongly assumed we're on the same wavelength, both physically and professionally?

Well, I know one thing: next time I have Reid alone I'll know whether our brief, sex-only fling is make or break.

CHAPTER SEVEN

Reid

I EXIT THE hotel and jog down the street, guilt and adrenaline charging my muscles with enough energy to run a marathon. What a fucking idiot. How could I have been so stupid, so thoughtless as to discuss Blair with my brothers where she might overhear? One look at her closed expression as she thanked Graham for lunch and bade us all farewell told me she'd not only overheard, but probably wanted to tear a few well-deserved strips off me too. And she'd have every right. Not only did she play along again with my father's mistake, something I know cost her, if the quickly concealed flash of hurt in her eyes was any indication, but she also showed how close she is to Graham and how invested she is in her relationships with all of us. She chatted to Mia and Kenzie, getting to know the newest two additions to the Faulkner clan, she teased Drake and Kit in the same way she's taken to teasing me and she even graciously lost a game of chess to Graham, even though I'm sure she has a hundred better uses for her Sunday afternoon.

She was relaxed and comfortable around us right up until I spoiled it with my thoughtless lack of tact.

I round the corner in time to see Blair unlocking her car door. A wall of relief slams into me and I slow to a brisk walk, allowing myself time to recover from the fear I missed my chance to make this right, but the fear that I've inflicted too much damage lingers, turning my blood to ice. I refuse to probe my motivations too closely—with anyone else I'd put up less of a fight, but for some reason, with her, I'm not ready to walk away. Blair is a breath of fresh air in my life I can't, and don't want to, ignore. And, whether I've sabotaged this or not, she deserves an apology.

I take a hard swallow and try to slow my breathing as I come to a halt at her side.

'Don't leave angry with me—let's talk it through.' My voice carries a pleading undercurrent that feels both alien and justified. The idea I'd get down on my knees, if that's what it takes, comes out of nowhere and takes root.

She turns, lazily lifting her gaze from the screen of her phone, as if she was fully aware I was pursuing her the whole time. 'I'm not angry. And I'd welcome the opportunity to discuss it with you in private—I'm not doing this in the road outside your family's hotel.'

I allow my lungs the barest recoil of relief that she hasn't shut me down. Yet.

'Perhaps a walk, then, or my place is just around the corner.'

She locks her car with a click of the remote. 'Okay—let's walk.' She sets off and, just like every time she's within arm's length, I want to reach for the hand closest, which swings by her side. Instead I shove my own hand in my pocket and curse my stupidity anew. She's smart, caring, funny and kind. I talked about her as if she meant nothing to me, insulting both of us, because that's not true, despite my divorcee's caution.

'I overheard you, Drake and Kit talking,' she says, aiming straight for the heart of the matter in her no-bullshit way.

I scrub a hand through my hair as my fear is confirmed. 'I guessed as much and I'm sorry. Sorry for being indiscreet and talking about you at all.'

She nods, but I'm still wriggling on the hook, the set of her full mouth tells me. 'I didn't want to eavesdrop, but when I heard my name I kind of wanted to know what you'd say. I accept overheard conversations can be misconstrued,' she says, 'so let me make my position crystal-clear.'

My respect for her, for her professionalism and maturity, ratchets up to new levels when I thought I'd reached the ceiling.

'I know you don't owe me anything—that all we've shared is a couple of orgasms—'

To hear the evening we'd spent together reduced to mere biology rather than the astounding night of connection it truly was, at least for me, stings like all-over nettle rash. But Blair isn't finished.

'I understand you may have trust issues—' A momentary flash of pain blazes through her expressive eyes, gone as quickly as it arrived.

I touch her arm, tug her to a standstill. 'It's not personal. I *do* have trust issues. A hangover of my divorce. In fact, I'm a suspicious old git, I'm afraid.'

She nods, not arguing and refusing to take the bait and tease me again about my age, and she continues as if I haven't spoken. 'But I'm a hard-working professional. I take my work very seriously. I'd never do anything to take advantage of you, your father or your hotel. I, perhaps naively, assumed your initial reticence for the renovations was down to it being sprung on you. And I thought we'd struck a deal that we wouldn't allow the sex to affect the work...'

She leaves the last dangling like a question, although it's very much a statement and it's as if our ages were reversed and I'm a schoolboy again, standing in front of the head for flinging insults at some bully who dared to pick on Kit or Drake. I want to rewind the past few hours, to walk into the lobby of the Faulkner again and show every scrap of the delight I felt at finding her there. To invite her to join us for lunch myself, not wait for Graham to do the honours. To whisk her out of there within minutes of the meal being served, take her home and lose myself in her again, because those impulses were strong, and now I can't think of a single reason I fought against them.

Blair mistakes my silence for apathy.

'But perhaps the sex was a mistake. Perhaps it's time to call this a day. We had a good time…' She swings her bag up onto her shoulder and crosses her arms over her chest.

The urge to hold her, to feel her body against mine, grows to impossible levels. I know how good it will feel. I know that nothing else will matter while she's there and all my worries will lessen. I know I'd do anything right now to ensure it happens.

'And if I don't want to call it quits,' I say, stepping a fraction closer, although not as close as I'd like, which is naked and inside her, making her eyes soften with pleasure.

That seems to startle her. The pulse in her neck flutters and the answering thud of my heart batters my ribs. 'Look,' I say, my voice strangled, 'you've been honest, so allow me to return the favour. I *was* thrown by your appointment to renovate the Faulkner, which Graham arranged without my knowledge. I run a tight ship, I always have, but now, with things…unravelling, with my always capable, energetic father behaving so erratically… you can understand how concerning—'

'Of course I can—'

I plough on. 'And despite all of that going on, I was blindsided by seeing you again. You've changed, or I've opened my eyes. I was reeling from my attraction to you and you were so capable, so vehement about your contract, so…driven and in control, and while I admire that trait in business—' I swallow, emotion thick in my throat '—if I'm brutally honest, I'm a little distracted by Graham's diagnosis. Bottom line, I was underprepared for you.' I wave my hand in her direction, encompassing the entire, spectacular Blair package. 'All of you.'

My words settle between us, charging the warm summer air with kinetic energy, until I'm certain something will need to break to snap the tension.

But I've never waited for something to come to me in my entire life, always making things happen, striving until I have what I want. I'm not about to start now when what I want is as tempting as her. I reach for her hand and she doesn't pull away, her fingers flexing against mine a soothing balm in more ways than one. But it's not enough. I want more of Blair Cameron for my own selfish reasons, reasons I refuse to examine too closely. Fuck, I hope she still wants me for hers.

Taking a leap, I tug her to my chest, wrapping my arms around her slim shoulders, dwarfing her physically even as she seems to envelop me—the scent of her hair carried in the hazy air, the crush of her soft breasts against my hard chest, her small hands on my waist holding me together where the shudders of something that feels suspiciously like fear seep from my every pore. I hold her until my own heart rate slows, not giving a fuck that she can probably feel it beating against hers, that she'll know how much I care, how sorry I am and how exposed it makes me. The feeling is so rusty, I can't name it, or choose not to.

I kiss the top of her head, and pull back a fraction so she can see the sincerity in my expression.

'I don't doubt you professionally and neither do Kit and Drake. They loved your plans for the renovations. Brothers just like to talk shit to wind each other up—it's a trait we've carried from childhood, I'm afraid.'

She nods, but her eyes are still haunted, her voice when she speaks flatter than I've ever heard it. 'They don't approve of us fooling around.'

I wince. I'd seen the way Kit reacted to my obvious closeness to Blair, but then, like now, I considered it irrelevant. 'I don't give a fuck. Do you?' The ugly swirls of fear return, my stomach twisting. If she says yes, that no-strings sex was fun, but family judgement is a distraction she doesn't need, that I'm too old for her after all, that we don't have enough in common or that's it's just not worth it... I grip her tighter. The reaction makes no sense—she's right, all we've shared is a handful of orgasms, but already this feels like more, feels as if we're heading into dangerous territory. Trouble is, I don't want to retreat. I'm selfish. I want her for as long as it lasts.

When she shakes her head, her chin lifted in defiance, I practically growl and press my mouth hard to hers as euphoria pumps around my body. Without interference or my own stupidity, our connection is simple—A plus B equals... What? A good time? If I'm honest, we've already surpassed simple physical gratification. She makes me feel invincible, makes me feel the optimism I associate with the man I was in my early twenties.

'Good. Come home with me.' I clutch her closer.

She laughs, a delightful sound that restores my equilibrium more than her words of reassurance or the lust simmering in her eyes.

'Just because I accept your apology doesn't mean I'm ready to forgive *all* your transgressions.' She tilts her pelvis and crushes my dick with her soft belly, bringing me back to life.

I grin; press a kiss to her irresistible mouth. 'I'm happy to pay for my crimes—there must be something you want in recompense.' I slide my hands over her hips and cup her arse, pressing her forward to increase the friction.

'Hmm…' She pretends to think, her eyes dancing. 'There might be one thing… But I'm not sure you're up to the job, being so old and set in your ways.'

My laughter blasts from me, draining any residual doubt. She's incredible—generous and caring and fearless. 'Well, if anyone can keep me on my toes, it's you. Why don't you give me a shot? There are worse ways to die than from pleasure.'

Malicious delight fills her expression. 'Who said anything about pleasure, especially yours?' Her teeth sink into her bottom lip as she grinds against my now hard cock, her actions contradicting her threats. 'I think your transgressions require a forfeit.'

Excitement pumps my blood harder, so I'm ready to give her anything. I was the minute she left the hotel without looking back. 'What's the forfeit?' I'm not used to handing over control and I'm sure I won't like it. But my blood pounds in case I fucking love it.

'The driver's seat.' She gives me no time to absorb her words before she spins, tugging me behind her towards my house. I sling my arm around her shoulder, caging her to my side while my mind sifts through her possible meanings. Does she want to tie me up? Blindfold me? Do I care? Any fantasy of hers is okay by me, because she's honest about what she wants.

But before I get carried away, I have more I want to say.

'Thank you.' I squeeze her closer, hoping she reads my heartfelt gratitude. 'For the chess. For playing along again. I'm sure it's upsetting that Graham seems to have forgotten how he knows you.' At her small shrug, I drag us to another standstill and kiss her again, trying to banish the slightly lost expression from her eyes. I linger over kiss after kiss until the atmosphere lifts, in no hurry to get home. She'll have to have her wicked way with me in the road. But all too soon we resume our walk.

'How did you know he played?' My father

taught all three of us to play, stating it fostered healthy competition without risk of coming to blows, although we Faulkner brothers managed to throw a few of those back when we settled things with our fists.

'We played at a Hoteliers Association conference I attended with my dad back in the days he thought I'd simply join the family business instead of pursuing my own dreams—not that there's anything wrong with family businesses, of course. Graham was there too. One day, he spied me sulking in a corner somewhere, challenged me to a game and then happily thrashed me. I always respected him more for not letting me win, and of course for taking the time to coax a moody teenager out of herself.'

Her tale is bittersweet, reminding me of the powerhouse Graham has always been, and how much I've relied on his always being so. 'He always wanted a daughter, I think.'

Blair's arm tightens around my waist. 'You're really concerned about him, aren't you? Are things worse than you've let on?'

'The honest answer is I just don't know, but we're all concerned. He has an appointment with the Harley Street specialist this week. Hopefully we'll know more about his prognosis then.' But I don't want to think about the future, about how a man I've always looked up to and relied upon may change, diminish before my eyes.

'That's good. I believe there are medications that can slow down the progression of dementia. And my father hasn't said a word, so perhaps only those closest to him are aware of the changes.'

'Thank you for saying that. For everything. I never realised just how close you two were.'

We walk the rest of the way in silence, perhaps each lost to our memories of the good old days when Graham was the rock, full of wisdom, sage advice and readily given support.

And, where only minutes ago I was certain Blair would be gone from my life as quickly as she'd entered it, it now feels like she's always been a part of our tight-knit little circle, and perhaps always should be.

CHAPTER EIGHT

Reid

THE MINUTE WE enter the house she spins and backs me up against the front door, until she's pressed against me, shoulder to thigh. I'm already hard because I've anticipated that the minute we touch, my doubts, my fears, the need to fix something out of my control will settle, the tension of stupidly almost losing her draining away.

She deserves better than me, better than an older, cynical, set-in-his-ways bachelor. She's bravery to my caution, laughter to my cynicism, sunshine and smiles and a hundred other fucking feel-good clichés, and one day, when she's ready, she'll move on to a relationship she deserves, perhaps marriage.

The thought sours my tongue but I swallow it down. I've had my shot and I'm on the slippery slope to forty. But by some miracle she's still here, willing to forgive me, albeit with a forfeit in mind, one I'm only too happy to pay.

'This time I'm calling the shots, my hands on the steering wheel—is that too challenging for you?' she whispers against my lips, her hips undulating so she's massaging my dick between our bodies with every move.

'You can steer this, as long as I can dictate the number of times I make you come.' It kills me, but I keep my hands hanging by my sides, when everything inside me fights to touch her, to make things right between us the only way I know how. But I want her to know I'm in this. That I can keep my promise, keep the sex separate, even if the demarcation, at least for me, blurs a little.

Her eyes flare and I want to start straight away, to chalk up an orgasm tally so long she loses the strength to walk. 'Okay, but this time we'll be banishing a few ghosts.'

'You know where the bedroom is.' My voice turns husky with the need strangling me, and it takes every ounce of control I possess to keep still.

'Hmm, that sounds kind of…middle-aged.' She grips the belt loops on my jeans and tugs my hips, dragging our lower halves impossibly closer. She knows exactly what she's doing to me. I see confirmation in her eyes, which dance with excitement and something wicked, something pure Blair—challenge.

'So what exactly did you have in mind?' If she stokes the fire in me any higher, we're going to burn ourselves clear through the door.

'I want to live out my sofa fantasy.' She doesn't wait for my response, merely takes my hand and drags me down the hallway and into the living room.

'You have a sofa fantasy?' I tilt my head in the direction of the cream sectional sofa that dominates this room. 'Not that I'm complaining—there are six pieces of upholstered furniture in this house and I'm happy to abuse each and every one of them for you, but didn't we cover that with the chesterfield in my office?'

'Humour me.' She releases my hand and inches closer to the furniture. 'Remember when I told you how I discovered Josh's cheating?'

Of course. She found him on the sofa… My stomach rolls with compassion, every thump of my heart promising retribution if I ever meet her ex. I tug her into my arms, ready and willing to give her some better memories. 'I'll give you anything you want, Blair.' I cover her mouth with mine in a slow, lazy exploration of our duelling tongues, because I'm weak where she's concerned, and I'm done being patient. I wrap my fingers around the back of her neck and hold her mouth on mine. Without breaking the kiss, I bend my knees, scoop my arms around her waist and lift her so she's plastered against me from shoulders to thighs. I kiss her until we're both panting hard and then I allow her to slowly slide down to the floor, so her breasts and the heat from between her legs slide all over me. I twist my mouth away with a groan. 'Fuck, you're so sexy. Get naked—let's abuse my sofa.'

She laughs, steps back out of reach, pressing one fingertip to my lips. 'Uh-huh. *You* get naked.' Her voice is breathy. Having me willing and ready to be her man-toy excites her so her nipples prod through her bra and T-shirt.

My hands settle on the swell of her hips. I want her close, at arm's length, as if our disagreement has left me craving a deeper connection.

She smiles a sexy half-smile. 'Touch yourself again.'

I lift one eyebrow, biting back my eagerness to comply. 'You like that?'

She nods, her breath hitching. 'I liked that you couldn't stop yourself the first time. That you wanted me that much.'

Something in my chest surges anew at her stark honesty, her embracing what she wants. She completely dismantles me. 'I want you more now.' Fuck, what is she doing with me—a distrustful, workaholic divorcee? There must be a thousand men her age lined up. That last thought has my jaw clamped so hard I hear my enamel creak.

'Show me,' she says, reaching for the hem of her T-shirt.

I yank my own shirt off over my head, pop my fly and release my cock, my heart thumping when her aroused stare drops to my crotch. I grip myself, lazily tugging while I shove my jeans and boxers down my thighs with my free hand. I stare into her eyes. 'I want you, Blair.'

She licks her lips. 'I see that. But do you trust me?' Her bold question hangs in the air as she slides her jeans down her legs and kicks them away together with her shoes.

'Yes.' The truth of that single word surprises me, but it's not a lie or false assurance to get laid.

Like this with her, just the two of us, I'm as authentic as I've ever felt.

'We'll see,' she says, wriggling free of her bra and swiftly adding her lacy underwear to the pile of discarded clothing on the floor, until she's gloriously naked, and every muscle holding me together strains her way.

'Look at you,' I croak out, my eyes gorging on her naked breasts, her tight nipples and the sweet haven at the top of her thighs. My chest tightens with repressed need. Need to go to her, to touch

her and make things one hundred per cent right between us, where words fail me. Because I'm not as
brave as Blair, not as open and fearless. But I want
to give her what she needs. This is about her—her
pleasure, her in control and me making amends,
no matter what it costs me.

'Don't stop,' she whispers.

I groan, the effort to be everything she wants
weakening my knees. She chews her lip, her stare
still torn between my face and my hand pumping my cock.

She joins me then, her hand slipping between
her thighs, and her fingers find her clit, her whole
body jerking in confirmation and her eyes half-
drugged with lust as we stand face-to-face. Open
and exposed and vulnerable.

'That's a wondrous sight.' I'm struggling to
talk, so good is the vision of her pleasuring herself while my dick is in my hand, but I don't want
to rush this. I want to show her that I care about her
despite the years that separate us or what anyone
else thinks. But we're on her timescale.

She sways, a flush staining her chest, and I'm
jealous of those slick fingers between her legs. I
want to be the source of her pleasure. I want her
moans and her ecstasy and her orgasm so she sees
the way I feel about her and her beautiful seduction, without words.

I pump faster, the needs of my body growing harder to ignore.

She rushes me then, the slam of her naked body colliding with me almost knocking me off my feet. Her mouth crashes to mine and I scoop an arm around her waist and fill my other hand with one deliciously round arse cheek, backing us up towards the sofa as I struggle out of the rest of my clothing while I walk and try to get my mouth back on hers.

At the last minute, I trip over my own shoe, my feet tangled up in my discarded jeans, and I lunge for the sofa, holding on to her waist and taking her down with me, so my fall ends with me on my back and her sprawled all over my chest.

We laugh and kiss and laugh some more. But as we emerge from the moment, the fire is still there between us, still there in her eyes, nicely banked.

'Perfect,' she says. 'This is exactly where I wanted you.'

I sober at the reminder she's in charge, my punishment for careless words. Not that lying under this naked woman is in any way a negative. But old habits die hard, and I can't help but wonder. 'What are you going to do with me?'

'I'm going to take care of you.' She kisses me, a lazy, decadent feast of lips and tongue and her sexy little moans. She straddles my thighs, loosening the hair tie from her hair so her ponytail spills

free. There are two of them. I watch in fascination and mounting excitement as she loops them
together and slips one around each of my wrists,
sparkling eyes returning to mine. 'It's symbolic—
I know you could easily snap them if you wanted
to.' Her hand delves between her legs, gripping
and tugging my cock. 'I'm going to make you feel
good.' She holds her breath for a beat or two and
then says, 'Is there any reason I can't take care of
you without the condom?'

I swallow hard, struggling to look away from
the exquisite and candid beauty of her eyes, the
thought of being inside her bare shutting down
at least eighty per cent of my brain. 'No—I care
about you.' I cup her face, my wrists still bound,
fighting the urge to pull her mouth back down to
mine for another kiss. 'I'd never put you at risk.'

'Me neither. And I'm on the pill.' She smiles
and then holds my face between her palms, her
fingertips gliding into the hair at my temple with
such tenderness I go completely still. 'I'm going to
remind you that it's okay to let someone be there
for you, to hold you up or catch you when you fall.
That you don't have to be strong alone. That's it's
okay to trust me like you say you do.'

She rises up a fraction, her eyes hypnotising,
and slides the head of my bare cock back and forth
through her wet folds, the friction almost too good.

'Blair—' I bite out a warning, clarity over what she wants from me, that she sees me so clearly, stripping me bare. Because physically I do trust her—fuck, I'd bend myself into a pretzel shape if that's what she wanted. But the emotional stuff? The feelings I'm too chickenshit to probe? Handing her that much power...?

Her hand slides across my chest, her fingertips trailing through my chest hair until her nails dig into my clenched pec.

Her voice when she speaks carries the same, hypnotic, lulling tone. 'You're so big and strong. Powerful and in control. You make me feel small, somehow cherished, just with a look or a simple touch. I want you to feel the same way.'

The fantastic torture to the head of my cock continues as she rocks her hips over me, and it takes everything I am not to plunge inside the tight, wet haven that awaits me. To take over, to block out her words, her caring until the pleasure swallows everything else—my concerns, my doubts, even my emerging feelings.

'You take care of everyone,' she says, 'carry more than your share of the load.' Her finger covers my mouth, stopping the interruptions sitting there. 'For the next few minutes you're mine, to do whatever I choose with. Don't speak unless it's to tell me how good something feels.'

And before I can agree or disagree she scoots lower between my legs and takes my wet cock into her mouth. My hips buck—I can't stop them—and she smiles, humming out encouragement and gripping the base of my erection until my vision tunnels. Everything stops—the noise of distant traffic and the hum of lawnmowers, the constant stream of thoughts and lists and ruminations plaguing my mind, even the shame of hurting this wonderful woman and the desire to make amends. Because everything becomes Blair and the wondrous things she's doing to me, the feeling of letting go and being worshipped.

My entire body is board-stiff under her, every muscle clenched as she sucks me down and watches my every reaction. Just when I start to buck my hips up off the sofa, chasing the paradise she promised, she stops, slides into position over me and sinks until I'm buried to the hilt inside her sweet, tight pussy.

I groan aloud, my mind blank, every brain impulse focused on the firing of pleasure centres. With a crunch of my abs I sit up, loop my tied arms over her head and drag her close so I can bury my face against her wild heartbeat and ride out the shock waves of ecstasy buffeting my body.

Her hands tangle in my hair and she holds me tight to her chest as her hips make the smallest of rocking motions. 'You fill me, Reid. You feel so good and I'm going to make you come.' I clutch her tighter, speechless, certain nothing in my life so far compares to this moment.

I raise my head, kissing her until she pulls away for breath, her rhythm choppy and uncoordinated. 'Come with me,' I say.

At her nod, her whimper, I dive for one of her nipples. At the first scrape of my facial hair over the sensitive bud, she cries out and squeezes my dick. I nuzzle her breast, lave all my attention on the nipple—sucking and licking and scraping until she's a panting, writhing mess, undulating in my lap while she clings to my shoulders, a fearless goddess guiding us towards oblivion.

She smiles, the astounding sight almost better than it feels to be deep inside her. I crush her close, until her breasts flatten against my chest and rub my lips over hers, needing more, needing everything.

She pulls away, ducks from between my arms, pushing them over my head. 'Lie back.'

I follow her command, sliding back onto the sofa, my hands itching to grab her arse and shunt her with me.

But she's there. She braces her arms beside my head on the sofa, her pleasure-drunk stare latched to mine shifting the organs in my chest. If ever I wanted a do-over at relationships, if ever I deserved a second chance, she'd be it for me—she couldn't be more perfect. I swallow back the lump of feelings in my throat and watch every move she makes so I can store every second of her in my long-term memory.

She starts to rock again, tossing her long hair back and forcing her breasts forward. I'm splayed, helpless, tied. I grit my teeth against the pleasure of her riding me, her moans of ecstasy growing more vocal.

'Reid.' She groans my name, reaching to cup both her breasts with her own hands.

My restraint breaks with the easily snapped hair ties. I can't take any more, can't watch and not touch. Can't deny myself the act of pleasuring her as she's driving me close to the edge. I'm greedy for her. I grasp the cheeks of her arse, gently parting them and slipping my fingers between to her opening so I feel myself sliding inside her tight sex with every rock of her hips.

'That's right, take what you want from me. Take what you need.' I want more hands to explore every inch at once—she's so fucking tempting—but I console myself with the two I have, filling one with her perfect breast while the other caresses her backside.

She starts to rock her hips in earnest, finding her rhythm again, and the sight of her above me, the feel of her clamped around me, makes me close to blowing. I bite back a curse, my jaw clenched as I will away the sharp gush of pleasure bathing my dick. She's driving, but I'm not going anywhere without her.

My thumb and forefinger roll her nipple as she picks up her pace. She takes my other hand, sliding it back between her cheeks.

'Touch me here.'

I obey, feather a fingertip lightly over her tight pucker so she's dragged back into a sensual haze I never want to see end. And then I'm lost, no longer caring who's in charge or who's letting go, as long as we finish together.

'Blair, you trust me, don't you?'

She nods on a strangled whimper. 'Yes.'

The glaze to her eyes tells me she's too far gone to care whose fantasy this started out as and who's in control.

'I trust you too.' Giving her what she wants is the easiest thing in the world.

She cries out, her hips bumping up and down on my lap. 'Yes, Reid.'

With every downward stroke, my finger skirts her rear, each fractured cry, each moan telling me I'm right on target to amp up her pleasure while staving off my own. Because I want her ruined, as she's ruined me. I want her broken and desperate and out of her mind, because that's where my head is.

Reluctantly dragging my eyes away from the sight of her riding me, her hair wild and her face flushed, I turn my head sharply to the left, catching our reflection in the mirror over the fireplace, our reflections erotic, like our own, private adult movie.

She looks too, as I'd known she would, her gasp followed by a long, low moan.

'Touch your nipples,' I order, because I need both my hands to finish this the way I want to. She obeys, her finger circling and pinching where mine have left off, and I grip both of her arse cheeks, adding upward tilts of my pelvis to her down-strokes so every thrust drags a cry from her arched throat.

'Reid, I've got you.' She tears her eyes from our wildly fucking reflections to stare down at me.

'I've got you too—come with me.' I pull her cheeks apart, grinding our hips together while my fingers probe deeper into her crease to stimulate more nerves.

She cries out, her orgasm wracking her entire body rigid and I feel her spasms around my dick and against the tip of my finger.

I buck up into her tight, clasping warmth a handful more times and join her with a roar of release that rivals any I've ever experienced.

By the time speech is possible once more, we've

been sprawled on the sofa in a naked tangle for several minutes. There's still a furnace bubbling inside me, but I spy goose pimples on Blair's arm, so I tug the throw from the back of the sofa over us. That's when I feel the rhythmic shudders of her chest against mine, which tell me she's laughing.

I lift her chin from my chest, forcing her to look up at me. 'Great...that's what every man wants after some of his best moves—to be laughed at.'

She covers her mouth, ungainly snorts she can't hold in escaping. 'I'm sorry—I just...' She presses her lips together and then gives up, freeing a cascade of chuckles.

I join her, although I have no idea what we're laughing at, but it's infectious. *She's* infectious, effortlessly worming her way under my skin and into my psyche. Offering tantalising glimpses of what might be, glimpses I'd thought I was long past craving. Dangerous.

'I've never met anyone who finds sex that hot funny,' I say, kissing the top of her head and breathing in coconuts. 'So hot my sofa is scorched.'

She collapses on top of me, kissing her mirth into submission. 'It's not that. I just... I can't believe you tripped over your shoe. It was hilarious.'

My ego could take a battering, but with her I don't seem to have any. I grin. 'Oh, good—I was aiming for sexy.'

'Oh, it was that, too. And I told you I'd catch

you.' She snuggles back into my side and a sigh of contentment leaves me, but doubts sneak in to fill the void, doubts that she could want more, because after that, after today with my family, seeing how perfectly she fits—I'm certain I want more than sex. But does she? Could she take this seriously outside of our sex-only arrangement? I've been so long entrenched in my single life, safe, secure, steady. Could I have more? Could I have it with this amazing woman? Would she want it with me? My track record speaks against me, and while our age gap works for a casual fling, would she want something more with a man my age? And surely the fact that she's still hung up on her ex's cheating, wanting to *banish ghosts*, as she said, means she's not fully over him.

Her fingers toy with the hair on my chest. I pull her hand away so I can kiss the tips of her fingers as I grapple with that last revelation. I should get up, make us a drink, suggest a shower, offer to drive her back to her car. I'm sure we both have a long day ahead tomorrow. But a part of me can't leave it alone, perhaps the part which feels the flicker of jealousy that while I'm imagining dates she's thinking about ways to exorcise her ex.

I choke out a question, the only honest thing I feel comfortable asking. 'So did you make some new memories?'

I feel her nod against my cheek and the whoosh

of air she eventually releases, and grip her closer on instinct.

'The day after Josh left me,' she says, 'I rushed out and bought a new sofa, knowing I'd never be able to look at the old one, let alone sit on it. But it's funny—no matter where I place the new one in that room, it never looks quite right.' She huffs. 'Or perhaps that's just my designer brain being a perfectionist.'

I stroke my fingers through her hair, trying to untangle some of the strands without hurting her. 'It's okay to be a perfectionist. It's who you are.' I allow the weight of my hand to settle between her shoulder blades before I add, 'Has he ever apologised?'

'Josh?'

Her body stiffens and I shift my leg so I can tangle it with hers to stop her escaping. 'Yeah.' I know he can't help the way he felt for someone else, but he should have come clean from the start instead of risking her finding out the way she did.

'I don't know,' she says in clipped tones, telling me she doesn't want to talk about this, that I've gone too far. But she's laid me open, used our attraction to each other and my growing feelings to pry confessions from me. Time to even the balance. And she can't be fully over him until she's had some closure.

'What do you mean? Has he tried?' Unease slides over my skin.

She shrugs, her eyes shuttering the emotion from the green-brown depths of her irises. 'I changed the locks after he left. I've never answered his calls or read his emails. I don't care if he's apologised because I don't want to hear it.'

My belly twists, banishing the last of the high from the incredible sex. She hasn't forgiven him, so she's not free to move on. Does she still harbour feelings after all this time? And where the fuck does that leave me and my newly acknowledged revelations?

I frame my words in a soothing tone. 'I don't want to patronise you, but until you allow him to apologise, what he did to you becomes compounded. You can't move on until you've given him the chance to at least say he's sorry for deceiving you.'

She raises her head and levels her bullshit look on me. 'Is that what worked for you with Sadie?'

Now it's my turn to stiffen, her attack close to the very heart of me, as exposed as I feel. 'That was different.'

'How? Because it happened to you?' She juts her chin, her barriers rebuilding.

A sense of claustrophobia presses in on me. Am I being a fool here? 'No—' I extricate my limbs from hers and slide to the edge of the sofa, restless with vulnerability and the hangover of literally having my emotions fucked from me. 'Because she attacked more than me. She went after my business, my family, my father in particular, and threatened the future of the Faulkner Group for Kit's unborn child and any children Drake and Kenzie might have.'

The room grows tense with our silence. When I look her face is ashen with shock, or perhaps revulsion that I allowed myself, my family and business to be so vulnerable. But if I believe the latter, I'll have to punch some inanimate object. Instead I stand and search for my jeans.

'How?' she whispers.

I've been exposed enough over the past hour, but the power balance has shifted, as if she's freed me somehow from holding everything inside. I'm not the only man on the planet to be taken to the cleaners by a greedy ex, and it's in the past. I've spent the years since Sadie dedicated to the Faulkner Group, repaying my father for rescuing me the only way I could—through hard work and sheer fucking persistence until the company is as safeguarded and future-proofed as possible. And now I have the more pressing concern of his health.

'She wanted out of the marriage and I let her go. She hired a ruthless lawyer and I didn't contend her claims. I was generous with maintenance because I felt guilty that I hadn't put in as much effort to making things work as I should have. Because she was right—I did put the business and therefore the interests of my family before our marriage.' I sigh past the shame trying to constrict my lungs. 'But then she went after the Faulkner.'

I grab my T-shirt, needing the protection it provides from her searching eyes, still wary. But she was correct about me—I do keep everything afloat. It's my job, my life's work. I'm good at it, determination to ensure this latest sideswipe is managed with the same single-minded focus returning, so I finish my tale.

'It was a stressful time. Kit had just lost his wife and Drake had just come back to the family business after leaving the army.' The words still taste foul, a reminder of the added worry and uncertainty I put my family through. 'If it wasn't for Graham bailing me out and paying her off, the legal wrangling would have likely dragged on for years.' I scrub at my face and level a look of challenge at her. She wants to play big league—well, this is it. She claims she can catch me—well, I come with baggage. She wants my trust—well, it's a two-way street, and now I'm certain she's hiding something. Better I know now, before this goes any further, before my feelings develop, if she still harbours feelings for her shithead ex.

But I'm out of luck. Her expression closes down, defences up, reminding me of the Blair who walked into my office and waved her contract a couple of weeks ago. 'Well, we're not that different, then,' she says.

'In what way?'

'We've both been betrayed—do the details matter?'

I collect her underwear and clothes from the floor and hand them over, trying to shove the disappointment back in, but it sticks, as if it's expanded and no longer fits the same space.

'I guess not.' Unless one of us is still holding on to the past when the other has glimpsed the future. I could push. I want to push. To wring her dry until she's as brittle as I feel, but I'm aware it's late and the renovations start tomorrow. I'll bide my time. And, in the meantime, guard my feelings more circumspectly. I've already shared more with her today than I've shared with anyone else, perhaps ever, so I let it drop and offer her a lighthearted wink and myself a route back to the casual safety zone. 'Only I'm older and more cynical. There's still time for you.'

She offers up a smile that doesn't reach her eyes, grasping the shift from confessional to conversational with a return flash of humour. 'Loads of time—I'm a spring chicken.' She tugs on her underwear and jeans. 'I'm going to head home—big day tomorrow.'

'You don't want to stay?'

She shakes her head and ducks into her shirt while I exhale the relief she's turned down my genuine offer. Perhaps we both need distance. Time to regroup.

'Thanks, but I have an early start tomorrow,' she says. 'And I don't want to upset my grumpy old client.'

I tug her to her feet, push her hair back from her still flushed face and swoop in for a lingering kiss I hope will banish the creep of doubts. 'I'm sure he'd forgive you. And I'll drive you to your car.'

'Didn't you leave your car at the Faulkner?'

I shrug. 'Us grumpy old men can afford more than one—we've been earning money for longer.'

'Great!' Her smile twitches but her eyes still carry the strain, which pulls me up short and reminds me there's as much at stake now as there was the last time I erred close to the kind of feelings germinating.

Question is, do I give them light and water, or rip them out by the roots?

CHAPTER NINE

Blair

I'M HEADING BACK to the Faulkner's rear staff entrance, having spoken to the team of carpet fitters working on the top floor of guest rooms today, when I spy Reid striding my way. I freeze, my pulse leaping double time and my face heating with remembered shame, which dilutes the excitement I feel at his appearance. Because I was a coward. I had the perfect opportunity to tell him I fully understood what Sadie had put him through—because Josh had not only done the same to me, but also gone one step further and actually succeeded in ruining my business—and I couldn't do it. Because the way he made me feel highlighted how invested I was in him. Not the work, or Graham, but Reid himself. I couldn't confess how naive I was. Not after the sofa session, not after he gave me the control I asked for, told me he trusted me.

That moment, a perfect moment when I saw past the Reid Faulkner he projects to everyone else. As he lay beneath me, naked, vulnerable and turned on all because of me, something cracked open, spilling inside me and filling me up until I could barely breathe. I not only wanted his trust, I craved it, validation I could have what I want, be who I want to be and never have to compromise again.

I was falling for him, addicted to *him*, the man I'd stupidly thought I'd known at eighteen, but now saw for who he really is with the clarity of a woman falling in love. And I didn't want him to think less of me, to think of me as anything but the competent, capable professional I've strived to become. I couldn't tell him what I haven't even admitted to my family—the full extent of Josh's betrayal for fear of *we told you so* recrimination.

The minute I hinted that my own betrayal wasn't that dissimilar to his, I sensed his barriers slamming back up. He said all the right things, but he withdrew, his reminder, albeit through humour, of our age gap and his experience and wisdom loud and clear. He said age wasn't a barrier to our sexual relationship, but perhaps it would be a barrier to us ever becoming more.

I search his face for evidence of his feelings, learning nothing. Perhaps he's not even here for me; perhaps his emotional withdrawal on Sunday means he's also withdrawn his trust. Perhaps he's checking up on me after all. It's his hotel—he has every right to keep an eye on the renovations and with any other client I wouldn't question his motives. But now, with my feelings growing harder and harder to ignore, I crave his belief in me more than I want his recommendation or his repeat business. Perhaps even more than I want the addictive, life-affirming sex. Because I crave all of him, the whole package, the man he is today. Is that, too, naive?

'Hi,' I say. 'Have you come to check on progress?' My stomach gripes with persistent, hard-to-shake doubts. I've been to the Faulkner three times this week, and each time I've caught myself looking for his tall frame and his dark head of hair. Each day as I've been driving home I've considered dropping into his place and allowing all my ugliness to spill, an insane act of bravery, which would tell me, one way or another, exactly how he feels about me, and whether we could have any serious future relationship. Every time I speak to the painters, I find myself smiling at his lime-green aversion. And passing any sort of upholstered furniture sends me up in flames as I recall me riding him on the sofa, our sweaty, carnal twins reflected from the mirror.

He presses a kiss to my cheek and then, as if thinking better of it, slides his mouth over mine while hoisting me up to his kiss with arms banded around my waist. 'No—I've been a little busy this week. And I've come to see *you*.'

'Oh? Why?' Pleasure at his words shudders through me, dampened by the cowardly secret hanging over my head.

'Well, one—' he presses a brief kiss to my lips '—because I've missed fulfilling your fantasies. Two—' he reaches inside his breast pocket and produces a business card '—because Mia wanted me to pass this along—she's serious about some decorating advice and wants you to call.'

He takes my hand in his and I try to contain the euphoria of how right it feels, how I want to keep it there all day. How I want to confess not only my darkest shame, but also my most enduring fantasy—him taking me, us, our relationship outside of the bedroom seriously. Him wanting me for keeps.

'And three—I wanted to invite you to the Hoteliers Association Gala on Friday.'

My heart beats a silly rhythm before I slap it back with some good, old-fashioned common sense. This doesn't mean anything. Just because he's missed the sex doesn't mean he's missed *me*. Just because he wants a date for Friday doesn't mean he sees relationship potential in us. And, of course, he feels obliged to invite me after Graham's suggestion at lunch.

'So you need a plus one?'

He grins as if he sees through my flimsy assurances. 'Sure. So, will you come? It's black tie. Dancing. Kit and Mia are going.'

'I…' My teeth catch my lip—this should be an easy yes. He's enough of a temptation dressed in one of his impeccable suits, this one royal blue. I love dressing up fancy and dancing. But somehow things have changed, and *I* changed them. Now I crave more of those moments when he lets his guard down and lets me in almost as much as I crave his sexy smile, his penchant for tugging me under his arm and kissing the top of my head, and his uninhibited laughter at my teasing. Decisions I'd have made in a heartbeat a week ago now require more serious consideration. More thought. Because now my feelings are involved, and I have no idea what he's feeling. But in order to find out, I'm going to have to be brave. To not only make myself vulnerable but also to confess I'm not quite the savvy businesswoman I've painted myself to be. Will I regret it? Will he be as disappointed in me as I am in myself?

'Don't overthink this, Blair.' His hand cups my face. 'You'd be doing me a favour, your presence turning a boring evening of talking shop with the industry's movers and shakers into a night out that I'm would actually look forward to.'

Still I hesitate. Because I want to be more than his date. More than someone spending an evening with him. I want all of him, and that will involve giving all of me and hoping he feels the same.

I stall for time. 'Is it being held at a Faulkner hotel? I don't think my parents have mentioned it this year...'

He shakes his head, sidling closer as if he knows he can persuade me with his physical touch alone.

'Well, maybe next year,' I say. 'In the newly renovated Faulkner ballroom, perhaps.'

'Maybe.' He shrugs, uncaring, eyes piercing through every defence I possess. 'Please come— if it's because you have nothing to wear I can juggle my calendar and we could go shopping if you want.'

I splutter then full-out laugh. '*You* like shopping?' The image of Reid wandering into some women's clothing boutique is too funny.

He grins. 'No, but I'll go with you, if it will help your decision. Plus, you have to come because Mia is about to give birth and she really wants to talk to you. Kit tells me it's not a good idea to upset a pregnant woman.' His lips twitch and I can't stop myself from kissing him. Because I've wanted to since the moment he walked into his hotel. Since the moment he drove away from me on Sunday evening. Since the moment he confessed that he trusted me, before the doubts crept in.

'Okay—you've convinced me.' My decision settles in the pit of my stomach but I ignore the pinch. It's just a night out.

'Excellent.' He looks at his watch. 'So four p.m. for our shopping trip?'

I laugh again, letting him off the hook. 'You don't need to worry—I have something I can wear.'

He visibly sags with relief. 'Thank God for that.' Then he winks, kisses me again and saunters off, leaving me freewheeling towards something I'm not sure I'm ready for, desperately searching for the breaks I'm certain are out of reach.

The dance floor in the grand ballroom of one of London's top hotels is packed with elegant couples dancing to swing classics played by a live band. Reid dances the way he does everything—with that sexy confidence, expertly leading me around to steps I'm impressed he knows.

'Who taught you to dance?' I smile up at him, my chest full to bursting with both the magical quality of the evening—a champagne reception followed by a four-course dinner and now dancing in the arms of the most handsome man in the room—and the sick-to-my-stomach knowledge I'm in serious trouble where my feelings for him are concerned.

'My mother insisted all three of us had lessons—we hated them, but it turns out it's a useful skill for impressing women.' He flicks up his brows and grins, tugging me closer so I'm doused in his delicious scent and fighting the urge to snuggle into his crisp white shirt.

I snort, avoiding temptation. 'Like you've ever had trouble in *that* area.' But now I'm curious. 'You don't talk about her much…your mother. I think I only met her one time.'

'No. She lives in Spain. We don't see much of her.' His face stays neutral but I feel tension radiate through his hands in mine.

'It must have been hard when your parents split.'

He shrugs. 'I was already pretty much a man—it was harder for Drake and Kit. I tried my best to keep them distracted with sports and sailing, and Graham tried his best to keep things…stable, but…'

'So that's when you became the caretaker?'

Another noncommittal gesture that tells me more than his words. 'We're family—I guess it made us closer as brothers.'

And now his role as caretaker is even bigger with Graham's dementia diagnosis at a time when he's head of the company and Kit and Drake have their own families to think about. 'Well, they're all lucky to have you. I'm almost certain my family will never see me as anything but the baby, inconsequential.'

The current song comes to an end, and I ignore Reid's frown and glance back at our table. A tired-looking Mia sits with Kit, who appears to be trapped in conversation with a man on his other side.

'I might go and keep Mia company.'

Reid nods and presses a kiss to my forehead. 'I'm just going to say hello to a colleague or two. I'll come and join you soon.'

As I approach our table, Mia smiles and pats the seat beside her. 'I'm so tired I could drop,' she says. 'But Kit's trapped talking to some old uni mate. Are you having a nice time?' Her eyes shine as she scans the room behind me, and I turn to see Reid in conversation with an older man, his eyes sliding my way every few seconds.

'I am. I can't remember the last time I got all dressed up.'

She eyes my dress—a black silk halter-neck, the bodice ruched around the breasts and hips. 'This is gorgeous. No wonder he can't keep his eyes or his hands off you.'

We laugh good-naturedly together and then Mia

sobers. 'You know, I haven't known him that long, but I've never seen Reid laugh or smile as much as he does when he's around you.'

I cover my internal glow at her words, brushing it off because it's too close to what I really want to hear, what I hope might be true. 'He just needed a date.'

She shakes her head, eyeing me with suspicion. 'I'm serious. Reid works—that's all I've known him to do. He's different around you.' Her eyes narrow and my colour rises. 'You really like him too, don't you?' Mia smiles like the cat that stole the cream and leans close to whisper, 'Are you falling for him?' Only another woman could be so perceptive to see what I've only myself just recently acknowledged.

I shrug. 'I care about him a lot. I'm just... We've both had our fingers burnt in the past and, well, I'm a lot younger than him...'

'I've heard you both joke about it—are you worried he cares? I don't think he does.' She touches my arm.

Maybe not for something casual, as we started, but for more than that...

She must sense my discomfort, because she grows serious. 'You know, Reid sees himself as the family guardian, the caretaker, if you like. Kit says he stepped up after their parents split up.'

I nod. 'Yes, that's who he is—a natural leader, someone to take charge of a situation.'

'Yes, and for a while Kit was in a pretty bad place after his wife died and Drake came home from the army with PTSD. He was their rock, their constant—they both agree he helped them through some pretty tough times.'

I choke up just thinking of Reid and the burdens he's shouldered, past and present, and how he feels he has to do it all alone because of one bad relationship experience. 'It's great that they have each other, that they're so close, especially in light of Graham's diagnosis.'

Mia nods, her hand stroking her belly as if soothing her unborn child. 'Yes, but Reid insists on taking on the lion's share of the burden.'

'He feels he owes Graham the most, I guess.' I feel defensive for Reid, although she's in no way attacking him—another sign, if I needed one, of my growing investment in the man.

Kit bids his companion goodbye and turns to Mia. 'Are you ready to go home?' He kisses her with such tenderness, I look away.

At that moment Reid returns, his hand caressing my bare shoulder.

'We're off,' says Kit. 'Mia is tired.'

The brothers hug and then Reid kisses Mia's cheek and helps her into her wrap.

Kit touches my shoulder and leans in to press his cheek against mine. 'I wanted to apologise for what you overheard that day at lunch,' he says, his voice low. 'My surprise—mine and Drake's—was for Reid; he's been so closed off for so long I was shocked and delighted that someone had finally broken through his shield and that it was you of all people. I know we used to tease you when we were younger, but, seriously, we couldn't be more thrilled for you. And Reid.'

I stare, too dumbstruck for speech. *Have* I broken through to Reid? Could Reid possibly care for me as I do for him? Could we ever be more than we are now? Could we be a serious couple with a future together?

'You're good for him,' says Kit, his stare sincere and as deep and dark as Reid's. 'Goodnight, Blair.' He collects Mia from Reid and they head off, their arms around each other, their love clearly on display.

I turn to Reid, who slings his arm casually around my shoulders in that way I love, but then tucks me into his side with a sigh and a protracted sniff of my hair. 'Want to get out of here?' I feel the weight of his question to the tips of my toes and see the fatigue and something else, something tantalising, behind his eyes.

'Yes.'

'Good, because I have a surprise.'

I lift an eyebrow in question, too touched by his smouldering delight and his thoughtfulness for more. I've already had a wonderful evening—with this level of attentiveness, he needs to be careful— the love Mia and Kit left wafting in the air could become contagious.

CHAPTER TEN

Blair

INSTEAD OF LEAVING the hotel, Reid heads for the lifts, a knowing smile twitching his sexy mouth. 'We're not going home?' I ask, my stomach swirling with anticipation and nerves, as if I'm still on the dance floor, spinning too fast.

He shakes his head as he selects the top floor and the lift doors close. 'I thought it might be nice to stay here.'

'Good idea.' Touched, I snuggle into his side, my arm gripping his waist inside his jacket. 'I had a wonderful evening. Thanks for inviting me.' Why is it so hard to tell him?

His deep voice rumbles against my cheek. 'So did I—thanks for coming.'

We arrive on the top floor and my head swims as Reid leads the way to the penthouse suite.

The door clicks open and he steps aside for

me to enter first. I gasp, one hand covering my mouth. The suite is in darkness, but for a million twinkling seed lights decorating every available surface. This would have taken a long time and considerable cost. That he's thought ahead and made such a romantic gesture gives me enough hope, my pulse ricochets. Would he go this far if he didn't care too? If it was just sex to him? That doesn't mean he sees a future for us though, and now I need to know, as much as I need to touch him. I'm not leaving this room until I cross that terrifying threshold and find out one way or another.

Reid shrugs his jacket off, an indulgent smile dancing on his lips as I fight the urge to cry at his thoughtfulness, or to blurt out my true feelings and completely scare him off. It's a good thing that I'm speechless.

Reid pours two glasses of champagne from a bottle chilling in ice and hands one to me with a sexy smile.

'To five-star hotels and chance meetings.' His eyes say what I desperately want to hear, but I calm my raging pulse with a swallow of delicious, ice-cold bubbles and force myself to simply live in the moment, to enjoy this. There's no need to rush my confessions—we have all night.

Coward.

I allow myself to be distracted as Reid steps close and skates his fingers lightly down my arm from shoulder to wrist, setting off a cascade of delicious anticipation. 'Tell me another fantasy.' His lips brush mine, the taste of champagne and him merging to create a sublime new flavour.

Tonight, it's easy. 'You're my fantasy. Being whatever you need to be.' *Having all of you.*

'I want you too.' He quirks one eyebrow, waiting, but I have nothing but honesty to offer.

'Then I'm yours.' *Show me how you feel.*

His eyes darken until the colour disappears and merges with his pupils. 'That's an intoxicating offer... A man could get used to that.'

My heart lurches and I place my glass on the table with a trembling hand, need burning through me. I want him physically, yes, as fiercely as ever, but I need more, and I need to know that he can give me what I need. Because if I do this, lay myself open, I'll want everything in return. No half measures, no settling for mediocre, and only complete, transparent trust.

Slowly I reach for his tie, loosening the bow and tossing it aside. All the while he watches my every movement, lazily sipping champagne, savouring it, his stare heavy with desire.

I undo the top few buttons of his shirt and press my mouth to his, keeping my eyes open to watch every nuance of his reaction. 'Why don't you show me what that, what *you* need, looks like?'

His pupils dilate and he rests his free hand on my hip, his fingers flexing, as if he can't not touch me. 'Keep going with the buttons.'

I smile to hide my nerves and get to work, ensuring I brush my knuckles over his exposed chest with every loosened stud, because I want to brand him for every woman still in the ballroom downstairs to see. To show him the depth of my feelings. To tell him without words and have everything reciprocated.

When I reach his waistband I look up, licking my parched lips.

One look from him and I continue. When I open his trousers and push down his boxers he steps back, denying me the prize of his thick, heavy cock.

'Take off the dress. Just the dress.' His command is gruff, thrilling.

While I rush to his bidding he grips himself with one hand, his thumb circling the head of his cock on every up-stroke and continues to sip his champagne. 'This is for you—I can't wait.'

My breath seesaws in excited gasps—he knows I love that he's greedy and impatient. He's so urbane, so decadent, so sexy standing there, his immaculate shirt and tailored trousers open, commanding our pleasure and spinning any fantasy I desire. He wants me physically, I've never doubted that.

I allow the dress to pool at my feet, my pulse surging anew at Reid's muttered curse. Beneath my dress I'm wearing a strapless bra, matching thong and suspenders. I smile for him, knowing the effect I'm having, because watching him stroke himself to produce a bead of pre-ejaculate does similar things to my weak body.

He jacks himself faster. 'Lose the bra. The rest stays, including the shoes.' He heels off his own dress shoes and knocks back the last of his drink, placing his glass beside mine.

I toss the bra aside and roll my shoulders back, presenting my breasts to their best advantage for his greedy stare.

He struggles, but manages to tear his eyes away. 'There's a very comfortable-looking sofa in here.' I follow his stare, waiting—the whole suite is sumptuous, elegant and luxurious. And the romance of tonight, the idea of giving myself to him in any way he wants and acknowledging the depth of my feelings, has me so turned on, he could take me on the parquet flooring for all I care.

'But, for now, I think we'll head to the bed.'

I precede him to the bedroom, allowing my hips to embrace the natural sway wearing sky-high heels provides. I'm rewarded with another groan from Reid behind me, and then I hear the clink of glass, looking back to see him collect our glasses and the bottle from the ice bucket.

'Lie down, Blair.' His sexy deep voice scrapes my nipples alive as I follow his command. While I wait on the bed he pours himself another glass and tops up mine, passing me the flute, watching me take a swallow and then leaning over me for a kiss, his tongue invading my fizzing mouth.

'Mmm…tastes better on you.'

I reach for his cock, my fingers gripping the base and my hand gliding to the very tip to capture that drop of liquid, as I know he likes, because I've watched him do it to himself enough times.

He pulls off his shirt, his stare bouncing between my mouth, which is wet from his kiss, and my hand pumping his erection. The lazy pace is killing me, I'm feverish, the ache between my legs is almost unbearable and my nipples are hard peaks, desperate for his touch. But it's his party. Whatever he wants goes tonight.

He seems to hear my desperation, because he slides his trousers and boxers over his hips and takes my glass from my free hand. 'Do you want to suck it?'

'Yes, oh, yes. Reid—don't make me wait any longer.'

He drinks from my glass, his eyes hooded. 'It's all yours.'

I pounce, there's no other word for it, bringing my mouth over the fat head of his cock to meet my still pumping hand. He grunts and his hips shunt forward as if out of his control, shoving him to the back of my throat. I pull back, my delight a hum in my throat, and swirl my tongue at the sensitive spot near the tip. He must have drained the champagne because he tosses the empty glass to the floor with a roll so it doesn't break. One of his hands finds my hair, tangling and gripping with possessive force while the other cups me through my damp underwear.

'And this is mine.'

It's not a question, but I nod frantically while keeping my mouth tight around him, because I love the way it sharpens his features with pleasure.

'I saw the way people looked at us tonight, like they were trying to figure out what you're doing with me, but I don't give a fuck, do you hear me? You're mine.'

It's so close to a declaration I'm desperate hear, I almost come there and then. But I can't enjoy his words for long, because he yanks his hips away and joins me on the bed, grasping my thighs and spreading them wide before tugging my thong aside and burying his face between my legs.

I cry out, the lance of pleasure is so acute, but his cock is right there, still straining and I manoeuvre my body so I can stretch and take him back into my mouth.

We're both groaning now, our mingled moans and sucking noises filling the air in an erotic aria. It's not my best blow job—he's eating me out with such thorough ferocity, his fingers plunging inside me while he tongues my clit, I'm surprised my lungs still work. But I'll die, if I have to, trying to give him as much pleasure as he's giving me.

And then it's over for me because he pushes the tip of a finger inside my rear while he flicks my clit with the tip of his tongue and my whole world detonates. I sob my orgasm into the mattress, my fingers still squeezing him as the jerks rack me.

And then he's sliding my underwear off and tossing my shoes over his shoulder. I'm his puppet, but I'm too languid to move for myself. His face tight with concentration, he removes one stocking and uses it to bind my wrists together before manoeuvring me onto all fours. His hands caress me from shoulders to hips, the strokes somehow both worshipful and possessive. 'You are every fucking fantasy I've ever had, Blair,' he says, pushing inside me so deep, I arch my back to take him the last inch. He pumps into me, one hand returning to my clit, where I'm still acutely sensitive.

'Yes. And you're mine.' I'm dizzy at once. It's close to what I want, but not enough, and I'm too wrung dry to act on anything besides instinct.

He pinches my clit between two fingers and I collapse forward onto my forearms as I absorb shock wave after delicious shock wave.

'But I want more than fantasy. I want reality, too.' He pulls out and I cry at the loss, but then he flips me onto my back and kisses me with a ferocious-sounding groan.

I lift my arms over my head out of the way and spread my thighs wide to cradle his hips. 'Yes, hurry.' I'm not above begging, and I'll give him anything in that moment.

He pushes my knees back and lines himself up at my entrance, pushing just the tip inside. I loop my tied arms over his head and drag his mouth down to meet mine, whispering his name over his lips and then pushing my tongue to meet his.

Reid braces himself on one strong arm and grips the back of my neck with his other hand to keep my mouth locked with his—not that I'm going anywhere. And then he's inching back inside, stretching me in that achingly sublime way that has me moaning and gasping into his mouth.

When he's fully seated, he breaks from our kiss with a grunt. His face is a study in fierce need that steals my air.

'I can't get enough of you. Even now, buried to the hilt, I want more of you.'

'Me too. Take more.' Take everything.

His fingers slip back into my crease and he touches my rear once more. 'I even want you here, but I don't want to hurt you, so we'll take that slowly.'

I gasp, welcoming the idea because I'm his already. 'You can have all of me.' I tilt my hips up so he sinks another inch and we gasp together.

My declaration seems to both thrill and galvanise him. He lowers his weight on top of me, balancing on his forearms while his hands push my wild hair back from my face. His lips brush mine and I wrap my legs around his hips as he starts to move.

It's slow, thorough, and so intense I want to weep. But face to face, without stares locked and our pants mingling, my universe shrinks to one, pinpoint focus.

Reid.

A man I love.

His pace picks up and he shunts me with him up the slope. I cling—my lips, my arms, my legs— desperate to go wherever he takes us. He comes with a harsh cry, his face pressed to the crook of my shoulder, and I spill after him, the words I so desperately want to say lost in my cries.

Reid rolls to the side, taking me with him,

spooning me from behind and enveloping me in his huge arms. His fingers loosen the stocking around my wrists while he presses kisses to the side of my face and neck. I snuggle into him, content beyond anything I could imagine, because he's just possessed me, claimed me, shown me all I need to know. He cares. He may not be there yet, as certainly as I am, but he cares.

I'm just drifting into a deeply relaxed space-out, lulled by the hypnotic way he strokes my arm with his thumb, when he speaks, the rumble of his gruff question vibrating through my back.

'Do you still have feelings for him?'

I freeze, even my breath. 'Who?'

'Your ex, Josh?' His voice is sleepy, as if he's making idle chat, but there's a tension in the arms banded around me.

I turn to face him so he sees the look of incredulity I'm sure is all over my face. 'No. Of course not. What makes you think that?' Irritation buzzes through my nerve endings even as I acknowledge that his question leaves him open and exposed, just like I want him.

'It's okay,' he says. 'It's hard to switch off feelings just because someone we love changes their mind.' He could be asking me if I still believe in fairies for all the emotion he displays and my blood runs cold so that goose pimples break out on my arms. Am I wrong? Can he really care if he thinks I'm still in love with my ex? Does he see me as someone too young to know herself beyond sexual infatuation? Will he ever be as deeply invested as me, or is this just marking his territory?

'I guessed you must still be hung up on the guy because you're still angry with him, still can't forgive him.'

I sit up, taking the sheet with me to cover my nakedness. 'I forgave him for cheating the day I caught him, Reid, more fool me.'

He frowns. 'What do you mean?'

I shuffle away from him on the bed, out of reach. If I have to do this now, like this, I can't have the distraction of his touch—not when I feel as if I'd have to slap it away, although some of my disappointment deflates, as I haven't been completely honest with him.

'Josh didn't *just* cheat on me. While the split was all rather amicable and, as you've already pointed out, incredibly mature of me, he wasn't content with one lie. We agreed to separate but to keep running our business together for the immediate future at least. So, imagine my surprise when I arrived at the office the following Monday morning to find he'd hightailed with most of our big-name clients, stripped our joint business account and left me with the outstanding bills.'

I take a minute's comfort in his ashen expression of shock, but plough on. 'So no, I can't forgive him for that, and no, I have no romantic feelings for him whatsoever. But yes, it does make me a naive idiot.'

'I'm sorry—I didn't know that part. I don't think you're a naive idiot, no more than I was with Sadie.' He reaches for my hand but I tug it away, too raw and too defeated at the reminder, my throat hot with the threat of tears. 'I'm going to take a shower.'

'Don't be angry with me.'

'I'm not angry.' I lie, because half of me is. 'I'm just humiliated.' And disappointed. I assumed, again wrongly, that his possession was a sign of his growing feelings, but was it simply jealousy…?

I head for the bathroom, his stare burning my back. With the water set to almost scalding I welcome the sting of the shower, which reminds me I might not have come as far as I'd thought in my recovery because, no matter how I might want it to be different, Reid doesn't seem to know me, to truly see me, after all.

CHAPTER ELEVEN

Reid

I PARK MY Jag in my designated spot in the Faulkner car park, a spot next to the empty one with Graham's name on it, the familiar pinch under my ribs reminding me tomorrow is D-Day—his appointment with Harley Street's most prominent dementia specialist.

The hotel is awash with contractors, the buzz of power tools and the smell of fresh paint filling the air. I've varied the time of my daily visits, but since our hedonistic weekend, where we only emerged from the bedroom to accept the regular room-service deliveries, I've managed to miss Blair every time. We've spoken on the phone every day, of course, but the easiness has vanished. And despite us both making our excuses, her busy with the renovations and me distracted by Graham's looming appointment, I've only myself to blame. I pushed her to tell me something she's clearly embarrassed by, and, rather than bringing us closer together, it pushed her away. Instead of telling her my feelings, I tried to sound out hers, idiot that I am.

I enter the foyer, amazed anew at how much more bright and welcoming the space is since the wall behind the old reception desk came down. Blair was right—the natural light works wonders. I can almost see it sparkling off the contemporary chandeliers she's going to hang.

My chest fills with pride. Whatever my father was going through health-wise, his vision for the flagship Faulkner Hotel and his belief in Blair hit the mark with his usual innate instincts. He was right to believe in her and she was right when she promised she could deliver.

Movement near the far wall close to the entrance doors catches my eye. I step closer to see a man wearing overalls, his long hair tied in a man bun as he sketches something on the freshly painted wall in broad, sweeping strokes.

'Hi,' I say, extending my hand when he spins to face me. 'I'm Reid Faulkner—I don't believe we've met.' What the hell is he doing?

'Oh, hey, man—Zach.' He tucks his pencil into his bun and shakes my proffered hand, his grip matching mine. 'I'm a friend of Blair's.'

My first reaction, a prickle of possession snaking down my spine—I've never heard of a Zach, and what the hell is he doing to a freshly painted wall, because he's not fitting a light fixture or hanging a print?—is replaced with a sense of foreboding I'm beginning to dread.

'So what are you doing *here*?' I point to the wall, at this distance noting what appears to be an outline of the Faulkner.

Zach smiles. 'It's the mural.'

I hide my frown, my dislike of being out of the loop on anything to do with my business, especially this hotel, making my jaw clench. 'Mural…?'

Zach's confidence wavers, his casual smile slipping a notch. 'Yeah—didn't Blair tell you?' He strides over to a small, paint-splattered table covered with a stack of art supplies and hands me a roll of paper. 'It's the tribute she conceived.'

At my blank look, he continues, only now his eyes are darting anywhere but at me as he fully understands I clearly have zero knowledge of any mural or tribute.

'You know—to Mr Faulkner…'

I unroll the paper, rage and sickening dread unfurling in my stomach with every inch that's revealed. Because what I see brings everything crashing down around me, as if my beloved hotel itself is crumbling.

It's a timeline. Scanned photos artfully blended together, from a youthful Graham cutting a wide red ribbon outside the Faulkner the day he re-opened it not long after purchasing the building, through a family portrait of me, Drake and Kit as boys, sitting on the reception desk, our grins missing various teeth, to a shot of Graham the day he officially retired next to the brass plaque he placed outside, which reads *A Faulkner Hotel, established 1979.*

My head spins with the flood of memories. These walls have housed almost every signifi-cant date in my life, and those in my brothers'. This…tribute, absolute confirmation that Graham is part of the Faulkner's past, not its future, may as well be an obituary for the violent reaction which courses through every cell in my body.

How could she do this without telling me? How could she plan to wipe Graham from the hotel's heritage with such finality? Why the hell would she think I'd want to see *this* every time I walk through the doors? A reminder of my father's past glory.

I grow aware of the time that has passed, swal-lowing hard to get myself back under control. 'Can I keep this?'

Zach nods, nervously. 'Sure, man. Of course. I have another copy.'

I roll the collage up, handling it as if it's a live snake. 'Why don't you take a break, Zach? Have the rest of the day off.'

He senses the unspoken in my words, offering a brief nod before turning to pack up his equipment.

Blair

I'm just entering the Faulkner Group building when a call comes in from Zach.

'Blair?'

'Hi.' I smile, excitement for the mural quickening my pace. 'I'll be with you soon. I'm just at the Faulkner Group offices.'

An ominous pause. 'I'm not at the hotel—Reid asked me to leave.'

I freeze, shock and outrage forcing my hand to grip my phone tighter.

'I just wanted to let you know,' says Zach.

My high at seeing Reid and making sure things are right between us dissolves, my mind shuffling through the implications of Zach's words and Reid's actions. But first I need details.

'What? Why?' I deflate, my heart sinking at the realisation that Reid has interfered, sent home one of my contractors without so much as a courtesy call, let alone a mature client-contractor discussion.

'He didn't say, but he didn't seem pleased,' says Zach.

I cringe. While I was preparing to see him again, sappily imagining I'd finally tell him how I feel about him and he'd reciprocate my love, he was checking up on me again, undermining my work and assuming he knows best. He simply couldn't trust me to do my job, even after I told him what Josh had done and its impact. My stomach falls and nausea grips my throat.

'Hey, it's not a problem from my point of view,' says Zach. 'I can resume the painting any time you're ready…but just to let you know Reid has settled my account in full, so… I don't know what that means for the mural.'

I do.

He hates it. He's vetoed it without discussion and despite its being personally commissioned by Graham. I swallow hard, fighting the burn of furious, frustrated tears. Why couldn't he have trusted me? It was supposed to be a surprise. But I should have known that, whatever progress Reid and I made in private, the trust element was an illusion. One I was a naive fool to believe.

'Thanks, Zach. Sorry for the confusion—I'll be in touch.' I disconnect the call while a strange numbness settles over me as I head inside the building. I won't jump to conclusions—perhaps he had genuine reasons for halting the work. I take my visitor's pass from the building's receptionist and turn for the bank of lifts, the tight, wooden smile on my face making my cheeks ache.

My body is restless, adrenaline pumping, but I stand before Reid's PA, my face tight with the effort of projecting an impression of calm professionalism.

'I'm sorry, Ms Cameron. He's out of the office at the moment,' she says.

I sigh, the delay in our showdown fuelling my frustration. Reid reacted with emotion. He should have called me first, not rushed in and paid off my contractor without consulting me. Of course, I understand he's protective of the Faulkner—it's home to him, his life's work and his father's before him. I get it, especially in light of Graham's diagnosis. But...

'I'll wait, thanks.'

I've barely taken a seat in Reid's empty office when the door swings open, revealing the man himself. 'Blair...'

Heat pours through me at the sight of him—last time I saw him he held me so tightly as we came together, I thought we'd become one person—only to drain away at the memory of what he did, at the knowledge that no matter how hard *I've* fallen, Reid still sees me as incapable, someone to be undermined and professionally embarrassed without thought. Shivers threaten to take hold. I clear my throat and stand tall. However this goes, I can fight my corner. I've done it before, despite the odds. I rebuilt something prosperous from the nothing left by Josh.

I accept his chaste kiss, which, for a moment, lulls me to believe everything is okay. That we're back in our hotel suite, still lost in those few blissful minutes when anything seemed possible.

Reid pulls back, his face drawn with fatigue and his eyes haunted with regret. My stomach twists and I look away, still clinging to denial for a few more minutes until I'm forced to face reality.

I take a seat in the same spot as I did at our first meeting, my body equally gripped by the conflicting visceral emotions, but my mind clear for the first time in years. 'You've halted the mural?' There's little point beating around the bush.

He nods, smoothing down his tie. 'Yes. I didn't know anything about it.' He wears the steely, cloaked wariness of our first meeting, and this drains more hope from me. 'Why is that, Blair?'

I ignore his question, too focused on the way my body wants to curl in on itself at his confirmation of what I suspected, but I tilt my chin. 'And you didn't think to call me? To discuss it with me before you paid off my contractor?' I can't help the accusation in my tone, because everything I've done has come from a place of love and respect for his family, particularly Graham, and if he can't see that he really doesn't know me at all or he's choosing to dismiss what he knows, and I can't tolerate either.

'I was going to call you. Look—'

I hold up my hand, blocking his words. I know they're going to hurt too much. Confirm my worst fears. I trusted that he'd respect my professionalism and my creative instincts. I trusted that when I told him about Josh, he'd understand how important my business is to me. I trusted that *he*, of all people, saw me as his equal, not some young, naive fool, playing with her little design projects.

'I assumed you'd finally handed control of the Faulkner renovations over to me, but now I see I've again been a misguided idiot. You may have been able to set everything aside to get laid,' I swallow hard, battling a wave of nausea, forcing out the words he hasn't said aloud that I can't allow to go unspoken, 'but you just can't do it, can you? You can't trust me to do my job. You can't trust me, full stop.' It's not a question. And the bigger statement refuses to emerge from my burning throat—that he can't trust *us*. That perhaps for him there never was an us, that too an illusion. That it was nothing more than sex, and even then he couldn't keep his promise to separate it from my work.

His eyes soften, but then he pulls back, once more the ruthless, in-control businessman. 'You're right—I should have discussed the mural with you. But when I asked Zach to stop, it wasn't personal against you. I felt threatened, I felt my business and my family's slipping through my fingers. And I put that first.'

My mind fills the blanks.

Before you.

Before us.

I force the emotion from my voice. 'You know, Reid, you're wrong. This *is* personal to me. My business is personal to *me*. And you knew that— I told you what Josh did. I've worked long and hard to claw something back from the wreckage. I thought you understood me better than that. You of all people, because you've been through the same with Sadie. Yes, I'm ten years your junior, but I know what I'm doing, and you've been keeping tabs on me from the start. You've never separated us from the contract between our companies. And, while you have the final say at the Faulkner, I'm in control of my life. So, you see, business is always personal to someone. That's what you know too, because of what Sadie did to you. But I'm not her. I just wanted to do my job.' Everything clicks into place, the blurriness becoming crystal-clear.

He can't trust me. He never did.

His hand scrubs at the spot above his eyebrow and I falter at the sight of his elegantly masculine fingers, wincing at the memory of his touch. His frown is so deep it conceals his eyes from view. 'I admit I messed up—look, if you give me a chance to explain—'

'Like you gave me a chance to explain the mural.' I breathe through the pain of a million jagged glass shards, fighting the sting behind my eyes. But I can compartmentalise. Time to wrap up this meeting and get the hell away from him, because just sharing air with him hurts—a bitter realisation after everything else I thought we'd shared. 'So, I'll finish the Faulkner renovations, as contracted. I'll expect your written confirmation, one way or the other, on completion of the mural and then I'll be out of your hair.'

I leave, my legs shaky but growing steadier with each step, unsurprised when he doesn't chase after me.

CHAPTER TWELVE

Reid

I HEAD AFTER her, my long strides only faltering as I answer my phone, which vibrates in my pocket.

It's Kit.

'The specialist called—he has a cancellation for this afternoon. Can you make it?'

I curse, skid to a halt and look at Blair's retreating back, but the worry in my brother's voice pushes everything else from my mind. 'Of course—I'll meet you at Dad's.' I toss my phone down on the desk and then grab it again, my grip surely threatening the glass of the screen. I should chase after Blair, explain why I put a halt to the mural. Tell her how it knocked me for six—visual confirmation that, whatever the outcome of today's appointment with the specialist, and however hard I try to make it different, to atone, I can't change a damn thing for Dad. He's part of the past in the business he founded.

I should have reacted differently, seen it from Blair's point of view, realised that, as much as I feel threatened by what my father's demise means for me and the family business, what I did made Blair feel threatened too, for Cameron Interiors. I stalk downstairs, pent-up frustration tensing every muscle in my body. The mess I made with Blair needs dealing with, but it will have to wait. Graham, my family, the Faulkner, as always, take priority.

After a gruelling two hours, I emerge from the specialist's office, drained. The prognosis for my father is uncertain, as expected. He's likely to continue to have good days and bad days, and, as today is fortunately one of the former, he's fully cognizant of everything the Harley Street specialist had to say. And the news reiterating that routines are helpful and the prescribed medication might delay a worsening of his memory loss is as I expected. Only the blow is amplified, because I can't share my concerns, my helplessness with the only person who makes any of this situation better, a person I want, a person who, despite everything, has become a part of my life, which is perhaps why her keeping the mural from me felt like such a knee to the balls after everything we've shared.

'Are you going back to the office?' asks Kit from the back of my car, his eyes a little tired.

I slide a glance at Graham beside me in the passenger seat, aware that someone should perhaps be with him after the news we've just received. I swallow, torn between comforting my father and rushing to Blair. 'I have something I need to do first,' I grit out, cursing my stupidity anew.

'Can you drop me off on Oxford Street?' says Kit. 'I'm picking up a gift for Mia.' He brightens at the mention of her name, and I literally wish I could kick myself up the arse, because that's how Blair made me feel and now I'm caught in a self-inflicted prison between a rock and a hard place.

'Sure.' Although I want to take it back, the urgency to make things right with Blair beating at me like shock waves.

We're in the car, heading towards Oxford Street, when Graham breaks the tense silence as he reaches for the rolled-up mural. 'What's this?'

I mutter a curse, wishing I'd thrown it in the boot, out of sight. The last thing I want to talk about is some tribute she saw fit to make a permanent feature, without my consent. A tribute which highlights the end of my father's role in the family business, as much as the depressing possible prognosis the specialist outlined in a fit of absolute disclosure.

'It's something I need to talk to Blair about.'

Graham unrolls the mural, his small smile a

blow, knocking the wind from me and telling me he's already seen it. 'Blair…she's an incredible woman, isn't she? I remember when she used to splash around in the Faulkner pool with you and Drake—such a cute little girl and so smart.' He directs this to Kit, who rolls his eyes and grins as he accepts the roll of paper and opens it up for a look.

'Did you know about this?' I ask, my eyes flicking between my brave father and youngest brother, so many emotions warring inside, it's a wonder I don't explode.

'Of course,' says Graham. 'She and I discussed it many times—it was *my* idea, but she came up with the mural concept. She has a talented artist friend. His work is amazing.'

Nausea pushes my heart into my throat. I grip the wheel tighter and mash my lips together, because if I speak I'll have to ask my brother and my father to get out of the car so I can go and repair what I've done.

Why can't my father stay as lucid as he is today for ever? What a terrible disease, robbing him of himself, and how selfish am I to think about what it means for me to mourn the man he was instead of simply celebrating the man he is still, even after the morning we've had—fearless, insightful and an inspiration?

'You're in love with her, aren't you?' Graham's

astute statement causes me to almost rear-end the car in front.

Kit snorts and Graham chuckles. 'You and Drake were right,' he says to Kit, and then to me, 'I think she loves you too. Mind you, she was always a bit smitten with you, so I suppose it's no surprise.'

My mind spins at the dizzying possibility of his words. Could it be true? Could someone as wonderful as Blair take a chance on me? A divorcee workaholic ten years her senior? Perhaps at one time, but not now I've fucked things up for the final, fatal time.

'I don't think so.' I slide Kit my promising-retribution look in the rear-view mirror, but he just lifts a mocking brow, as if I'm the last person to catch on.

I sigh, wishing Graham's words were true and the mess I'd made of everything could be that easily rectified. 'Well, regardless, after today I think she'll be done with me.' And I don't blame her. She gave me all of herself, she was there for me, she even tried to give Graham the love and respect he deserves through her tribute, and I steamrollered in, assuming the worst, belittling her and acting as if I knew best, when all along she's been wiser and more open, and at times shown more integrity.

My palm slaps the steering wheel. 'Fuck!'

Kit chuckles. 'I know—it sucks to realise you've been a total knob, but it's not too late to make it right.'

'It feels too late.' What if it is? I knew what her ex did to her, and I let her down too. In a worse way. All because I like control and need to be at the helm of the business. But do I like it enough to be without Blair for the rest of my life? Would I walk away from the Faulkner Group if it meant she'd give me another chance?

Yes...

My father's hand grips my shoulder and I focus on the traffic to stop myself from hurling.

'Don't be stuck in the past. I know you feel like you have to take care of us all, but we're a family, one I'm proud of. You boys have grown into fine men. In fact, your younger brothers seem to have their shit together a little better than you these days. Perhaps you should follow their example. Take care of *your* needs. Take care of the woman who loves you. You've worked tirelessly by my side to ensure the business is as solid as ever—it's okay for it to take a backseat in your life.'

I'm stunned silent, reeling at what others can see when I've been blind and desperate to reveal my fate, to see if it's one revelation too late. We arrive and I pull into a No Waiting spot, frantic now to shove Kit out of the car and race to find Blair.

'Do you want to join me shopping, Dad?' says Kit, as if sensing my urgency.

'Sure.' Graham pops his seatbelt, casts me one last look, so reminiscent of teacher, mentor, boss Graham I've spent my whole life learning from, I sit up taller, praying I can do him proud in this challenge—the fight for Blair's love.

'Do you want me to wait for you?' My offer isn't heartfelt, my thigh jiggling with impatience.

'Nah, we'll get a cab home,' says Graham.

I pull back out into traffic, formulating a plan. Then I abandon the plan—trying to control everything is what landed me here in the first place. Time to simply trust my feelings, which have been pointing the way since Blair came back into my life.

I love her. I think I knew the minute she challenged my father to a game of chess. How could I have been so stupid as to focus on the things that matter the least? The Faulkner, while important to me, to our family, to the business, is just a building. Bricks and mortar.

People matter. People you love.

Blair matters.

CHAPTER THIRTEEN

Blair

I FLING OPEN the door, my heart pounding in my throat when I see Reid filling my doorstep.

'Can we talk?' He shoves his hands in his trouser pockets, his hunched shoulders the only sign of hesitation, every inch of him gorgeous and urbane and painful to my eyes. Because no matter how much I wish it could be different, I won't settle again.

'No—I'm on my way out. Mia just texted me— she's gone into labour.' I swallow, proud of the steadiness of my voice. It stings to look at him, my eyes burning, and in the same breath I want to drag him inside, to hold him, to feel his arms big and strong and vital around me. But I'm done being naive and trusting the wrong person.

Reid's face registers surprise, but then his eyes harden, telling me he's about to issue some command or try to control something. But it won't be me. 'Is Kit with her?'

I nod.

'Mia's in good hands—they have each other. They don't need us right now. But I need…to talk to you. To apologise. Please? You can visit when the baby's born.'

Still I hesitate. He's right—it's likely to be hours before the baby arrives and I don't want to get in the way. But that doesn't mean I should invite him in. In the flesh, as opposed to in my mind, he's so much harder to resist. The lure of his closeness, the edge of vulnerability in his expression, the urge to pretend I can live with his lack of trust, live with him underestimating me and riding rough-shod over anything he feels he knows better and simply have whatever scraps of himself he's willing to give me, is too strong. But I can't go there again. This time there's more at stake. My heart is in greater danger. Because I love him as I've never loved before. Because any weapon thrown by him has double the power to inflict damage. Because I don't think I could ever bounce back from the ultimate betrayal from *this* man.

'Okay,' he says, done waiting for my reply. 'I'm just going to say what I need to on the doorstep—I *wanted* to chase after you earlier, to explain prop-

erly, but my father's appointment came through—
the specialist had a cancellation.'

I waver, compassion warring with self-preserva-
tion. 'Is he okay?'

He nods and his eyes hold such vulnerability I
want to reach out and catch him the way I said I
would. I curl my fingers into my palms.

'The news was as we expected,' he says. 'Certainly nothing new to add. He's having a good day
today though, waxed lyrical about you and put me
straight on a few things, just like the old powerhouse Graham we know and love.'

'Oh?' Hope flutters in my chest. Stupid emotion. I don't need hope. I'm mistress of my own
destiny. I don't need Reid. I just want him, but only
if he wants me as fiercely.

He swallows hard, so I know something mo-
mentous is coming. 'You were right about me. I
couldn't trust.'

'Okay.' I rest my hip on the doorframe, blocking the entrance, uncertain if it's to prevent him
entering or me leaving, my breaths shallow at his
confirmation of what I already know.

He rushes on. 'But it was myself I couldn't trust,
not you. I kept myself closed off, busy, thinking
my business, my family needed me, which they
do, to a degree, and that stopped me looking too
closely in the mirror. Because I've been hiding for

years, keeping busy so I don't have to face what a mess I made of my personal life, unwilling to admit that my family, the business—they don't need me. Certainly not as much as I need *you*.'

My pulse leaps. I want so badly to believe him.

He reaches for my hand, but then drops his arm back to his side before making contact, and every cell in my body strains his way. 'I did doubt you at first, because I was trying to keep a lid on everything—my father's diagnosis, the business. On us. Trying to protect myself.' He sighs and rubs at a spot above his eyebrow. 'And I interfered with the mural because it freaked me out to see my father almost become a part of the Faulkner's history—it felt like I was already losing him, and I reacted with emotion, not thinking to talk to you, or explain. But you were just helping him to leave the legacy he's worked for his entire life, a legacy I'm proud to carry forward. I see that now and I'm sorry I undermined you. But I need you by my side as I carry that legacy, because you're already a part of the family I was trying so hard to protect. Not just any part either, but the vital part. The part I need to breathe, to be whole, to cling to every day for the rest of my life, if you'll let me.'

Heat builds behind my eyes. These are the words I wanted to hear, and I feel his pain. I ache for him and his family and Graham, because loving him means caring for them.

'You make me a better version of myself, Blair. You make me laugh. You make anything seem possible. You make sense. You push me and support me and catch me. And you were right—I don't need to carry everything on my shoulders. I'm allowed to find happiness for myself. But I want that happiness with *you*. I've found it with *you*. I just allowed other stuff, trivial stuff, to get in the way. I trust you with my life, Blair. I trust you with my fucking hotels, even my family's lives. I trust you. Is it too late? Please don't let it be too late...'

I step back, too close to flinging myself into his arms as I breathe and try to untangle my matted feelings. The past longing, the present yearning to be loved as I love and the future possibilities. Can I have everything I want? Can I truly have this man for ever? I'm speechless for so long a million emotions cross his handsome face. Perhaps as many as there are building inside me—a torrent. But one persistent thought emerges, time after time.

I love him.

Time to tell him.

'I don't know, Reid... I'm done settling. I've fallen in love with you.' My sad smile knocks the joy from his, which followed my declaration. 'But

I want you to want me with the same fierceness with which I want you. I don't want half measures or broken promises.'

He steps one foot onto the doorstep and reaches for my hand. 'I agree. You deserve to be loved like that. But what if I love you *more*? What if the burden of my love, the weight of it, is too big for me alone, and I need—?' His voice breaks, and I almost reach for him then. 'I need you...to help me carry it.'

I let out a long sigh, squeeze his hand, trying and failing to contain my euphoria. He's laid himself open, as open as me, and I see what I need shining in his eyes.

'Well, that's not how I saw that fantasy play out.' I can't resist teasing him a little more—after all, if we're going to be together, he needs to get used to it.

'What fantasy?' Hope flickers in his eyes. A ghost of a smile.

'The fantasy where you tell me you love me and you'll never, ever be a dick again, for as long as you live.'

His full-blown smile threatens, but he pulls back, as if he can't quite believe the turn of events, can't quite believe *me*. He opens his beautiful mouth to speak and then closes it again.

But I'm impatient now. 'Come in,' I say, swinging the door wide. 'You need to show me.'

'Show you what?'

'The fierceness of this love you claim to feel.' My lips twitch with the barest hint of amusement.

'Oh, I feel it.' He steps inside the doorway and scoops me into his arms, kissing me as if he's forgotten how it feels and needs to remind us both.

I break away. 'Close the door—I want you now. I want you always and for ever.'

Reid kicks the door closed and wraps one arm around my waist, lifting me from the floor.

'Thank fuck for that, because that's exactly how I want you.' He presses his forehead to mine, his eyes open so I see the sincerity shining there. 'I love you. You're the best thing that's ever happened to me. The day you walked into my office changed my life. I want it all with you—I'm already way ahead of myself, plotting our own family. Kit's baby will need a cousin.'

I laugh, wrapping my arms around his neck to stop him escaping. 'You are? Don't you think you should ask me if I even want children?'

'I should. Do you?' he says, his grin wide. 'Although I don't care either way. You're enough for me, in every way. Perhaps too much for me in some ways, but I'll die trying to satisfy every fantasy you have.'

I try to keep a straight face. 'I want six actually. A big clan of Faulkners.'

He splutters. 'Six?'

'Yes.' My lips twitch. 'Up to the task? Because you're not growing any younger.'

He throws his head back and laughs. 'Whatever you say.'

'Good, let's get started, then—trial run.' I head for the stairs, dragging him behind.

We strip and kiss and touch. When he pushes inside me and grasps my face in his palms so there's nowhere to hide, he slides his mouth over mine and whispers, 'Did you ever fantasise about me loving you?'

I nod, too overwhelmed, too full of Reid and our love, to speak.

'Don't worry,' he says, lacing his fingers with mine and holding me tight. 'I'm going to make the reality of loving you so much better than any fantasy.'

Slowly and thoroughly he proves it to me with a hundred tender touches, and I believe.

EPILOGUE

Three Months Later

Blair

I'M TOO HAPPY, my cheeks aching with the wide smile that just won't leave me. Drake and Kenzie's wedding, an intimate family affair in the newly renovated Faulkner ballroom, has been a day I'll never forget. Drake had both Reid, Kit and Graham as groomsmen, the four of them dashing in morning suits. Mia and Kenzie's sister, Tilly, were bridesmaids. And me? Well, I had the best job—taking care of my godson, Ryan Abbott-Faulkner.

Of course, he's breastfed and teething, only wants his mother, and I'm relieved to hand him back after the ceremony. But that's mainly because I need both hands for holding Reid.

'Did you cry?' He presses a kiss to the top of my head.

'A little. It was a beautiful ceremony. They're so in love, aren't they?'

He nods, tugging me closer into his arms, an indulgent smile playing on his lips. 'Let's get some champagne and check on the wedding breakfast.' He leads me towards a waiter and we take our glasses out into the foyer, which is filled with light on this beautiful day.

'I'm sure everything is in order,' I say, taking a sip and remembering a thousand Reid-flavoured champagne kisses I've tasted since the first one. 'You don't need to oversee everything.'

He pulls me to a stop and kisses me. 'You're right. Just like you were right about this space and knocking down that wall.'

I give him my best I-told-you-so face, but then he distracts me with his lips on mine, which are soft but demanding, as they were this morning when we made love, and champagne-flavoured. A thousand and one...

'And we need as much light as we can get in here,' he says, 'so I can see your exquisite face.'

'Okay, charmer.' I laugh. 'What are you after, because we have a whole wedding reception to get through before we can go home?' Although it's a tough one to call—Reid is as addictive as ever.

'Well, I wondered if you'd ever had the particular fantasy I've had in my head for a while now...?' He quirks one eyebrow, his eyes sparkling.

I shrug, stare searching for a possible hidey-hole and mind calculating how long we have before we'll be missed. 'Personally, I'm happy with any fantasy—mine or yours.'

'Mmm... I think you'll like this one better than all the others,' he says.

'I will?' My pulse roars.

He nods, a wicked twist to his mouth. Confident, sexy sod. 'It goes like this.' He leans close, his mouth millimetres from mine, and holds up a black velvet box as if from nowhere.

I'm struck dumb, my eyes burning and my mind blank of even the most basic functions of breathing and heart beating.

Reid opens the box and drops to one knee. 'Blair, will you marry me? I promise to fulfil your every fantasy to the best of my ability until the day I die.'

I cover my mouth, holding in ecstatic laughter. But what else is there to say, because we're exactly where we're meant to be?

'Yes.'

* * * * *

SHE DEVIL

CHRISTY McKELLEN

MILLS & BOON

This book is dedicated to my incredibly talented
editor, Vic Britton, whose encouragement, support and
insight has brought out the best in my stories and in
me as a writer.

CHAPTER ONE

April

SEX ISN'T ABOUT love and connection; it's about power and control.

That's what I've come to realise over the last ten years.

Yes, okay, I accept that it can also be used for the purposes of procreation and continuing a lineage—or, in my father's case, providing an heir to his vast business empire—and I know that some people even *think* they're doing it for fun but, take it from me, sex is just a tool we use to manipulate each other.

And, yes, it is true what people say about me—and when I say *people* I'm specifically talking about Jamie De Montfort here—I am a total and utter bitch.

Because I've had to be.

'Hard as nails' is one of the things I hear people say about me behind my back.

I like that.

Nails are useful items—essential, even. Structures would fall down without them.

'As cold as a polar bear's arsehole'—that one I'm not quite so keen on.

But I wouldn't have risen to the position of Chief Operating Officer at DH Worldwide, my father's aforementioned multinational corporation, if I hadn't developed the ability to ignore what people say about me.

Except this time when I say *people* I don't mean Jamie De Montfort because I've always been uncomfortably aware of what he thinks of me. Let's just say that ever since my mother died and I was forced to step into her role as matriarch of the family—much to my sister Maya's disgust—my relationship with Jamie has been on less than friendly terms.

Because it's had to be.

I've never been able to tell him exactly why I finished our eighteen-month relationship during our third year at St Andrew's University, so he's chosen to think the very worst of me—and to make sure everyone knows it too.

But that's okay. It's had to be. For both our sakes.

If I told him why I'd been forced to do what I did it would destroy him—and me too.

Because I loved him.

But not any more. Not after the way he's treated me since then.

Unfortunately we end up running in the same social circles a lot nowadays and he never misses an opportunity to let me know exactly how little respect he has for me now.

Like he did last night, for example.

Except in the end, last night turned out to be completely different from all the other times. In fact, thinking back, I can hardly believe it happened now. It feels more like a dream—or perhaps a nightmare, depending on how you choose to interpret it.

I'd gone to a charity fundraiser that my business associate's wife had organised to raise money for a children's charity that's very close to her heart, having agreed to attend at the last minute after a meeting in Rome had fallen through and I'd found myself without anything to do that evening.

Which is why I had no idea that Jamie De Montfort was compèring the event.

As a world-famous former tennis champion, securing him as the host was quite a coup, and it was clear from the reaction to his obsequious, crowd-pleasing performance there was going to be a lot of money dropping into the charity's coffers that evening.

At least from my seat near the back of the room I was able to observe him without feeling the usual compulsion to turn away.

I grudgingly have to admit he was looking good. Very good, in fact. His athletic physique was very much in evidence, despite being encased in a dinner jacket. He's always had a great body, even in his early twenties, when I knew him best. And by 'knew him' I mean when I'd seen him naked on a regular basis.

Prohibiting my body from reacting to those memories, I attempted to study him with a dispassionate eye. He'd grown his strawberry-blond hair a little longer since the last time I'd seen him a few months previously so it curled around his collar at the nape of his neck and fell in tousled strands over his forehead. It reminded me of the way he used to wear it when we were dating, when he'd had to push his fringe out of his striking blue eyes whenever he'd turned to look at me. That simple idiosyncrasy had never failed to conjure a need in me that I've never been able to explain in words.

His strong jawline was very much in evidence that night too, because he was clean-shaven for once, seemingly taking a break from the designer stubble he's famously sported in the ads he's starred in for his own line of men's sports clothing.

He's always been demonstrably aware of how

attractive he is, so it doesn't surprise me at all that he has no qualms about using his looks for monetary gain.

The self-important narcissist.

I think that's why he was so incredulous—and unreasonably malicious—when I called a halt to our relationship. He couldn't believe I'd had the nerve to dump someone as *outstanding* as him.

But dump him I did. And I don't regret that decision. Even now, ten years later. Especially when I see him flirting shamelessly with every single woman in the room, even the women I know he's already talked into his bed—including some of my friends, I might add—but still treating me like the scum of the earth.

But I don't care any more.

I really don't.

Ironically, it happened to be that exact thought that was racing round my mind when the person sitting to my left—who I think was one of the organiser's good friends—leaned over to me and whispered, 'Did you hear about Jamie De Montfort's father, Cliff?'

Just the mention of that name sent a shiver of unease through me.

'No,' I managed to reply, even though my mouth felt like someone had just filled it with rocks.

My dinner companion shook her head sadly,

her eyes wide with compassionate dismay. 'He had another heart attack and passed away a few days ago. Jamie was devastated, apparently, but he was determined to still come and host tonight.' She nodded towards where Jamie stood proudly on stage, shaking the hand of the director of the children's charity as everybody clapped. 'That man is the definition of a true hero,' she shouted above the sound of the applause, admiration shining in her eyes.

A thin smile was all I could manage as blood thumped in my temple and my stomach did sickening somersaults.

So Cliff was dead. And Jamie had still turned up for this gig. I couldn't quite get my head around that. Jamie had idolised his father and, even though I had no kind feelings towards him any more, I understood how much he must be hurting right then. The news brought back a flood of painful memories from when my mother had died after a skiing incident, swiftly moving on to remind me of the dread and fear I'd felt when I heard that my own father had been in a near-fatal car accident only a month ago.

Yes, I knew exactly how he felt.

Frighteningly alone.

Especially because he was now the only De Montfort left. The last of his kind.

A wave of something like nostalgia crashed through me—undoubtedly in response to my own tormenting memories—and I had to excuse myself and stumble out of the room to drag some air back into my lungs. I meant to go towards the bathrooms, but there appeared to be a stream of other women doing the same thing ahead of me, so instead I diverted to a nearby office, which was mercifully empty. I didn't bother switching on the light and strode straight over to the window, cracking it open so that the cool evening air rushed over my heated face.

My heart was pounding like I'd just run a mile at full pelt and my whole body hummed with agitation.

Cliff was *dead*.

I wondered whether my father had heard and if so why he hadn't told me.

I jumped as the door to the room opened behind me, flooding it with light from the corridor.

I blinked at the outline of the tall, broad-shouldered man who stood in the doorway, instinctively knowing who it was even before my eyes adjusted and I was able to make out the familiar features of his face.

'Good evening, Jamie,' I said with as much indifference as I could muster. I didn't want him to see me in this weakened state, and I knew if I gave anything away he'd jump on it immediately. I hoped, once he realised it was me alone in there, he'd just turn and walk away.

But it was not to be.

'April, fancy finding you here skulking in the dark.'

Irritation clawed up my spine at the disparagement I heard in his tone.

'I'm just taking a moment out. It's so hot in there,' I said blandly, keeping any emotion out of my voice so he had nothing to comment on, hoping he'd soon get bored and go away.

But of course he didn't. This was Jamie, after all. The man who never passed up an opportunity to torture me.

Instead, he closed the door behind him, throwing the room back into shadow, and walked over to where I stood stiffly by the window.

Right at that moment I was immensely grateful for both the darkness and the cold breeze.

'Is there a reason you chose to do it in my dressing room?' he asked, the streetlight from outside casting his face into light relief.

'I thought it was an empty office. I didn't realise it was your room,' I countered, aware of my face flushing with embarrassment at my unlucky *faux pas*.

'Is that right?' he replied, his scepticism clear.

There was an awkward pause as I tried to think of something to distract his attention away from my obvious discomfort.

'I was sorry to hear about you father passing away,' I said, deciding I might as well tackle the subject head on. No doubt it would come up at some point soon anyway. Jamie already thought my family was responsible for everything bad that had happened to his father and would no doubt try to pin this heart attack on us as well.

If only he knew the truth…

The air in the room had become very still, and I thought I caught a flash of pain cross his face, but in the semi-light I couldn't be sure. My stomach still swooped at the thought. Jamie hadn't shown me any real emotion—apart from anger—for years.

'You heard about that, huh?' he said eventually.

'Yes, just now at dinner. I was surprised I hadn't heard about it sooner.'

He shucked off his jacket and tossed it onto the back of an office chair that was tucked under a nearby desk. 'No, well, my father didn't want his death spread around like gossip. He'd had enough of that shit, thanks to your family.'

I had a lot of trouble biting my tongue at that, but somehow I managed it, despite the usual resentment building inside me. He'd have a very dif-

ferent attitude if he knew how much I'd done to
protect both Cliff and him from gossip. And worse.

'Speaking of which, I hear your father's been
spending time in hospital himself recently,' Jamie
went on, tugging undone his bow tie and popping
open the top button of his shirt.

'Yes, he was there for a week or so, but he's
back at home now recuperating,' I said stiffly, trying not to think about how distractingly arousing
it was to witness him messing up his neat formal
attire.

'You mean he's actually taking some time off
work? I thought I'd never see the day.'

I forcibly had to restrain myself from crossing
my arms. 'He's not well enough to be back in the
office yet and probably won't be for a few months.
He's in constant pain and the painkillers he's taking make his head too fuzzy for him to concentrate for long periods of time.'

Jamie nodded, his hair falling into his eyes. I
watched him push it away from his forehead and
my disloyal pussy gave a throb in response.

'So he's taking a break from terrorising his em-
ployees? That must be a relief for them all.' He
tilted his head, his gaze boring into mine. 'Or have
you muscled straight in to take over that role?'
The hostility emanating from him made my whole
body prickle with an edgy, disturbing tension.

'I'm acting CEO at the moment, if that's what you mean, but I'd like to think I'm a fair and approachable boss.'

He snorted. 'Approachable? You?'

And there it was, the inevitable slide into insulting me. Even though I'd been preparing myself for it, it still stung. I blinked hard, banishing the hot tears that pressed at the back of my eyes. No way was I showing him an emotional reaction. He'd only use it against me.

He took a step closer and I had to steel myself not to take a pace away, especially when his familiar musky scent hit my senses, making my head reel and my body pulse with an unwelcome carnal ache.

'How does it feel to finally be allowed to stand on your own two feet without Daddy calling all the shots?' he murmured, his bright-blue eyes searching mine, clearly looking for weakness in me.

Which I was *not* about to show him.

I let out a withering sigh and rolled my eyes. He might have just lost his father but that didn't give him the right to be so vile.

'You don't change, do you? Still reeling out the same old, tired lines.'

'Well, if you ever manage to do something new that was even vaguely worthy of my attention instead of being so fucking boring and *soulless*,

I'll finally be able to change my repertoire,' he bit back.

Despite my resolve not to react to his contempt, I still flinched at that.

For one breathless moment I thought I saw something like regret pass across his face, but I wasn't prepared to hang around and find out. I was too afraid my insouciant front might completely crumble, so instead I pushed back my shoulders and said, 'Well, Jamie, it was predictably unpleasant seeing you again. If those are all the snide remarks you have for me this time, I think I'll be leaving now. I don't want to keep you from your doting audience. I know how much you need to be adored.'

'April. Wait...'

As I turned away I saw him reach out as if to try and stop me leaving but, instead of his hand landing squarely on my arm, his fingers caught the thin spaghetti-strap of my dress. In my determination to get away from him I was moving too fast to give him a chance to untangle himself and I felt a sharp tug, then the strap give way on one side of the dress and slither down my back.

I sucked in a breath of agitation and turned back to glare at him.

'Oops.' The twitch of a smile at the edge of his mouth was more than I could stand.

'This is a five-thousand-pound, custom made, Eva Verdano dress!' I yelped, anger and frustration at his unapologetic amusement making my voice unsteady.

'It's not as if you can't get Daddy to stump up for another one,' he said with a condescending flick of his eyebrow.

'I can afford to buy my own clothes, you arrogant prick,' I couldn't help but retort, despite hating the fact I was rising to his goading, 'Because I happen to be one of the highest paid businesswomen in the country.' I pointed a shaky finger at him. 'And before you try and say *Daddy* just handed me the job I'll have you know I worked my arse off to be where I am today!'

'Yeah, you keep telling yourself that, if it makes you feel better,' he growled back.

And that was it. I'd had enough of him. A blistering anger rose through me and without thinking I reached out and grabbed the front of his shirt and pulled with all my strength. The material must have had a high silk content because the top four buttons easily tore away, leaving his shirt gaping open and giving me a spectacular view of his muscular chest.

Neither of us reacted at first, both of us too shocked by what I'd done. Then, before I had chance to stop him, Jamie reached out and grasped the front of my dress and did the same thing to me, tearing a deep valley down the front of it and exposing my breasts, which unfortunately I'd chosen not to encase in a bra that evening so as not to ruin the line of my outfit.

I let out a low scream of frustration, not just because he'd totally ruined my beautiful dress, but because I was now completely exposed to his mocking gaze.

Through the red haze that descended over my eyes, I saw him lift a hand in apology. 'Shit, April, sorry, I didn't—'

But I didn't want to hear it. I was way past trying to make any kind of peace with him. I wanted to hurt him, like he'd hurt me. Repeatedly. For *years*. But the words wouldn't come. I couldn't think of a single thing to say that would penetrate that thick hide of his so, in the absence of a better idea, I pulled back my arm and slapped him hard across the face.

The violent sound of it rang around the small room, but somehow still failed to penetrate my rational consciousness. I seemed to be in some sort of incensed rage that incrementally had been building for years, so I simply swung my arm back again and attempted to repeat what I'd just done.

This time he was too quick for me and managed to grab my wrist before my hand made contact with his cheek again. He gripped me tightly, staring into my eyes and shaking his head in silent warning. But I wasn't having it. I wasn't going to let him subdue me. So I raised my free arm and swung that towards the other side of his face.

He seemed to be anticipating this, though, and managed to grab hold of that one as well then twist us round and pin me against the window, holding both of my wrists in his large hands, effectively confining my wrath.

'Stop!' he ordered me as anger and something that looked suspiciously like desire flashed in his eyes.

We were both breathing hard now, the sound of it loud and raw in the otherwise silent room.

I should have felt scared and defenceless, alone with him and physically overpowered like this.

But I wasn't afraid. In fact, I felt weirdly jubilant.

I had the strangest urge to push him as far as I could, just to see what he'd do. I wanted to force him to act, force him to the very edge of his comfort zone, and perhaps even past it. To make him feel as off-balance as I did right then. I was determined not to be the only one fighting to stay in control.

'What are you gonna do now, huh?' I growled at

him. 'Now you have me trapped here, half-naked and vulnerable.'

I stared into those striking eyes of his, hyper-aware of my bare breasts rising and falling only centimetres away from his own exposed chest. My nipples were rock-hard and felt super-sensitised and I was intensely conscious that it wasn't just the cold breeze that was responsible.

Something flickered in his eyes and they appeared to grow darker as his pupils dilated.

It suddenly felt as if we were on the cusp of something—something new and dangerous.

And my whole body ached for it.

But to my frustration he loosened his grip on my wrists and backed away from me, his handsome face drawn into a deep scowl but his eyes still betraying a heated longing.

A moment of pure, sweet wistfulness hit me as a memory flitted through my mind of how he used to look at me with the same kind of unadulterated need.

We'd had a wild time together what felt like a lifetime ago now, experimenting with all kinds of crazy stuff—mostly power-play and some BDSM—which I'd loved at the time but had never wanted to do with a partner since. It reminded me too much of the time I'd spent with him—a happier, simpler, more naïve time, and one I'd been determined to forget. I'd needed to be emotionally rock-solid for my family's sake since breaking up with him so I'd boxed up those desires and never peeked at them again.

Until now.

But to my raging disappointment he just shook his head and said, 'I'm not going to do anything. I have zero interest in continuing this pathetic exchange, because I have zero interest in you. I don't waste my time with cold-hearted bitches. Not any more.'

The words stung like a thousand paper cuts and the red mist of anger swelled in me again.

How dared he act as if this meant nothing to him? As if I meant nothing. Because I knew I did. He wouldn't have acted this way towards me if he really didn't feel anything.

Without conscious thought, I strode forward and braced both hands against his shoulders, using the surprise of my attack to catch him off-balance so I was able to push him against the nearest wall.

He let out a grunt of surprise as I pressed myself into him, jamming my pelvis up against his, jubilant to discover that his cock was as hard as I'd imagined it would be.

'It doesn't *feel* like you're not interested in me,' I goaded.

He let out a huff of a laugh and, before I could

register what was going to happen, he wrapped his arms around me and swung us around on the spot so that now it was me with my back against the wall. Not wanting him to get the jump on me, I pressed myself backward, trapping his arms between my body and the wall so he couldn't get away.

Looking up into his face, I saw both fury and confusion in his eyes, which only made me more determined to win this battle.

'Now what are you going to do, huh? What's your next move?'

Knowing his hands were securely trapped behind my back, I slid my fingers inside his open shirt and ran them up his chest, making sure to graze both of his nipples when I reached them, gazing into his face the whole time to check his reaction.

His sharp intake of breath and frustrated glare made my heart leap with satisfaction. I knew his body so well, even after all this time, and that knowledge made me unreasonably happy.

I felt his hands shift behind my back and realised they weren't as trapped as I'd thought.

But he still didn't try to release them.

He wanted me to do this.

So do it I would.

Skating my hands lower, I pressed the tips of my

nails into the flesh of his torso, feeling him twitch and shudder under my touch. I watched with satisfaction as he closed his eyes, his breath juddering through his throat and catching each time I dug my nails into him a little harder.

And then I was at the top of his trousers, where I hung out for a moment, running my fingertip across the hard muscles where his taut belly met the leather of his belt.

'Fuck!' he moaned, his eyelids still squeezed shut. 'Go on, then.' He opened his eyes and looked straight into mine. 'Do it.'

It was half challenge, half plea.

And I didn't need any more encouragement than that. Laying the flat of my hand onto his chest, I pushed until he was forced to take a step away from me, giving me enough room to reach down and slide the soft leather out of his buckle. His arms fell to his sides as I pulled the belt free then popped open the button on his trousers and tugged down the fly so I was able to slide my hand easily into the waistband of his boxers, my eyes never leaving his.

I wanted him to know I was still in charge of things here. That despite his repeated attempts to bring me down he hadn't succeeded. I was still directing the play. This was only happening because I was letting it.

His cock was hard, but his skin felt silky smooth as I wrapped my fingers around his shaft, drawing another guttural groan from him. I began to move my hand up and down, giving a little twist as I reached the tip and getting a short, satisfying pant of appreciation from him each time I did it.

I was aware of heat emanating from his body in waves now, warming my skin and causing goose bumps to rush over me, but I ignored my response, not wanting it to distract me from what I was doing to him. I wanted to revel in this, to enjoy the sense of power I was experiencing from totally being in control of his pleasure.

In control of him.

Heady with triumph, I increased both the pressure and speed of my movement and was rewarded for my efforts when he closed his eyes, dropped his chin and clamped his jaw shut, as if losing himself in what I was doing to him.

His chest heaved as his breathing became more laboured and I took great satisfaction in the knowledge that I knew exactly what he needed right at that moment. I sensed he'd been keeping his feelings about losing his father bottled up and this angry confrontation with me was a release for his pain. A way to hand over responsibility for the way he felt to someone else, if only for a short time.

I was the only person who knew how to give him what he needed.

And how.

Because I *knew* him.

I'd always known what he needed most.

Remembering how much he used to love me going down on him, I sank to my knees and took his cock in my mouth, delighting in his groan of appreciation as I used my tongue to find the spot he loved having licked. Cupping his balls in one hand, I used my longest finger and thumb of my other hand to form a ring around the base of his shaft, pressing firmly as I slid it up and down in time with my mouth.

I smiled to myself as I felt his body begin to tremble. He was completely under my influence. And I loved it.

'Look at me,' I heard him whisper, his voice a guttural rasp.

But I wasn't going to let him start leading this now. I didn't want him telling me what to do. Not any more. That wasn't how this was going to work.

So I kept my gaze on what I was doing and continued to move my mouth on him, sliding his cock deep into my throat then pulling him all the way out again so I could play with my tongue around the head—just as I used to, to drive him crazy. I could tell he was getting close to coming by his short pants of breath and the way his hands were clenched into tight fists at his sides.

And I revelled in the idea of being in control of that.

I was so caught up in the powerful satisfaction of what I was doing to him I didn't anticipate what he was going to do next—which was to let out a loud groan of frustration, suddenly withdraw from me then stoop down to grab me under the arms and lift me up, pressing me back against the wall and trapping me there with his hands on my shoulders.

He stared into my eyes for a moment, as if trying to centre himself, before flashing me a wicked sort of smile. Then before I could react he reached down and bunched the skirt of my dress in his hand so he could slide it up my body and roughly push his other hand between my legs. I let out an involuntary gasp of surprise as his fingers pressed into the desire-soaked material of my knickers.

'It seems like you're pretty interested in getting something out of this too,' he muttered, leaning towards me so his words whispered over my lips, making them rush with intoxicating sensation. He slid his hand into my knickers and rubbed the backs of his long fingers over my mound, then pressed his thumb firmly down the line of my pussy, making my clitoris throb with the need to be touched more intimately.

'I don't need anything from you,' I tried to protest, my heart thumping like a jackhammer as I tried not to let myself be pulled under by the erotic desire he was triggering in me.

But I could see from the amusement in his eyes and the sceptical raise of an eyebrow that he didn't believe a word I was saying.

Frustration at losing my authority over this game built inside me, but I was suddenly at a loss to do anything about it as he dipped one long finger inside me, sliding it deep then drawing it out slowly, catching every erogenous spot I had.

I bit my lip hard to stop myself from letting out a moan of pleasure, but I could tell from the smile in his eyes that he knew exactly what he was doing to me.

And he wasn't about to stop.

This time he used two fingers, curling them towards him to press on a magic area inside me, shooting tendrils of pure pleasure through my body. Then slowly he slid them out of me again, using the slickness of my desire to smooth his way back up to my needy clit.

'Admit it, you want my cock inside you,' he insisted, gently flicking his fingertip over the hard little nub of nerves there. 'More than you've ever wanted anything.'

'Fuck you,' I moaned, barely able to think straight now.

'What's that? You want to fuck me? Yeah, I thought so,' he ground out, twisting his fingers into my knickers and tugging on them so hard the fragile lace around the band ripped and they slithered down my legs to the floor.

That was the moment I should have walked away. I should have said that I didn't want this, that I wanted him to leave me alone.

But right at that moment I couldn't. Even though, intellectually, I knew I should.

Because my body wanted the exact opposite. Desperately. Like it had been starved for years and he was the most delicious meal in the world just ready and waiting to be eaten.

Which I suppose is why, instead of backing off, I closed the small gap between us and kissed him hard.

The moment our lips met it was clear to me he wanted the exact same thing because he opened his mouth and slid his tongue deep inside me, his groan of approval vibrating around the cavern of my mouth.

And it felt so incredible. Hot, dirty and urgent. His tongue firmly stroked against mine, over and over again, as if this was a duel he was trying to win, but I gave back as good as I got, pulling back to bite at his lips then suck the lower one into my mouth.

He gave a moan of what sounded like frustration, then pulled away from me to stare into my eyes, his expression fierce.

'You want this?' he demanded, his voice a growl of desire.

'Just as much as you do,' I murmured back. There was a hot, raging need inside me, something I'd been subduing for years, but it was out now, free and determined to get what it wanted.

I felt him slide his hands under my buttocks and lift me up. Instinctively I wrapped my legs around his waist, exhaling with satisfaction as his hard cock pressed between the folds of my pussy. He began to rock his hips, rubbing himself against the sensitive nub of my clit, and my whole world narrowed to that one sweet, lascivious sensation.

We were both panting hard now, our breath rushing in and out of our lungs from both the physical exertion and the intense need to fuck.

As much as I wanted to get back on top of this situation, I was aware I was losing the battle. My mind was hazy and overrun with an overwhelming desire to finish what we'd started, so it felt completely right when I felt the head of his cock pressing against the entrance to my vagina, then firmly and insistently pushing inside me.

I sucked in a breath as he slid deeper, my body stretching to take the impressive girth of him. He didn't pause there but immediately began pounding into me, his powerful hips thrusting against my body as he took himself deeper.

And I loved it. Needed it. Needed more of it.

I began to rock my body in unison with his, taking his hard thrusts and urging him on for more of them.

I was wild. Abandoned. Not the controlled, tactically driven woman I usually was when having sex. I was suddenly a person I only vaguely remembered being all those years ago. A woman who had let herself enjoy fucking for the sake of it. Who had been capable of feeling love and affection.

Then suddenly, shockingly, he stilled. His cock was still buried deep inside me, but he was holding the rest of his body rigid, not moving a single muscle. I nearly screamed in frustration, wriggling my hips and trying to get him to start moving again.

But he didn't.

Instead he leant back and cupped my chin in his hand, turning my head so I was forced to look straight into his narrowed eyes.

'This is why you really came in here tonight, isn't it?' he murmured. 'You can't keep away from me. Wherever I go these days, there you are, hanging around at the edge of my vision like a mournful ghost,' he teased, the words loaded with triumph as he began gently to rock back and forth again, the pressure of his pelvis against my clit sending echoes of pleasure through me. 'I knew it. I knew you still wanted me. You've wanted me back for all these years but you've been too much of a coward to admit it.'

And that was the moment that reality and sense rushed in.

His jubilation killed dead the eroticism of the moment and in my anger and intense frustration I put my hands against his chest and pushed him hard away from me. I felt his cock slide out of me as he was forced to take a step back and I dropped my feet to the floor.

My whole body gave a throb of regret at the loss of intimate contact with his and an agonisingly familiar grief began to build inside me. But I knew I had to quash it quickly before my emotions got the better of me. Before he saw the pain and sadness I'd been hiding from him for all these years.

'Don't kid yourself,' I said with all the disdain I could muster, pushing down the skirt of my dress. 'This wasn't about wanting you. It's just a hate fuck. Something we've been dancing around for years. Which frankly has become very boring. It just felt like a good opportunity to get it over with and get each other out of our systems for good.'

He stared at me with his eyebrows pinched together, seemingly amused by my statement. 'You're really going to give up the best orgasm of your life to maintain your overblown pride?'

My laugh was scornful. 'I wasn't even close to coming then. You could *never* make me orgasm.'

He snorted in disbelief. 'I seem to remember doing just that, quite a few times, in fact, back when you used to behave like a human being instead of a business-driven robot.'

I wagged my finger at him. 'Newsflash. You didn't make me come then, either. I faked it every time because I felt sorry for you and didn't want to damage your fragile ego.'

This wasn't entirely true. While I'd had trouble at first relaxing enough to orgasm, and had pretended I had out of shame at not being able to do it, I'd definitely come regularly once we were past the awkward new-relationship stage and we'd got to know each other's bodies a whole lot better.

'You're a fucking liar,' he said, pulling his trousers closed and buckling his belt.

'Am I?' I gave him my haughtiest look, one that reputedly could freeze people to the spot. 'Honestly, you meant nothing to me then and you mean nothing to me now. You're just a minor nuisance with a big mouth and an obvious lack of self-esteem. Perhaps it's time you took a long, hard look at yourself.' I straightened my shoulders, fighting back a wave of shame when I was certain I saw hurt flash across his face this time.

My gut clenched. What was wrong with me? The man had just lost his father and I was laying into him in the most vicious and hurtful way.

But he didn't give me an opportunity to backtrack. He just looked me up and down with his jaw set, taking in my dishevelled state with a cool gaze, then turned, grabbed his jacket off the chair and threw it towards me.

I was too slow to catch it, so it just slithered down my body and landed in a heap at my feet.

'You're going to need that more than me. We wouldn't want you getting any colder,' he said before turning and walking away, slamming the door shut behind him.

I kept his jacket for far longer than I should have done.

It just sat there, on the back of the armchair in my bedroom, taunting me for the next few days.

I'm ashamed to say I ignored my better judgement at one point and picked it up and held it to my nose to remind me of the scent of him. I'm not sure why. Something deep and dark inside me compelled me to do it. An instinct to punish myself, perhaps. A form of self-flagellation.

It was wrong to have had sex with him. So wrong. Foolish and weak. And the shame of it infected me like a virus, waking me up night after night in a hot, feverish state.

Eventually, five nights after it happened, when I was still having trouble sleeping, I got up and angrily shoved the jacket into a carrier bag to be sent to the dry cleaners the next day.

It was funny, but as soon as it was out of the house I immediately felt better. As if I'd exorcised a malevolent spirit.

But of course I knew deep down that wouldn't be the end of it.

Life didn't work like that.

And, of course, I was right.

CHAPTER TWO

Jamie

I'VE FELT SO much anger towards April Darlington-Hume over the years, it's impossible to quantify it.

At least, I think it's anger.

It certainly feels like it most of the time.

Except for the times it doesn't.

I've never known what to do with those feelings, though, so mostly I've tried to ignore them.

Which hasn't been easy.

I fucking *adored* her ten years ago, imagining that we'd stay together after we graduated from university and make a real go of it. It would have been challenging, sure, with me travelling the world one way to take part in tennis championships and she the other to build her career in the business world, but we could have done it. If she'd been brave enough.

It was her father that got in the middle of us.

I'm pretty bloody sure of it. He never thought I was good enough for her and in the end she clearly gave in and decided he must be right—even after I tried so hard to be there for her after her mother died. I knew exactly how much pain she was in because I'd been through the same thing in my teens when I'd lost my own mother—who had chosen her love of alcohol over her desire to stay alive and in my life and had succumbed to liver disease. I did nothing but send April letters, gifts and offer support and generally put my life on hold for her in case she needed me.

But she didn't.

Instead she dumped me, without even giving me a decent reason, then proceeded to act as if I didn't exist any more. She wouldn't take my calls or come down and meet me at the door when I turned up at her house. And, when I finally managed to confront her when she left the house one day on her own, rather than hiding away in her chauffeur-driven car, she refused to talk to me, telling me to leave her alone and that it was over between us.

That she didn't love me and she was moving on. That I would be a hindrance to her family responsibilities and her career.

That was all the explanation I got. After a year and a half of growing so close to her I seriously thought we'd get married one day.

Because she'd been my best friend as well as my lover. My other half.

But it turned out I'd meant nothing to her. Less than nothing.

It's no wonder I lost the plot for a while after being treated like that. I'm not especially proud of my actions at that time but I was hurting and so fucking angry with her, I could barely think straight.

And now we've gone and raked it all up again.

I've not been able to stop thinking about her since that night at the fundraiser. Her words have turned over and over in my mind, especially the part about her faking her orgasms with me. I don't believe that's true. It can't be. I would have known. I'm sure of it.

Wouldn't I?

I've never had any complaints from women before.

But, despite being ninety-nine per cent certain I'm not misremembering our time together, that one per cent has planted a seed of doubt in my mind. Which has been fucking with my head ever since—so much so I've had trouble thinking about anything else.

That is until the letter from my father was handed to me by the executor of his will.

I'd been summoned to the solicitor's office in Kensington a few weeks after I'd buried my fa-

ther in the De Montfort family plot on a clifftop
graveyard just outside St Ives—where we'd laid my
mother to rest fifteen years before. The solicitor,
Phil Clary, was one of my father's oldest school
friends and it was he who handed me a thick cream
envelope with a sad, supportive smile.

'Your father wrote this after his first heart attack a year ago and wanted you to have it a little
while after he'd been laid to rest.' He nodded towards the envelope. 'I think he wanted to give you
a bit of time to grieve first.'

I have to admit, I was intrigued. He'd already
willed everything he owned to me, including the
entirety of his prosperous software business, so I
was at a loss to think what could be in this letter.
It had to be something seriously important for him
to have had it delivered to me in this way.

After ripping it open and sliding out a single
sheet of paper, I took a breath before starting to
read my fathers achingly familiar handwriting, my
heart in my mouth.

Son,
If you're reading this it means my damaged
heart has finally given up on me and I'm in
the ground. In a lot of ways this will be a re-
lief. There have been many times in my life
when I've prayed for an easy way out of the
despair I've often found myself sucked into,

particularly since losing the woman I loved more than life itself.

Please don't think for a second that this means I ever wanted to leave you, though. You are the one and only thing I did absolutely right in my life and I'm so proud to call you my son. You turned out to be a better man than I could ever have hoped for.

I'm sending you this letter now because I need you to do something—something I was never able to ask of you while I was alive. Go and ask April Darlington-Hume to tell you what really happened to her mother.

What they reported in the papers wasn't the whole story. Not even half of it. I've wanted to tell you about it so many times, but it's proved impossible for me.

You'll understand what I mean by that when you finally hear the long-buried truth. Even though it may be distressing to hear, I've come to realise that you knowing everything is the most important thing in the world.

It will finally give me peace and hopefully you too, eventually.

Take care of yourself, Jamie.

Be happy. That's all I've ever wanted for you.

Your loving father,
Cliff

I stared at the piece of paper in my trembling hand, holding back an onslaught of emotion that brought back the memory of the excruciating mental agony I'd experienced as I'd watched his coffin being lowered into his grave.

Despite the distracting weight of my grief, I was still intrigued by this posthumous missive. Why on earth did I need to know what had really happened to April's mother? And why couldn't he have told me when he'd been alive? Had April's father, Maxim, been blackmailing him all these years so he hadn't been able to tell me what he'd obviously felt I now needed to know? As far as I knew, Maxim had taken great pleasure in bankrupting my father's first business not long after Isabella Darlington-Hume had died, but was there more to the story than that? And, if so, why hadn't April told me about it at the time? Why, instead, had she cut all ties with me? Had her father forced her to do it?

It seems incredible that something like that could have happened. But then, you never did know with Maxim Darlington-Hume. He'd probably happily use his daughter as a shield if he thought it would let him get away with something.

Is that why my father wrote me this letter—to ask me finally to get justice for him? Or for me—so I can finally get closure?

But of course that means connecting with April again.

Something I'm reluctant to do after our last clash.

Being inside her again, so physically close when my feelings about losing my father were still so raw, had been electric. I'd needed it so badly, that intimacy, that primal, life-affirming connection. But I hated that it was hcr I'd needed it with. In those moments I'd let my emotions control me, something I'm very careful not to do any more, and it had scared the crap out of me, how good it felt to fuck her. To be close to her. To connect with her again. I was on a razor edge of ecstasy and despair. And it was dangerous. Really bloody dangerous.

Which is why I'd forced myself to turn the situation back into a game. Perhaps it had been a way of punishing her for making me feel like that. I don't know. It was a fucked-up situation through and through.

And not one I should consider revisiting.

But I know my father would hate to think she'd beaten me into submission and that I was just moping about, feeling sorry for myself, now that he's gone. I'm the last living De Montfort without a steady partner or children and perhaps he was afraid I'd never be able to commit to someone if I was still hung up about my disastrous relationship with April. That I would spend the rest of my life alone.

So I'm going to take his challenge and run with it. To be the man he was so proud of and get him the justice he deserves. I'm finally going to make April tell me the truth then nail that bastard Maxim to the wall for what he put my father through—even up the score between our two families. Then maybe I'll finally be able to move on from my hang-ups about April Darlington-Hume.

But all this means I need to find a way to see her again.

I need some sort of bait. But in order to make that work I'll have to offer her something she can't refuse. Something she has no choice but to deal with herself.

Maybe then I'll finally be able to put this thing between us to bed once and for all.

I choose to roll out my plan on my private island off the coast of Greece, deciding it'll be the best way to secure her complete attention for as long as I need it.

Now I've retired from professional tennis and I'm in a position where I can run my sports-clothing company remotely I like to spend a lot of time here on Palioph. It's small compared to the rest of the Greek islands, with only three miles between its coasts, but to me it's six and a half square miles of paradise.

It only has one residence on it, a two-storey, six-bedroomed Greek mansion with a balcony that wraps all the way round the house, giving me three-hundred-and-sixty-degree sea views. It's right on the northern coast, and has a white sand beach directly in front of the house and a small harbour just a five minute walk away where I keep a small yacht moored for trips to the mainland. In a complex next door to the house I also have a gym, an Olympic-sized open-air swimming pool and both lawn and clay tennis courts.

You can see why I like to spend so much time here.

And, if all goes to plan, April's going to be more than happy to spend some time here with me. For a handful of days, at least. I'm hoping that's all the time it'll take to get the information I want from her.

Thankfully, the lure of the business proposition I've set in motion has caught her attention and I'm expecting her to arrive here on a private-hire yacht any minute now.

I pace the room as I wait to hear the sound of the boat's engine as it approaches the harbour, aware of my blood thrumming through my veins.

To my great annoyance I'm actually nervous about seeing her again. I guess it's because I know I probably only have one chance to get this right.

If she senses how important this information is to me, she'll use it against me by deliberately with-holding it, and I can kiss goodbye to fulfilling my father's dying request.

Which I'm not going to let happen.

I owe him that much.

I turn and look out of the floor-to-ceiling win-dow as the sound of a boat's motor breaks the still air of the living room where I'm waiting. It's her. I can see her standing on the deck of the small yacht, looking towards the house. The sun is making her blonde hair shine like spun gold and I'm struck by how proudly she holds herself, as if she's keenly aware of the power she holds. Because she does. I've witnessed it first hand: the way people's eyes are drawn to her whenever she enters a room. She's a beautiful woman, after all, but there's more to it than that. She has a formidable presence.

Trouble is, she knows it too well.

Tearing my eyes away from her, I go to the kitchen and pour myself a cold drink, trying to get the image of her out of my mind. But it deter-minedly stays there as I close my eyes and tip back my head to drink the ice-cold water. All I can see is her hair streaming behind her in the breeze and the magnificent swell of her breasts pressed against the soft material of her blouse as it plasters itself to her body. She's wearing a white trouser-suit, for Christ's sake, and she looks incredible in it.

Fuck.

I'm really going to have to watch myself around her. The last thing I need is to allow myself to indulge in some stupid fucking fantasy where we reform the connection we once had. After the way she's treated me over the years, I know that's impossible. That I can't trust her for a second.

It's ten long minutes before there's a loud, assertive knock on the front door—so very April— and I'm finally able to pace through to the hallway and swing the door open to admit her.

She stands on the doorstep for a moment, her cool blue eyes assessing me, as if trying to figure out my game plan before she enters.

Good luck with that, sweetheart.

'April, good of you to come all this way.'

She raises one perfectly shaped eyebrow, then gives me a wry smile. 'You didn't exactly give me a choice. Your broker made it clear you were only interested in seeing prospective buyers here on your island.'

I nod. 'This is where I run my businesses from now.'

The look in her eyes is discerning, as if she suspects she's been brought here on false pretences.

Shrewd woman.

'So you're really serious about selling your father's company?' Her eyebrows twitch upwards. 'I have to admit, I'm surprised you're happy to potentially sell to DH Worldwide, considering our history.' She moves her finger between the two of us to make it plain she means *us* personally.

I shrug. 'I just want the best deal I can get for it. I can't let my personal feelings get in the way of the most intelligent business decision to make.' I lean against the doorjamb and fold my arms. 'But, before you get too excited, I have to point out that you're up against some stiff competition, so there's a good chance I won't be selling to you anyway. Unless you can offer me a deal I can't refuse.'

I can tell she's trying not to frown at that, but I don't allow the smile that's pushing at my mouth to surface. I want her to think I'm deadly serious about selling De Montfort Software and that she's in with a real chance of securing the sale.

'I know you won't want to lose out, though, April. And I'm damn sure your father won't either. I'm guessing it'll put a real dent in his confidence in you taking over the CEO role full-time if you can't close this deal. Am I right?'

She doesn't answer this, but I can tell from a slight, momentarily unguarded expression of worry that flashes in her eyes that I've hit the nail on the head. I'd specifically made sure her father heard about me putting up my father's business for sale so she'd be forced to respond to it. I knew Maxim Darlington-Hume wouldn't be able to pass up an opportunity to take another of my family's businesses from us. Especially one that would be so beneficial to his company's portfolio. And it appears I was right.

She glances over my shoulder as if looking for something—or someone—inside the house.

'Have my rivals arrived yet?'

'They've been and gone already.' I keep my expression blank so as not to give away my ruse. 'You're the last one to turn up.'

In reality, the others haven't actually been invited to come yet. I'm still trying to decide whether I actually want to sell my father's business right now, or try running it myself for a while first, but she doesn't need to know that.

She frowns and it's clear the idea of being last to the table frustrates her. 'Oh, I see. Well, I'm here now, so perhaps we should get straight down to business, then.'

'I'd expect nothing less from a professional such as yourself,' I say, waving her inside with a sarcastic flourish.

She gives me a stiff sort of nod—I can tell it's killing her, having to try and be so unnaturally friendly towards me—stalks past me, then pauses in the middle of the hallway, waiting for me to close the door and show her in which room we're going to be doing business.

I lead her towards the library, which is my favourite room in the house. I've had it stocked with hundreds of books, both fiction and non-fiction—a lot of which I've read and enjoyed over the years I've lived here.

Her face is a picture as she gazes around the room, clearly surprised I would own such intellectual things as books.

'Don't tell me, you had no idea I could read,' I tease her.

She visibly tenses, as if I've hit a nerve, then holds up a hand in supplication.

'Look, Jamie. I know we've not exactly had the best of relationships over the years, but can we put that aside for the time being? What happened the last time we saw each other was a mistake, I'm sure you'll agree. It was clearly a time of heightened emotions and a culmination of a lot of pent up anger which I think we're both mature enough to move on from now.'

'Perhaps you're right—fucking each other against a wall wasn't a great idea,' I agree, walking towards her so we're standing only feet apart. 'I guess the resentment between us finally reached a point where something had to give.' I flash her a grin. 'And it turned out to be your underwear.'

I see something flare in her eyes and heat rushes through my body, making my cock throb with interest at the memory I've just described. I tamp down the feeling, knowing I need to keep my head on straight here.

'But, seriously, I agree it was a moment of madness,' I say. 'If I hadn't been off my head with grief after losing my father, I would never have even entertained the idea.'

Her throat moves as she swallows, and I wonder whether she's trying to gulp down a retort she wants to make but knows she shouldn't.

'So can we talk seriously? Business person to business person?' she asks stiffly.

Is she feeling the same sexual tension I am? I bloody hope so. It'll make my job a lot easier if she's distracted by her desire for more adventures against the wall.

'Of course. That's what we're here for. Business,' I murmur, smiling at her.

She looks disconcerted by my affability, but I'm guessing she assumes I must be hard up for money to cover my father's death duties if I'm trying to sell his business so fast, and that therefore as a potential buyer she has some power over me.

Think again.

'And we can put our personal differences aside for the duration of this meeting?'

'I can if you can.'

A flicker of doubt in her expression tells me she's sceptical about that.

It seems I have some work to do here.

'Okay. Well, putting all my cards on the table, I'd like to buy your father's business and I'm absolutely positive that DH Worldwide will be able to top any offer you've already been made,' she says, giving me the sort of determined gaze I've come to know well over the years.

'Oh, I don't know. I've had some pretty interesting offers made already.'

'But you're still open to hearing an offer from me.' She delivers this as a statement, as if she's sure there's no way on earth I'd even consider cutting her company out of the running. Typical April—completely convinced she's right, no matter what.

'To be honest, it's going to take more than money to convince me that your company is a fitting contender.'

'What do you mean?' She genuinely looks baffled by that.

I fold my arms. 'I mean you're going to have to convince me that you're the best person to nurture and grow my father's business. It meant a lot to him personally and I know he'd hate to think I was selling it to just anyone. Especially after what your father did to his first company.'

For just a moment she lets down her guard and I see a hint of panic flash across her face. 'That was years ago. Surely you recognise that the business world can be cut-throat and not every company survives? At that point I believe there was only room for one of us to provide that particular service and it so happened my father managed to take the crown.'

'He did everything he could to sabotage my father's company until he was forced to file for bankruptcy,' I point out.

She shifts on the spot and I notice she's bunched her hands into fists. 'You need to understand that he was in a very dark place after my mother died and wasn't as considerate in his business dealings as he could have been.'

'He's never considered other people in his life,' I counter, interested by the fact she suddenly looks so uncomfortable. But I know now isn't the right time to bring up the questions surrounding her mother's death. I need to bide my time. But at least I have a way into that conversation now, given she was the one to bring it up. But later. When she's relaxed and off-guard.

Her hackles are up now, though, I can tell, but

she knows she's in a tricky position here. If she keeps arguing for her father's past actions, this meeting's going to be over before it's begun and she'll be travelling back to England with her tail between her legs, which I'm sure her father won't be at all pleased about.

It seems I'm right because she forces her mouth into a strained smile and says, 'I can assure you, this time the integration of your father's business will be treated with the respect it deserves. It'll become an integral part of our portfolio. I promise you, it has a strong and profitable future with us.'

'Is that right?'

'Yes. It is. I accept that your father and mine have had their differences in the past, as have you and I, but we can't let that get in the way of a deal that'll benefit both families in the long run. Anyway, I think your father would have liked the idea of you fleecing my family for every penny you can get.' She flashes me a conspiratorial grin, as if we're in on a joke together.

I can see why she's so good at her job. She has a way of putting real conviction behind her words that instinctively makes you believe she's going to make whatever needs to happen bloody well happen. It's actually pretty arousing.

She takes a couple of careful steps towards me, her hands raised and her palms towards me, as if trying to show me there are no tricks up her sleeve. That she's as genuine as they come.

Yeah, right.

'Okay, look, Jamie, just tell me what I can do to persuade you to sell to DH Worldwide and I'll do it. Let's find a way to make everyone happy.'

I take great pleasure in leaving a long, thoughtful pause hanging in the air before I speak again, seeing the tension mount in her shoulders as I draw this out for as long as I can.

'You can let me make you come,' I say finally.

She stares at me, obviously wondering whether she's misheard me, her hands jerkily returning to her sides.

I suppress the grin that's pushing like mad at the corners of my mouth. I need her to believe I'm deadly serious about this.

'I'm sorry, did you really just say I have to have an orgasm in order for you to sell your father's company to me?'

'I did. And it has to be me that gives it to you.'

She lets out a broken laugh and shakes her head. 'Wow. I had no idea you could stoop this low just to try and prove a point.'

'Okay, well, if that's the way you feel then there's nothing left to discuss,' I say, walking away from her, over to my desk. 'I'll happily sell to your biggest rival instead. I know they'd be delighted to have De Montfort Software for their portfolio.'

Her hands shoot up again. 'No. Wait. I didn't refuse the deal, did I? I was just surprised by it.'

'So is that a yes?'

She looks properly confused now. 'Why, though, Jamie? Why on earth would you want something like that?'

I shrug, as if it's of no real consequence. 'Let's just call it closure, shall we?'

'Is this because of what I said at the fundraiser? About you never being able to make me come?'

'If that's what you want to believe.'

She gives me another smile, which I think she thinks is warm but actually comes across as beleaguered. 'Because I was only messing with you, you know.'

I lean back against the edge of my desk and take a moment to thoroughly assess her. 'I'm not sure I believe you. In fact, I'm not sure you're actually capable of letting go enough to orgasm.'

'Well, I am!' I can see I'm making her angry now but she's desperately trying to fight it to keep this meeting on a businesslike footing.

Satisfaction surges through me, but I know I need to keep my triumph under wraps if I'm going to gain her trust so she'll tell me the secret she's been keeping from me all these years. I think at this point she'd tell me any old pack of lies if she thought it would help close this deal and that's exactly what I don't want to happen. I need to get her to a point where she's emotionally compromised and weak enough to let me back into her good graces. I want to turn her upside down and inside out with lust, to make her so befuddled by desire she'll happily tell me anything I want to know.

So she'll tell me the truth.

I push away from the desk and walk over to the window, pretending to stare out at the view, though all I can see is the image of her confused face blazed across my vision like a light trail. I force down a sting of unease, which comes at me from out of nowhere.

'I'll let you have a few minutes on your own,' I say, gesturing outside towards the path from my house that leads down to the cove, as if I'm thinking of taking a stroll there. 'Give you some time to think it over.'

I turn back to see she's standing ramrod-straight in the middle of my library, as if turned to stone. She's paralysed with confusion and frustration.

Just the way I hoped she'd be.

CHAPTER THREE

April

A BEAD OF sweat trickles down my spine as I stand there, frozen with indecision about what to do about Jamie's indecent proposal.

It's not as if I have a moral objection to using my sexuality to attain something I feel will be beneficial. Hell, I was prepared to go through with a marriage of convenience a couple of months ago because I could see the clear business benefit—not that I ever had a chance of making that happen, because my potential suitor turned out to be the only man capable of taming my wild sister, Maya, who's now completely in love with him, and he her—but Jamie's an altogether different proposition. There's history between us. Twisted, messy history with a potential for *challenging* emotions to resurface.

He's the last man on earth I should be letting into my bed.

But I wouldn't be the successful businesswoman I am today if I hadn't been able to handle challenging situations.

Evidently Jamie needs to restore his manly pride after I took it to pieces then gave him no recourse to prove me wrong.

Which I can understand. He always did let his dick lead his actions.

But I can deal with all that.

As previously mentioned, sex to me is just a tool, a means to get what I want. So having sex with Jamie again—because it's not as if we haven't done it before, and recently too—will be absolutely fine. I can keep any lingering feelings—mostly of annoyance at him—at bay. Just until he's given me what I came here for.

At least, I think I can.

I'm going to have to if I'm going to be successful here.

Unfortunately, he was absolutely right about my father making it clear that if I wanted to keep hold of the CEO role—a role I've hankered after for years—I'd have to secure this sale to prove to him once and for all that I'll be capable of making a success of running DH Worldwide on my own.

Up to this point we've not managed to produce our own product to the same standard as De Montfort Software's and it's currently hurting us at the acquisition stage. It frustrates me to say it, but Cliff's software is still by far the best on the market despite our best efforts to replicate it. If one of our biggest rivals manages to secure this business it could be very bad for us. One company in particular has been chasing our tail a little too closely for my liking recently and I don't like the numbers I've been seeing.

So I'm going to give him what he wants. It'll involve some highly skilled and possibly demeaning play-acting—but I'm okay with that. It's a means to an end. Everyone makes sacrifices to get their golden ticket. Don't they?

Yes. They do.

So I'm going to make this work.

No matter what it costs me to do it.

Anyway, as soon as the deal is signed I'll be able to walk away and never need to see or speak to Jamie again.

And he'll be getting his closure and soothing his precious ego, so he'll probably never want to see or speak to me again either.

It's a win-win.

'Wait, Jamie, don't go,' I say as he starts to walk past me towards the door to the hall.

He stops and turns back to face me, his eyebrows raised in question.

I try not to let myself be distracted by how spectacularly sexy he looks today. He's wearing casual trousers, which hang low on his hips, and a form-fitting light-blue shirt which is open at the neck and showing a tantalising amount of his toned chest. The chest I've had trouble not obsessing about since I last ran my nails down it.

I give myself a mental shake. I have to stop thinking about him that way. This needs to be a clinical thing, without any warm and fuzzy emotions attached.

So, yes, okay, practically speaking he's a very attractive man. And, yes, my body reacts instinctively to him whenever I'm anywhere near him. But that doesn't mean I should let that get in the way of what I'm here to do. This will be a business transaction, nothing more. A semi-pleasurable one, sure, but short-lived and to the point.

I can give him the type of performance his ego's looking for then get the hell back to London and back to business.

I walk towards him, seeing his eyes flicker with interest as I smile and nod.

'Okay. I'm happy with that deal.' As soon as I'm close enough, I raise my right hand and slide it against his jaw, feeling the beginnings of his stubble prickle my skin, then push my fingers into his thick hair, tilting my head up and urging his head down as I angle my mouth towards his and plant a whisper of a kiss on his firm lips.

My mouth rushes with tingles as the warmth and the scent of him assault my senses and I allow myself to let out a small gasp of pleasure. I need to convince him I'm enjoying every moment of this in order to keep up the pretence that he's capable of giving me the satisfaction I need. That I'm desperate for him to give me release from the pent-up sexual energy only he can stoke in me.

I press my lips harder against his, opening my mouth and sliding my tongue against his. There's a low throb building deep in my pelvis as my body reacts to my proximity to him and the thought of what he's going to do to me. Shifting my body closer, I crush my breasts against his solid chest, inviting him to wrap his arms around me, to pull me to the floor, rip off my clothes and make the magic happen.

But he doesn't.

He just stands there with his arms hanging loosely by his sides, taking my kisses but not reciprocating.

As soon as I realise this, I pull my mouth away from his and frown, seeing his eyes are open and free of any kind of expression of desire.

'What's wrong?' I ask, trying not to sound worried, though I don't think I get away with it. My voice has a giveaway shake to it that sends a sting of horror through me. 'I thought this is what you wanted.'

He raises one eyebrow and looks at me as if he thinks I've lost my mind.

'You don't really think I'm going to just throw you down on the floor right here and now and that'll be the end of it?'

He sounds incredulous, as if I'm being the biggest idiot alive.

Heat burns in my cheeks. 'I don't understand. I thought that's what the deal was,' I say, taking a step back and smoothing down my rumpled suit jacket, desperately trying to save face.

His snort is full of amusement. 'I'm not twenty any more, April. I like to take my time over sex these days. Give my partner the maximum amount of pleasure possible. That means build up. Foreplay. Anticipation. Rushing into things is never a good idea. It's all over way too soon and neither of us has the opportunity to properly experience it. The end result is so much more enjoyable when it's been hard won, don't you agree?'

His smile is wide and wicked and it suddenly occurs to me exactly what he's doing.

'So how long are you expecting me to stay here with you before you finally decide to give me this

holy grail orgasm?' I demand, nerves and frustration getting the better of me, making me snappy.

He shrugs his wide shoulders. 'I'm not sure. A
couple of days? Three? Four? As long as it takes
to satisfy me you're not just "faking it again".'

He puts the last three words in disdainful air
quotes. I curse myself for having said that to him
now. It's caused more problems than I ever could
have anticipated.

Bloody men and their *bloody* male pride.

'I don't have three or four days to spare,' I
argue. 'I have a company to run.'

'And a huge and very competent team working
for you who can handle you not being there breathing down their necks for a few days,' he argues
back, not unreasonably.

I know my team can handle me being away for
that long—but can I? Especially if it means being
here with Jamie twenty-four-seven.

I stare at him, hating him for doing this to me,
but at the same time feeling a weird sense of pride
that he's going to such lengths to have me. I can
see from the small tick in his jaw that he's feeling
the tension here too. He's a little afraid that I'll refuse to stay and he'll never be able to satisfy himself that he's good enough to get one over on me.
That he can beat me.

I suppose I can stay long enough to convince

him he has. It's no big deal, really. Just a couple more days of play-acting.

I can do that.

I give him an assured nod. 'Okay. Fine. I'll stay for a couple of days. Three maximum. That's all I can afford to have away. We're very busy at the moment and things start to fall apart if my team can't get hold of me when they need quick answers to things.'

'Well they're just going to have to cope,' he says with a lopsided grin, evidently feeling he's won this battle. 'You have to promise not to make or take any business calls while you're here. I want your undivided attention.'

I swallow hard. That's going to be tough. I'm usually on the phone all day long when I'm not in the office, but I guess I can cope if I'm able to brief everyone first.

'Agreed,' I say. 'As long as you give me an hour now to prep everyone.'

'Okay. You have one hour,' he says with a slow grin full of wicked promise. 'Then you're all mine.'

Jamie

I've done it. I've convinced her to stay. Which means I have a real shot at getting her to open up to me.

I'm going to take a lot of pleasure in teasing and

provoking her, getting her all hot and bothered, dazed and befuddled with lust.

Then I'm going to take great pleasure in breaking her.

It's going to be a lot of fun.

And hopefully it'll finally give me the peace and closure I've been craving.

'I'll let you have the room,' I say, strolling past her. 'But I'll be back in one hour exactly.'

I don't turn around and look at her again, imagining her expression of determination to make this work, no matter what she's going to have to put up with from me.

But she needn't worry. I'll be kind. In fact, I'm going to be the perfect host. Friendly and courteous, generous and fair.

I'm a gentleman, after all.

I pace away from the library, through the hallway, then open the front door and walk towards the beach. Despite the knowledge that my plan is going well, I'm still filled with a nervy sort of energy. Being in such close proximity to her back there in the library has put me on edge. It was like torture, holding myself back from returning her kiss and ignoring the firm press of her body up against mine. My cock ached to conclude what we'd started a few weeks ago, but I know it would've been disastrous to give in to my carnal need, to strip that sexy white suit off her and make her moan right there, laid out across my desk.

Fuck.

I have to take a deep, calming breath and focus on the horizon with its fluffy white clouds dotted in random patterns across the brilliant azure blue, to snap my thoughts away from that particular fantasy. I'll get to do it at some point. Just not yet.

The sea is calm today and gently laps at the sand as I stroll up and down the beach, matching my breathing to the rise and fall of my feet to bring me back to a state of composure. The water looks inviting and I imagine how fantastic it would feel, rushing over my overheated skin.

Hell, I don't know why I'm stopping myself. I have some time to kill, after all.

So I strip off. Everything. There's no other island even remotely near enough from where I can be seen and boats rarely sail close enough to my shore for anyone to spot me flashing my dick at them.

As I anticipated, the cool water on my skin feels incredible as I wade into the sea, pushing against the rhythmic swell of the waves. Shivers of pleasure rush through me as I go from the searing hot heat of the day to the cold depths of the clear, aquamarine water.

I'm intensely aware of my heart thumping against my chest as I begin to swim away from

the shore. She's done that to me, April, with her
attempt to seduce me into completing the deal before I was ready. I'm feeling a mixture of irritation,
sexual frustration and longing now and I know I
need to pull myself together before I face her again
or I might end up doing something I regret later.
Timing is everything here.

I manage to work off most of the adrenaline
surging through my veins by swimming hard up
and down parallel to the shore, changing my stroke
on each turn. Finally, breathless and thoroughly
worked out, I turn back towards the shore and
let the waves carry me back towards the beach.
As soon as it's possible, I put my feet down onto
the ever-shifting sand and stand up. The water is
still chest-deep and as I straighten I feel my hard
cock—which has refused to go down despite the
vigorous exercise and my attempts to try and blank
my mind of her—bob against my stomach.

Instinctively I reach down into the water and
take it in my hand, giving it a firm tug, trying
to placate my need to be touched. But it's not
enough. Not nearly enough. Now the memory of
April pressed up against that wall at the charity
fundraiser with me thrusting inside her, her mouth
slack and her eyes wide with desire, spins into my
head and I can't help but give my dick a couple
more rough tugs in response to it.

The look she'd had in her eyes reminded me of the way she used to look at me when we were together. With such open heat and devotion. One of my favourite recollections from that long-ago time was when she was on her knees in front of me with my cock deep in her throat, her eyes open and fixed on mine. Totally subservient. Totally turned on. Totally trusting as I slid in and out of her mouth, feeling her tongue working hard at the end of my cock, catching a spot in a way she knew sent me crazy.

I turn away from the house and face out to sea, the memory playing on repeat in my mind as I work my dick in serious strokes now. I need the release from the erotic thrall she has me in so I can go back in there and maintain control over the situation. And this seems to be the only way to get that.

Closing my eyes, I concentrate on the image of her taking my cock in her mouth again, satisfying my greedy need. My hand works frantically, my thumb catching the head, and I imagine it's her mouth and tongue on me, sucking, licking and swallowing. Taking me deep, her eyes staring into mine with a look of utter reverence.

I come hard, my body shaking with blessed relief, my semen mixing with the salty body of water and floating away with my happy memories and crushed dreams.

Hell, I miss what we had.

CHAPTER FOUR

April

I FINISH MY final phone call fifty-five minutes after Jamie left me alone in the library and turn the ringer off before slipping my mobile into my bag. I'm not going to turn it off fully, just in case there's an emergency, despite agreeing not to take any calls. Not that Jamie needs to know that. I'll be discreet.

I turn to look out of the wide windows which afford a magnificent view of the sea, showing only a couple of small islands in the far distance. We really are cut off here. Alone together. A shiver rushes over my skin, but it's not fear. I think it's actually nervous expectation. Or something like it. It's been a long time since I took any kind of holiday and, even though I'll be *on* the whole time I'm here with Jamie, at least I'll be doing it on a sun-drenched island.

My gaze snags on a movement in the distance. There's something in the sea, right in front of the white sand beach I'd seen as the yacht had come in to dock at the island's small harbour.

I peer harder. It's not a some*thing*, it's a some-*one*. It's Jamie. He's chest-deep in the water, his bare, broad back to me, and he appears to be staring out to sea as if transfixed. But there's a strange movement happening. His right arm and shoulder are jerking up and down, making the muscles in his powerful back bunch then release.

It takes me a moment to realise what's going on. He's masturbating.

Is that because of me? Of what could have happened here in the library before he stopped it? Before he told me he wanted to build the anticipation? Is he, in actual fact, having trouble with that notion himself?

The thought of it sends a surge of relief through me. So it's not just me struggling with the tension between us. Good. That gives me more power here than I thought I had. I can use that.

I can't tear my eyes away from him, though. I'm transfixed. Hot pressure pools at the juncture to my thighs and I feel my pussy swell and throb with interest. I've not felt this turned on in years. I've had plenty of sex since I broke up with Jamie, but my sex drive hasn't been the same, and I often

don't orgasm, or orgasm well. Not that it's bothered me that much. I've put it down to using all my
sexual energy for working as hard as I do, which to
me has been a fair trade-off. But my libido seems
to have come raging back to life since that night
at the charity ball. The *coitus interruptus* has left
me with a strange, hollow sort of ache inside me.
One I've not been able to sate by myself, no matter how many times I've tried.

Thanks to Jamie and his tormenting games.

The obnoxious bastard.

His movements seem to reach a crescendo and
a wave of electric lust crashes over me as I see his
shoulders first stiffen, then slump in relief.

Strange echoes of what I imagine he must be
feeling ripple through me and I'm almost jealous
of him. I suddenly want to be that abandoned.
That un-self-conscious and free to enjoy my desires again.

As I used to be when I was with him.

A memory sidesteps into my mind of how he
used to send me sexually charged text messages
an hour before he was due to arrive at my place.
He'd describe in explicit detail what he was going
to do to me when he arrived, then he'd demand I
go into my bedroom and masturbate until the point
I thought I was going to come. As soon as I felt

on the cusp of an orgasm I had to stop, save it for him to finish when he arrived.

At first I laughed off the idea of doing this, embarrassed by the idea of him knowing I was masturbating—a subject I'd never discussed with anyone before because I'd thought of it as a private and somewhat shameful act. But after some persuasion he'd convinced me it would be a fun game and that I shouldn't feel at all bad about the idea of giving myself pleasure. That it was a basic human right to give ourselves orgasms.

So I'd tried it, feeling foolish at first. But once I'd pushed past the primal shame and embarrassment it had become exciting and illicit. Because it was something only the two of us knew about: a personal, secret world of pleasure that we shared. It had deepened the connection between us because it was a true exercise in trust.

And I came to love it.

I have to admit, it became really bloody tough as time went on, holding myself back from the release I desperately needed after an hour of self-denial, but it was so worth it. The orgasms I'd had once he finally allowed me to have them were out of this world...

I'm dragged out of my erotic reverie as I realise he's turning around to face the house again, his magnificent chest sparkling in the brilliant sunshine with drops of sea water. I can see the power emanating from his well-worked-out body from all the way over here. All those hours training and playing tennis have left him with a physique to die for. I'm having immense trouble taking my eyes off him, but I don't want him to know I've been watching him, so as soon as he starts to push through the water and back towards the beach I move swiftly away from the window and face into the room.

I pace the floor as I wait for him to return, my knickers distressingly damp. I want to touch myself. To ease the pressure of need that's built between my legs, making my pussy throb with a yearning to be attended to. But I daren't risk it. I have to project an image of cool detachment here in order to maintain my pride. I can't let him catch me, either with my hand in my pants or with a healthy flush from the orgasm that's now screaming for release.

Damn it.

Why did I let myself stand there for so long and watch? As soon as I realised what he was doing I should have looked away.

But I hadn't and now I'm paying the price.

The library door opens and Jamie comes strolling in, his shirt clinging enticingly to his still damp-chest and his hair hanging in wet strands across his forehead. A bead of water escapes the hollow of his collarbone and runs down between his pecs, vanishing into the material of his shirt.

My breath catches in the back of my throat.

'Time's up,' he says in a low, seductive tone which my pussy immediately responds to.

Hell, this is challenging. My whole body is vibrating with tension as he stands there and assesses me with that astute gaze of his.

Can he sense how I'm feeling right now? It wouldn't surprise me. He always had an uncanny ability to read me, even when I was outwardly trying to not give him a reaction.

I take a mental breath and reach for a calm place in my head. Force myself to think strategically.

Actually, maybe it's a good thing I'm so turned on. If he makes any kind of move on me now it'll be easy to reach the orgasm he's so intent on getting out of me. There won't be any play-acting needed. All I need to do is think of him as a warm body, an orgasm machine, a very large vibrator or man-sized sex toy, perhaps.

A smile pushes at the corners of my mouth at the thought of that.

'Something funny?' he asks, advancing towards me. My mouth dries instantly as I catch the scent of him in the air. It's his natural musky fragrance mixed with the smell of the briny sea: fresh, sharp and seductive.

'I'm just speculating about what you're intending to do to me for the next few days,' I counter. 'And I'm wondering whether you've got the balls to go through with it.'

His eyebrows shoot up. 'Believe me, I have the balls and I'm not afraid to use them.'

I nod, keeping it cool. 'I only ask because it looks like the heat's getting to you.' I give him a taunting smile. 'Have you just taken a cold shower?'

His hand goes to his damp shirt then back down to his side, where he clenches it into a loose fist. Is he wondering whether I saw him?

'I've been for a swim in the sea,' he says roughly. 'You should try it. It's a great way to relax.'

I suppress a knowing grin.

He moves even closer, so close I can feel the whisper of his breath on my skin, and my inner smile vanishes.

I think of all the things he could do to me right now to make me relax.

My body throbs with interest.

Perhaps he'll tear at my clothes, like he did in the office at the fundraiser, then lower me to the floor and push my thighs apart to give him easy access to my needy pussy. Or maybe he'll demand I do a slow striptease for him, watching me the whole time with a superior smile before beckoning me towards him and burying his face between my legs.

Oh, God, my nipples are rock-hard and pressing distractingly against the cups of my bra, as if they're very interested in the idea of being free and available to his touch.

My breath feels ragged in my throat and is coming out in small pants, as if my body's being starved of oxygen.

But it's not oxygen I'm craving.

I moisten my dry lips with my tongue and see his gaze shoot to my mouth.

Is he going to kiss me now? God, I hope so. I'm desperate for him to take what he wants from me so I can get the hell away from his tormenting presence.

We're standing so close I swear I can feel his heartbeat moving the air between us. It's a heavy, erotic pulse which matches the insistent throb of need between my legs. The scent of him is deep in my nostrils, penetrating my resistance, drawing out my desire.

Please just kiss me. Please. Get this started already...

'Speaking of relaxing, let me show you to the bedroom you'll be staying in while you're here,' he says, startling me with his businesslike tone. 'Give you some time to freshen up before dinner.'

The sudden change in atmosphere makes me blink and I instinctively cross my arms over my chest, feeling like an idiot. He's really not going to touch me yet, even though I'm aching for him to do so. This is just another way to torture me.

He's pretending to be a gentleman about it all, but I know that's just a ruse.

He's play-acting too.

Playing me at my own game.

Okay, then, fine. I guess it's time to regroup and rethink my battle plan.

I nod in brisk agreement. 'That would be great, thanks.'

He looks at me for a couple more beats, as if expecting me to say something else. Perhaps beg him to give me that orgasm he's promised right now.

Never going to happen.

'Follow me,' he says finally, and I'm sure I catch a flash of disappointment in his face.

He leads me out of the library and up a sweeping staircase to the wide landing, which leads left to three doors and right to three more.

'You're the farthest room on the right,' he says, gesturing in that direction. 'You'll find clothes in your size in the wardrobe if you'd like to change into something a little more casual. I'm guessing you didn't bring your suitcase to the island with you.' This time he gives me a warm, joshing sort of smile, as if I'm a friend who's decided at the last minute to stay on for a fun weekend.

'Thank you,' I say stiffly. I refuse to smile back and play his game. We're not friends now and we never will be again. He might know my clothes size but it doesn't mean he knows me. Not any more.

'I'll arrange to have my suitcase sent over from my hotel suite on the mainland,' I add.

He nods. 'If you like, but I have everything you need here.' He starts to walk away, leaving me staring after him. 'Food will be ready in an hour. We'll eat on the terrace,' he shouts over his shoulder as he saunters to the top of the stairs.

As soon as he reaches them I stride to the room he pointed me towards and shut the door firmly behind me, leaning against the reassuringly solid wood and letting out a long, low breath of frustration.

I hate him, *hate* him, for putting me through this. It's revenge, I know it is, for the way I finished our relationship all those years ago. Not that he hasn't already punished me for it after the way he acted afterwards, sleeping with as many women as he could possibly fit into his bed, knowing it would get back to me.

And the vicious rumour about me that went around afterwards had his fingerprints all over it. Not that I demeaned myself to ask him about it. I didn't want to give him the satisfaction. I had more important things to worry about at that point in my life, such as preventing my family from falling apart.

And now he's doing this to me—making me feel all sorts of things I thought I'd escaped from. Forcing me to confront what I gave up in order to do the right thing.

I haven't felt this turned on in years. I'd forgotten how much I could ache for my body to be touched, stroked and played with. Explored and dominated.

But he's going to make me wait.

He's such a bastard.

I walk over to a mirror positioned above a large oak dressing table and study my flushed face, seeing the strain of the situation reflected in my eyes.

I don't look good. I look wired and out of control.

Ah, hell. I think I'm in serious trouble here.

Jamie

I'm aware of my fingers twitching by my sides as I descend the stairs and stroll towards the kitchen to begin cooking the evening meal.

Fuck, that was hard.

It had taken all my willpower to ignore the insane eroticism of the moment, as well as the lingering sense of loss I was still feeling, and bring our focus back to practicalities. She was so temptingly *there*, with her wide, defiant eyes and her damp, kissable mouth. I wanted *so fucking much* to avenge my younger self's misery by taking her the way I've been dreaming about since that aborted fuck a few weeks ago. But I know it wouldn't have worked like that. She's not ready to give me what I'm looking for yet. I want her to want it—*need it*—to happen so badly she begs me for it. Only then will I feel that I've redressed the balance between us.

So more pleasure-delaying it is. For now.

I made the deliberate decision to give my housekeeper and chef the next couple of days off so April and I can be alone together. I want to gain her trust by cooking for her myself, reminding her there's more to me than she's come to believe. I actually really enjoy cooking for people. I taught myself how to do it a few years ago and I find it a soothing activity. I think I'm pretty good at it too. My meals are something else about which I never get complaints from the women I entertain.

My blood spikes with adrenaline as I remember her disdainful expression when she'd thrown that barb at me about not being capable of making her come. I'm glad I'm getting the opportunity to put that fallacy to bed, even though I consider it an added extra compared to my real reason for getting her to stay here with me.

I can tell she's still very much on her guard, which isn't surprising, considering my rather unusual demand. Not that it seems to have fazed her at all. As I suspected, she's willing to do anything in order to get what she wants for her family's business. To further her career. She's that mercenary. Though I guess I've no room to talk at the moment, considering the way I'm acting.

But it's a means to an end. An opportunity to put everything right and move on. To get a major source of hurt and stress out of my life.

This *thing* between us has followed me around for too many years now, like an abused but loyal dog, and I'm coming to recognise how unhealthy it is. It's coloured every single relationship with a woman I've had, in one way or another. I think subconsciously I've compared them to her and they've all come up wanting. Not that I can put my finger on why, exactly. She's not that special. But, despite my continued attempts to forget what happened between us, I've never been able to put it to rest and move on.

But now it's time to do exactly that.

CHAPTER FIVE

April

THE CLOTHES HE'S picked out for me are surprisingly demure.

When I pull back the wardrobe door I expect to see a selection of clingy, provocative outfits to pull me further out of my comfort zone, so fingering through the beautifully cut, classy designer garments gives me both a thrill of pleasure and relief.

While I hate the idea of him dressing me, I can't help but feel grudging approval at his good taste.

Not that I should allow that to affect my opinion of him. I've always known he's one step above most men I've ever met, but he's also self-obsessed and wily, and I need to keep my guard up around him at all times. Even though I know he's taking great pleasure in 'teaching me a lesson', I can't help but wonder whether there's more to his demand that I stay on his island, cut off from outside communication. I'll need to stay vigilant, just in case he's trying to sneak something past me while I'm here. I wouldn't put it past him.

I've experienced too much betrayal and disappointment in my life not to be paranoid at every turn.

After taking a refreshing shower in the aquamarine-tiled *en suite* bathroom, I use the powerful showerhead between my legs to try and relieve some of the sexual tension that's been plaguing me for the last hour, but to my frustration I can't quite get there. Something's stopping me from reaching that peak and I get out of the water with the craving for release still clawing through me.

Once I've dried my sensitised skin I select a simple but elegant silky-feeling slip dress in royal purple. As promised, it's in my size, and when I slip it over my head and do up the zip at the back it fits perfectly. Like a second skin.

I dry my shoulder-length hair, which takes longer than usual in the humid heat of the Greek evening, then twist it into a neat bun and pin it up, leaving my neck exposed. It feels good to have the cool air from the open window breeze across it.

Okay, I'm ready.

Body humming with nervous energy for the battle of wills I'm sure I'm about to face this evening, I make my way down the stairs to find Jamie.

My taste buds tingle as I make my way deeper into the house to where I imagine the kitchen to be. There's a delicious smell wafting from that direction and it lures me towards it like human catnip.

But when I step inside the large, lived-in-looking room, with its terracotta-tiled floor and white-washed walls, it's free of human presence. The oven is on, with a couple of dishes on the shelves inside, and there are plates laid out ready to be filled. Cooking is still in progress, it seems.

So I go in search of Jamie, not wanting him to find me dithering about in there, looking out of place and uncomfortable.

There's a warm glow coming from a room opposite the library and I stroll towards it, hyper-aware of the kitten heels of my shoes clicking on the polished tile floor. I walk into a large, simply decorated sitting room and look around. Nothing in this house is for show, it all has a useful purpose, though I'm sure it's all top-quality merchandise. On the other side of the room there are bi-fold doors pushed wide open, giving a stunning view out across the sea. A warm breeze plays over my skin as I make my way towards them and I see there's a terrace out there with a large dining table and chairs set out on it. The sun is beginning to set in the distance and there are lanterns hanging from two posts that are holding up a canopy of sweet-smelling grapevines heavy with their purple fruit. The flames from the lanterns flicker gently in the breeze as I move towards them and I experience a sudden uplift in my mood. It feels good to be out of the city, I realise, breathing the fresh sea air deep into my lungs.

'Come and join me,' Jamie says as I walk further onto the terrace. He's lounging in one of the cedar-wood dining chairs with a glass of what looks like gin and tonic in his hand, watching the sun setting in the distance.

'Thank you,' I say stiffly. I take a seat opposite him, then turn to look out to sea too.

'Here, I fixed you a drink. G and T,' he says, pushing a cut-glass tumbler towards me. The liquid fizzes and glints in the early-evening sun, a slice of vibrant green lime jostling against ice cubes on the surface.

'Thanks,' I say, picking up the glass and taking a tentative sip.

'Don't worry, I haven't poisoned it,' he jokes, his eyes alive with wry mirth.

'I should hope not. You'll never get to soothe that poor ego of yours if you do away with me first,' I retort, not quite able to match his relaxed tone. Again I wonder what sort of game is afoot here. I don't know what I was expecting, but it wasn't out-and-out friendliness from Jamie.

'That dress suits you. I knew it would,' he says.

I clear my throat, disconcerted by the compliment.

'I have to say, I'm impressed. You did a pretty good job of picking out the sorts of clothes I'd choose for myself,' I say, forcing myself to join in with the friendly banter. To be honest, it'll probably make this evening so much less stressful if we're not sniping at each other the whole time.

And I can do civilised. No problem. I'll just follow his lead. But I'm not going to allow myself to get too comfortable, because that's when he'll go in for the kill. I've experienced it before, so I know what I'm talking about.

He nods, his gaze fixed on mine, his firm lips drawn into a playful smile. 'Well, I figured I owed you a dress,' he murmurs, his voice warm with flirtation. He's referencing tearing off the last one he saw me in, of course, and the memory of it has my body right back on high alert, craving a repeat performance.

'What's for dinner?' I ask, in an attempt to distract my thoughts from wandering that way. But all I can think about now is the naked desire on his face as he thrust into me, pinning me against that wall...

Oh, God, I know I'm going to have real trouble eating tonight when he's sitting so close. His musky scent is in my nostrils and I'm so very aware of those long, skilful fingers of his wrapped around the glass. I know exactly what he can do with those hands. How much pleasure he can give me.

Stop thinking about it!

'It's baked white fish with roasted Mediterranean vegetables,' he says.

Despite my nerves my stomach still growls as I remember the delicious smell in the kitchen.

'Sounds great.'

He stands up. 'Speaking of which, it should be just about ready.'

I go to stand up too.

'No, you stay there and enjoy the sunset. I'll bring it out to the table.'

So he's cooking and serving the meal himself. As I'd started to suspect, his staff aren't just discreet, they're not actually here. It seems we're totally alone on the island.

An electric prickle rushes over my skin and I sit back heavily in my chair again.

I watch him walk away, hyper-conscious of his athletic grace. It looks as though he's taken a shower since I last saw him because he's changed his clothes and his hair is shiny and swept back from his closely shaved face. He's still casual, in a short-sleeved linen shirt and navy combats, but seriously the man can make anything look a million dollars when it's on that incredible body of his. He's so bloody virile it's sickening.

It appears he can cook, now, too. Something he'd never done when we were together. We'd always gone out for meals, choosing to spend our time together in bed at each other's houses.

I have a suspicion he's deliberately trying to impress me, but I have no idea why. He's the one holding all the cards here.

The idea of spending the next few days in his company is frankly unsettling, so I take a big swig of my drink to calm my nerves before he comes back, then another. The alcohol warms my chest then hits my empty stomach, immediately filling me with a false sense of well-being.

I should be careful how much I drink, though. I don't want to compromise my control over this situation.

I wonder if he's thinking the same way. Is this his first drink, or one of many?

He used to drink a fair amount when we were together at university, though not to extremes, but after we split up there were some stories in the tabloids about him being drunk and lary in a few London nightclubs. Not that I allowed myself to pay much attention to them because there had always been a beautiful party girl involved and it had been too painful to think about him being with other women. But, come to think of it, I've not heard about any bad behaviour on his part since then so I guess he must have pulled his drinking back.

On a whim, I lean forward, pull his tumbler towards me and take a tentative sniff. It doesn't smell alcoholic. I frown, then pick up the glass and take a small sip. Nope. There's no gin in here. It's just tonic.

Interesting.

Footsteps sound behind me and I hurriedly push his drink back across the table top to where he was sitting and turn around just as he walks out of the living area and onto the terrace with plates loaded with food in each hand.

He puts one in front of me and one at his place, then reaches into a side pocket in the leg of his trousers to produce cutlery.

'Voila,' he says, waving his hand with a proud flourish towards the meal.

'It smells delicious,' I say, because it does. Despite the fact my stomach's jumping with tension, my mouth still waters with anticipation.

'Would you like some wine to go with it?' Jamie asks, gesturing towards a silver bucket at the other end of the table with the neck of a bottle of white wine peeking out of it.

'No, thank you,' I say, 'But don't let me stop you if you want some.'

He shakes his head. 'I don't drink any more.'

I blink at him. 'You don't drink wine, or any alcohol?' I ask, wanting clarification on that point.

'Alcohol. Not since my early twenties.'

'Why did you give it up?' I'm intrigued about the reason for this.

He looks away and I get the sense he's uncomfortable talking about it.

'Mostly because it interfered too much with my tennis training. There's nothing worse than running round a court with a hangover being bellowed at by your coach,' he replies, picking up his knife and fork and cutting into his fish. He's still not looking at me and I could swear his shoulders and jaw have tensed.

Then it hits me. Of course. His mother died from liver failure. Although he never explicitly said so, I got the impression she was an alcoholic and that's what had caused it. Which actually makes a lot of sense to me after what shook out after my mother's death.

Jamie had very rarely talked about his mother, who he'd lost when he was only fifteen, and whenever he did mention her I'd got the feeling he'd struggled to come to terms with it—he'd certainly become very morose whenever the subject had come up—so I'd never pursued it.

And I wasn't about to delve into that sticky topic now. Too personal.

I pick up my knife and fork and begin to eat, savouring the soft, creamy texture of the fresh fish in my mouth.

Thinking about it, perhaps something happened to make him think he was heading towards alcoholism too. Perhaps it was after what happened with us.

A hot rush of distress hits me.

But I can't let myself think like that. I'd done what I'd done to protect him. To save him from losing everything that had meant something to him.

Anyway, it was probably just the training, like he said.

'I heard you've given up playing professionally,' I say to distract myself from the sinking feeling in my gut. 'What happened?'

He looks up at me, his brows pinched together. 'I had a bad fall on the court during a training session a couple of years ago, which my shoulder never fully recovered from, and it put paid to my winning streak.' He rolls the shoulder in question as if the mere thought of it had sent a throb of pain through him. 'Even after a year of physiotherapy the mobility in my shoulder hasn't entirely returned so I can't put as much power behind my strokes any more.'

He shrugs. 'I still play a bit, though, when I get a chance. I sometimes do stints of coaching for kids from underprivileged backgrounds through a couple of sports-focussed charities, to give them opportunities they might not ordinarily have. And I run scholarship programmes to help with club and coaching fees if they show talent and interest.' He flashes me a self-depreciating smile. 'At first I thought it would drive me insane, watching all those bright young things priming themselves to take my crown, but actually it's been incredibly rewarding.'

I realise I'm staring at him, a forkful of food en route to my mouth. 'I didn't know all that,' is all I can think to say, caught off-guard. I didn't realise he had philanthropic leanings, but then I've avoided him—and even conversations about him—as much as possible over the last ten years.

He laughs at my surprise, his whole face lighting up.

My breath catches in the back of my throat and warmth pools in my belly at the sight of it. He looks so different when he's not being angry with me. I'd forgotten how much his smile affects me. How my whole being responds to it, as if I'm being shot through with pure pleasure.

Another thing to watch out for.

'There's no need to look so shocked. I know you think I'm just some self-obsessed playboy, but that couldn't be further from the truth,' he scolds me, dipping one eyebrow in mock consternation.

'Yes, well, we haven't exactly spent a lot of time around each other recently, so I'm going on past experience.'

I have to look away from him after that and concentrate on forcing down some more of my food so he doesn't see how much this conversation is bothering me. It was hard enough being around him when he was being cruel and offensive, but now he's actually acting like a human being I don't seem to know what to do with myself.

It's a charm offensive, all right, but I'm not sure where it's leading.

He chooses not to respond to my jibe and out of the corner of my eye I see him continue to eat his meal.

The silence is tense and as soon as we're both finished and have carefully placed our cutlery on our empty plates he gives a frustrated sigh and shakes his head.

'Look, April, can you at least try to relax? I'm not that much of a bastard, am I?'

'Relax?' I scoff, crossing my arms and leaning back in my chair. 'How do you expect me to do that when you have me captive here, just waiting to exert your will?'

He waves a dismissive hand at me. 'You know that's bullshit. You could leave any time you like. I won't stop you. Just say the word and I'll sail you straight back to the mainland.'

'But then you won't sell me your company,' I point out.

'Well, no. That was the deal we made. Which you agreed to,' he says with a wolfish grin. 'So don't try to make out I'm some sort of sexual deviant. This is a business exchange. Where we both win, remember?'

'You're only doing this to pay me back, Jamie. Don't try and pretend it's anything else.'

He lays his hands on the table and fixes me with a serious but friendly look. 'Think of it as closure, April, pure and simple. So we can both move on. Losing my father forced me to reassess my life and I've decided it's time we put our resentment towards each other to rest. Don't you agree?'

I pause, wanting to refute this, to say I can never get past it. That too much has happened between his family and mine for that to be possible. But I don't. Because that would inevitably open up a whole new conversation with him that I really don't want to have. I buried the past ten years ago and there's no way I'm going to exhume it now.

Nothing good can come of talking to Jamie about it. Especially so soon after losing his father. He'll only hate me more for my involvement in it and I can't afford to let that happen.

'Yes, I guess this ridiculous feud has gone on too long,' I say slowly, uncrossing my arms and placing my hands neatly onto my lap. 'We're adults now. We should be able to handle being around each other without fighting. Let's agree that we both made mistakes, but it was a long time ago. I can forgive if you can.'

'Good,' he says, a wide smile flattening his lips. 'Then let's forgive each other.'

But I'm not that stupid.

I know this is just a trick.

Jamie

She looks guarded, sitting there all prim and proper, as we both lie through our teeth to each other.

I know there can be no way she's actually forgiven me for the way I behaved after we spilt up, and I certainly can't forgive the anguish she put me through when she so callously cut me out of her life.

But perhaps we can put it to one side, if only for this evening.

In all honesty, having her here on the island has made me realise just how much I miss the April

I used to know—at least the person I thought she was, until she turned her back on me. We'd had such a good time together when we were young. We'd fitted. And for some unknown reason life keeps throwing her back in my path.

It's really fucking with my head.

'Want to go for a stroll on the beach before we lose the light?' I ask as an awkward silence descends between us again.

Is she thinking the same things I am? Wouldn't that be something?

I'm not quite sure how I feel about it, to be honest.

'Sure,' she says, standing up from her chair and smoothing down the skirt of the dress I knew she'd look incredible in. She has the most perfect body. It's all soft curves and strong, toned limbs. I remember the glorious sensation of her long legs wrapped around my waist and her arms circling my shoulders as I held myself still inside her in that dark office and my body heats with the promise of what's still to come.

Or who. Hopefully both of us.

We follow the path across the chamomile lawn I've had planted in front of the house and down to the beach. Birds leisurely swoop across the darkening sky, getting in one last blast of exercise before bedding down for the night.

The sea is still calm and makes gentle lapping sounds against the wet sand as we walk down to the shoreline.

April's hair shines in the dying rays of the sun and I can't help but stare at her. I can barely believe she's actually here with me. I never thought I'd see the day when we were alone together and not fighting.

How has my life come to this—where I've practically had to kidnap her in order to find out the real reason why she left me the way she did ten years ago.

'It's a beautiful island,' she says, dragging me out of my musing.

'Thank you. It was completely deserted when I first bought it, with just an old ramshackle house and one hell of an overgrown mess. It's been quite a challenge to get it to the state it's in now.'

She raises an eyebrow. 'How long have you owned it?'

'I bought it at the pinnacle of my tennis career, five years ago. Winning the French Open and Wimbledon in the same year meant the sponsorship money came flooding in, and then the opportunity to set up my own sports clothing line came about, which I grabbed with two hands.'

I glance at her, but she's looking down at the sand, her brow set in a small frown.

'My father suggested I invest the money I made, rather than fritter it all away, which I thought was good advice,' I go on, feeling a need to fill the silence. 'But I also really liked the idea of having a place where I could both train and holiday away from prying eyes. The press seemed to be particularly interested in me at that point and I found it exhausting trying to go about my day-to-day business in England.'

She stops to take off her shoes and pushes her bare feet through the sand, her colourful toenails disappearing then reappearing again like shy sea creatures. 'It must be nice to have somewhere you can hide from the rest of the world,' she says, turning to look at me now.

Am I imagining it or is that a wistful look on her face?

'It is,' I agree. 'It never occurred to me that my private life would become such public property before I started winning major tournaments, so it's been great to have a place where I can get away from the press and relax. I only ever wanted to play tennis. I've never been interested in the fame that comes with it.'

She doesn't say anything to this but I sense her internally raising an eyebrow at that and I'm sure I see her mouth twitch at the corner.

'It's been ten years since we knew each other,

April. Don't you think it's possible there's more depth to me now than you're willing to acknowledge?' I chide, experiencing a jab of hurt at what feels like unfair judgement.

There's a small pause while she seems to contemplate this. 'I guess there's a chance you might have changed since then,' she grudgingly admits, shooting me a reluctant small smile of acknowledgment.

A grin twitches at the corner of my mouth. I get the impression she's still struggling with having to play nice with me. But she's going to have to do a lot more of it before our three days together are up. I'll make damn sure of it.

As if she's sensed me thinking this, she slowly moves towards me, her gaze intent on mine, closing the distance between us till we're standing only inches apart.

'You know, since we've forgiven each other there shouldn't be anything stopping us from moving on with our deal now,' she says, reaching out a hand to brush away a leaf that's snagged on the shoulder of my shirt.

My heart relocates to my throat at the touch of her fingers and the atmosphere suddenly becomes charged with promise.

She reaches behind her and slides down the zip at the back of her dress, keeping her eyes fixed on mine, daring me to react.

I stare back, a pulse ticking in my jaw.

Once again she's trying to force things to move on before I want them to.

But I'm going to make sure this happens on my terms. I won't let her control it. No matter how much I might want to kiss her right now.

Defiance flares in her eyes as the dress slithers down her body to expose the black balconette bra she's wearing underneath which pushes her breasts upwards into two generous mounds.

I struggle not to give in and look down.

Reaching behind her, she undoes the clasp and slides first one bra strap, then the other down her arm until it falls away from her body and she's standing brazenly in front of me, half-naked, her face set in an expression of dignified purpose. And it's so fucking hot.

The sound of our ragged breathing is the only noise in my head and it takes all my willpower to keep my hands at my sides and give her a bland smile. 'You can't let go, can you? You can't stand not to be in charge for one second,' I tease her.

'Of course I can,' she retorts, as if I've just made the most ridiculous suggestion ever.

I shake my head. 'That's not how this is going to work. I thought I made it clear earlier, I'm not interested in a quick fuck. I want us to get to a point where we can stand to be in a room together again and in order to do that we need to reconnect properly. I want to know there are no issues left between us so I can finally put the past to bed.'

'And you think proving you can make me come is going to achieve that?'

I flash her a grin. 'It's worth a try, don't you think?'

She lets out a snort, which could either mean she agrees, even though she thinks it's a crazy idea, or she just thinks I'm plain crazy.

'But not tonight,' I say, reaching forward to snag her dress between the finger and thumb of each hand and slide it back up her body, holding out the arm holes so she can grudgingly slip a hand through each one. Once she's done this, I glide the straps back up her arms towards her shoulders. She gives a little shiver as the front slips over her beautiful bare breasts, the material catching for a moment on her erect, rose-pink nipples, and I feel a sting of regret as they vanish from sight.

I'm so close to her like this, I can feel the heat radiating from her body. She lets out a small, unguarded sound in the back of her throat, like a strangled cough, as I push the straps of the dress back onto her shoulders, my thumbs grazing the soft skin of her collarbone.

Perhaps this is harder for her than she's willing

to admit. Perhaps my delaying tactics are getting to her, the anticipation making her crazy.

I hope so. Because I don't know how much more of this I can take myself. I long to touch her, to see her give in to the desire she so tightly controls. To reignite a part of her I know is still burning on low inside. To see the April I used to know again.

I force myself to take a step away, my body aching with regret.

'I think it's time we retired for the evening,' I murmur, trying not to react when I see frustration flash across her face.

'You should have everything you need in your room,' I add. 'I'll see you in the morning.'

Without another word, I give her a casual nod of goodbye and walk away, feeling her perplexed gaze boring into me the whole way back to the house.

CHAPTER SIX

April

I HADN'T BEEN expecting that—the gentle redressing of my body, as if he was concerned for my dignity. And I certainly hadn't expected to be left standing alone on that beach, my whole body throbbing with unsatisfied need.

Once Jamie disappears into the house I take some deep, shuddering breaths and try to get my hands to stop shaking.

He's turning me into a half-crazed mess.

But perhaps that's his plan. He wants to see me lose my legendary cool.

Can he really be that shallow? I can't quite reconcile it with the Jamie I'm starting to get to know all over again. The philanthropic businessman. The talented cook and attentive host.

A man I'd told myself he wasn't capable of being.

But I can't let that knowledge sway me. So what

if he doesn't appear to be the shallow arsehole I thought he was? It doesn't mean it would be a good idea to get emotionally involved with him again. It doesn't mean he's not playing a sadistic game of cat and mouse with me.

I trudge back to the house, bra in hand, hyper-aware of my sensitive nipples rubbing against the soft material of the dress like a caress. Everything I've sensed, seen or touched since I've been here in his company has felt sexualised, as if Jamie's ministrations, or lack of them, have put my body on constant high alert. The empty space between my legs throbs with the need to be filled. To feel the heavy weight of his cock inside me again.

Damn it. I'm letting him get to me and that can only end in disappointment and pain. Just like the last relationship we had. Men are self-ish, self-serving beasts and Jamie De Montfort is no exception.

Like father, like son.

As soon as I get back to my room I take another cooling shower before retiring to bed.

I sleep fitfully till the early-morning sun bleeds around the shutters on my windows waking me up.

Getting out of bed, I stretch my tired muscles and take some deep centring breaths, preparing myself for a brand new day of tactical engagement, my stomach fizzing with nerves.

* * *

Jamie is nowhere to be seen when I make it down-stairs, dressed and ready for battle in a pair of blue silk shorts and a simple white cotton vest-top.

I make my way to the kitchen, where I find fresh aromatic coffee and a plate full of pastries waiting for me. I pour myself a large mug of black coffee and take it with a custard-filled filo parcel through the living area and out to the terrace where we'd sat the night before. Even though the sun isn't fully on that part of the house yet, it's lovely and warm, and I sink into a dining chair and sip my coffee as I stare out to sea.

It really is beautiful here. I can see why Jamie bought this island. There's an air of serenity about the place, a calmness that's impossible to find in London. It's been a long time since I've just sat and stared, I realise. Usually I'm looking at my emails while eating my breakfast. My stom-ach gives a nervous roll at the thought of what's happening—or more to the point, what isn't—without me.

It's so hard to turn my brain off from work. I seem to eat, sleep and breathe it nowadays. No wonder I'm finding the quiet and stillness of this place so unnerving.

I've just finished my delicious pastry when there's a movement in the corner of my eye and

Jamie strides onto the terrace in gym shorts, his glorious torso naked and gleaming with sweat in the soft morning sun. My stomach swoops and my face immediately heats as though someone's just directly aimed a furnace at it. Reaching for my coffee mug, I take a long sip to give me a moment to compose myself.

My God, he looks good after just working out. Hot, virile and so bloody healthy.

'Morning. I hope you slept well,' he says, his tone practically winking with innuendo. He must know how much his teasing game of slow seduction is getting to me.

'Very well, thanks,' I say coolly. It might be visibly obvious that I'm struggling with his half-naked presence but there's no way I'm vocally going to admit to it. I need to maintain some vestige of pride here. 'I hope you don't mind—I helped myself to breakfast,' I add.

'Of course not. I put it out so you could.'

So we're still alone, then.

He takes a seat opposite me, his eyes never leaving mine. 'I want you to relax while you're here. Take a break from the rush of your life. Focus on one thing for once, instead of a million of them.'

'Focus on *you*, you mean?' I say with a wry smile.

His shrug is nonchalant. 'Yes. I do. And in order

to do that you need to calm that overactive brain of yours. That's why I wanted you to stay for a few days.'

'Are you trying to tell me you're doing this for my health now?'

'Partly, maybe. But I'm also interested in seeing the April I used to know. Back when you weren't driven by profit and loss. When you could laugh at yourself and actually enjoy life.'

Thinking about the person I used to be makes my chest contract.

'She doesn't exist any more. She died the day my mother did,' I say, keeping my voice brisk and dispassionate.

His gaze locks with mine and an expression of sadness crosses his face.

'I don't believe that,' he says quietly. Leaning forward, he braces his hands on the table. 'I think she's still in there somewhere.'

My laugh is strained and cynical. 'Well, if she is, I can't find her.' I swipe my hand through the air, swatting away the notion. 'Anyway, I wouldn't want to be that naïve again. I'm proud of the life I've made for myself. I have everything I've ever wanted now.'

'Everything?' he asks.

I feel my heart starting to beat harder in my chest. 'Yes,' I lie.

'I remember you saying that to me once before, when we were together.'

My throat dries as I remember exactly the time he's talking about. We'd spent the weekend together, mostly in bed, only getting up to eat then go out to a gig at a local pub. We'd been sitting at a sticky table with pints of lager in front of us, relaxed and happy in our cosy world of private jokes and dreams for the future. A future together.

That moment had felt perfect in its simplicity.

I *had* had everything I wanted.

I'd had Jamie.

And I'd thought that if we were together then everything would always be okay.

How wrong I'd been.

'That was a long time ago,' I murmur, the words rough in my throat. 'A lot's happened in the meantime. Like growing up and having adult responsibilities.'

'What responsibilities?'

'My sisters, for one.'

He frowns. 'But they're adults too now. I'm sure they're totally capable of looking after themselves.'

I sigh, feeling the weight of my family's dysfunction pressing down on me. 'You'd think so, wouldn't you? But Maya is so irresponsible and Juno always seems to have her head so far up in the clouds she doesn't notice life going on around her.'

'I thought they were both happy with partners now. That's what I heard.'

I pause before I speak, mulling this over. 'Yes, they are. That's true. But I suppose I'll always think of them as kids needing my support. They were both so young when our mother died and I was the one they looked to to step in and fill that role. I suppose I've never shaken it off.'

He stares at me, his brow a little pinched, as if something's just occurred to him.

'It sounds like it's time to do that now, though— let go a little?'

I shrug, feeling uncomfortable. This conversation is a little too close to the bone for my liking. 'Perhaps.'

There's another weighted pause.

'Come for a swim,' he says, suddenly getting up from his chair and looking at me expectantly.

'I don't have a swimsuit,' I point out.

'Yes, you do. There's a bikini in your wardrobe.' He steps away from the table. 'I'll see you in the pool in half an hour,' he says in a no-nonsense tone, striding away before I have time to respond.

I stare after him, feeling a mixture of irritation at being told what to do and disgruntled respect for his absolute conviction that I'll do exactly what he tells me.

That kind of confidence is a strength I've not seen in many men.

And I like it. It impresses me.

It always has.

And I guess I need to play by his rules of engagement for the time being, even if the idea of slipping and accidentally showing something real of myself terrifies me.

But I won't let that happen.

I can't. It'd be a disaster.

So I guess I'm going swimming.

Jamie

I've already done fifty laps of the pool before April shows up, a towelling robe wrapped around her and her long swathe of hair pinned up on top of her head.

I take a break at the edge of the pool and watch her unwrap herself and lay the robe neatly onto one of the sun loungers at the side of the pool.

I surmise from an almost imperceptible stiffness in her movements that she's keenly aware of me watching her, but when she turns to face me there's no hint of discomfort in her expression.

She's a pro actress. I'll give her that.

Her body is lithe and toned, as I knew it would be, and my heart judders in my chest as I watch

her walk to the edge of the pool and execute a perfect dive into the deep end. She remerges about
fifteen feet away from me after swimming most
of the length underwater. Standing up, she swipes
her hands over her face to clear the water from
her vision.

Water droplets cascade down her shoulders,
arms and between her breasts and I find I can't
tear my gaze away from her. She really is a breathtakingly attractive woman. Not just physically, but
in the indomitable way she conducts herself. She's
totally in command of every move she makes.

I itch to break that strict control and free her
from the constraints under which she puts herself.

'Come here,' I suggest with a grin when she
raises a cool, laconic eyebrow at my examination
of her.

But she doesn't, damn her. Instead she gives
me a shrewd sort of smile that tells me she's not
just meekly going to follow my instructions. She's
going to make me work for it.

My cock hardens at the defiance I see in her
eyes.

'Come here,' I repeat, with more command in
my voice this time.

'I thought we were just having a swim together.'

'Not any more.'

I can practically see her mind warring with itself as a whole range of emotions flits across her face. Half of her wants to hold her ground and keep an iron control over what happens here, but the other half knows that would be counterproductive. It's clearly been way too long since she let go and allowed things to happen *to* her.

But I know she knows if I'm even going to contemplate selling my father's business to her she's going to have to give me what I asked for in exchange. We had an agreement, and April Darlington-Hume is not the kind of woman to welch on a deal. She has a reputation to maintain, after all.

So she moves towards me, her agile body cutting through the water as though it's air, until she's standing right in front of me.

Her face is bare of make-up now and she looks younger and more approachable for it. She looks like the woman I used to know before she took on this awful corporate persona. Before she smoothed herself out so much none of her former personality remained.

I experience another wave of nostalgia for that April—the woman who would allow me to see her softer side. Who would smile, laugh and enjoy the simple things in life. Who wasn't driven by power, status and the demands of her family.

Where has she gone?

My heart gives a heavy thump against my chest. I want her *fucking* back.

With only that thought in my head, I reach towards her, cupping her jaw in my hands and pulling her mouth towards mine. She lets out a small gasp of surprise and stiffens—but only for a second. As soon as I open my lips against hers and slide my tongue into her mouth, I feel her body melt against me. I kiss her greedily, my mouth pressed firmly to hers, my tongue exploring the hot softness of her mouth. Our bodies slip and slide against each other in the water as I wrap my arms around her back and pull her closer. I feel her breasts crush against my chest and experience a fierce surge of longing to explore them with my hands and mouth. I want to hear her moan for me like she used to.

Moving us to the side of the pool, I pull the bow loose at the back of her bikini top where it's tied around her neck. Then, after I push her against the side, I take a step back so the straps can slither down her body and the two triangles of material fall away, revealing her breasts in all their glory.

And they are magnificent. Firm and voluptuous, with those rose-pink nipples which are currently erect and just begging for my attention. I bend to kiss first one, then the other, hearing her ragged intake of breath as I let my hot breath tantalise her skin before sucking down hard. Her body bucks against me as if I've hit a pleasure point—which I know, from past experience, that I have.

I use both hands to scoop her breasts together and I move my head between them, first running my tongue round and round each aureole before sucking down on each nipple in turn, until I feel her whole body shuddering under my touch. She has her back pressed up against the edge of the pool and both arms splayed on either side of her to keep her balanced. When I glance up her head is tipped back, her eyes shut and her lips parted as soft breaths sigh in and out of her.

She looks glorious there, in the bright morning sunshine, her skin perfect and smooth, the tall column of her throat elegantly extended.

I want to do more to her. To see, hear and feel more of that carnal need.

Sliding my hands down her body, I curve my fingers under her buttocks and lift her up onto the side of the pool.

She lets out a gasp of surprise as I push her legs apart and roughly tug aside her bikini bottoms. My gaze locks with hers and she gives me a nod of approval. 'Go ahead,' she whispers in a hoarse voice.

I don't need any more encouragement than that and lower my mouth to her exposed pussy, which gleams with moisture in the brilliant sunlight.

Using my fingertips, I gently open her up to reveal the hard nub of her clitoris to my greedy gaze before flicking my tongue over it.

Her legs jump beside my head and she lets out a soft yelp of approval. So I do it again, then slide the tip of my tongue down between her folds, exploring every part of her pussy, before moving back up to swirl my tongue round and around the periphery of her clit, until I feel her desperation for more direct contact, which I give her after another moment's pause.

The low, guttural groan she lets out causes my already hard cock to give a throb of extreme interest. But I ignore my own need and continue to focus on hers, lathing my tongue between her folds then dipping a finger inside her to locate the spot I know drives her wild. Her whole body jerks when I press hard on it and her hips twist with pleasure as instinctively she tries to get me to do it again.

But I want to hear her say it. To ask me for what she wants. To plead with me to give her what she needs.

I know she's enjoying this. I can tell. I know her body so well, even after all these years. But I want to hear it from her lips.

When we'd first started having sex, she'd been coy and hesitant—she'd been a virgin, in fact—and I'd taken great pleasure in teaching her everything I knew. And she'd responded so well—once she'd allowed herself to give in to her desire. That's how I knew she'd been lying about not orgasming with me. I knew her tells—her uninhibited displays of abandon—for what they were.

Like now—the way her fingers are gripping the sides of the pool and the little gurgles of pleasure in the back of her throat. I know them. They make sense.

I remember.

Come on, April, lose it for me. Tell me how much you want me, even though you're desperate not to let me know.

But she doesn't. She doesn't say a thing. She just takes what I'm giving her. And I sense her resistance.

But I'm not prepared to give up just yet. I know it's possible to get what I want from her, if she'll just let go a little...

I continue to stroke her hard with my finger, making a beckoning motion to catch her G spot every time while using the flat of my tongue to lap her clit.

She's shaking with the intensity of the pleasure I'm giving her, but she's still not letting go. Her lips are clamped shut and her eyes closed, as if she's fighting this—fighting her need. She doesn't want to give me the satisfaction of seeing her losing her shit, so she's still holding back.

I ramp up both the speed and pressure of what I'm doing to her and I'm rewarded with a low gurgle in her throat. But it's still not enough. She's not abandoned, as I want her to be.

And then, out of nowhere, I feel her coming against my mouth. Her legs shake next to my head and I look up to see her whole body is tense and straining with the effort of keeping herself upright on the side of the pool.

Her eyes are screwed shut, but she's not making any noise. She's completely internalised it.

This orgasm is for her only. As if she's just been using my mouth to masturbate.

I feel cheated. Tricked. Like she's snuck this orgasm in under the radar without allowing me the satisfaction of giving it to her.

She's taken it, but she's not given me anything back. It's as if I've just performed a practical service for her.

Fuck!

Why is she so afraid to properly to let go with me? Has she locked herself up so tightly over the last ten years she's worried she'll never be able to put herself back together if she comes apart?

Is she scared she'll start to have feelings for me again?

A fizzing, electric surge of emotion rushes through me at this thought. Do I want that? And, if so, is it only so I can then reject her and finally get my pride back? So I can balance the scales that have been tipped against me for ten long years now, weighing me down, reminding me *every fucking time* I see her how she'd broken me and turned me into the kind of man I despise?

A weak, selfish bastard.

I still as the reality of that thought sucker-punches me in the gut.

What the hell am I doing? Am I really so pathetic I'm actually more interested in getting my own back on April than finally getting to the bottom of what my father wanted me to know?

Regret stings the back of my eyes and I pull away from her. I need to regroup and find another way to gain her trust. I sense, deep down, that I'm going to have to give her something first—an apology, I guess—for the way I acted after we broke up.

But I can't do that right here, right now.

I need some time to think first. To put some space between us so I can get my thoughts straight.

Putting my hands on her hips, I pull her back into the water.

Her self-satisfied smile vanishes when she sees that I'm not entirely happy with what just happened here.

'What's wrong?' she asks, confusion clouding her eyes. 'Wasn't that what you wanted from me?

'Not even close,' I reply, shaking my head and moving away from her.

I feel her gaze hot on me as I put my hands on the side of the pool and haul myself out of the water.

'What—what do you mean? I don't understand,' she stutters, sounding utterly bewildered.

'I'll see you later,' I say as I walk away, my muscles tight with frustration. 'Enjoy your swim.'

April

I stare after Jamie as he strides away from me, his powerful body tense with what seems to be anger.

I'm floored with shock.

What the hell just happened? I was giving him what he wanted: my acquiescence. At least, mostly. I'm aware I was keeping part of myself back in order to deal with the intensity of the situation, and perhaps he'd felt that resistance and hadn't liked it. He seems to want me completely under this thrall.

But I can't allow that. Not if I'm going to keep my sanity and presence of mind.

Feeling his mouth on me had been electric, though. I'd had to fight hard not to give in to the joy of it and beg him to make me come.

Oh God, even though I've only just had an orgasm my whole body is aching for more of his attention. I can still feel the ghost of his mouth between my legs, lapping me hard with his expert tongue in exactly the way he knows I like. He hasn't forgotten. Even after all these years he still knows how to make me crazy with pleasure.

But he seems intent on making me crazy in other ways too. He's torturing and tantalising me until I think I'm going to go mad. He's taking down my defences bit by bit.

He's trying to break me.

I stare in the direction in which he disappeared, my head spinning with tangled fears.

The worst thing about all this is that I'm afraid I might let him.

CHAPTER SEVEN

April

OKAY, NO MORE pussy-footing around, I decide as I take my second shower of the day.

I need him to know I'm not going to keep putting up with this inconsistent, harrying behaviour. I know he's doing it to put me off my game, to pay me back for the pain he thinks I put him through, but it's time to get this ridiculous charade over with now. It's time to get down to business.

In honour of this, I tame my hair into a neat chignon and put on the white trouser suit I arrived in to project a renewed statement of my position. I love this suit. It always gives me a lift of self-esteem and helps put a spring in my step, which is exactly what I need right now.

I stride downstairs and search the living area, the terrace and then the library, looking for Jamie, determined to confront him about the game he's playing and to find a way to resolve this situation once and for all.

A strange tension begins to build behind my eyes when it becomes obvious he's not in the house. Maybe he's back at the tennis courts or in his gym?

After checking both of these, and the pool too, I trudge back to the house feeling my previous chutzpah slipping away. He seems to have abandoned me here.

The thought that he's punishing me by leaving me alone with just my scrambled thoughts for company sends an arrow of fear through me.

Would he really do that?

Probably, I decide—in order to take control further out of my hands. He's reminding me that I'm on his turf and that he gets to decide how this plays out.

As I walk back towards the house I notice a movement on the terrace and my heart leaps when I realise it's Jamie. He appears to be laying out food and drinks for lunch.

So he hasn't abandoned me here after all.

Relief rushes through me, as does a twisted sense of exhilaration at the sight of him. He's changed too, into casual baggy khaki shorts and a white V-neck T-shirt. He looks good. Relaxed and at home.

I experience a rush of jealousy for the life he's made for himself here. God, I'd love to have an island to hide away on when life gets too much. Where I could turn off my raging brain and just *be*.

With him?

I stop dead in my tracks, aware of my fists bunching at my sides, my nails digging into my palms.

Where the hell had that thought come from? It's ridiculous to think we could get back what we had all those years ago. Too much has happened to allow for it. And I can't be with him, not properly, knowing what I do and deliberately keeping it from him. If he ever found out...

I shake the thought from my head. That's not going to happen. I told myself ten years ago to bury the truth—for everyone's sake.

'Are you hungry?' I hear Jamie shout. He's spotted me standing there staring at him as he lays the table for lunch.

I swallow hard and raise my hand in acknowledgement, then start walking towards the terrace.

He flashes me a smile and I drag in an involuntary breath as the beauty of it hits me full-force. The memory of his mouth on me, teasing and torturing me into a frenzy of desire, fills my head and I feel my legs wobble as blood rushes to my head and my pussy simultaneously.

Being in a constant state of arousal for the last couple of days has really messed with my mind. And my balance, it seems.

'It's gazpacho,' he says, waving towards the bowls of chilled soup and a big mound of soft rolls on the table as I step onto the terrace.

'Great,' I reply, keeping my expression blank and my mind on the challenge of not reacting to his allure in any way.

He's all relaxed again now, as if the scene in the pool never happened. Well, fine, I can act as if it didn't either.

I take a seat opposite him and pick up my spoon, annoyed to find my hand is shaking. I put the spoon down again and pick up a bread roll instead, tearing it apart to give my twitchy fingers something to do.

'I owe you an apology,' he says, startling me.

I look up to see him assessing me with that shrewd gaze of his.

'Oh?' I say blandly. I'm not going to give him the satisfaction of a response until I've heard what he has to say. This could just be another trick, a way to unnerve me further.

'I need to explain why I acted the way I did after we broke up.'

I blink at him, completely surprised by this. I was expecting an apology for him walking away from me like that in the pool, not about his behaviour ten years ago.

'Okay. I'm listening,' I say warily.

'Okay.' He blows out a long, low breath, as if readying himself to do this. He picks up his spoon and swirls it through the soup as if needing something practical to focus on while he speaks. 'When you finished with me so suddenly I felt like my whole world had fallen apart,' he begins.

He pauses and looks at me, as if checking this is a safe subject, so I nod, encouraging him to go on with his story, my heart thumping in my chest.

'I knew that your mother's sudden death had been a horrific shock, and that you'd need time alone with your family to get through that period, which is why I gave you the space you asked for at first.' He pauses again, his eyes filled with sadness. 'But I couldn't understand, when I came to you later to let you know I was there for you whenever you needed me, how you could just turn your back on what we had.' He grips his spoon harder, his knuckles turning white.

My stomach gives a swoop of regret as I see the pain he's remembering flicker in his eyes.

It had hurt me too, more than I'd ever let him know.

'I didn't understand what had gone wrong. What

I could have possibly done to cause that. It made me crazy. I felt so fucking *powerless*.'

He sighs and shakes his head. 'After what we'd shared, I really thought we were solid. That we cared for each other. Loved each other.' He looks directly into my eyes again and I have to steel myself not to react to this.

My chest feels like it's been trapped in a vice, and my heart aches with the emotional pain I'm experiencing, but I can't let him see that. I can't. I *can't*.

'But I guess I was wrong,' he carries on when I don't say anything, resting his spoon on the side of his bowl, apparently not hungry any more. 'I guess our lives were destined to go in very different directions from that point. But I couldn't accept it at first. I thought—naïvely, I now realise—that if you heard I'd been seeing other people it would make you jealous. That you'd decide you'd made a mistake and want me back. And when that didn't work I was so fucking frustrated I did the most stupid thing in the world.' He runs a hand over his creased brow. 'I started drinking heavily.'

There's a loaded pause while we both reflect on the implications of this.

'You remember my mother died from liver failure, right?' he says quietly.

I nod, not able to speak, my heart in my throat.

'So I'm sure you've put two and two together
by now and figured out that she was an alcoholic.
She couldn't control her urge to drink and keep on
drinking. I thought I was okay with alcohol, but it
turns out a traumatic event can turn me into someone I had no idea I was capable of being. Someone weak and needy. And when I started drinking
heavily I couldn't stop. I had no off-switch. There
are weeks from around that time that I have no
memory of. I know I behaved badly because my
friends were honest enough to tell me about it. And
I know that I told one of the women I was fucking
at the time—who it turned out had a real grudge
against you, for some reason—about you begging
me for anal sex.'

He's referring to a sex game we used to play
and at least has the decency to look thoroughly
ashamed at blabbing about this.

'Which I recognise was a terrible abuse of trust
and I know resulted in a lot of unkind gossip flying around about you,' he adds.

He holds up a hand and shakes his head, not
able to meet my eyes now. 'Shit, I'm so sorry about
that. It was unforgivable. But I was so angry with
you for rejecting me, and half-crazy with frustration and alcohol poisoning at the time, I did nothing to quash it. I guess in my addled, fucked up

state I told myself you deserved it for hurting me so badly.'

He picks up his spoon again and jabs it into the rich liquid in his bowl. 'So, yes, you're absolutely right about me being ego-driven and self-serving. And, of course, that's why I don't drink alcohol any more. I stopped before it ruined my tennis career and the rest of my life.'

He leans back in his chair and folds his arms, studying me with a steady, contemplative gaze. 'The shame I felt about it has dogged me for far too long now. It's been a really destructive force in my life and I don't want to carry it with me any more. I'm done with pandering to my resentment about what could have been with us. It's time to move on.'

The smile he gives me now is tinged with remorse.

'The truth is, I wanted you to stay here so I could prove to you, and to myself, that it's possible. That I've changed. That I'm over you and what we had. What happened at that charity fundraiser was a real wake-up call. I let my grief about losing my father get the better of me and lost my mind. I was still pretty raw then and probably shouldn't have gone that night. I definitely shouldn't have ripped your dress. And I shouldn't have fucked you like that, especially because I didn't even stop for one second to think about using a condom. That was irresponsible and really fucking stupid.'

He shoots me a look of apology, which morphs into concern. 'You're not pregnant, are you? I realise I never asked. I guess I thought you'd let me know if that was the case.'

I shake my head, his apology ringing in my ears. 'I'm not pregnant. I've been on the pill for years. And, just so you know, I did all the sensible tests they recommend after unprotected sex, so I know there are no other issues we need to deal with either.'

'Good to know,' he says with a relieved smile. 'And, in the spirit of sharing, I did them too and got the same results.'

I suddenly realise I've reduced my bread roll into crumbs as he's talked and I pick up my napkin and wipe my fingers to give myself a chance to look away from him for a second.

His confessions have knocked me for six and the tension that's slowly been mounting in my chest since this morning has grown and grown until my heart feels like it wants to explode.

The problem is, I've used his anger and cruelty towards me as a shield from my real feelings for him for so long—even though I've never allowed myself fully to admit it—and now I've finally heard an apology for the way he treated me

I don't know how to protect myself any more. It's as if he's peeled back a shell I've been relying on and now I'm raw and vulnerable to his charm. I'm reminded of my longing for what we used to have. A feeling that's never really gone away. It's bubbled there, under the surface, permeating my every thought, my every action.

He's like a dangerous drug. Addictive and sanity-threatening.

'So, come on, since I've been so honest with you, don't you think it's time you were honest with me too?' he says with a provocative smile, picking up his spoon again.

My chest gives a throb of panic. 'What do you mean?'

'I mean are you ever going to tell me why you really dumped me back then?'

I clear my throat, then clear it again, playing for time until his penetrating gaze becomes too much for me. 'I told you at the time why it wouldn't have worked between us long-term,' I say, my voice sharp with nerves. 'Our lives were going in different directions and I had to look after my father and sisters after my mother died. My father went completely to pieces. The whole family was in turmoil. I had nothing left for you. For us.'

He leans forward, his expression insistent now.

'I don't believe you. I think there was more to it than that.'

My heart thumps harder. Even though we're outdoors I suddenly feel trapped and claustrophobic, as though a cage has unexpectedly fallen down around me. 'You can believe what you want. You always did think you were right, no matter what,' I bite out. He knows I'm lying. I can sense it. I can see it in his eyes and it frightens me.

His gaze remains fixed on mine for what feels like eternity, neither of us saying a word, locked in a battle of wills with neither of us willing to lose. So much passes between us in that silence, so much pain, hurt and regret.

But I can't back down. I can't tell him what he wants to know. It would destroy the safety of the world I've built around me since that terrible time.

I jump as Jamie suddenly lets out a low growl of frustration and flings his spoon into his bowl of soup, where it makes a great splash, sending droplets of brightly coloured pureed vegetables flying through the air which land on the front of my white suit in a shower of splatters.

I stare down in horror at the mess he's made of me. My beautiful power suit. He's ruined it. Just as he ruined my dress. He seems determined to destroy every beautiful thing I own.

'Shit!' he says, springing up from his chair. Before I can say anything, he grabs a napkin and starts rubbing at the stains, smearing the bright-red soup further over my front and only making things worse.

I sit there, shaking my head in disbelief. Then I knock his hand away from my chest, stick my fingers into my own bowl of soup and take great pleasure in running them down his white T-shirt, marvelling at the elegantly swirled pattern I make.

He freezes and stares down at what I've done, one eyebrow raised.

'There you go, now we're even,' I say.

Without a word he leans over, picks up my bowl of soup and proceeds to pour it from a great height down into my lap. I give a shriek as the cold liquid trickles between my thighs.

'No, *now* we're even,' he says with relish.

'Right!' Jumping up from my chair, I make a grab for his bowl and manage to get my fingers onto the rim before he can reach over and stop me. I throw the soup towards him, managing to catch him a little on the face as well as all down his neck and chest.

'Fuck!' he shouts as soup drips from his chin and soaks into his clothes.

He's a mess too.

Such a mess.

Tension hovers in the air between us. At this

point it could go either way: tip towards anger or laughter. And we both know it needs to go somewhere.

I start to laugh. I can't help it. It comes from deep in my belly, radiating upward through my chest and out of my throat in great gusts. And, now I've started, I can't stop. It pours out of me, making me bend at the middle from the force of it, my whole body shaking, my eyes watering. I can barely breathe, and I know my face must be as red as the soup I'm covered in, but for once in my life I don't care.

Because he's laughing too.

This moment is perfect in its madness. And it's the ideal antidote to the tension humming between us.

Finally, my hysteria starts to subside and I straighten up, smoothing my hands down my soup-stained suit, suddenly not caring whether it's ruined. It was worth it just to feel like that again.

Happy, carefree and alive.

If only for a few minutes.

When I look at Jamie he's not laughing any more. Instead he's gazing at me with a puzzled but gratified sort of frown, as if he's seeing me again for the first time in a long time.

'There you are,' he whispers fiercely, reaching up to slide his hand against my jaw, his eyes dancing with delight. And something else—lust. Longing. 'I knew you were in there somewhere,' he murmurs before bringing his mouth down hard onto mine.

The last of my laughter dies in my throat as I open my mouth to kiss him back, my heart thundering against my ribs.

And this kiss feels different. It's no longer a quest for dominance or a battle of wills; it's a meeting of minds.

I know it's the most dangerous thing in the world at this point, but I can't bring myself to stop it. Because I want this so much. This connection. This elation I'm feeling.

The kiss goes on and on and we press ourselves closer, deeper, tighter, till I can feel the beat of his heart against my chest and the insistent press of his erection against my stomach.

And, oh, God, I ache to feel him moving inside me. It's all I can think about.

I'm suddenly aware of him stooping down a little and in one fluid movement he scoops me into his arms, his hands holding me firmly behind my knees, his other arm pressing me against his chest.

'Let's take this inside, shall we?' he says, though it's not a question; it's a statement of intent.

He strides through the open bi-fold doors and into the living room, where he drops me onto the large leather couch. I watch in rapt fascination while he strips the soup-stained clothes from his body until he's standing naked in front of me. His cock is hard and clearly very ready for action.

My whole body zings with a mixture of excitement and apprehension and blood rushes straight to my pussy, the pressure of my need making me crazy. I sit up and begin to strip off my own clothes as fast as I can, the movement of my fingers clumsy with eagerness.

I'm so afraid he's going to stop this at the crunch point, just to tease me, I can barely stand the tension. I think I'll go completely crazy if he does. I'll lose my goddamned mind.

But it doesn't seem as though that's his intention this time because as soon as I've stripped off the last of my clothes he lets out a growl of approval and grabs my hands to pull me off the sofa and down onto the rug with him. The moment I'm down on the floor he rolls on top of me, his arms braced on either side of my head, pinning me under him.

I'm his prisoner through and through.

'Tell me what you want,' he demands, moving down my body to kiss my neck, my breasts, my belly. I feel his lips hot on my skin, his tongue damp and insistent on my nipple, his teeth gently biting my shoulder, sending small currents of ecstasy all the way through me. But he doesn't touch the part of me that needs his attention the most. He's nowhere near sating the hot ache between my thighs.

'I want…inside me,' I say, my voice a whisper of desire.

'What's that?' he teases, moving his mouth over my ribcage, his breath leaving trails of burning sensation in its wake.

'I want something. Inside me…'

'What do you want? Say it. I need to hear you say it.'

I screw my eyes shut. 'You! Your cock! I want your cock inside me,' I moan. 'I need it. Please. Please. I need it.' I arch my body upward, hoping, praying, for contact. I shiver with relief as he moves up my body and lowers his hips so his erection presses firmly against my left leg. I wiggle my shoulders, trying to push my body higher up the rug to get the kind of contact I'm desperate for.

His knee nudges between my legs, signalling me to spread them wide so he can kneel between them, which I waste no time in doing.

He stares into my eyes for a moment, his pupils blown and dark with desire, before lowering his head and crushing his lips against mine. His tongue plunders my mouth, his kiss deep and forceful. I feel him rock to one side and then suddenly there's delicious pressure at the apex of my thighs as his cock finds my entrance, which is slick and ready with desire for him, and he pushes forward, opening me up to his gentle thrust, filling that aching gap between my legs.

Finally, finally!

His cock is hot and hard inside me and it feels so good, so *fucking good*, as he moves deeper, taking himself all the way to the hilt so our pelvises clash and my needy clit receives the contact it's longing for.

'Oh…' we both groan happily as our bodies lock together for one sweet moment of ultimate pressure, with him so deep inside me I feel absolutely complete. And then he begins to move, slowly drawing himself out then pushing back, making every nerve I have come alive with pleasure. He keeps his thrust gentle to begin with, but I can tell from the shake in his arms that he's having trouble holding himself back.

'Harder! I want it harder,' I demand, tipping my pelvis upward to meet his next thrust, encouraging him to do as I say.

'Fuck!' he groans, holding himself still inside me for one heart-stopping moment, then he seems to give in to the urge he's been so carefully controlling and begins to pound into me hard, as if he no longer has power over his desire and is allowing it to take him along for the ride.

This wonderful, brain-melting ride.

Our bodies crash together, over and over, until we find the perfect rhythm with his cock hitting a spot inside me that makes me shiver with pleasure, and his pelvis catches my clit with every thrust.

This is going to be fast. I know it. There's no time for changing of positions. But that's fine with me. This is exactly where I want to be right now. Beneath him, around him, moving with him in the kind of sync we've not been in for ten long years.

I hear his ragged breathing in my ear and I know he's close too, so close. And that knowledge pushes me over the edge and breaks into a sparkling tidal wave of ecstasy, the shocks of it crashing through my body and sending a roaring pleasure through my head.

I have no idea if I've made a sound—my hearing is too full of my own internal joy—but as it starts to subside I become aware of a low, frantic sound coming from Jamie's throat and he pounds into me a few more times, his body jerking above me, the sinews in his neck taut and his jaw clamped as he comes inside me.

In that one moment everything is absolutely perfect. Still. Calm. Serene.

And then out of nowhere hot tears suddenly press behind my eyes and a wave of emotion hits me hard. I'm crying, unable to hold back the persuasive release of tension. Hard, wracking sobs escape from my throat and fat tears run down my cheeks and into my ears.

'Hey, hey, it's okay,' Jamie says, a concerned frown creasing his perfect brow. 'Shh…' he soothes. He places feather-light kisses to my nose, lips and cheeks, using his tongue to smooth away the tears streaking my skin.

After another few minutes of this madness I'm finally able to get myself under control and I give him a wobbly smile.

'Sorry, I don't know why I'm crying. I think it's just the relief of finally getting that life-changing orgasm you've been promising me for far too long now,' I joke to cover my embarrassment.

He's still frowning at me, though I'm not sure it's with dismay. 'As long as you're crying with appreciation rather than disappointment.'

I can't help but smile at that, my tears finally drying on my cheeks. 'Definitely appreciation,' I whisper. *Definitely.*

'Well, that's okay, then,' he says, rolling off me then pulling me into his side and wrapping his arms around me. Holding me close.

I feel on the edge of a transformation, as if I'm

finally reaching the kind of freedom I've been longing for. For so, so long. But, like everything good, I know the feeling will be short-lived. He can't really be mine. This is only temporary. An illusion. A means to an end.

As soon as he's given me what I want I'll have to let him go again.

I tighten my arms around him and bury my face deeper into his chest, breathing in the reassuringly familiar scent of his skin, committing this moment to memory.

Because I'm not ready to let him go just yet.

Not yet.

CHAPTER EIGHT

Jamie

SHE'S STILL HOLDING back her secrets from me. I know she is. But right at this moment I can't bring myself to care.

I lie on the rug in my living room with her warm body pulled tightly against mine, feeling the slow and steady rhythm of her breath on my chest where she's buried her head against me. I can barely believe she's here, in my house, pressed securely to my body. A thing I'd never thought would happen again.

And I've proved I can make her come hard, just as I'd promised I would.

I'd been so caught up in the moment, so determined to get the reaction I wanted from her, it hadn't exactly been my most skilful performance. It had been more fast and furious than finessed—but that seemed to be what we both needed.

I don't feel bad about it, anyway. These last two days have been one long session of foreplay. And I know I was successful because she cried—something I'd never dreamed I'd see April do.

I'd been horrified at first, feeling a jab of guilt for pushing her towards such an extreme reaction, but then it occurred to me that maybe it was a good thing. She held her feelings so tightly to her, so hidden, maybe this was cathartic. A response to the relief she felt at finally being able to let go.

Sex—*good* sex—was therapeutic for her. And if that was the case I was more than happy to counsel her some more while she was here. Perhaps after a couple more days of stunning orgasms she'll find it easy to give in and tell me what I want to know.

My plan might work after all.

Perhaps then I'll have the peace I'm looking for.

It's funny, but I was surprised to find it had actually been a massive relief to apologise to her. To admit out loud that I'd made mistakes and that she'd been the victim of them. That it had been wrong for me to act like that—whether or not she'd hurt me first.

It was liberating finally to be free of that shame.

One huge step closer to throwing off the chains of my past.

She shifts against me.

'Are you okay there?' I ask.

I feel her nod. 'Yes, fine, but I could do with a few minutes out,' she says, pulling away from me, not meeting my eye as she rolls to one side and sits up, her back to me.

I want to reach out and stop her from leaving, disappointed that this new closeness should be interrupted when I was enjoying it so much, but I know that would be a bad idea. And, honestly, I could probably do with a few minutes to recover too.

Things have been pretty intense around here lately.

I watch her stand up—still so graceful and self-assured, even when she's completely naked—and walk out of the room, her once-neat hair falling down her back in messy tendrils.

God, she's sexy when she's messed up.

Even though I've come very recently my cock still hardens at the sight of it. It seems my body's not entirely satisfied with that one quick fuck and is hoping for more.

Much more.

And why shouldn't I indulge that impulse? It's clear that both of us were completely into what just happened. And this physical contact is bringing us closer, which will help my strategy to get her to trust me again so she'll talk.

I pull my stained shorts and T-shirt back on,

smiling at the memory of our sexual-tension-fuelled food fight—that had been a lot of fun—and pick up a crossword to do a couple of clues in an attempt to distract myself from the pressing quiet of the room now she's not in it.

After a few minutes, I throw the paper down and pick up a book I've been trying to read—unsuccessfully—since she's been here. Her presence seems to have fried my brain to the point where I can't concentrate on anything cerebral for long and I've ended up reading the same page over and over again.

But that's no good either.

I get up, book dangling from my fingers, and pace around the room, staring out of the windows towards the sea, waiting for her to come back.

But she doesn't.

It's been at least twenty minutes since she disappeared upstairs. Is she okay? Or is she regretting what happened now? Perhaps she's embarrassed about crying in front of me. Showing me weakness. Something she's been so careful not to do for so many years now.

I throw the book back onto the coffee table. *The hell with this.* I can't hang around here while she's up there alone, pulling that hard shell around her again when I've only just cracked it open. I've worked too hard to get her finally to relax around me to let this opportunity get away from me now.

I make my way upstairs, my mind racing and my body buzzing with a strange kind of nervy energy. What the hell's making me feel like that? Is it the worry that I've not capitalised on the progress I've just made and that it might all slip through my fingers from here? We've just concluded the agreement I proposed, after all, so she might just try to pin me to it and demand I sign the documents she's bound to have brought with her, in true April style.

I can't let that happen, though. I need to distract her. Or make up a new condition.

My heart lurches as I climb the last couple of steps and turn towards the door to the room she's staying in. To my relief I see it open as I approach and she steps onto the landing and pulls the door closed behind her.

So she was coming back after all.

Relief trickles through me, but a surge of desire quickly takes its place as she turns and spots me, giving me a wide, friendly smile, as if she's pleased to see me.

She's changed into a pale-green strapless sundress that stops mid-thigh and showcases her incredible legs. Her hair has been tamed into a neat bun at the base of her neck. She's put her armour back on, I realise. Exactly what I'd feared she'd do.

I need to get her out of it again as soon as possible.

Striding towards her, I tilt my head in a gesture of concern. 'Is everything okay? I was worried about you.'

Her smile widens. 'You were worried about me?' She seems genuinely touched by this notion.

I push away a wave of unease. That's how I wanted her to react, so why do I feel so uncomfortable about it? Is it because it makes me happy actually to hear it?

No. I can't let myself fall down that rabbit hole. This thing between us can't go anywhere after this. I know how ruthless and self-centred she's capable of being and I don't want to put myself in a position where I might have to deal with that again. This is a short-term thing only.

Seeming to read my racing thoughts, she takes a step towards me and cocks a questioning eyebrow.

'Are *you* okay?'

'Yes, I'm great,' I say in a casual tone. I can't let her think for a second that this is unnerving me in any way.

'So are you satisfied that you can make me come now?' she murmurs with a wry smile.

'*Fairly* satisfied,' I say, deadpan.

She raises her eyebrows. 'Was I not convincing?' She seems to be genuinely concerned about this. But then this is a woman who hates to be thought of as anything but exceptional in everything she does.

'*Pretty* convincing,' I reply, in an equable tone. 'But I'm the type of person who likes to do a comprehensive evaluation of something before I'm satisfied that I've done it to the best of my ability. To make sure the first time wasn't a fluke.'

Reaching out, I run my fingertips lightly over her collarbone to the hollow of her neck, seeing her shiver as I caress her soft skin there.

Her breath catches in her throat as I move my hand lower to skate over the swell of her left breast, where her hardened nipple is pushing into the soft material of her dress, giving her own interest away. I play my fingertips over that tight little nub, seeing her chest rise and fall with her accelerated breathing before moving my hand lower, down over her stomach to the hem of her dress. Sliding the dress up her legs, I slip my hand into her underwear, and she leans back against the wall behind her and widens her stance so I can glide my fingers over her mons and dip a fingertip into the hot, wet heat of her pussy.

'Are you changing the terms of the deal on me?' she whispers, but I can tell from the catch in her breath and the way she rocks her hips back and forth, pushing my finger deeper inside her, that she's not totally averse to the idea of extending the terms of our agreement. She moves against my touch like this for a few seconds, her breathing deepening and the movement of her hips becoming more pronounced.

'I don't remember stipulating that it only had to happen once,' I murmur, flashing her a provocative grin.

Her eyebrows shoot up. 'So what are your new terms?'

'Similar to before. You stay for two more days and I'll see how many times I can make you come in that time frame.'

Her eyes widen.

'That's a bold proposal.'

'I have confidence in my abilities,' I say, pressing my thumb against her clit and smiling as she draws in a sharp intake of breath. A low moan resonates in her throat as I draw tight circles around the sensitive little bud.

Her legs start to shake and I become aware that this isn't the best place to conduct our next adventure.

I pull my hand out of her underwear and she looks at me like she wants to kill me.

'Please don't start that torturing shit again!' she

hisses, sounding thoroughly pissed off about the interruption.

It makes me pity the poor fools that work for her.

'Don't worry, it's just a short interlude while we change locations,' I tell her.

Before she can protest, I scoop her up into my arms and march us into my bedroom on the other side of the landing, kicking the door shut behind me before I deposit her on my bed.

'Take your clothes off,' I tell her, pulling my T-shirt over my head and moving straight onto my shorts. By the time I'm buck-naked on the bed, she's removed all her own clothes and is stretched out on the mattress, looking at me with those intelligent, discerning eyes, just daring me to take this further.

I take a moment to gaze at her, soaking in every detail of her gorgeous body, every curve, every dip, every smooth plane, and I consciously have to shake myself out of the erotic trance I've put myself into imagining all the things I want to do to her. Letting out a growl of appreciation, I start to kiss every bit of the body I've just inspected so thoroughly until she's moaning softly and writhing with pleasure under the pressure of my mouth.

I straddle her, then use my knee to push her thighs apart so she's forced to spread her legs for me. Then, reaching under the bed, I bring out a box of toys I'd ordered especially for her visit here, just in case. I'm actually pretty delighted that I'm getting the chance to use them.

I pluck out a small silver tub the size of my palm and screw off the lid.

She tilts her chin to look down at what I'm doing. 'What the hell is that?' she asks with a tremor in her voice—but it's one of keen interest.

'Just something to heighten sensations,' I say cryptically.

Her eyebrows twitch, but she doesn't question me further. It seems she's prepared to trust that she'll like whatever it is I'm going to do to her. And she will. I'm confident of it.

Rubbing my finger over the smooth, oily substance, I make sure I've got a good amount on my fingertip before applying it to both of her nipples, spreading it thinly over the areoles and then the peaks, which are pointing upwards with wanton attentiveness.

It takes a moment or two for her to feel it, but when she does she draws in a short, ragged gasp.

'Oh! Oh!' she breathes, her mouth forming a wide, appreciative smile. 'That feels cold. And tingly.'

'That's the menthol doing it's work,' I say with a grin, then I bend forward so my mouth is only inches away from her left nipple and gently blow a cool breeze over it.

'Ngh!' The sound she makes is like an aphrodisiac to my brain.

I move to the other nipple and give it the same treatment, and I'm rewarded with the same show of pleasure.

Then I breathe hot air over her breasts instead to alter the sensation.

'Oh, my God, God, God!' she moans.

'Are you ready for it on your clit?' I ask, lacing my voice with dark intent.

'Wait—what?' she says, lifting her head from the bed and starting to move, as if she's not sure she likes the idea of that.

'Trust me,' I say, putting a hand on her belly and gently pushing her back down. 'You're going to love it.'

She looks at me as if she's not entirely sure she wants to trust me, but I keep my expression fixed in a look of absolute self-assurance and she finally submits and flops back down onto the bed.

After slathering some more of the oily balm onto my finger—taking my time doing it, to tease her some more with the anticipation of waiting for it—I carefully put the pot onto the bedside table before returning to kneel next to her on the bed.

'Spread your legs wider,' I order her.

She does as I ask and I see that she's trembling a little now.

But this is going to feel so good. And I know for a fact she's going to love what I'm going to do to her next.

Her fingers grip the sheet on either side of her as I lean forward and gently part her folds to expose the neat nub of her clitoris to my gaze, then I stroke her there with my loaded finger, once, twice, three times.

Again, it takes a moment for the sensation to hit, but when it does she gives me the same beautiful reaction as before.

I bend my head and blow on her there, hot, then cold, then hot.

Small gasps of air are escaping from her throat as I continue to tease her like this for a few minutes, changing the sensation over and over again until I sense she's going a little crazy from it.

'Jamie, I need—I need—'

Clearly she doesn't quite know what she needs, but that's okay, because I do.

I move away from her and reach into the box again, extracting a beautifully made clear glass dildo from it, which has ridges along the shaft, each one spaced an inch apart. It's a thing of beauty and feels perfectly weighted in my hand. It's heavy, solid and substantial. A sex toy of kings.

A tube of lube is the next thing to appear from the box.

She raises her head and watches me with rapt fascination as I smooth lube over the head of the dildo.

'Where are you going to put that?' she asks breathily.

'One of two possible places,' I say with a wry lift of my eyebrow as I move it between her legs, running the cool, smooth head over her clit and then down through her folds—taking my time so she can appreciate the quality of my tools—to the bridge of smooth skin between her vagina and asshole, where I gently press it into her with tantalising intent.

'You really would have that reputed stick up your ass if I put it in here,' I joke as I move it fractionally closer to her tightly puckered hole.

She wriggles her hips a little, as if trying to get me to move it lower. Daring me to go through with my threat.

'But maybe not just yet,' I say. 'Maybe I'll put something better in there later.' I can tell from the flash of interest in her eyes that she likes that idea. She always did like anal play, as I so childishly let slip all those years ago. That hadn't been a lie. But that's what had been so awful about it. I'd let loose her most private desires.

I push the thud of guilt away. I've apologised for that now. And she seems to have accepted my apology. I'll just make sure to give her as much pleasure as I can right now to distract her from the memory of that mistake.

Moving the dildo back up to the slick entrance of her vagina, I play with it there, pushing it forward a little so she starts to open up and take the rounded glass head inside her.

Her stuttering inhalation of breath makes me smile.

I push it deeper, then deeper still, fascinated as I watch the ridges disappear one by one inside her.

'How does that feel?' I ask, fascinated by the way her body twitches and writhes with pleasure as I increase the pressure.

'So good. It feels like I'm being penetrated over and over again as it goes in,' she answers in a husky voice. I can tell from the flush on her cheeks that she's thoroughly enjoying this.

I lean towards her again and blow on her clit as I continue to move the dildo in and out of her, picking up the pace a little as I see her stomach begin to tense. She's close to orgasm already, I can tell.

'Oh fuck, Jamie, yes. That feels so good. Don't stop!' she pants, her eyes screwed tightly shut.

And I love the sound of my name on her lips.

Love it.

Barely a moment later, she bucks and twists her hips, her hands screwing the sheet into balls at her sides and lets out a long, low scream of pleasure, completely lost to the orgasm I'm giving her.

Because that's exactly what's happening here. I'm giving this to her. I'm totally in control of her pleasure.

And I really fucking like that.

It takes a few moments for her to come round from her private world of gratification, but when she finally opens her eyes I can see her mind has been blown.

'Wow…' She groans. 'That was intense.'

I can't stop the smile that's pulling at my mouth.

I gently draw the dildo out of her and discard it onto the floor beside the bed.

'I feel like I should return the favour,' she says, propping herself up on her elbows, a seductive, hazy look in her eyes. 'I hate to think this was all going to be one-sided. It's not my style to be selfish in bed.'

My body heats with interest, my already hard cock bobbing against my stomach as I think about all the things she could do to pay me back. One thing in particular springs to mind. But before I can even voice it she rolls onto her side then gets onto her knees and crawls towards me, lowering her head in readiness to take my cock into her mouth. And it's as though my ultimate fantasy has come true—the one I'd thought about in the sea. She pokes out her tongue and flicks the end of my cock with it, sending shivers of electric sensation through me.

'Kneel up,' she tells me, looking up at me with those beautiful, determined eyes.

I do as she says without a murmur and am immediately rewarded as she takes my dick into her hot, wet mouth, sliding me deep into her throat.

She looks up at me, her expression heated and totally trusting.

And, oh fuck, I'm lost.

April

Now we've started having sex, we don't seem to be able to stop.

It's bizarre, but I feel as if I've been given a shot of some kind of lust drug so that the moment he leaves the room all I can think about is him coming back so I can have him inside me again.

Giving myself over to Jamie was terrifying at first, but then totally exhilarating. Letting him take the lead—something I've not allowed any of my sexual partners to do in the last decade—seemed perfectly right.

He's the first and only man ever to break my tightly held control.

I've never wanted anyone like this before, not even Jamie when we were together. Perhaps it's the knowledge that we have finite time together that's driving it. Whatever it is, it's making me think about sex in a whole new way. And I've decided, to hell with it. I'm just going to go with it for now. It's not as if I don't deserve to have some fun. The last ten years have been spent doing the right thing and, while I'm here on Jamie's secluded private island away from real life, I've decided I'm going to do the wrong thing.

Just this once.

I'm going to be the woman I can't be anywhere else.

So we have sex. A lot of it. For the rest of the day and most of the night.

In the morning I wake up to find him lying next to me, having fallen asleep after our sex marathon, finally sated and exhausted. But somehow I still seem to be able to find the energy to have his cock inside me again as soon as he wakes up and rolls over, discovering me there next to him.

I beg a little time on my own after that, needing it in order to get my head together and do some kind of exercise that doesn't involve my vagina.

Normally, I go to the gym for an hour every

day before work and do yoga for half an hour in the evenings, but just a short blast in Jamie's gym is sufficient to satisfy my exercise needs today.

Funnily enough, I've found it easier than I thought I would to refrain from checking my phone for news of work all the time. It seems the sky hasn't fallen in without me, which is heartening. It makes me determined to take more holiday in the future than I've allowed myself in recent years.

Later he finds me in the library, curled up on his red leather Chesterfield sofa, reading a science fiction novel that had caught my interest.

He brings me a glass of champagne to drink and puts it onto the small side table next to where I'm sitting.

'Thanks,' I say. It gives me a warm sort of feeling in my chest to have him looking after me like this.

'I didn't have you pinned as a sci-fi nerd,' he teases, sitting down next to me and checking out the front cover of the book. 'I thought you preferred romance novels.'

'There are lots of things you don't know about me,' I point out with a wry smile. 'Ten years is a long time.'

I pick up my drink as a distraction from the tense atmosphere I've created with that comment and take a sip. The bubbles go up my nose, causing me to cough and the glass to tip a little in my hand, spilling champagne down the front of my sundress.

'You don't seem to be able to keep your clothes clean at the moment,' he says with a wry grin.

'Yes, well, normally I'm absolutely pristine and totally in control of my appearance, but it seems whenever you're around I can't help but make a mess of myself.'

'I like seeing you all messed up,' he says, his voice deepening to a sexy drawl. 'It's hot.' His eyes darken with desire and my pussy gives an immediate throb in response.

This gives me an idea. One I think he'll like.

Lifting the flute above my head, I tilt my face upward and open my mouth. Then, with a wink towards him, I tip the glass so the fizzing liquid pours over the rim and cascades down towards my mouth, some of it hitting its target but most not, so that the whole front of my dress is soaked with bubbling alcohol.

I give a small, delicious shiver as I feel it run down between my breasts and soak into the front of my knickers.

'I can't believe you just did that,' Jamie growls, then gets up from the sofa and kneels in front of me, between my legs, putting his hands on my waist and sliding me closer to him so he can run his tongue first over my lips, then down my chin to my throat. He laps at my damp skin, moving downward with every lick until he's deep into my cleavage.

I can't help but laugh with delight at the reaction I've drawn from him.

'This is the only way I ever want to taste alcohol again,' he mutters against my breasts.

I freeze as the stupidity of what I've done suddenly occurs to me. I put a hand on each side of his head and pull his head away from my breasts, forcing him to look up at me. We stare into each other's eyes for a moment, both aware of my unsaid apology in the air but neither of us wanting to tackle that subject right now and kill the mood. To his credit he doesn't pick me up on my lack of tact and reaches up to place a hot, searching kiss on my mouth.

My heart throbs hard with a new, warm affection for him. And I'm suddenly nervous, jittery— afraid of the feeling that's rising in me like a tide about to break.

I need to refocus my thoughts. Sex them back up. That's what I'm here for, after all: pure carnal satisfaction.

I pull away from him and glance down.

'Oh dear, I seem to have made a mess of your lovely sofa too,' I say with unconvincing remorse.

'Yes,' he says, surveying the spatters of alcohol on the leather seat. 'Let me show you what happens to women who make a mess of my things.'

Grabbing me behind the knees, he pulls me off the sofa and manhandles me round so I'm now kneeling in front of it with my back to him. He tugs up the hem of my dress and yanks my knickers down to my knees, exposing my buttocks to his greedy gaze. Then he puts the flat of his hand onto my back and pushes me down so I'm forced to press my chest onto the sofa seat.

I'm now bent at the waist with my ass in the air, obediently waiting for him to do what he will to me.

And I love it.

My pussy is already puffy and slick with need and I feel my juices run down my legs as I wait, my breath coming fast and my whole body trembling with anticipation.

There's a resounding silence in the room before he brings the flat of his hand down sharply onto my left buttock, leaving a delicious sting in its wake.

I let out a groan of pleasure and ready myself for the next contact. It comes quickly, again and again as he slaps my ass hard, sending a rush of blood to my skin there and making my pussy throb with an overwhelming desire to be filled.

He moves on to the other buttock, giving it the same treatment, causing endorphins to rush through my system, taking me into a world of beautiful, edgy pleasure.

And then it stops.

I wait, my heart in my mouth and my buttocks burning deliciously, to see what he'll do next.

'I think you're enjoying your punishment a little too much,' he teases, and I shiver with pleasure as he skates his fingers up the inside of my thighs to my pussy, which hums with anticipation for his touch. He doesn't make me wait for this, though, and I feel one of his long, thick fingers penetrate me, pushing in a knuckle-length at a time until it's buried as deep as it can go. Then he adds another finger. He plays them both there, widening them to open me up, then sliding back and forth, setting my nerve endings on fire.

And it feels so *good*.

I pull in a startled breath as he suddenly pulls his fingers out of my pussy and slides them straight up to my asshole, using the slick, silky moisture of my desire to ease his path. He plays around a little there, teasing me, sending raptures of joy through my body as he presses around the tightly puckered hole. Then he slowly slides one finger inside me.

I suck in a ragged breath, the illicit sensation of his rude invasion driving me a little wild.

He adds a second finger and an eager moan rumbles out of me. I love this. I've always loved it. And he knows that only too well.

He uses these two fingers to stretch me out, moving slowly in and out of the tight channel until I stop resisting. Then he pulls them out and a second later I feel his cock pressing against the entrance to my pussy. Without a word, he slides his cock deep inside me, then begins to pound into me, his breathing quickening in sync with my own.

But it seems that's not the focus of his end game and he pulls out of me after a few strokes and slides the head of his cock up to my ass.

I let out another moan of excitement as he draws more delicious thrills of sensation from the sensitive bundle of nerves there, sliding himself over and over me till I think I'm going to die with want.

'You ready for this?' he murmurs.

'Yes, yes, do it!' I groan, not caring about anything except the thrill of finally experiencing something so thoroughly indecent and tawdry. So unladylike. So contrary to the civilised, controlled veneer I have to project in my day-to-day life.

It's such a turn-on for me and I ache for it.

My slickness is still coating his shaft so he slides into me fairly easily, opening me up to his intrusion, though he takes it slowly, giving me time to adjust to his substantial girth. His path burns through me, but it's a good pain, one I'm enjoying more than I can express in words.

It's so filthy. Lewd. Illicit.

To me it's the ultimate carnal act. There's something about the vulgarity of it that really turns me on. It's rude, crude and dirty, and I love it. Love giving myself over to it.

Once he's as deep inside me as he can go, he holds himself there for a moment, seeming to enjoy the power he has over me and my needs, before drawing slowly out of me again, making me shiver with delight before pushing back into me again.

I no longer have control over the guttural groans of pleasure coming from deep in my throat as he works my ass, sending dizzying quivers of elation racing through my entire body.

A wave of emotion rushes through me as he continues to take what he wants from me and I suddenly feel the need to ground myself before I totally lose control.

'Want to know a secret?' I whisper.

He stills his movements and his fingers dig into my hips, his body pressed hard against mine, as if it's taking all his willpower not to keep moving and listen to what I have to say.

'Yes,' he says in a low, fervent tone. 'I do.'

'I've only ever done this with you,' I murmur, my voice guttural and saturated with pleasure. I want him to know that I'm putting my faith in him with this. That I trust he won't let me down by spilling my secrets again.

He leans down and kisses me between my shoulder blades, his breath hot on my back. 'That makes me very happy,' he murmurs against my skin before resuming the exhilarating sensation of his thrusts inside me, taking me to the edge of ecstasy over and over again until I can't stand it any longer and have to move my hand down between my legs to stroke my finger over and over my clit for release from it.

I come hard, seeing stars and patterns in front of my eyes, my world a kaleidoscope of colour. It's the most breathtakingly fierce orgasm I've ever had and a low, animalistic sound resonates from deep in my lungs, rudely breaking the heavy tranquillity of the air around us.

This seems to arouse Jamie even more and through my haze of pleasure I feel him pound into me harder and faster until he lets out his own low, angry-sounding growl and finally shudders to a halt, his cock buried deep inside me.

'Fuck. That was incredible,' he says after a few moments when neither of us seem able to speak or move.

He slides his hands under my body and wraps his arms around my waist, pinning me there under him, as if he's claiming me for his own. As if I'm not allowed to leave until he says so.

My heart leaps with happiness at the sensation of feeling so wanted, so cherished, so coveted.

I really believe now that he's truly sorry for what he did to me, and for the way he's behaved ever since. For all the pain he's caused me.

As I lie there under him, enjoying the feeling of being trapped by his powerful body, I wonder whether he was right about this being a way for us to make things right between us. Something that's been impossible during our brief, angry clashes in London, where we've circled around each other like angry dogs snapping and spoiling for a fight.

The simple, serene atmosphere on the island has done my state of mind so much good.

Positivity rises through my body, riding a wave of optimism. Does this mean we could get to a point where the two of us could be close again? Where we could actually consider being together? Once my father hands over the business to me, I'll finally be free of his tyranny. I'll be the one in charge, both of the company and my life.

It's time for me to break away from the life I thought I wanted in London and start living it the way I always wanted to when I was younger.

With Jamie by my side?

Perhaps.

If he feels the same way I do.

Which I think he might.

It certainly feels possible right now with him pressed to me, his arms encircling me as though he never wants to let me go.

But then I've been wrong about him before, I remind myself.

I can only hope that this time my instincts are sound.

CHAPTER NINE

Jamie

AFTERWARDS WE TAKE a bath together.

She sits between my legs, her back to my chest with my arms wrapped around her.

It feels right, our bodies melded together so perfectly.

The intensity of our fucking over the last couple of days has both surprised and fascinated me. I had no idea I could reach the highs I have with her. No idea I could reach a state where my body physically aches for hers to be pressed against, beside or around me.

Her total trust in me, downstairs in my library just now, pretty much blew my mind.

I still feel a bit unnerved by it, to tell the truth.

The way she looked at me after I said that stupid thing about only wanting to taste alcohol when it was on her skin had shaken me at the time. Because I realised it was too romantic a thing to say. Too personal and weighted with feeling. Which is why I'd flipped the mood into one of me dominating her instead. I'd wanted to show her I was still in charge of my feelings.

But then that had got away from me too when she told me that that filthy, intimate act was all mine—that most personal sacrifice of her body. All mine. And I realised she was totally giving herself to me. Trusting me.

In those profound, emotionally raw moments it seemed as if she was only just stopping short of saying *I love you*.

This should have delighted me—persuading her to fall for my charms had been my aim in getting her here, after all—but it didn't. It scared me. Because of what it might mean.

And now, lying here in the water with her, I'm intensely aware of the pressure of time ticking away.

Tomorrow is our last day together and then our deal is complete.

I still need to ask her the questions that I've been avoiding touching on until I'm satisfied she trusts me enough to answer honestly. But I find now that I'm not so sure I want to know. Or if I want to act on the information any more, whatever it turns out to be. Whatever April's father did, it doesn't matter so much to me any more. Though perhaps I should have it, just so I can mentally put the past to rest.

What matters is that we've both been given a chance to move on. To wherever that might be.

But I don't want to ask her about it right now. I can't bring myself to ruin this feeling of peace I have inside me.

So it'll be tomorrow, then.

Tomorrow I'll get out of her what my father wanted me to know.

'Tell me about your life now,' I say to her as I run my fingers over her wet, soapy skin—from the magnificent swell of her breasts to the gentle jut of her hip bones. I suddenly can't imagine not being able to touch this body again.

'It's mostly work, work, work,' she murmurs. 'The job I do is usually so intense, there's not a lot of time for fun.'

'I'm sorry to hear that,' I mutter against her hair, breathing in the fresh, intoxicating scent of her, committing it to memory.

'You know, I haven't had a proper holiday for about five years, so my time here has actually been very welcome.'

'I'm glad it hasn't been an entirely horrific experience,' I say with a wry lilt to my voice.

She turns her head to look up at me, her expression filled with warmth.

It's so beautiful.

She's so beautiful.

'Barely horrific at all. Apart from the terrible, tormenting pleasure I've had to put up with from you,' she says with a frowning sort of grin. But I can tell she's not really angry about that. If anything, she's enjoyed it more than she ever thought she would. Because she likes to be challenged and have her boundaries pushed—something no other men have been brave enough to try, I'm pretty damn sure.

I smile and bend down towards her, kissing her soft mouth, loving the unique taste of her.

But *I* am. I'm brave enough.

Because I understand her. I know what she needs better than anyone else on the planet and I love seeing her reaction when I give it to her.

I *love* it.

April

I wake up the next day with Jamie lying in bed next to me, his arm slung protectively round my waist.

I feel him stir as I shift a little against him.

'Morning,' he murmurs into my hair.

My skin rushes with goose bumps as I feel his hand begin to caress my stomach then move up to graze my breasts, his fingertips playing with my instantly erect nipples.

I'm not sure how he's done it, but he's turned my body into an instrument of sexual pleasure and I can't get enough of him playing with me.

I slowly turn to face him, smiling at his sleep-worn face. He's such a handsome man, and the memory of his dreams still in his eyes and his jaw rough with stubble takes away none of his appeal.

I could gaze at his face for ever.

As if sensing my thoughts, he reaches up to stroke his fingers over my cheek and down to my lips, where he plays with his fingertip for a moment, leaving a delicious shimmer of sensation in the trail of his touch.

Without a word he rolls on top of me, not breaking eye contact for a second, and slides his thighs between mine, opening me up to the demands of his body. I let him, feeling my pussy pulse with the urgent need to have him inside me again, as if it's been an age since he was last there. He's already hard and after a small adjustment he pushes his cock deep inside me, his eyes locking with mine, his mouth hovering above my lips as I draw in a deep, satisfied gasp.

We move together, our bodies and minds as fused as they could ever be, our gazes never leaving the other's.

It's such a blissfully complete connection, where our bodies are speaking to each other without us needing to utter a word. We thrust and grind ourselves together, needing it faster and harder as we get closer to our goal of mutual pleasure.

And still we don't look away.

It's so intensely intimate, staring into his eyes like this as he brings me to climax, that I experience what I can only describe as a brain orgasm. It rushes through my head, then down, deep through my body, taking my breath away.

He comes a moment after I do, finally screwing his eyes shut as he shudders above me, lost in his own climax of ecstasy.

'Oh fuck, that was intense,' he murmurs after a moment of calm, his body still pressed into mine. He leans back and smiles into my eyes and I can't help but smile back. It's like an instinct I can't fight any more.

This is such a perfect moment, I can't bear to think it might be the last one I ever have with him.

'I've really enjoyed being here with you. It's been wonderful to have a break from real life,' I say, though I have to force it through a throat that's uncomfortably constricted.

'All those responsibilities seem miles away right now, huh?'

'They do,' I say with a pained sigh. 'But I guess it's time to get back to them now.'

I rub my eyes, feeling the weight of my life back in England begin to press in on me.

If only I could stay here for ever…

'Tell me something,' he says, propping himself up on one elbow and supporting his head with his hand while he gazes down at me, his eyes searching mine as if he's looking for more of my deepest desires in them.

'Hmm?'

'What was it about your mother's death that meant it had to be *you* to hold your family together? Why did your father go to pieces like he did?'

I stiffen, my heart suddenly racing a mile a minute, and I swallow hard as my throat tightens in panic. I wasn't expecting that question right now and I feel blindsided by it.

'He was in shock for a long time. A loss like that can affect people in very different ways,' I bluster, but I can tell from the look in his eye that he knows I'm lying.

Suddenly I'm too hot, my skin is burning and lungs no longer seem to be able to take in as much air as they need. I try to shuffle out from under him so I can breathe again.

He resists me, but only for a moment, before letting me go.

I slide out from under him and sit up, but the edgy heat doesn't recede.

'Was he more involved in what happened to her than he's ever admitted?' Jamie says, sitting up too.

'What do you mean?' I ask, trying to keep my voice breezy, as if I genuinely have no clue what he's talking about, as I get out of bed and reach for my underwear, pulling it on with fumbling fingers.

'I mean, I get that it was a terrible shock to lose her so suddenly, but was there more to her accident than was made common knowledge? What made your father shut down like he did? It seems odd for a man like Maxim, someone who's so emotionally cold and always in control of everything he does, to react in that way.'

'What are you trying to imply?' I'm shaken, unnerved. There's a new, cunning look in his eyes that I've not seen before. I'm sure I'm not imagining it. And it's scaring the hell out of me.

'I think there's more to the story. And I think you know what it is. But you've kept it from everyone. What are you protecting your father from? Jail time? Or social condemnation?'

'I don't know what you're talking about,' I say, but there's a giveaway tremble in my voice.

I feel trapped now, panicky. What the hell is going on here?

Jamie seems to sense my anxiety because he gets up from the bed and comes towards me, taking my face between his hands and looking into my eyes, his gaze steady and determined.

'Tell me what really happened to your mother.'

'I can't.' I shake my head loose from his hold and turn away from him to grab my dress, which I pull over my head with trembling hands.

'I know there was more to it,' he says forcefully behind me.

I spin round to look at him. 'How do you know?' I demand. He can't know. Who would have told him? Only three of us know what really happened and I know for damn sure my father would never have said anything to anyone.

'My father sent me a posthumous letter alluding to the fact there was more to the story and that *you* know about it.'

So Cliff had finally decided to let Jamie in on the dark, shameful secret we'd all been carrying around for the last decade but he hadn't told him himself—oh, no—he was leaving it up to me. The selfish *bastard*.

'I need to know what it is, April, so I can put him to rest. Your father is a cold, callous bastard. We both know it. So stop trying to protect him.'

A pulse beats hard in my throat and my whole body rushes with unwelcome, prickly heat, as if I'm being stabbed all over with pins.

I can't tell him, though. I can't do it.

I've spent ten long years burying my memories of that horrific day. I don't think I'm capable of facing them again right now. Not when I'm feeling so vulnerable here with him, on his territory.

'You don't want to know, Jamie. Trust me,' I bluster.

'Trust you? How the hell am I supposed to do that?' He's angry now that I'm still resisting him, refusing to give him what he wants. 'You've been lying to me for ten years! I want to hear the truth, April. You owe me that much. I know my father was involved in some way and I want to know how. Stop being such a fucking coward and tell me.' His face is a mask of frustration. 'Tell me!'

I can tell from the determined look in his eye that he's not going to leave this alone. He's going to hound me for the rest of my life until I tell him what he wants to know.

I feel sick at the thought.

It's suddenly clear to me that he's brought me here to his island on false pretences to seduce me into telling him what he wants to know. It's all been a game, a performance, in order to get what he wants from me. To trick me into trusting him so I'll give away my secrets.

And I fell for it.

How could he do that to me after what we've shared here? It felt so special, so real. But it wasn't. It was all just a lie.

Anger surges through me.

'Is this what this seduction has been about? You're trying to get some damning information about my father out of me so you can destroy him?'

He has the good grace to look a little shame-faced. 'Maybe at first. And why not? He had no problem destroying my father. And our relationship.' He shakes his head. 'I can't believe you're still defending him after all this time. After everything he made you do.'

'He didn't make me!' I shout, my control snapping. 'He begged me not to see you any more. He couldn't stand the thought of it after what *your* father did!'

There's a ringing silence in the air after I shout this when we stare at each other in shock.

'What are you talking about? What did my father do?' Jamie asks quietly, his voice dangerously low and incredulous, as if he thinks I'm lying.

I suck in a breath, attempting to centre myself. Okay, then. I guess it's out now. If he really has to know the sordid details, I'll tell him. If it's so important to hear the truth, no matter what it costs him. No matter how much it's going to hurt him to hear it.

I'm through protecting him from it.

'If you really want to know, it was your father's fault that my mother died,' I say in a shaky voice.

His face pales and he shakes his head, his brow furrowed in angry confusion. 'What? No. Don't be ridiculous. How could it have been?'

I draw in a shuddery breath, feeling it catch painfully in my throat. 'They were having an affair, Jamie. Your father and my mother.'

There's an agonising silence in the air that throbs with tension.

'What makes you think that?' Jamie asks eventually, though I can tell he's having trouble accepting such a preposterous suggestion.

I walk back over to the bed and slump down onto it, forcing myself to look at him so he'll know I'm telling him the truth.

'Your father was at the hospital with her when my father and I arrived after her accident,' I say. 'He was sitting outside her room in a terrible state. He was drunk and distraught. He admitted to us that he'd found her passed out in her hotel room. He'd gone there to apologise for a row they'd had the day before. Because he and my mother had been lovers for years, even before we were born.

They were supposed to be going on that skiing holiday together. My mother's friend was going to cover for them—the one my father made go to France to pick up Maya and tell her that her mother was dead as punishment.'

I twist my fingers together in an attempt to stop my hands from shaking. It's so unbelievably hard for me to talk about this after burying it so deep for so many years, but I know now I've started I have to get it all out.

'Maya had messed up their plan to be together by getting expelled so my mother felt forced to take her instead,' I explain. 'Your father had been angry about this—that she was putting her selfish teenaged daughter's needs before his—and he'd followed her there. She'd told him to go home and they'd had a terrible row.' I take a breath, steeling myself to continue, even though my chest feels as if it's folding in on itself.

'He'd been drinking heavily in a nearby bar when he spotted first Maya then my mother go up to one of the dangerous black slopes later that day and had followed them up there. Apparently my mother was about to take the lift back down to meet Maya at the bottom instead of skiing down the slope that she wasn't experienced enough to handle—until she saw Cliff. They had another row and he threatened to tell my father about

their affair. Apparently, in her anger and desperation to get away from him, she skied down the
slope—and he chased her. That's when she fell
and smashed her head. That's why she died. Your
father hounded her to her death because he was
jealous and selfish.'

Jamie has remained standing rigidly in the middle of the room, staring at me with angry tears in
his eyes as I've told him all this, but now he shakes
his head, his jaw set. 'I don't believe my father
would do that.'

'It's all true, Jamie,' I whisper with sad exasperation. 'I was there at the hospital. I heard it
from his lips. He told us all about it while she was
fighting for her life in the room next to us. There
was no reason for him to lie.' I sigh as I remember
the terrible aftermath that followed his confession.
'I had to forcibly restrain my father from beating
the shit out of him.'

The unrestrained dismay on his face makes my
stomach turn. He can't believe he's hearing this.
It clearly isn't what he was expecting to find out
about the father he's worshipped for all these years.
But he asked for it. He forced me to this point of
honesty, even after I warned him he should let it
go.

Still, I experience a stab of guilt as I see pain
and confusion flash through his eyes. It's a dev-

astating blow and he's having trouble standing up straight now, as if he's been belted in the stomach.

'That's why I could never tell you the truth,' I say shakily, suddenly feeling the need to soften the blow in any way I can. Because I know how painful it must be to hear this—I've been through it myself.

I stand up and move towards him, but he backs away from me and leans against the wall behind him, holding out a hand to stop me from coming any closer.

'How could we have stayed together at that point, both knowing your father was responsible for my mother's death, Jamie?' I plead, desperate for him to understand how much it's affected me. To get why I felt forced to act the way I did.

'Our relationship wouldn't have survived it. But I couldn't tell you that because I didn't want to put you through the same pain and anguish I'd gone through. I cared about you too much to hurt you like that.'

His face is a mask, rigid and unreadable, but I sense his anger simmering beneath.

I wrap my arms around my middle and hug myself tightly, desperate for any kind of comfort. 'It was all so messed up. I could barely look at you after that, knowing what your father had done. It felt so icky and wrong knowing that *your fa-*

ther and *my mother* had been lovers. So screwed up. It tarnished everything we'd had, made it feel seedy. I was terrified we'd all be treated like lepers socially. Everyone would have been whispering and laughing at us behind our backs. Wondering whether we were actually related.'

He looks at me sharply. 'What the hell are you talking about?'

'Did you not hear what I said? The affair had been going on for *years*.'

He looks absolutely floored.

'That's why I broke things off so sharply and wouldn't see you. I wanted to wait until I had the DNA test results back, just in case.'

'And are we?' he asks, his voice a deep growl.

'Are we what?'

'Related.'

'No. My DNA test came back as a match to my father.'

'Well, that's something at least,' he says with a cold, cynical smile.

I hesitate, but now the truth is out I know I'll have to tell him the other thing that's played on my mind for the last decade.

'I strongly suspect Juno might actually be your half-sister, though—as does my father, I think, though neither of us have ever said so out loud. I'm sure my father believes it because of the way he acts around Juno. He's either cold with her or he acts as though she's not even present in the room. It breaks my heart to see it, but I can't do anything about it. Thank goodness Juno is so grounded and mostly able to shrug it off. I've seen her literally do that many a time.'

'Was this affair going on when my mother was still alive?' he asks roughly, though I suspect he's already figured out the answer to this.

'I think so, yes,' I say with a sigh. 'I suspect that's why she drank. Or at least it might have contributed to it. Your father thought she knew about the affair. He blamed himself for her depression and alcoholism.'

He drops his head into his hands and stares down at the floor, his body rigid with shock.

'All these secrets and lies. It's utterly disgusting.'

'I know. That's how I felt when I found out too.'

He looks up at me again and I suck in a sharp breath at the loathing I see in his face. 'I'm talking about you deliberately keeping this from me for all this time.' He rounds on me, his eyes flashing with anger, and I take a step backwards in shock.

'How dare you decide whether I got to know this stuff or not? To make that choice for me? You put your and your father's pride before our relationship!' he shouts at me.

'That's not why I did—'

'It wasn't your decision to make, April. You should have trusted me. Trusted in us.'

He's pointing an angry finger at me now, his eyes wild.

My body floods with adrenaline. My pulse is racing in response to his anger, but I know I need to keep calm. It's the only way to get through this.

'You took away the opportunity for me to deal with what my father had done while he was alive,' he says. His shock now seems to have turned into full-on fury and it's all focussed on the one person he has left to blame. Me.

'I can't even talk to him about it now. It's too late. How am I supposed to come to terms with that? To try and forgive him? Clearly you thought I was too weak to handle it.' He points his finger at me again. 'That's what hurts the most. You had no faith in me. You took my power away. And I can't forgive you for that.'

Before I can respond to this he brushes past me and swings open the door to his bedroom, turning back to look at me with such coldness in his eyes I actually shiver.

'I want you off my island. I'll arrange for the transfer yacht to pick you up in one hour.'

I can't believe this is happening. But then, also, I can. This is exactly what I was afraid of.

It's all such a mess. A horrible, painful, tangled mess. Just as I knew it would be.

Not that it stopped me from coming here. Apparently the potential of that wasn't enough to make me ignore the lure of spending time with him.

'What about the sale of your father's company?' I ask in panic, trying to delay being thrown off his island and out of his life for as long as I can, though I feel like the most shallow, unfeeling parasite in the world, using our former deal as an excuse. But I need something practical to focus on right now or I think I'm completely going to lose my mind.

The look of disgust he gives me shakes me to my core. Because I think I know deep down that I deserve it.

'*That's* your greatest concern right now—that you'll lose this deal?' He shakes his head, distaste clear on his face. 'I can't believe I thought you were capable of being anything but a cold-hearted business bitch, just out for what she can get,' he snarls at me. 'You can have the fucking company. I don't want anything of his any more anyway. You and your father are welcome to it. I'll have my lawyers draw up the sale documents as soon as possible. Let your jackals pick over the flesh of his dead body.' There's no expression in his face now. He's completely blanked himself of all emotion.

I take a step towards him and reach out a hand, wanting to touch him, comfort him, though I know there's no way he'll let me do that.

'Jamie, will you be okay?'

Anger flashes in his eyes. 'What the hell do you care? You only came here to get your hands on my company.'

'Maybe to begin with,' I argue weakly. 'But I feel like things changed between us recently.'

He waves away my words with a gesture of disgust and looks at me with utter revulsion in his eyes.

'You mean absolutely nothing to me. This was all just an attempt to force you to finally be honest with me. So I can move on with my life and never have to see or think about you again. Because that's exactly what I want.' He leans in closer and whispers, 'I *never* want to see you again.'

And I know for sure, right then, that he means it.

That this is the end.

I wait at the small harbour in a numb state of shock for the transfer yacht to pick me up. I'd barely brought anything with me, so it didn't take me long to pack.

It's been painfully easy to leave.

Everything seems so quiet and still, as if I'm

waiting at the end of the world for the sky to come crashing in. It's just me left here now, alone with my racing thoughts.

After delivering his final dénouement, Jamie simply walked away from me, his broad back tense with anger, and all I could do was stare after him, wondering how the hell I'd allowed myself to get into this mess.

I know how, though. I'd wanted it. Encouraged it, even. Because I'd craved spending more time with Jamie. I'd enjoyed being here with him.

I felt as though I'd come home.

I shake my head, fighting back the tears that threaten to spill from my eyes.

What the hell had I been thinking—that I could seriously pretend I was someone else while I was with him and that would protect me from my feelings? That here on his island everything was different? That I was different? That he was?

I think what hurts the most is that for those handful of glorious days I'd felt like the woman I used to be: playful and full of positivity and fun. Someone who didn't take herself too seriously, who enjoyed life and wasn't weighed down by her cynicism.

A woman who could imagine allowing herself to love someone and to accept and believe that they could love her back.

But it had all been an illusion.

A trick.

So now she's vanished again, leaving behind the same hollow shell I've had to live in for the last ten years.

And all I can do is sit on this cold, hard harbour wall and grieve for her.

CHAPTER TEN

Jamie

I KNEW IT was true. As soon as she said it. I just didn't want to believe it.

But it made sense to me. Everything I'd wondered about in the past but hadn't had answers for suddenly fell into place: the way my father had behaved after Isabella Darlington-Hume's death—and, come to think of it, before it too whenever she was around him. There was always a strange atmosphere between them when they were together—an electric sort of frisson in the air.

I also remember how my father had very rarely talked about my mother, as if he was trying to forget she existed. Because of his guilt? I could only guess if that was true.

And the way he'd just rolled over when Maxim had gone all out to bankrupt him.

And then there was his insistence that I just let

April go and move on 'to pastures new' when she left me. He'd never been particularly keen on our relationship, now I come to think of it, though he'd stopped just short of advising me against being with her. And now I know why.

The revelations went on and on in my mind.

I sit in my living room staring out to sea now that she's gone, feeling as though my whole world has been flung upside down, scattering every belief I thought I had, wrecking every truth I believed in.

My father had lied to me for *years*.

He wasn't the man I thought he was.

As the shock finally begins to wear off and I start fully to process what April told me an hour ago, I slowly begin to accept that, actually, it was he who had been the coward, not April. Even at the end of his life he'd not been brave enough to tell me what he'd done and had forced that awful task onto her. And I'd blamed her for it, like a blind, self-involved, fucking idiot, not wanting to believe that my father could be such a shit.

But he was. Because for all these years he'd let me think it was something to do with Maxim rather than him that had kept April and I apart.

Looking again now at his letter to me, it strikes me how differently it reads now that I know the truth.

But then maybe he'd sent it to me hoping it would force me to talk to April again. To try and bring us back together now that he's gone.

Maybe.

I'd like to think so, anyway.

I can't believe now that I went along with that fucking ridiculous revenge plan, telling myself I'd be fine at the end of it—because it was bound finally to finish things between us. But I wasn't fine. Not even close. Because deep down I didn't want us to be finished.

I *don't* want us to be finished.

I want her back. I need her, I realise now. My heart had been hollow since the day she'd first cut me out of her life, but it felt full again while she was here with me.

I'd been happy.

I get up and pace the room, feeling the lack of her presence here like a deep abrasion on my skin.

I'm not really angry with April, only angry with myself for letting her down and putting her in the position where she felt she couldn't confide in me.

It was the fact that she hadn't been able to tell me that hurt me the most. That she didn't trust me. But then of course I'd gone and proved her right when I'd acted in such a cruel, insensitive way after we split up.

No wonder she's shut herself off from love and

relationships for all these years. No wonder she can't trust anyone with her heart. I hurt her so badly and I wasn't there for her when she needed me most.

All I did was think about my own selfish pain.

What a fucking mess this all is. It's not surprising she shut right back down as soon as I showed her my anger. She must have been expecting me to turn on her, and I did. I proved her worst fears about me to be right.

But I won't do it again.

I'm going to change the pattern of my behaviour from this point. Do the right thing by her.

I want to be the man I should have been all those years ago—supportive and understanding.

Because there's no point trying to deny it any more: the truth is we're meant to be together. I know it. I knew it the moment she stepped onto my island.

I can't let her go back to England thinking I hate her. Because I don't. In fact, I feel the exact opposite. I always have.

I know what I have to do now: I need to find her and stop her from getting on that boat. I have to ask her to stay so we can work this out. If she goes back to England I might never get a chance to be close to her again. I have a feeling she'll make sure of that. She's the queen of icy resistance.

Striding out of the living room, I walk straight to the front door and out to the path leading down to the harbour.

My pulse thunders in my throat.

I might just make it. The boat wasn't due to arrive till about now. She might still be here.

Hoping to God that my epiphany hasn't come too late, I run towards the harbour, my heart in my mouth.

April

I see the yacht in the distance making its leisurely way towards the island, its stern bobbing gently up and down in the gentle waves.

The closer it gets, the lower my heart sinks.

Jamie hasn't appeared and asked me to stay and talk as I'd hoped he would. It's obvious he hates me now, even more than before, now that I've confirmed what a shallow, uncaring bitch I am. I never should have brought the conversation back to our deal about his father's company but I'd been on the back foot, scrabbling for control, and putting on my business head was the only way I knew how to get through that painfully emotional scene. I'd well and truly reverted to type.

I stand up with a bone-deep sigh of despair,

feeling my whole body aching from holding my-self so stiffly for the last hour.

I'm about to start walking to the end of the jetty when I hear a sound behind me that sounds like a shout.

Blood thundering in my ears, I slowly turn to see Jamie running towards me, his legs working hard to cover the ground between us.

'Don't go,' he pants as he reaches me, skidding to a halt a few feet from where I'm standing.

Bending at the waist, he props his hands on his knees, his chest rising and falling rapidly with his accelerated breathing.

I stare at the top of his head, my nerves thrum-ming, trying not to let myself get too excited at his appearance here. He just might have come to deal one last cruel blow to my pride then send me on my way again after all. I need to be prepared for that.

It only takes him a moment to get his breath-ing back under control and he unfolds his large body and takes a step towards me, holding out both hands to me, palms forward, as if he's attempting to tame a wild beast.

'What do you want, Jamie?' I ask, my voice frosty and controlled. I'm not going to let him see how much I'm hurting. I have to protect myself from this. Just in case.

'I'm sorry about the way I reacted,' he says levelly. 'I was so shocked and angry I couldn't think straight and I took it out on you.' He raises both hands higher in a gesture of apology. 'That was wrong of me. It was a classic case of shooting the messenger.'

'Your reaction was actually a blessing,' I say stiffly, not wanting to trust him. This could all still be a ruse to get something more out of me. 'It's actually easier for me if we're enemies. To know how much you despise me. So I can stay well away from you and give us the space we both need to put this fucked-up relationship down in a dignified, humane way.'

'That's not what I want, April.'

I stare at him, trying to convey the full extent of my scepticism. 'Really? Because it seemed to be exactly what you wanted when you said that I mean nothing to you!'

'I didn't mean that,' he says, exasperation roughening his voice. 'It was a defensive reaction because I felt so fucking impotent back there, so irrelevant. I should have been given some power in that situation instead of being left hanging, wondering for the rest of time what the hell I'd done wrong when it wasn't my failing at all. You should have told me, let me in on the secret, instead of leaving me out in the cold, feeling like a fucking failure, rejected and unwanted!'

'Your father begged me not to tell you!' I shout back at him in frustration, not caring about how crazed I must seem now. 'He was terrified of losing you. He loved you too much to hurt you like that. He just wanted you to be happy, Jamie. You'd already lost your mother…he didn't want you to lose him too. To be alone. He loved you more than anything in the world!'

He lets out a low, exasperated sigh, slumps down onto the low wall I'd been sitting on previously and puts his head in his hands. 'I just wish I'd known about this when he was alive. Now I'll always have this anger gnawing away at me. Ruining every memory I have of him.'

I sit down next to him, drawing my knees up to my chest and wrapping my hands around them.

'I did it because I wanted you to be happy, Jamie,' I say more calmly now. 'At the time I thought it was better to have you hate me rather than him and have your entire world crash down around you as well. I've thought about telling you so many times, just to have a chance to connect with you again, but as the years have gone by and you've acted as if you have no respect for me whatsoever it's got harder and harder to say anything to you.'

My voice breaks on the last word and to my horror I suddenly begin to sob, long-held-back tears streaming from my eyes. The utter bleakness of the situation overwhelms me.

'I'm sorry. I'm so sorry. I thought I was doing it for the best. I was so lost after it happened. Afraid. Alone. My father was a fucking mess and I was the only one left to look after my sisters. I had to be strong for everyone. I had to put them first.'

I'm aware of him still sitting there with his head bowed, but I can't look directly at him. I'm afraid if I do I'll never be able to stop crying.

'You were right. My father did ask me to stop seeing you,' I said once my sobs have subsided a little. 'He couldn't stand the thought of being linked to your family in any way. He told me I'd be betraying him and my sisters if I continued to see you. But I think what he actually meant was that he didn't want anyone to know his beautiful, perfect wife had betrayed him. The humiliation would have killed him.'

I took a shaky breath.

'He said you'd turn out to be the same as Cliff, that you'd do the same to me eventually given half the chance. "Like father, like son", he said. I defended you. I argued that you wouldn't, because you loved me, and then you proved him right by letting me down the way you did to get revenge for your damaged ego. I decided you weren't the person I thought you were if you could really be that overtly cruel to me. So then I had to cut myself off from you and everything I felt for you because I couldn't cope with the alternative. I had to shut down every emotion I had, except for anger. You made me feel too much. Which is why I was always so cold to you. I had to be like that, otherwise I would have fallen apart, and I really couldn't afford to do that. I had too many people relying on me.'

He finally raises his head and turns to look at me, his eyes red-rimmed with held-back emotion.

'I'm so embarrassed about the shitty way I behaved after we split up,' he says in a shattered tone. 'You broke my heart when you left me and I guess, in my stupid, fucking naivety, I thought you were just one more woman that I loved who was choosing something more precious to them than I was. For my mother it was alcohol, for you it was your career. But I was wrong on both counts. I know that now.'

He reaches out a hand and lays it gently over mine.

'Even after all these years the pain of losing you has never gone away. I thought it would. I hoped it would. But it didn't. And I hated you for making me feel like that. I've never been able to love anyone else, April, because of you.'

He draws in a ragged breath, on the edge of tears.

And my heart breaks.

'I'm sorry. I'm so fucking sorry for being such a selfish asshole.' He squeezes my hand hard. 'I miss you. I've missed you for ten fucking years, April. It's driven me crazy, seeing you and knowing you didn't feel the same.'

'But I did feel the same. I *do*,' I say, putting my other hand over his.

'You know I love you, right?' he says, looking straight into my eyes now. 'I've always loved you. I always will.'

'I love you too,' I say in a shaky voice, desperately trying not to let my emotions get the better of me. Now I've finally tapped into them, I don't seem to be able to stop them from surging through me in waves every other damn minute.

'I'm so fucking happy to hear that,' he says with a great sigh of relief, putting a hand behind my head and pulling me towards him, kissing me so hard it's as if our mouths are fused together. I feel him trembling in my arms and I realise just how hard it's been for him to come here and risk his heart and his pride to tell me this.

A feeling of utter, blissful relief crashes over me and I pull him tighter, digging my fingers into his back, not wanting ever to let him go now we're finally together again.

When reluctantly we break apart, I whisper,

'I've been trying to make up for my mother's bad behaviour and selfishness for too many years now. Perhaps to prove to my father, and myself, that I wasn't like her. But it's time I look after myself now. Make myself happy. And I think being with you is what I need to make that happen.'

'I promise I'll make you happy if you'll let me. I swear to God I will,' he says fiercely, pulling me against his chest and tightening his arms around me so that for the first time in a very long time I feel truly safe again.

After a few minutes, when I feel as if I'm finally in control of my emotions again, I draw away from him and look into his gorgeous, compassionate gaze.

'You know, I found out recently that Maya's been blaming herself for my mother's death for all these years because she went up to that slope in the first place. I know I need to tell her that's not true, but I haven't been brave enough to tell her the truth in case she hates me for everything I've done and everything I've kept from her.'

He frowns. 'April, you know that's not fair, right? You have to tell her.'

'I know, but this all came out just before my father's accident, so I was distracted by that, and she's been so happy recently since she got together with Benedict. I wanted her to have some time to enjoy that without the past impinging on it. I know she's going to be furious with me for not telling her the whole story and I can't stand the thought of being estranged from her. She might annoy the hell out of me but I still love her. If I'd known before now that she blamed herself for our mother's death, I'd have put her straight a long time ago. The same with Juno. She's in a good place right now and I don't know how she's going to respond to the fact that she might not be our father's daughter.'

'You need to tell her. Let her decide. She deserves to know the truth. She'll thank you eventually, take it from me.'

'I know that, logically. I know I've been a coward, avoiding all this, but I've genuinely only kept these secrets to protect the people I love. My mother left one hell of a mess when she died which I've been trying to manage ever since. Not that I've made a great job of it.'

'You have to stop trying to control everything. It's destructive,' he says with a compassionate smile, running his hands over my hair and cupping my face.

'I'm so afraid the truth might destroy our family completely, though.' I take a shaky breath. 'But you're right. I need to be brave and face it. I'll tell Maya and Juno everything. They're not kids any more and they deserve the truth. No matter how much it might hurt them. Perhaps then we can all move on.'

'I'll do it with you,' he says with utter conviction in his voice.

'Really? You'd do that for me?'

He smiles and raises his eyebrows, then strokes his fingers against my cheek. 'I'd do anything for you.'

And suddenly the hurricane in my mind goes quiet because I can tell from the naked sincerity in his face that he really means that.

I'm not alone any more. We're going to face this together.

EPILOGUE

April
Six months later

I BARELY RECOGNISE the life I was leading before I set foot on Jamie's island now.

So much has changed.

After we'd had some time fully to enjoy our recoupling, then work out the boundaries of our new relationship, Jamie formally agreed to sell his father's software company to me so it could be integrated into DH Worldwide's portfolio. I gave him a good price for it too, in the interests of professional fairness, and he's going to use the proceeds to develop his scholarship programmes, offering more opportunities to young athletes from underprivileged backgrounds. So the future looks bright for both our businesses.

And I finally did what I should have done years ago and stood up to my father, telling him if he wanted me to continue to run the family business then he had to give me complete control—no provisos or tests—and not only over my professional decisions, but over my personal life too.

He'd agreed more readily than I'd expected, but then I think the woman he seems covertly to have fallen in love with—the woman who started out as his nurse and has apparently become his lover—has been a wonderful, calming influence on him.

He actually seems to be happy for the first time in years.

They're both here today, holding hands and smiling—something I've very rarely seen my father do—and I can't tell you how wonderful it is to see it. They look so comfortable together, so *right*, it's hard to believe they've only been in love for a short time.

He deserves to have this after what he went through with my mother.

It wasn't easy, telling my sisters the truth about her. Seeing the shock and pain pass across their faces when they realised she wasn't the saint they'd thought she'd been was hard. Maya reacted the most strongly, understandably. I hadn't realised quite how much her guilt about the incident had affected her life until I saw her un-Maya-like reaction.

Luckily her partner, Benedict, was there to talk

her down from an attack of panicky hyperventilation and hold her afterwards, soothing away her tremulous tears.

Most surprisingly, once we'd sat down together and I'd fully explained my actions and decisions, she wasn't angry with me. In fact, she was the reverse. She said she was grateful to me for everything I'd done to keep our family together. It's going to take a while for her to get past all the angst she's been carrying around for all these years, but she's working on it.

Feeling emotionally close to her for the first time in years made me realise how much I've missed my sister's love and affection. But I think the two of us are going to be okay now.

She's here today with me, looking stunning in the sky-blue bridesmaid dress I picked out for her, so that's a good start.

As for Juno, she took the whole revelation about the question over her paternity in her stride, in the calm, intelligent way with which she seems to deal with everything. She went straight ahead and had a DNA test done, which to my surprise—and I think everyone else's too—showed that my father really was her biological father after all. I suspect rogue genes, way back down the family line, must be responsible for her striking red hair and creamy pale skin.

She and my father have seemed a lot closer since the revelations—at least he acknowledges her now when she walks into a room—and I've seen them talking a lot more than usual, though I think it's going to take quite a bit more time for them really to become comfortable around each other. They're perhaps a bit too dissimilar in personality for that to happen easily.

But she's happy, at least. And she seems very settled with her partner, Sandro, whom I can tell, from the way he treats her, is deeply in love with her. They're standing together now, hands locked tightly, talking quietly as we wait for the photographer to take the family pictures.

As for me, I'm happy, properly happy, for the first time in ten years.

Standing at the altar today, with Jamie looking at me as if I was the most incredible thing ever to happen to him, I couldn't quite believe my life had turned in this exciting and satisfying direction.

But I'm so glad it has.

It took Jamie a while to get past the fury and disillusionment he felt towards his father. But, despite still being angry with Cliff for his cowardice in not having told him what he'd done while he was alive, he's come to believe that he sent that letter so that he and I would have another chance to connect—and fall in love again.

Deep down, neither of us believes Cliff was a bad person; he was just besotted with my mother and made some very bad decisions. Keeping silent about them had been his way of protecting Jamie, because Cliff had loved him more than anything in the world. I truly believe that. He genuinely wanted the best for him. For him to be happy and secure.

Accepting this as truth has helped Jamie come to terms with his father's actions and enabled him to begin to forgive him, I think.

As it has for me, too.

I'm no longer weighed down by the resentment I've been carrying around with me for all these years.

I've chosen to move on from the mistakes of the past and look to the future.

Because I have my Jamie back.

I've told him every day since we've been a couple again how much I love him. How grateful I am for the second chance we got to be together.

Because now I *truly* have everything I've ever wanted.

* * * * *

COMING SOON!

We really hope you enjoyed reading this book. If you're looking for more romance, be sure to head to the shops when new books are available on

Thursday 22nd August

To see which titles are coming soon, please visit

millsandboon.co.uk/nextmonth

MILLS & BOON
DARE

Sexy. Passionate. Bold.

Sensual love stories featuring smart, sassy heroines you'd want as a best friend, and compelling intense heroes who are worthy of them.

LET'S TALK
Romance

For exclusive extracts, competitions
and special offers, find us online:

- **f** facebook.com/millsandboon
- **🐦** @MillsandBoon
- **📷** @MillsandBoonUK

Get in touch on 01413 063232

For all the latest titles coming soon, visit
millsandboon.co.uk/nextmonth